A TIME TO HEAL

A Novel

by

Darryl M. Bloodworth

Book 2 of the Jordan & McKenzie series

All scripture quotations are taken from the New Revised Standard Version Bible, copyright © 1989 by the Division of Christian Education of the National Council of the Churches of Christ in the United States of America.

All references to The Book of Common Prayer are to Rite II, The Book of Common Prayer and Administration of the Sacraments and Other Rites and Ceremonies of the Church: together with the Psalter or Psalms of David According to the Use of the Episcopal Church. New York: Seabury Press, 1979.

Cover Designer: Robert Ousnamer

Cover Photo by Darryl Bloodworth

ISBN: 978-1-963611-85-4
Library of Congress Control Number: 2024925189

Fiction: Legal drama
Fiction: Christian Romance
Fiction: Cyberbullying
Fiction: Family Life

Published by EABooks Publishing a division of
Living Parables of Central Florida, Inc. a 501c3
EABooksPublishing.com

ENDORSEMENTS

"Darryl Bloodworth has hit a home run with *A Time to Heal*. The story presents the modern struggles of professional life as David deals with the loss of his wife and the challenges of a single parent, while Jesse attempts to overcome the wounds of a past relationship that threatens her future with her fiancé. All of this occurs while their clients face an existential threat from a vengeful large corporation. You can learn from their journey and from the sources of their strength—their family, their faith, and their friendships with their colleagues. A truly wonderfully written and inspiring novel."

> — Max James, author of the award-winning book, *The Harder I Fall, the Higher I Bounce*—a business memoir for today's entrepreneurs and executives. He is a serial entrepreneur best known as the founder of American Kiosk Management, dubbed the King of Kiosks by Fortune Magazine, and a former Air Force rescue helicopter pilot.

"A captivating story told by a seasoned trial attorney with all i's dotted and t's crossed, including precise facts, deeply felt emotions, and the consequences of personal choices. Darryl Bloodworth masterfully weaves together a spectrum of real-life circumstances highlighting the values of family, faith, and a time to heal."

> — Terry Isaacson, author of three novels and several non-fiction books, a former all-American football player and wrestler, and 27-year Air Force combat veteran.

"Looking for a worthy challenge? Could you . . .defend an executive and six managers who leave a company at a critical time, taking inside knowledge and contacts to a competitor? . . . stop cyber bullying in a middle school when popular bullies hide behind a virtual private network and an anonymous email provider? . . . land an Air Force jet with radio failure when the weather is too low for an instrument landing and the plane doesn't have enough fuel to divert to another airport?

In *A Time to Heal,* Darryl Bloodworth draws on his experience as a lawyer and pilot to weave such conundrums into a fascinating narrative. Without violence or catastrophe, this novel is a delightful read that makes a winning case for the principled practice of law as perhaps the best hope for a just society.

> — James C. Gaston, former Professor of
> English at the United States Air Force
> Academy, and former F-100 and T-38 pilot
> and combat veteran.

"In Darryl Bloodworth's sequel, *A Time to Heal,* attorney David Jordan tackles a complicated legal case while still struggling to move on in life with his daughter after the death of his wife. Amid the drama of family issues and romantic tensions, David and his law partner, Jesse's, legal expertise skillfully unravels the intricacies of a complex case involving a series of thorny relationships and legal entanglements. For those who enjoy legal suspense, Bloodworth has crafted an engaging drama, devoid of artificial Perry-Mason-like rescues, to impressively capture the authenticity of courtroom drama. An accomplished lawyer himself, the author provides a realistic look at the dramatic tensions and revelations that can take place as a lawyer prepares for trial. The legal suspense, plus the story's well-developed characters and engaging side stories, give readers a rich and thoroughly enjoyable reading experience.

> — Linda W. Rooks, author of *Pieces of Dark,*
> *Pieces of Light,* Carol Awards semi-finalist,
> and *Fighting for Your Marriage While*
> *Separated,* Golden Scroll Non-fiction Book
> of the Year.

Dedication

This book is dedicated to the memory of my son David, for whom life did not afford the opportunity to mature into the outstanding lawyer he could have become.

Chapter 1

Jessica McKenzie's fitful sleep was shattered by a lightning strike so close the acrid smell filled her nostrils, and the sizzle in the air tingled on her skin. The sound of the lightning strike was followed almost immediately by the crash of a large limb from her immediate neighbor's oak tree, sending a shudder through her townhouse as it landed only a few feet from her front door. She jumped from her bed to the window to see whether the limb had hit her house.

"Thank God it missed my house," Jesse, as she was called, muttered to herself. She noticed with relief the limb also avoided the entrance to her garage where her BMW sedan was housed. She had a temporary injunction hearing scheduled for 9:00 AM, which had been the cause of her fitful sleep all night. *The last thing I need is to have no car to get to the courthouse. Judge Long will have my head if I show up late for the hearing.* Judge Long was a good judge, but she was also a no-nonsense judge who would not hesitate to censure a lawyer who failed to show up on time.

As she headed to the shower, Jesse glanced at her alarm clock. It was only 5:30 AM, thirty minutes before the alarm was to go off. The early spring line of thunderstorms had been forecast to sweep across the Orlando-Winter Park area around the time her hearing was to begin but had accelerated overnight.

Jesse stripped off her pajamas and stepped into the shower, getting the water as hot as she could stand it to wake up. She glanced at herself in the mirror through the clear shower door, pleased that the result of the recent increase in her workouts was evident; she had lost the extra ten pounds she gained several months earlier when she and her law partner, David Jordan, tried a four-week jury trial in neighboring Seminole County. She also was beginning to adjust to her new, short hairdo. Jesse had had long, light blond hair since high school, and she thought it was one of her better features. But the demands of a heavy trial schedule left little time for constant attention to her hair, and it had become too burdensome to maintain, resulting in the new short cut. *Not a bad look for a thirty-five-year-old woman lawyer,* she admitted to herself as she stepped out of the shower.

She quickly dressed in her standard courtroom attire—grey suit with a light blue blouse, a single strand of pearls, and medium heels—and went downstairs for a light breakfast while reviewing her notes for the hearing.

The plaintiff in the case was National Material Handling Company, usually called NMH. It was a subsidiary of National Manufacturing Company, a publicly held company, with NMH being headquartered in Orlando. The plaintiff sued Jesse's clients, Mark Conboy and six others who previously worked for NMH with Conboy. The plaintiff also sued Brandon Associates, Inc., the company that hired Conboy and the other employees away from NMH.

The complaint was obviously hastily drafted because it was a mishmash of allegations that were confusing, rambling, and at times contradictory. The gist of the complaint, as best Jesse could determine, was that her clients had been employed by NMH in their material handling business. That business involved designing and installing systems to automatically locate, retrieve, and deliver items in a warehouse to a customer, similar to the systems e-commerce companies use. One of NMH's customers was the U.S. Postal Service, for whom NMH had developed and installed a system in Tampa for scanning and automatically directing mail to its intended destination. Mark Conboy had been the NMH vice-president in charge on the project, and the other six individuals being sued worked for Conboy.

Brandon Associates was a privately owned Georgia company that for years had been in the warehouse construction business. Additionally, Allan Brandon was a consultant who advised customers on how to design and operate material handling systems, which were often necessary for the businesses operating from the warehouses they built. For years, Brandon Associates didn't actually build or install such systems, preferring instead to recommend other companies for such purposes to their customers. Recently, however, they decided to expand into the material handling business because many of their customers had urged them to do so. Their customers preferred to have one company build the warehouse and install the material handling system as well; otherwise, the customer had to deal with two separate companies rather than one that could handle the entire project.

When Allan Brandon, sole owner of Brandon Associates, decided to go into the material handling business, he knew exactly who he wanted to lead that business—his old college friend, Mark Conboy. After Conboy left NMH for Brandon Associates, the other six employees on NMH's management team soon followed, leaving NMH with almost none of its managerial staff. Within several months Brandon Associates' new material handling business had many new, lucrative contracts and was highly profitable, whereas NMH's business languished—so much so that National Manufacturing considered closing or selling NMH and getting out of the material handling business entirely.

NMH's response to these events was dramatic. They filed a one hundred page complaint in the Circuit Court for Orange County, Florida, alleging: (i) tortious interference by Allan Brandon and Brandon Associates with the relationship between NMH and its employees; (ii) tortious interference by all defendants with NMH's relationship with its clients and potential clients; (iii) conspiracy by all defendants to illegally take and use NMH's trade secrets and proprietary information, including customer lists, to unfairly compete with NMH and unjustly enrich themselves; (iv) unfair competition by all defendants to take away NMH's business; (v) breach of Conboy's fiduciary duty to NMH by misusing NMH's confidential information and soliciting its employees and customers; and (vi) breach of all of the individuals' duty of loyalty to NMH by misusing its confidential information and soliciting its employees and customers.

I'm surprised NMH didn't claim my clients pilfered the kitchen sink on the way out, Jesse mused as she finished reviewing the complaint. She then turned to the motion for a temporary injunction that NMH's lawyers had filed, which was the subject of the hearing today. The motion reasserted the facts alleged in the complaint and asked the court to enjoin Conboy and the six other individuals from continuing to work for Brandon Associates, or any other company engaged in the material handling business, and from disclosing NMH's confidential information to anyone else. NMH also asked the court to enjoin Brandon Associates from continuing to employ the individual defendants or otherwise do business with them. *In short, if NMH prevails in its motion today, my clients will be out of a job, with slim prospects for continuing to work in the material handling business. Their lives will be destroyed.*

"This is a case in which David and I should both be heavily

involved," Jesse said out loud to herself as she continued to review the file. David Jordan had been her mentor at Smith & Bridges, the large national law firm where they both worked until they formed their own firm some five years ago. When they worked together on a case, David was usually the first chair attorney, although they normally split the handling of witnesses. However, since David's wife, Carol, died five months ago—leaving him the sole parent of Jenna, their twelve-year-old daughter— David had not been the same. In the four-week jury trial they recently handled, David insisted that Jesse be the lead attorney, with him playing the assisting role Jesse usually played on cases they jointly handled. Although he performed well in the case, he was not quite the old David, and it pained Jesse to see him struggle at times, clearly suffering from the loss of his wife.

David's struggle was personal to Jesse. He wasn't just her law partner; he was also her first cousin, once removed. Her grandfather and David's mother had been brother and sister. But she viewed their relationship more like siblings than distant cousins. That was one of the primary reasons she joined Smith & Bridges right out of law school—where David was already practicing—and she had never regretted her decision. David apparently felt the same because when he made the decision to form his own firm over five years ago, he asked her to join him as his partner. Together they built Jordan & McKenzie into the formidable law firm it had become. Seeing her cousin and law partner suffer over Carol's death felt to Jesse like the slow drip of water torture without any end yet in sight.

Carol's death was also personal to Jesse for other reasons. She and Carol had become as close as sisters, and Carol's death was as crushing to her as the loss of her own sister would have been. Plus, Jesse had always been the doting aunt to Jenna, Carol and David's twelve-year-old daughter, and Jesse now felt a greater responsibility to this remarkable young girl who lost her mother at a critical stage of life. With David's encouragement, she had become the most important woman in Jenna's life, spending at least one evening a week with Jenna, and taking her phone calls at all hours. But none of this was a burden to Jesse; she loved Jenna deeply. *Jenna isn't the only one benefitting from this relationship,* Jesse acknowledged to herself as she got up to pour herself another cup of coffee.

One area in which Jesse *did* feel an increased burden as a result of Carol's death was with Women's Crisis Center. WCC was a non-profit corporation providing a safe sanctuary for battered women and children, as well as for women dealing with drug addiction. Carol was the founder of WCC and had served as its president until her death. She had convinced Jesse to serve on its board of directors, but now with Carol gone, Jesse had become the chairman of its board. WCC's board—with David's help—found an experienced person to serve as its president and chief executive. But Jesse's role—and time commitment—had greatly expanded, especially with the construction of a new facility about to begin as the result of a generous gift from David's client, Max Foster. *I couldn't say no when the board asked me to serve as chairman, but how am I going to find time to carry out my duties at the firm, handle my case load, be available to Jenna, and be an engaged chairman of the board of WCC?*

As Jesse pondered these questions, while still thumbing through her notes for the hearing, another thought crept into her consciousness, one she had suppressed every time it had bubbled to the surface previously. There was another relationship that was demanding her attention, one she was eager to explore. During the past year she represented Dr. James Faulk, an orthopedic surgeon who had been sued by his former employer, Orange Orthopedic Surgeons, when he left to set up his own practice in Sanford. His former employer claimed he violated the non-compete clause in his employment contract and demanded that he cease practicing at his new Sanford office because it was within the thirty-mile radius where competition was prohibited. Jesse successfully defended Dr. Faulk, and his former employer dismissed the case following an unsuccessful hearing on a motion for an injunction against Dr. Faulk. When Dr. Faulk showed his gratitude by asking Jesse and her associate Steve Cutler to celebrate at dinner, Steve was wise enough to glean whom the client really wanted to have dinner with. He left after drinks, leaving Jesse alone with her then-former client so they could get to know each other better.

Although there were no sparks flying that night there were at least some smoldering embers, Jesse recalled. James must have felt the embers also because he asked her out the following week, and they dated regularly thereafter. By agreement, they decided to go slowly and not announce their relationship to their close friends. "That would only put more pressure on us," Jesse recalled both of them saying at the time. However, when Carol died Jesse asked James to accompany her to the funeral. He seemed to recognize the funeral was a profound event in Jesse's life, and her asking him to attend it with her was an indirect way of asking for a deeper commitment to their relationship. James readily agreed, and without stating it out loud, they both recognized they wanted to see where this relationship might go.

As the months passed since Carol's funeral, their stated preference to go slowly had not been a problem. Jesse's increased responsibilities had taken up so much of her available time that finding even one night a week to get together with James had been a challenge—especially with James on call three to four nights a week as he was attempting to build his medical practice. The result had been frustration for both of them. They both professed a desire to see where the relationship would go, but so far the embers were barely smoldering, and Jesse feared they might go out entirely if she and James couldn't find more time to be together.

James is a good man, and I'll regret it for the rest of my life if I don't give sufficient attention to this relationship to see where it might go, Jesse admitted to herself for the first time. *And at my age, I don't know how many more chances I'll have to find the right man. But how am I going to find the time for James and still do justice to my other commitments?*

With this newly admitted but somewhat depressing thought in mind about James, she put her breakfast dishes into her dishwasher, gathered her notes into her briefcase, and went to her car to head to the courthouse for the temporary injunction hearing.

Chapter 2

David Jordan was in the middle of a dream in which he was trying to figure out who was the culprit in a detective mystery of the type he loved when he felt something wet on his face. Still in the middle of the dream, he looked about for the source of the wetness, mystified as to where it was coming from, while wondering how it might be a clue to solving the mystery. An insistent bark, however, brought his eyes open, and he was startled to find himself eyeball to eyeball with Molly, the white Labradoodle puppy he had given Jenna for her Christmas present. Molly was licking his face, apparently spooked by the thunder and lightning from the line of thunderstorms tearing through central Florida. Although she usually slept on her own doggy bed in Jenna's room, this was not the first time Molly had run to David's bedroom and jumped into bed with him when thunder frightened her.

"Jenna, come get your dog," David yelled as he glanced at the clock on his nightstand. It was only 5:45 AM, forty-five minutes before the alarm was to go off. He was still bone tired, as he had been when he went to bed shortly before midnight. Following Carol's death, he felt tired most of the time. Even his exercise routine of running three or four times a week, which had previously energized him, now just seemed to add to the fatigue.

David shooed Molly off the bed as Jenna shuffled down the hall to get her.

"Sorry, Dad. The thunder and lightning must have frightened her. Remember, she's still just a puppy . . ."

"That's no excuse, Jenna. She's still your responsibility," David said—although softly and with a slight smile—as Jenna scooped Molly up to take her back to their bedroom. David was finding it quite difficult to get too upset with Molly no matter what she did. She had been a great comfort to Jenna, especially on afternoons when Jenna got home before David did. Jenna clearly loved the dog, but as Molly grew from a puppy to a fifty-pound bundle of energy over the past few months, Jenna was finding it difficult to keep her out of trouble. Just last week, David was dressing for a court appearance when he discovered Molly had chewed through the toe of one of the dress shoes he was about to put on, requiring a complete change of clothes and shoes, and initiating a few colorful words to Molly from David.

Today, however, David was trying to be more magnanimous toward Molly. *As Jenna said, she's still just a puppy, and Jenna loves her dearly, but had I known all this would entail, I may have found a different Christmas present for Jenna.*

Recalling that Molly was Jenna's Christmas present reminded David when his condition—which he could only describe as a funk—began. It was around Christmas. Carol passed away in early November. Despite the shock and sense of loss, he and Jenna were doing about as well as could be expected during the ensuing weeks following the funeral. All their friends and church members had surrounded them with so much love and support David had come to believe his life would soon return to something resembling normal, although admittedly with a big hole in it from Carol's absence. But when the Christmas tree went up and traditional Christmas events rolled around, the enormity of his loss hit him head on once again and overwhelmed him.

I'll never hold her again. She will never be there for me when I so desperately need the counsel and comfort of the woman I love. Without her, I don't know how I'll be able to raise Jenna.

Every significant event surrounding Christmas triggered a reminder of his loss, depressing him further. He felt like he was under a heavy wet blanket that was depriving him of the joy of his family life, his work, and his relationships. And here he was, months later, still unable to navigate his way out of the fog of depression, struggling to be the father he wanted to be, and the lawyer he used to be. *How long will this go on? Will I ever get past the loss of Carol?*

David stepped into the shower and felt the soothing flow of hot water over his head and shoulders, bringing relief from the tension in his shoulders his self-criticism had aroused. But even as he felt the tension ease, a fresh reminder of his recent failures popped up, bringing the tension back. He and Jesse had agreed to handle their recent four-week jury trial together in their usual manner. David would take the lead with *voir dire*— jury questioning—opening statement, and final argument; Jesse would handle half the witnesses and address various motions during trial. However, only two weeks before trial David realized he was not up to fulfilling his usual role and dumped the lead counsel role on Jesse. She was gracious about the last-minute reversal of roles, and performed beautifully at trial, but David felt guilty every day of the trial.

I can't imagine how I would have felt if we had lost the trial. The client was perturbed at me for the last-minute change of roles, changing his mind only when we got the favorable jury verdict. I have got to get back to being my old self soon or all my clients will start looking elsewhere.

***

David had just finished dressing when their Puerto Rican housekeeper called out from downstairs, "Breakfast is ready, Meester David."

David had hired Angelita Ramon earlier in the year when he realized he simply couldn't manage his law firm duties, be a good father, and run the house all by himself. That became painfully apparent as trial preparation heated up, requiring long hours at the office.

Angelita was a godsend. She was a fifty-five-year-old woman who had recently lost her husband, Jorge. They had moved from Puerto Rico to the Orlando area six years ago to rebuild their lives after a category five hurricane had destroyed their home and most of their possessions. It also destroyed the factory where Jorge worked, leaving him without a job. When they arrived in central Florida, he was able to get a job as a field manager with a large agricultural business, and she worked as a cook at a local diner that catered to the expanding Puerto Rican population in central Florida. With both of them working full time, they were able to rent a one-bedroom apartment and purchase a 15-year-old used car.

It was a tough life, but they were getting by, until Jorge had a heart attack and was dead before they could get him to the emergency room. Angelita was devastated, and also destitute without Jorge's income. She was considering moving back to Puerto Rico, where she still had relatives, when a friend from the company where her husband had worked told her about a lawyer who was looking for a full-time housekeeper.

David recalled her interview. She was dressed simply but neatly, of medium height and slight build, with calloused hands— someone who looked like she had worked hard all her life. Her

12

dark hair was flaked with grey, and the wrinkle lines around her eyes contributed to a happy, outgoing persona, although David suspected it masked a difficult life. Her English was quite good, even if she occasionally lapsed into Spanish when she couldn't recall the English word she was searching for.

As soon as she mentioned her husband had recently passed away, David felt a bond with her that immediately changed the tone of the interview. For twenty minutes they exchanged stories of their struggles since their spouses had died. She seemed particularly interested in David's stories about Jenna. Angelita had no children of her own but told David she had often cared for her nieces back in Puerto Rico. She also warmed up quickly to Molly, who met her at the door with David, and, tail wagging, sat close to her throughout the interview, staring at Angelita with her enormous brown eyes.

By this point in the interview, David was quite sure he wanted to hire Angelita. He had already interviewed four other women, none of whom seemed right for the job. He didn't want to let her get away.

"So, Angelita, what are your salary requirements if you take this job?"

"Meester Jordan, I must make at least $3,000 a month to afford my apartment in Oviedo, buy gas and insurance for my car, and buy food. This area is so much more expensive than Puerto Rico."

"How many hours a week would you expect to work for that amount of money?"

"I would work from 8:30 to 5:30 each day, with lunch included."

"What if I have to be out of town? Could you stay overnight with Jenna?"

"Yes, Meester Jordan, but only for more pay."

David lightly tapped the kitchen table where they were sitting as an idea formed in his mind, vague at first, but quickly coming into focus.

"Angelita, the more we talk the more I realize your driving back and forth from your apartment in Oviedo for a normal workday of about eight hours isn't what I need, and it isn't what Jenna needs. What we need is someone who lives here and is available to our family, including Molly, throughout the week. Is that something you might be interested in? I think you would be perfect for the job if you are interested."

"What are you thinking, Meester Jordan?" Angelita responded, obviously puzzled by the changing nature of the job she had anticipated.

"We have a garage apartment out back which is fully furnished; you would live there, rent free, utilities included. Since you will be driving Jenna to school and back, you will have a car available for your use, all at my expense. Part of your duties will include buying food for all of us, including Molly, and preparing breakfast and dinner for Jenna and me, Monday through Friday. You will have a credit card for buying food, and your own food can be charged on that account. Additionally, I will pay for health insurance coverage for you and get you a cell phone that you can use for personal reasons as well as your job. Finally, your salary will be $1500 per month; you will receive $750, less taxes, on the first and fifteenth of each month. How does that sound?"

Angelita just stared at David, blank faced, for a long

moment, apparently taken aback by the generous offer. As David was about to repeat his offer, Angelita said, "May I see the garage apartment?"

The inspection of the apartment only took six minutes before Angelita declared it good— more than she expected. "Meester Jordan, I like the apartment and your offer is good, but I can't say yes until I meet Jenna. Unless she is okay with me, this won't work."

Angelita's response just further confirmed David's belief this was the right person to be their housekeeper. "Well, why don't you come with me. I'm going to pick her up from Maitland Middle School in a few minutes, and we can come back here to let you two get better acquainted."

Twenty minutes later David and Angelita picked up Jenna from school. By the time they got back home, Jenna and Angelita were happily chatting in a mixture of English and Spanish. Jenna clearly liked the idea of having someone to help her with Spanish, which was her most challenging subject.

After talking further around the kitchen table for a short time, Angelita said, "Meester Jordan, I say yes to your offer. How soon you want me to start?"

"As soon as you can get moved in. However, there is one more condition to my offer."

Angelita's face fell with this comment, apparently thinking the offer had been too good to be true. But David continued with a smile, "You have to call me David, not Mr. Jordan. Can you do that?"

She quickly returned the smile and said, "Yes, Meester

Jordan . . . I mean Meester David.”

***

Angelita had cooked one of David and Jenna’s favorites—huevos rancheros—for breakfast. Angelita was a master not only with Puerto Rican food, but also many Mexican dishes. She even gave Molly a small taste of the eggs on her dog food, which, judging from the increased tail wagging, was greatly appreciated. As they all sat down to breakfast, Angelita and Jenna chatted in Spanish to make sure Jenna was ready for her quiz in Spanish class today.

Seeing the two of them so engaged lifted the fog of depression that had been haunting David, but only slightly. Even the slight lifting, however, gave David hope that life may someday go back to normal—whatever that might be without Carol.

Jenna’s voice brought David out of his thoughts. “What are you up to today, Dad? Anything exciting on tap?”

David noticed Jenna was aware of his depression and tried to cheer him up whenever she could. He was doing his best to be cheerful, but Jenna apparently knew him too well; she seemed to know when his cheerfulness was put on, masking his true feelings.

“I have a deposition at 9:30, the firm attorney meeting at noon, a client conference at 2:00, and a meeting with Jesse at 4:00 to discuss a new case of hers that I may become involved in. All in all, a busy day ahead, but I should be home by 6:00.”

He sounded more excited about the day ahead than he actually felt. His depression might recede intermittently, but it was always there lurking in the background—even during those times when he hoped he was on the way back to his old self. When Jenna nodded in agreement that it was a busy day, he patted Molly, kissed Jenna on the cheek, and headed to his car for the commute to the office.

Chapter 3

"All rise. The Circuit Court for the Ninth Judicial Circuit of Florida is now in session, the Honorable Judge Sally Long presiding."

The bailiff's declaration brought everyone in the 18th floor courtroom to his or her feet. Jesse and her associate, Steve Cutler, sat at the counsel table on the far left, facing the bench where Judge Long was taking her seat, with the empty jury box located beyond the other two counsel tables to Jesse's right. Also seated with Jesse and Steve was Mark Conboy, with her other six clients seated directly behind them but in front of the bar separating the lawyers and clients from courtroom observers.

Judge Long opened a file on her desk, poured herself a glass of water from the pitcher in front of her, then announced, "We're here on Plaintiff's motion for a temporary injunction against all defendants in National Material Handling versus Brandon Associates, Inc, et al. Would counsel please announce your appearances and introduce those with you, beginning with Plaintiff."

From the far-right counsel table a tall distinguished-looking man with greying hair, immaculately dressed in a pinstriped navy-blue suit, maroon tie, and black wingtip oxford shoes stood and stated with a slight New York accent, "Karl Stanton, of Paul & Ramey's Miami office. Together with me is my associate, Seth Rigdon, and Rhonda Robinson, the general counsel for National

Material Handling Company."

Stanton had introduced himself, his associate, and Ms. Robinson to Jesse and other counsel present before the hearing began. He explained that he was admitted both to the New York and Florida bars, and he split his time between Paul & Ramey's New York and Miami offices. Jesse's first impression was that he was a typical senior partner in a large national firm. He would likely be highly competent, outwardly courteous and ethical, but he would raise every issue that could possibly be raised and concede nothing that might make the case move along more smoothly. Given the firm the plaintiff company had chosen for this case, she anticipated she would be in a fight that would consume most of her time, and probably much of the time of other lawyers at Jordan & McKenzie.

Jesse had no strong initial impression regarding Stanton's associate, but she *did* have a visceral negative reaction to Rhonda Robinson, NMH's general counsel. First, she was cold as ice during introductions before the hearing began. Jesse even noticed her arguing with Stanton after all counsel sat down at their own counsel tables for last minute preparations. She appeared not to even acknowledge the presence of Stanton's associate and had an air about her that instinctively told Jesse that Ms. Robinson would be an unpleasant presence throughout the case.

As Stanton sat down, Bart Mayfield arose, and announced in a soft south Georgia accent, "Bart Mayfield, of Mayfield & Pines, Valdosta, Georgia, appearing on behalf of Allan Brandon and Brandon Associates, Inc. With me is my associate, Regina Paxton. We are both members of the Georgia Bar and have filed a request to appear *pro hac vice* in this case, your honor. All counsel have informed me they have no objection to my request. Also seated with me is my client, Allan Brandon."

As Judge Long said, "The motion to appear *pro hac vice* is granted," Jesse recalled her telephone conversation with Mayfield the previous week when she first learned of this lawsuit. Mayfield called to ask her to represent Conboy and the other six individuals.

"Ms. McKenzie, we need the best counsel we can get to defend Mr. Conboy and the other six individuals in the suit filed in your jurisdiction. NMH seems to have a vendetta against Brandon Associates and Allan Brandon."

"Why is that?" Jesse asked.

"My client previously sent some material handling business to NMH before Brandon Associates got into that business. When Conboy and the others left NMH to join my client, it apparently put the continuation of NMH's business in jeopardy. There are rumors that NMH's parent company—National Manufacturing Company—is looking for a buyer for NMH, or may just shut it down, and NMH's management isn't happy about that. Rhonda Robinson—NMH's general counsel—called me just before the suit was filed, demanding that we immediately fire Conboy and his compatriots, or NMH would come after us in court, 'until Hell freezes over,' in her colorful words. Of course, Allan Brandon is committed to paying your fees to represent Conboy and the other six individuals."

Jesse recalled that she discussed the allegations with Mayfield, satisfied herself that Mayfield would be a good co-counsel to work with, and agreed to take on what promised to be one of the largest cases she had ever handled.

Jesse noticed that Judge Long was staring at her and quickly stood up. "Jessica McKenzie of Jordan & McKenzie appearing on behalf of Mark Conboy and the other six defendant employees of Brandon Associates who are present with me. Also with me is my associate, Steve Cutler."

Judge Long nodded as the appearances were completed, glanced at her notes, and said, "We are here on Plaintiff's motion for a temporary injunction. However, I don't see where counsel noticed this hearing to be an evidentiary hearing. Mr. Stanton, what do you have to say about that?"

Stanton quickly stood up and said, "Your honor, we filed an extensive affidavit signed by Ms. Robinson which verifies all of the essential facts giving rise to this lawsuit. As outlined in detail in the memorandum of law we filed with our motion, we've set forth in the affidavit evidence to support every element of our claims, and we're entitled to the relief sought on this motion. We saw no need for testimony in addition to the affidavit to support our motion."

Jesse noticed that Judge Long had a dubious frown on her face as she glanced back at the pleadings on her desk, then said, "But the relief you are seeking is for this court to bar these seven individuals from working for Brandon Associates, or anyone else in the material handling business, and you want me to grant your motion without any cross-examination?"

While still looking dubiously at Stanton, Judge Long said, "Ms. McKenzie, would you like to address this issue?"

At once, Jesse was on her feet. "Yes, your honor. First, I would point out that none of my clients signed a non-compete agreement with NMH, and there is no allegation that any such agreements ever existed. Without the existence of a non-compete agreement there is no basis for entry of an injunction prohibiting my clients from working for Brandon Associates, or anyone else they want to work for. They were all at-will employees who were free to leave NMH at any time, and Brandon Associates was free to hire them."

"How about that, Mr. Stanton," Judge Long said as she turned to address Stanton. "Ms. McKenzie's argument accurately states my understanding of Florida law."

Jesse glanced at Stanton. Rhonda Robinson was whispering something in his ear, as Stanton strained to hear what Judge Long was saying to him. He quickly held out his hand toward Robinson to indicate he needed to listen to the judge. This apparently infuriated Robinson who clearly didn't like the way the hearing was going.

Ignoring Robinson, Stanton stood and said, "It's true there were no non-compete agreements, but we have alleged a breach of the individuals' duty of loyalty to their former employer—NMH. They all left en mass to Brandon Associates, taking with them all of NMH's confidential information, which enabled Brandon Associates to unfairly compete with NMH. The damage my client has suffered is substantial and ongoing. This can't be allowed to continue, your honor."

Judge Long returned her gaze to Jesse, who responded, "Without non-compete agreements, all Plaintiff has is allegations of wrongdoing, as yet unproven, which could lead to nothing more than a money judgment for damages. Even in the unlikely event Plaintiff could prove all of their allegations, it would only entitle them to a judgment for money damages, not an injunction, and an injunction is all we are here to address today, your honor."

As Judge Long nodded in apparent agreement with Jesse's argument, Robinson stood and said, "May I be heard, your honor?" As she did so, Stanton's head snapped around toward her, surprise plainly visible in the expression on his face.

"Ms. Robinson, we already discussed the fact this is not an evidentiary hearing, so you will not be permitted to testify today," Judge Long calmly said, although she said it through slightly clenched teeth, indicating she wasn't happy with the request.

"I want to be heard as a lawyer, not as a witness, Judge. I'm a member of the bar of Virginia, and request that I be allowed to be heard on behalf of NMH."

"But you haven't filed a motion to appear *pro hac vice*, Ms. Robinson. Only those who are members of the Florida Bar, or those admitted for a specific case *pro hac vice* can argue in this court." As Judge Long said this, Jesse noticed that small splotches of red were spreading across Judge Long's neck. It was well known among local lawyers that Judge Long seldom got angry on the bench, but if her neck became peppered with red splotches, she was furious and the lawyer inciting her should look out.

"Then I hereby request that I be admitted *pro hac vice* to be co-counsel with Mr. Stanton and his firm for this case." Stanton's shock at this request was written all over his face, but he managed to resist objecting to his own client's request as Judge Long stared at him, apparently dumbfounded over his apparent loss of client control.

Judge Long then turned to Jesse and Bart Mayfield and dryly asked, "Do *any of you* have an objection to Ms. Robinson being admitted *pro hac vice?*"

Jesse and Mayfield glanced at each other, then turned back to Judge Long and in unison said, "No objection, your honor." As the judge looked back down at her file, apparently considering how to proceed, Jesse muttered to Steve under her breath, "This should really be good. Ms. Robinson is violating a cardinal rule of trial lawyers: don't piss off the judge, particularly at the first hearing."

"In the absence of any objection, I will grant your motion, Ms. Robinson. However, let me remind you that as counsel admitted *pro hac vice*, you are required to be familiar with the Florida Rules of Civil Procedure, the Florida Evidence Code, the Florida Rules of Professional Conduct, and the rules of this court. Should you violate any of these rules, your permission to appear *pro hac vice* can be terminated at any time. Do I make myself clear?" The judge was as stern as Jesse had ever seen her. Jesse's visceral reaction to Ms. Robinson was proving to be prophetic.

"Perfectly clear, judge," Robinson responded with a slight tilt of her head that Jesse—and apparently Judge Long—viewed as arrogant. "May I proceed with argument?"

A long pause as Judge Long leaned back in her chair, exhaled, and then said, "You may."

Robinson's lips curled into something between a smile and a sneer as she began her argument. "My client had a successful material handling business that was growing steadily. Our clients included the U.S. Postal Service and numerous public and privately owned companies. NMH even had contracts with Brandon Associates to install material handling systems in warehouses they built. Once Brandon Associates learned my client's trade secrets and confidential information, they swept in and lured away nearly all of our management, and started up their own material handling business, devastating ours by using our confidential information."

As Robinson said this, her voice was becoming increasingly strident, and loud, taking on an air of outrage over a perceived gross injustice.

"Overnight, Brandon Associates knew all the customers of NMH, the price points for the different types of material handling systems NMH installed, and NMH's confidential knowledge about potential customers. Judge, this situation is similar to a thief breaking into the home of a famous chef, stealing all his recipes, and then offering his lead cook twice the salary to start up the thief's new restaurant."

Judge Long's dubious expression deepened with Robinson's last comment. But Robinson pressed on, apparently oblivious to the effect she was having on Judge Long.

"The defendants' conduct is so egregious they should all be in jail. We are simply asking the court to enter an injunction prohibiting the individual defendants from continuing to rob my client and enrich Brandon Associates, which under the circumstances is a reasonable request." Robinson was almost shouting, and she paused to catch her breath.

By now, the red splotches were all over Judge Long's neck. Jesse thought she was about to explode. But Judge Long kept her composure, and intervened as Robinson was catching her breath. "Is it true that none of the defendants have a non-compete agreement?" the judge asked.

Robinson appeared taken aback by the question, her puzzled expression suggesting she thought the question was irrelevant, before responding, "Well, yes, but. . ."

Judge Long cut her off and pressed on. "Can you cite to me any Florida case in which a temporary injunction was entered terminating defendants' employment and prohibiting them from working elsewhere in the industry where there was no non-compete agreement?"

"Uh, no, not at this time, your honor. . ."

Robinson started to resume her argument but Judge Long raised her right hand to stop her. The judge remained silent for a long moment as she appeared to be trying to control her anger and contemplate how to proceed. Finally, she looked directly at Robinson, and said, "The motion for a temporary injunction is denied."

"But judge. . ." Robinson began before the judge cut her off.

"Ms. Robinson, I have ruled. Once I make my ruling, counsel is not to argue further. Is that understood?" The expression on Judge Long's face left no room for optimism she would entertain further argument.

After a stunned pause, Robinson said meekly, "Yes, judge, I understand."

As Robinson sat down, Judge Long paused, stared at all counsel one by one, and then, looking directly at Stanton and Robinson, said, "I can see from today's hearing this is going to be a contentious case. All counsel are advised to review the professionalism standards which this court expects; they can be found on the website for the Ninth Judicial Circuit under my name."

All counsel nodded, as Judge Long continued. "Furthermore, I am moving up the pretrial scheduling conference to two weeks from today. By then, I expect counsel to have come up with an agreed-upon discovery schedule that will expeditiously get this case ready for trial. Are there any questions?"

When all counsel nodded negatively, Judge Long said, "Then we are done for today. Ms. McKenzie, please prepare an order confirming my ruling, and circulate it among counsel for their approval before sending it to me." As Jesse nodded that she would, Judge Long closed her file and exited the courtroom through the door behind her bench, which led to her chambers.

Chapter 4

The attorneys at Jordan & McKenzie meet every Monday at noon to go over administrative matters, new developments in the law, and their cases. The office manager, Sarah Garcia, always joins them, at least for the administrative portion of the meeting. David chairs the meetings, but any of the lawyers can raise an issue for discussion. Maggie Price, the young black associate who works primarily with David, always leads the discussion about new developments in the law and is responsible for keeping up with new case law or new statutes.

Today, Sarah Garcia led them through a 30-minute discussion of changes to the firm's 401(k) retirement plan while the lawyers finished their lunch—pizza from their favorite Italian deli. As soon as Sarah left the meeting, David turned to Jesse and asked, "How did your hearing go this morning? I know we're meeting at 4:00 today to discuss it in detail but give us a brief overview."

"To say it was an unusual hearing is an understatement," Jessie replied as she set aside her coffee.

"Amen to that," chimed in Steve, as David and Maggie's expressions said, "Tell me more."

"The first thing that was unusual," Jesse said, "was that an experienced attorney like Karl Stanton would attempt to obtain a temporary injunction banning our clients from working for

Brandon Associates, or anyone else in the industry, without scheduling an evidentiary hearing. He just submitted a lengthy affidavit by Rhonda Robinson, NMH's general counsel. The Paul & Ramey firm has a good reputation, but Stanton didn't get off to a good start with the judge in this case with that blunder."

"Get on to the good stuff," Steve said to Jesse with a sly smile.

"Steve's right. What was really unusual about the hearing was that Rhonda Robinson, the general counsel for National Material Handling, took over the argument for the Plaintiff in the middle of the hearing. When she saw the hearing wasn't going well for them—and apparently without any discussion with Stanton beforehand—she stood up and asked to be heard, even though she hadn't filed a motion to be admitted *pro hac vice.* This irritated Judge Long, who nevertheless allowed her to appear in the case *pro hac vice* after Ms. Robinson's verbal request."

"Wait. You didn't object to her being admitted *pro hac vice?"* Maggie asked.

"Are you kidding? Of course not," Jesse said. "We could see how Judge Long was responding to her. Those splotches Judge Long gets when she's getting angry? They were creeping up her neck. Bart Mayfield and I took about two seconds to say we had no objection. Stanton looked like *he* wanted to object, but he didn't."

A knowing smile spread over Maggie's face. "I get the picture."

"Well, that was only the beginning. In her argument, Robinson compared our clients to thieves who should be in jail for stealing NMH's secrets and confidential information."

"What secrets and confidential information did she claim our clients stole?" asked David.

"Who knows?" Jesse replied with a shrug. "Despite a 100-page complaint, they didn't specifically identify what any of the secrets or confidential information were, except in the vaguest of terms."

"I can imagine how Judge Long responded to calling our clients thieves," David said with a smirk, then took another bite of pizza.

"Oh, her splotches were so prominent by then I thought Judge Long was going to explode and hold Ms. Robinson in contempt. But the judge maintained control, quickly asked a series of questions which demonstrated how unprepared Robinson was to pursue a temporary injunction at this time, and then denied the motion."

"So, all went well with the hearing?" Maggie asked.

"Not quite. Judge Long apparently wants to move this case along and keep control over it. She's moved up our initial pre-trial conference to two weeks from today. As you know, counsel must come up with a discovery plan and identify potential witnesses; it appears that's going to be quite a job."

"Why is that?" Maggie asked, looking up from her yellow note pad.

"Well, when the hearing was over, Bart Mayfield and I met with Plaintiff's counsel to discuss a schedule for getting our discovery plan together. Robinson was still seething from how the hearing went. She seemed angry with everyone—the judge, our clients, even her own counsel, Stanton. And get this, she says they intend to take at least fifty witness depositions, plus expert witness depositions, scattered all over the country."

"Isn't that a little excessive?" David asked. "Are there really that many witnesses that have relevant information about the case?"

"I have no idea at this point," Jesse replied, "Bart Mayfield seemed as surprised by the number of depositions as I was. We may have to ask Judge Long to put a limit on the number and length of depositions each side can take. Perhaps you and I can discuss this issue when we meet this afternoon."

With this comment, David turned the discussion to other cases.

***

As Jesse and David agreed, they gathered at 4:00 in the conference room. By then, Jesse had spoken further to Bart Mayfield about the discovery plan, and she had an idea of how they might staff this case.

After David poured coffee for both of them, they settled around the conference table. Jesse quickly reviewed her notes from the morning hearing, then looked at David with a weary smile, and said, "David, it's clear to me this case is going to require most of my time and a substantial portion of yours over the coming months. Judge Long will probably expect us to complete all discovery within six months of our pre-trial scheduling conference. After speaking to Bart Mayfield earlier this afternoon, we've concluded that between the plaintiff and the defendants we'll likely have over sixty depositions, including experts, unless Judge Long limits the number of depositions. That's ten a month, and they're going to take place all over the country."

"Why so many?" David responded, shaking his head in disbelief. "This case doesn't seem *that* complicated to me. And the ultimate issue—for our clients at least—is a simple one: whether our clients violated any duty to NMH by going to work for Brandon Associates."

Jesse shook her head also. "At this point I can only guess why NMH wants to take so many depositions. First, I think they're fishing for any helpful evidence. By now, they realize they'll have a difficult time convincing the judge and jury our clients violated any duty to NMH, since they had no non-compete agreements. Their plan is apparently to find out whether there are any witnesses out there who might testify that our clients steered work away from NMH to Brandon Associates. If so, they'll try to convince the jury this was a plot all along between Brandon and our clients to steal NMH's business."

"That sounds plausible," David responded, nodding in agreement. "But based upon NMH's behavior so far, it also appears they're trying to make this case so expensive that Brandon and our clients will throw in the towel early and settle on terms favorable to NMH."

"Oh, I think there's no question about that," Jesse responded. "Rhonda Robinson has already hinted at that several times. She told us following the hearing this morning they are prepared to litigate this case, 'until Hell freezes over,' repeating a threat she made earlier to Bart Mayfield."

David paused, looking out the conference room window, apparently considering his response before turning back to Jesse. "As unjust as that is, it's an approach large companies sometimes take when suing a smaller company. Since Brandon Associates is paying for the defense of all of the defendants, this case could become very expensive for them."

Jesse met David's gaze, and said, "Don't think I haven't thought about that, particularly after meeting Rhonda Robinson."

"So, I have two questions for you," David responded. "First, do you believe Brandon Associates has the financial wherewithal to see this case through to conclusion, which could take several years, including appeals? And second, do you believe Allan Brandon has the will to see the case through to the end? As you well know, litigation takes a toll on management of any company, but it especially takes a toll on smaller companies where the senior management has to stay heavily involved in the lawsuit while also performing all of their other duties."

Jesse pondered David's questions for a long moment, glancing at the ceiling before looking back at David. "As to the wherewithal to see the case through, my tentative opinion is *yes*. Brandon Associates' material handling business has exploded—in a good way—since our clients joined them. Unless NMH is able to get Judge Long to enter an injunction prohibiting our clients from working for Brandon Associates, Brandon should be able to afford a complete defense. So far, the chances of NMH obtaining an injunction appear quite low to me."

David nodded agreement, and said, "And as to the second question . . . ?"

Jesse paused, grimacing slightly. "That's a tougher call for me. Based on my limited conversations with Allan Brandon and his counsel, Bart Mayfield, I *think* the answer is *yes*, but at this point I'm not as confident about my response to this question as I am about Brandon Associates having the financial resources to see the case through."

David took a long sip of his coffee, then said, "Not surprising, Jesse. We don't really know how much determination to fight a client has until the pressure is ratcheted up. We'll get our answer to this question when the bills start rolling in and Mr. Brandon's time is being dominated by this case. In the meantime, we need to ensure Brandon Associates keeps paying our bills on time, and we'll need a cost deposit for all of the out-of-pocket expenses we'll incur."

"I've already made that point with Brandon and Mayfield. I don't anticipate a problem."

"Now, let's discuss staffing," David said, checking off an item on his yellow pad. "As you probably recall from our last trade secret case, before any depositions can be taken regarding trade secrets, the plaintiff has to describe with particularity any trade secrets they contend were stolen, which they have obviously not yet done. Otherwise, we won't know who to depose or what to ask the witnesses about. My suggestion is that we get Maggie working on a set of written interrogatories, and comprehensive requests for production of documents. We don't want to start depositions until we have responses to the interrogatories and receive the documents we request."

"Agreed," Jesse responded, jotting notes on her yellow pad. "My suggestion is that we ask Steve to analyze whether we should file a motion to dismiss the complaint, or simply file an answer. He would take the lead in drafting those documents for our review. If you will work with Maggie on the discovery documents, I will work with Steve on the pleadings."

"Perfect," David responded.

Jesse looked at David for a moment, deep in thought, then said, "I like the idea of our having all hands on deck for this case.

More than any other case we've had in the firm, this one is going to require all of us to work together."

David nodded in agreement as they brought the meeting to a close.

Chapter 5

When David arrived home that evening, Angelita met him at the door, plainly concerned about something judging from the expression on her face.

"Meester David, I worry about Jenna. She went straight to her room after getting home from school today, and not come out. She look like she been crying. I ask what's wrong, but she don't want to talk about it."

"Really? She was in such a good mood this morning. Something bad must have happened at school today. Thanks for letting me know, Angelita. I'll speak to her."

As David headed up the stairs to Jenna's bedroom, he could hear Molly from inside Jenna's room, barking to welcome him home. David knocked lightly on the door and said, "Jenna, can I come in?"

From inside, David heard a muffled response that he assumed was a *yes,* although he wasn't sure, but he slowly opened the door anyway. All lights were out, and the wooden blinds were almost closed, leaving the room dark, apparently in sync with Jenna's mood. She was lying on the bed, but Molly had jumped down to greet David at the door.

After petting Molly's head to acknowledge her greeting, David sat on the side of the bed, and just looked at Jenna for a long moment, assessing the situation, but saying nothing. Jenna sat up, with her back against the headboard; her medium brown hair was pulled back into a ponytail. Her enormous blue eyes were bloodshot, visible even in the dim light seeping in through the blinds. She had taken off her glasses, and despite the glum expression on her face, David caught his breath as he noticed afresh how beautiful his young daughter had become.

"Are you OK, Jenna?" David finally asked as he reached out for her hand. "Did something happen today?" The fact Jenna was usually so upbeat caused David to fear something was seriously wrong as he took in the depth of her depression.

Jenna didn't respond immediately, obviously struggling to control her emotions before answering her father. Her bottom lip trembled slightly, and she pulled Molly close to her as she jumped up on the bed to snuggle with Jenna.

After a long pause, with her head still down, Jenna mumbled so softly David could barely make out her words, "It's not just today, Dad. . ."

"What's not just today, Jenna? Has someone hurt you?" David's imagination began running wild with what could possibly have caused Jenna to be so despondent, and he felt the anger begin rising deep within him over the possibility of someone hurting his precious daughter.

"No, not physically, Dad. But people can be just so mean sometimes," she hissed, shaking her head.

Slightly relieved, David quietly asked, "How so, Jenna? What did someone do, and who did it?"

Jenna was still trying to control her emotions. She was

obviously in pain and seemed to be struggling to express what she was feeling—her thoughts not yet formed, and words rumbling around aimlessly in her head. David waited quietly until she was ready to talk. Finally, she took several deep breaths, pushed a lock of hair out of her eyes, and said sternly, "My friend Wanda Sparling and I are being bullied and harassed, and we're sick of it."

"What? How? Who's doing this?" David asked, incredulous this was happening.

Jenna finally looked David in the eye before saying, "It's all happening online, Dad. But I know it's coming from someone at school. We don't know *who* is doing this because it's all being done anonymously. It started a few months ago, just a few catty statements at first, but it's been getting progressively worse ever since. We laughed it off initially, but that was a mistake; it's only gotten worse."

Jenna paused, dropping her gaze to the bed again as she struggled once more to control her emotions. David could feel his jaw tightening as he ground his teeth to control the anger bubbling up within him again at the thought of someone harassing Jenna and her friend.

"Give me some idea of the kind of things they're saying, Jenna."

After another momentary pause, Jenna seemed relieved to finally have an adult to discuss this problem with and sat up in her bed ready to talk to her father. "As I said, initially it was just catty stuff, like criticizing our clothes or saying we thought we were better than everyone else, but it was constant. Wanda's on the girls' soccer team with me, and we've been playing pretty well lately, winning a lot of games. We get a lot of praise and attention from our teachers when we win, which this person *really* doesn't like. The comments have gone from just catty stuff to ridiculous stuff—like saying we're taking drugs to play better, and we've been having booze parties when we win. Just ridiculous stuff!"

"Have you tried to talk to this person to find out what the problem is?"

"Dad, you don't understand. . ." Jenna said, the frustration palpable in her voice. "All this is being done *anonymously*. The Jerk—let's just refer to whoever's doing this as the Jerk—is using an anonymous email account, and also using a VPN to ensure his identity remains a secret."

David suddenly realized he was in over his head. "What's a VPN?"

Jenna's expression seemed to David to say, "Really, Dad, don't you know *anything*?" But she just stared at him momentarily, then seemed to remember who she was talking to, and said, "A VPN is a virtual private network. If you have a VPN account with, say, CyberGhost VPN—like the Jerk does—you can avoid exposing your real IP address. So, you can then use an anonymous email provider like Mailfence—which the Jerk is doing— to keep you completely private and untraceable."

David just looked blankly at Jenna; he would have understood as much if she had told him this in Chinese. "But if we have to, we can subpoena CyberGhost or Mailfence to find out who the Jerk is, can't we?" David couldn't imagine harmful online bullying could be kept secret.

"Dad, my understanding is that such companies don't keep tracking information, so you can remain anonymous . . . but I could be wrong. I never thought I would have to worry about something like this." Jenna's gaze returned to the bed as she slowly scratched

Molly's neck while apparently imagining what she would like to do to the Jerk for treating her this way.

"I can see I need to talk to Maggie about this," David commented, shaking his head over the helplessness he felt for being unable to deal with—or even fully understand—Jenna's problem. Maggie Price was the associate who worked with David on all his cases. She was the Jordan & McKenzie expert on electronic discovery and all things digital. Maggie was also very adept at translating technology issues into language David could understand.

After thinking about the questions he had for Maggie for a few moments, David returned his gaze to Jenna, and asked, "So what happened today to get you so upset? You've just told me this has been going on for a few months, but I haven't seen you upset like this before today."

"That's because nothing like this has ever happened before today, Dad. Everything before today has been irritating, but Wanda and I have been able to laugh it off, hoping the Jerk will finally get tired of his silly games and stop. But today, the Jerk—who goes by the alias Ghostwhoknows—posted the results of a fake student questionnaire on the student bulletin board on the school website. The first few questions were about the school lunchroom, the library, and various school programs, so it looked like a genuine questionnaire with a tally of the responses, which of course it wasn't. The last question was, 'Who are the sluttiest girls in Maitland Middle School?' Below the question it listed Wanda's name and mine, with it showing 89 percent of the respondents listing Wanda's name, and 92 percent listing mine."

David was so shocked and surprised he didn't know how to respond. After a few feeble attempts to say something, he blurted,

"Surely no one is going to believe something like this."

"Who knows what all my friends and classmates believe, Dad?" Jenna said, about to burst into tears. "But they're all having a blast posting on Facebook and texting one another about the questionnaire and the newly crowned two sluttiest girls in school. Everyone in the school now knows about this, and when they see Wanda or me, they just laugh. It's no fun being the butt of such a school-wide joke."

Still mystified by the situation, David asked, "Are your teachers and the principal aware of this?"

"Yeah, sure. But the fake questionnaire was posted about 1:30 today. The principal's office didn't find out about it for nearly an hour, and then they couldn't figure out how to take it down from the electronic bulletin board for nearly another hour. When word got out about what had been posted in the questionnaire, every afternoon class I was in was buzzing about it. Our teachers totally lost control of the classroom; I understand that's what happened in all the other classrooms, too. It was awful!"

"I can imagine, Jenna," David said with resignation, as the full scope of what Jenna and her friend were experiencing came into focus. "I'm so sorry you have to deal with this. How's your friend Wanda holding up?"

Jenna's shoulders slumped as David asked this question. Turning her gaze again to David, she said, "That's another thing that burns me up, Dad. Wanda's been going through a tough time. Wanda's mom and dad got a divorce last year. That's when Wanda's mom moved them to Maitland to be closer to her mom's family. I only spoke to Wanda for a few minutes after school today, but I've never seen her so down. The Jerk's bullying has affected Wanda more than it has me. She was crying and said, 'I just can't take it anymore.' I'm not sure what she meant, Dad, but I'm worried about her."

David was impressed once more with how his daughter, in the midst of her own pain from the Jerk's actions, seemed as concerned about her friend as she was about herself. If Jenna was that concerned about Wanda, he was also. After considering his options for a few brief moments, David said, "I think this situation has to be addressed immediately before it gets entirely out of hand, and permanent harm comes to someone. I'm going to talk to Maggie tomorrow; she's familiar with the law regarding cyberbullying. Then Jesse and I may have to go speak to the principal."

Somewhat to David's surprise, Jenna didn't object at all to David's comment. She also seemed to realize that someone's silly prank had gone way beyond the bounds of silliness, and if the Jerk wasn't stopped soon, someone—probably Wanda, but possibly even herself—could be harmed beyond repair.

After another brief pause while David and Jenna held hands and just looked at each other, Jenna put her arms around David and warmly hugged him. She said, "I love you, Dad."

"I love you too, Jenna," David replied as he, Jenna and Molly got off the bed and headed downstairs to see what Angelita had prepared for dinner.

Chapter 6

The following morning David arrived at the Jordan & McKenzie office shortly after 8:00 AM and asked Jesse and Maggie to meet him in the conference room at 9:00. David was already pouring coffee for them when Jesse walked in.

"What's up, David?" Jesse asked. "I don't have a meeting scheduled for us on my calendar this morning. Do we have a new case?"

"I'm not sure yet," David replied, as Maggie walked in, also expressing surprise at the unscheduled meeting David had called. David gave them each their coffee, black for Jesse and one sugar for Maggie, and gathered them around the conference table, as they looked expectantly at him.

After taking a sip of his coffee, David began, "Last night I learned for the first time that Jenna and a friend of hers have been cyberbullied and harassed at school over the past few months. It was nothing serious until yesterday when the perpetrator posted on the electronic bulletin board on the Maitland Middle School website a fake questionnaire with fake responses to the questions. The key question was, *Who are the sluttiest girls in Maitland Middle School,* and the responses were shown as Wanda by 89 percent of the respondents and Jenna by 92 percent. No other names were listed. You can imagine the impact that had on a couple of middle school girls."

"Oh, my God, David!" Jesse exclaimed. "I had no idea such shenanigans were going on in *middle* schools."

David noticed that Maggie wasn't as shocked as Jesse. "I'm sorry to hear that also, David," Maggie quickly added, "although I'm not surprised. I've been dealing with cyber-bullying issues in several of my legal aid cases recently. The problem is far more pervasive than most people are aware of. This issue is even arising in some elementary schools now, but the problem gets worse in middle schools and worse yet in high schools and beyond."

"Yeah, that's what I've come to realize," David replied, then hesitated before continuing. "After thinking about it, I believe we need to get involved to bring this episode of cyberbullying to a stop, and quickly. Jenna's upset, but she told me her friend Wanda is really distraught; she's worried about Wanda."

David looked directly at Jesse, then to Maggie, and back to Jesse. "I wanted to bring you up to date, Jesse, so you would know what's going on in Jenna's life. She may want to discuss this with you the next time you see her." Turning to Maggie, he said, "I need your expertise, because you know more about the technology issues involved here than anyone else I know."

"Sure. I'm glad to help, David," Maggie replied, not at all hesitant to pitch in even though this was not a billable hour project for her. "It would help me come up with some suggestions if you would go over when this began and what happened before yesterday."

Jesse nodded in agreement, and David recounted for both of them, in detail, his discussion with Jenna the previous night. "Frankly, I was mystified when Jenna mentioned the harasser was using a VPM."

"What's a VPM?" Jesse interposed, apparently as puzzled as David had been when Jenna mentioned it.

"Correct me if I'm wrong," David said, looking at Maggie, then turning to Jesse. "A VPN is a virtual private network. If the user has an account with a VPN, he doesn't have to expose his IP address for his email and can use anonymous names. This perpetrator is using 'Ghostwhoknows.'"

"Let me guess," said Maggie. "I bet Ghostwhoknows is also using an anonymous email provider. Mailfence?"

"Spot on," David said, relieved to see Maggie was as knowledgeable as he thought she would be about these issues. He asked, "So apparently someone can use a VPN account together with an anonymous email provider to keep his identity completely private and untraceable?"

Maggie took a long sip of her coffee before nodding, and adding, "Yes. There are some good reasons why this is legally permissible, but it's very frustrating in the cyberbullying context."

"So, bring us up to date on what the Florida law is regarding cyberbullying," David said to Maggie.

"Sure," Maggie responded. She picked up a volume of Florida statutes and turned the pages until she found what she was looking for. "Section 784.048 of Florida statutes deals with stalking and cyberstalking. It defines cyberstalking as follows: 'To engage in a course of conduct to communicate, or cause to be communicated, directly or indirectly, words, images, or language by or through the use of electronic mail or electronic communication, directed at or pertaining to a specific person, causing substantial emotional distress to that person and serving no legitimate purpose.'"

"That pretty well defines what Jenna and Wanda have been going through," David said. "I'm pleased the legislature has addressed this issue. How serious an offense is it?"

"That depends," Maggie replied. "If the cyberstalking doesn't include a credible threat to the person being cyberstalked, it's a misdemeanor of the first degree, which could involve prison for up to a year, and possibly a fine. If it does include a credible threat to the person, it's a felony of the third degree, which could result in up to five years in prison, plus a fine."

"I don't think we yet have what can be considered a credible threat . . . but that could come at any time," David mused.

"I was just getting to that point," Maggie replied as she turned the page in the statute book and found the section she was looking for. "As it turns out, it doesn't matter whether there was a credible threat in this instance because section 784.048(5) provides that anyone who cyberstalks a child under 16 years old has committed a felony of the third degree."

"That's helpful," David said, nodding with satisfaction.

Jesse, who had been taking notes on a yellow pad, suddenly appeared to have an epiphany moment, looked up and said to David, "Based upon what you've told us so far it sounds like Ghostwhoknows is probably a minor—one of Jenna's classmates. What effect would that have on what action can be taken against the person doing this?"

"Good point," David said. "Maggie?" David asked as he turned to her.

"Jesse has raised a key issue. Although it's possible for a minor to be tried as an adult, that's unlikely in this case. If the perpetrator is a minor, law enforcement would probably file a delinquent complaint in circuit court, and the case would proceed under juvenile court rules. Many such cases result in a diversionary program, especially for first time offenders. Of course, we don't know whether a minor is doing this, although I agree with Jesse that it sounds like a classmate of Jenna's is the culprit."

David, Jesse and Maggie all pondered the situation for a few moments before David spoke up. "One more question, Maggie. It looks like Jesse and I should go speak to the principal of Jenna's school. Are there any other rules, regulations or statutes we should be aware of before speaking to the principal?"

"I'm not familiar with all of the rules and regulations of public schools, but I am aware of one other statute that should be helpful. The legislature passed section 1006.147 of Florida statutes last year. It specifically prohibits cyberbullying in schools, including the use of any computer or computer networks within a public school. Since the most recent instance of bullying took place through the school's computer network and website, this statute should be helpful."

"Anything else we need to know?" David asked.

"Well, there is one thing," Maggie said after thinking about it for a moment. "The statute I just mentioned requires each school district to adopt and review at least every three years a policy prohibiting bullying and harassment, including cyberbullying, and the principal of each school must implement the plan. If the principal appears not to take this situation seriously you might let him or her know you're aware of this requirement and ask about its implementation."

"I like the way you think, Maggie," David said with a smile, and brought the meeting to a close.

After Maggie left the meeting, David picked up the coffee cups to take them to the kitchen. He casually asked Jesse, who was lingering, "How are things going with Dr. Faulk? I haven't seen him lately." David didn't intend to pry, but Jesse was like a sister to him, and they had become even more like siblings since Carol died and Jesse became more involved with Jenna.

"To be honest, I don't know, David," Jesse said, shaking her head with a faraway look in her eyes. "We've both been so busy we haven't seen each other in two weeks. Yeah, we've texted and talked by phone, but that isn't the same as being with someone, is it?"

As David quickly agreed it was not, Jesse continued, "It's funny you ask, though. James and I are meeting for dinner at Antonio's tonight. I think I'm going to ask him how he thinks our relationship is going."

"Well, good luck," David said as they left the conference room.

Chapter 7

Jesse agreed to meet James at Antonio's in Maitland at 7:00 that evening, but due to traffic being light she arrived fifteen minutes early. Instead of asking to be seated right away, Jesse went to the attractive upstairs bar just off the entrance to have a glass of wine and plan her strategy for the evening. *I need to find out whether I'm wasting my time with James or not. I don't want to find myself still wondering where this relationship is going a year from now.*

As she sat at the bar and ordered a glass of Pinot Noir, Jesse remembered her first real date with James. They had come to Antonio's that night as well, at her suggestion. It was her favorite restaurant, and she hoped it would become one of his favorites as well. She chuckled to herself as she recalled that James was ten minutes late meeting her because he was waiting downstairs in Antonio's deli and wine shop, expecting to meet her there. The aroma of all of the classic Tuscan dishes floating in the air had convinced him he was where he was supposed to meet her. Only after texting her that he was at the restaurant did he learn he was to meet her upstairs at Antonio's upscale restaurant and bar.

Despite the fact there was a party in one of the private rooms that night, the noise was only a low hum in the main dining room, and they quickly tuned out everyone but each other. Jesse had learned a lot about James' background in the medical field while representing him, but that evening she was anxious to learn more about his personal life. He had grown up in a suburb of Chicago and attended Northwestern University. After slogging through the brutal Chicago winters for so long, he decided to come to Orlando to attend the University of Central Florida's relatively new, but highly regarded, medical school. He was able to stay in the Orlando area after med school when he got a five-year orthopedic surgery residency at Orlando Regional Medical Center, part of Orlando Health's sprawling hospital system, with coverage throughout central Florida. It was following his residency that James joined Orange Orthopedic Surgeons, the entity that sued him when he left, leading to his retaining Jesse to defend him.

But more than just getting to know the when and where of his life to that point, Jesse felt she had really connected with him that night. Unlike some of the physicians she had met, he was warm and kind. He spoke fondly of the relationship he had with his mother, a nurse, and with his sister, a schoolteacher. Although his sister was still back in the Chicago area, he was close to her children—his niece and nephew. They even face-timed most weeks. The clincher, though, was that he looked directly in her eyes as they talked. He was tuned in and seemed anxious to get to know her, not just as a successful lawyer, but also as a woman with whom he might be interested in having a long-term relationship.

As all of this came back to Jesse, she had to admit something else that colored her feelings about James. He was perhaps the most handsome man she had ever met. He was tall and muscular, with jet-black hair, the palest blue eyes, and classic features that caused everyone who saw him for the first time to stare—at least briefly—perhaps thinking he must be someone famous. The fact this beautiful and accomplished man was also rather humble, personable and interested in her had blown her away during that first date. By the end of the evening, she had definitely decided this was a relationship she wanted to pursue. She thought he felt the same way.

Indeed, over the ensuing months they saw each other as often as they could. By unspoken agreement, neither dated anyone else, but once Carol's illness became known, and Jesse's responsibilities at the law firm, with WCC, and with Jenna increased, she had less time to devote to James. Although she repeatedly apologized to him for being unavailable so often, she sensed he felt she was pulling back, unsure whether she wanted to commit fully to the relationship.

As she sipped her wine, Jesse remembered when she first sensed James was questioning her commitment to the relationship. After their first few dates, they had become physically affectionate with each other. There was no consummated sex, but there was a strong physical attraction—lots of kissing, hugging, and what on one particular occasion strongly resembled foreplay. When Jesse brought their passion to an unrequited end, James was plainly surprised, and they both were frustrated. What had caused Jesse to bring their lovemaking to a premature conclusion, though, was no lack of desire for James, but rather a flashback to the only other serious relationship she had had since high school.

The earlier relationship had occurred during her second year of law school at Emory University in Atlanta. After she and one of her male classmates flirted throughout their freshman year, they began dating in the fall of their second year. The relationship quickly became physical, with Jesse spending most weekends at his apartment. She had never been in such an intense relationship before, feeling at times overwhelmed by her emotions and consumed by her desire to be with him constantly. Her grades suffered; on a few occasions she even skipped classes—something she had never done before—so they could be together all day at his apartment. Although they had never discussed marriage, Jesse began thinking about it constantly. If he felt anything close to what she was feeling, how could they not get married?

Then, as suddenly as they started the intense relationship, it all fell apart. After one of her close friends told Jesse she had seen her boyfriend with another woman at a popular bar the previous evening, Jesse confronted him, and he promptly dumped her, saying it was time for both of them to move on. Jesse was shocked and humiliated; she felt she had been used, just a fling to keep him amused while going through the grind of law school. She felt worse about herself than she had ever felt in her life, and she swore she would never allow herself to get in such a situation again. The only good thing about the breakup was it forced her to realize how off track her life had become—especially regarding law school. Fortunately, it occurred early enough in the semester for her to catch up, but her grades were still the lowest of any semester in law school.

Jesse recalled now that she didn't tell James the real reason she brought their intimacy to an end that night. She just said they needed to slow down. After she came on so passionately to him, Jesse's abrupt about face clearly had James mystified, as well as frustrated, and the evening had come to an awkward end. There wasn't much passion in their dates after that night, although they were still somewhat affectionate with each other.

Jesse hoped that asking James to accompany her to Carol's funeral would let him know she was still committed to their relationship, and he seemed to recognize this, although neither of them actually verbalized it. But after Carol's funeral, they both had been so busy with their other commitments they had less and less time for each other. She wasn't dating anyone else, and she didn't think James was either, but James was acting more defensive, in her opinion, apparently protecting himself against the possibility she was pulling back. Something needed to change, or they both were wasting their time, going nowhere.

As Jesse took another sip of her wine, she checked her watch. It was 7:00, and James should arrive at any moment. Jesse was excited about seeing him, but fearful at the same time. It seemed an important part of her life was at a crossroads, and she didn't know which path tonight's events would send her down.

***

James Faulk pulled into the parking lot for Antonio's restaurant at 7:00 PM on the dot. He anticipated getting there a little earlier, but traffic from his office in Sanford to Maitland had been horrific. He had ruminated the entire way about his history with Jesse. He recalled well his first meeting with her as his attorney; he was stunned she was so strikingly beautiful—as much so as any movie star. But he was also equally impressed by her intelligence and her attention to detail as they went over the facts of his case. As a highly trained physician, he recognized professionalism and competence when he saw it, and before the meeting was over he realized he was fortunate to have her representing him. He smiled inwardly as he recalled how smitten he was from the moment he met her, but she maintained a strictly professional demeanor throughout the case, and he reluctantly felt he had to also.

He recalled how he was finally able to get a date of sorts with her. It was last year after they had an evidentiary hearing on Orange Orthopedic Surgeons' motion for a temporary injunction that, if granted, would have required him to move out of his office and relocate outside a thirty-mile radius from Orange Orthopedic's offices in Orlando. Jesse was magnificent during that hearing. Her cross-examination of his former boss, Dr. Edwards, and of their economist expert, gutted their case. What impressed him even more was the moxie Jesse showed to insist that Orange Orthopedic settle the case then—over the lunch break—or there would be no further settlement negotiations in the case. If Orange Orthopedic eventually lost the case they would have had to reimburse him for all his attorneys' fees and expert witness costs, which by the end of the case would have been in the hundreds of thousands of dollars. They caved to Jesse's demands and dismissed the suit that day. All he gave up was the right to be reimbursed for his attorneys' fees to date, which were not significant that early in the case.

James was beyond ecstatic. On a day he could have been enjoined from continuing his medical practice from the office into which he had sunk all his life savings—and would then have been sued by his landlord, probably putting him in bankruptcy—he walked out of court the victor, all his legal problems behind him. He was overjoyed, and by the next day he realized this was the perfect opportunity for him to try to connect with Jesse personally. So, he called her to invite her to a celebratory dinner. But not to be too bold, he invited Steve Cutler, Jesse's associate, as well. Thankfully, Steve was prescient enough to cut out after drinks, leaving Jesse and him to enjoy dinner alone.

James felt they really connected that night on a personal level. They were comfortable with each other and in a celebratory mood, which encouraged the openness they each expressed about their dreams in life, including family life—hypothetically, of course. Along with the wine, the banter flowed as it does when a man and a woman are enjoying being in each other's company and signaling their enjoyment to each other. By the end of the evening, they were making plans to get together again.

Their first official date was at Antonio's, which James fell in love with immediately. The evening convinced James that what he felt during the celebratory dinner was real, and he was determined to pursue a serious relationship with this wonderful woman. Over the next few weeks they got together for dinners, a day at the beach, and even a round of golf—which they both vowed never to do again.

In James' view the relationship could not have been going better. They were becoming more physically affectionate with each other while also becoming more verbally affectionate. And then, one night after they both said they were falling in love, which led to steamy foreplay, Jesse abruptly seemed to freeze. She pushed him away, saying they should slow down, which was the exact opposite of every signal she had sent to that point. He was completely taken aback, not to mention frustrated, and unsure how to respond to her. It also did something else; it reminded James of the last serious relationship he had, and specifically reminded him how it came to an end.

Not long after beginning medical school, James had met a woman going through nursing school at UCF, and they dated each other exclusively for the next two years. Although they never moved in together, they frequently spent weekends at his apartment, and they talked openly about the possibility of getting married some day. James was so committed to her that he was about to formally propose, when he sensed she was beginning to distance herself from the relationship. That feeling began shortly after he told her that although he was fully committed to her, he felt he should graduate from medical school before they marry. There was no immediate reaction to his statement, nor any arguments from her about why they shouldn't wait, but he sensed this wasn't a timetable she was prepared to accept. She soon had other priorities on weekends. When they were together, she wasn't as tuned in to him as previously; again, nothing he could put his finger on, but rather a gnawing feeling that she was withdrawing from him.

As he turned off the radio in his car, James recalled how prophetic his vague feeling was. Only three months after James told her he wanted to wait until after medical school to get married, she broke up with him—with a text message no less. It was a profound disappointment to him. The woman he believed he would spend the rest of his life with had essentially kicked him to the curb because she wasn't willing to wait until he completed medical school. It wounded his confidence that he could tell when a woman really loved him, but it strengthened his confidence that he could tell when a woman was pulling back from him.

That same uneasy feeling that his girlfriend was pulling back from him is what he had been feeling lately from Jesse. *Should I tell Jesse that I feel she's pulling away from me, and that I'm particularly sensitive to that because of my past experience with my former girlfriend?*

James pondered those questions for a few moments— without formulating a clear answer—before opening the door to his car and heading up the stairs to meet Jesse for dinner. He wasn't at all sure how the evening would turn out, but he had to know how she felt about him. He didn't want to continue in what felt to him like no man's land, where the only woman he cared about seemed to be losing interest in him.

***

Jesse was still at the bar when she saw James come in. Just as he approached the maitre'd, Jesse caught his attention, inviting him into the bar. They exchanged a somewhat formal hug, although Jesse felt the expression on his face indicated he was happy to see her.

"Do you want to get a drink at the bar before we're seated?" Jesse asked.

"No, I'm hungry; I missed lunch today. Let's be seated."

Jesse had asked the maitre'd for one of the few booths in the restaurant. It gave them slightly more privacy than the tables did, and she definitely wanted more privacy tonight. As they were seated, James asked the maitre'd to have a waiter bring him a glass of Pinot Noir, the same brand as Jesse had. They discussed their respective day's events as they reviewed the menu and awaited James' wine. Although they were friendly with each other, Jesse felt there was a distance between them, with each cautiously probing the other for any hint of the other's expectations for the evening. When James' wine finally arrived, they both told the waiter they were ready to order. Once they had ordered, they sipped their wine and just gazed into each other's eyes, each apparently reluctant to begin the conversation that they both knew had to take place. Finally, Jesse decided to take the first step.

"James, do you remember our first date here at Antonio's?" As she said this, Jesse braced herself for what the answer may be.

"I do. I thought it was one of the most enjoyable evenings of my entire life."

That was a better response than she expected, so Jesse ventured further, "Do you mind my asking why you thought it was so enjoyable?"

James seemed surprised by this question and hesitated before responding. "It was enjoyable for me because I was with the lawyer who had just won a case for me that had a profound impact on the rest of my working life. Your efforts literally kept me out of bankruptcy."

This wasn't exactly the answer Jesse was looking for. She tried to hide her disappointment, but feared she didn't succeed. She just nodded her head as if to say, "I thought that was the primary reason."

But after she didn't respond verbally, James continued, "It was also enjoyable because I was in the company of the most beautiful woman I knew, a woman who seemed to meet every expectation and hope I've ever had for a woman I would come to love."

This response was much more in line with what she had hoped for, and Jesse felt her heart skip a beat as she pondered what he had just said. After looking warmly into his eyes for a long moment, Jesse cautiously asked, "Do you feel the same way about our date here tonight?"

Jesse perceived that James was taken aback by this question, as though he was being asked to reveal something he wasn't yet ready to reveal. He said nothing for what seemed to Jesse like several minutes or more, although it was surely less. After apparently searching for the right response, he said, "I want to be perfectly honest with you, Jesse. The answer is both *yes* and *no.*"

"What do you mean?" she asked, fearful of what the response may be.

"My answer is *yes* because I still feel you are the most beautiful woman I've ever known. I expect I will always feel that way. My answer is also *yes* because I still believe you meet every expectation and hope for the woman I will come to love, with one exception."

When James paused after saying this, Jesse waited for him to continue, but he didn't, apparently reluctant or unsure of what more to say. Finally, Jesse couldn't wait any longer, and said, "What's the exception, and what's the reason for the *no?*" As she said this, Jesse had a strange feeling not unlike the feeling she usually experienced as the jury returned to announce its verdict. At that point in a case, she had done everything she knew to do for her client, and she was then helpless to do anything more than await the verdict. It was always an emotional moment—a happy one for her, as well as for the client, if the verdict was favorable; otherwise, it was a miserable one. In this instance, her emotions were magnified because the verdict would affect her personal life in a profound way. She felt her heart rate speed up as she awaited his answer.

James didn't hesitate with his response, and his expression was more serious than she had ever seen it. "The reason for the *no,* and the reason for the exception I mentioned are the same. One of my hopes and expectations for any woman I love is that she be committed to me body, soul, and spirit. When I marry, it will be for the rest of my life, without question. And I want my wife to be as committed to me as I am to her."

Jesse just nodded as he said this, not sure how to respond in view of her perception that he felt she was not that committed to him. So, James continued, "Frankly, Jesse, I've had the feeling for some time now that you're pulling away from the relationship. Regardless of how beautiful and wonderful I think you are, I can't commit myself fully to a woman who doesn't return that total commitment."

Jesse was silent, realizing her perception of what James

was thinking was as she feared, before meekly asking, "When did you first come to believe I was pulling away?"

"I remember very specifically when it was. You remember the night, I'm sure, when we were about to make love when you put a stop to it. Please understand, Jesse, I don't want to make love to you until you're totally ready, and I'm willing to wait however long that may be. But all the signals you sent up to that point indicated you were *more* than ready; then you abruptly stopped us, and you've been a little distant ever since. Or at least that's my perception."

Jesse's emotions were about to overwhelm her, and she fought back tears as she realized what she had to do. It was time for her to be totally honest with James, as well as with herself. "You're correct that something changed that night, James. And I have to apologize for not telling you the real reason I stopped us and for unconsciously putting distance between us. Please believe me, though, it wasn't because I don't have feelings for you. I do, and I want more than anything for our relationship to go forward to that total commitment you're looking for."

"Well, what *is* the reason, Jesse? Don't you trust me enough to be honest with me?"

His comment hurt—and startled her. The thought never occurred to Jesse that the reason she didn't tell James why she pulled back was because she didn't trust him. She was just ashamed of how she had allowed herself to be taken advantage of previously, and how fearful she was it might happen again if she committed herself totally to someone. But as she listened to him, the realization hit her that, at least subconsciously, maybe she did have trust issues with James—or any other man she might be involved with. In any event, it was time for her to be completely honest with him.

"The reason I stopped us is I had flashbacks to my relationship with a boyfriend while I was in law school. I told you I dated someone during law school; in fact, it was more than just dating. For the only time in my life, I became consumed with a relationship with a man—and not in a good way. Soon after we started dating, we entered into a sexual relationship. I thought it was much more than that, but he apparently didn't. After several months of practically living together and being inseparable, I learned he was cheating on me. When I confronted him, he dumped me. I've never been so humiliated and embarrassed in my life. . ."

Jesse fell silent as she bit her lower lip, trying to tamp down her emotions. She glanced up, unable to hold her gaze with James, then took a deep breath before exhaling slowly. She continued, "This was a man I had begun to think would be my husband. Instead, I was just a plaything to entertain him while he was going through law school. I can't tell you what that did to my self-respect. I thought I had gotten over that episode in my life, but that night as we were about to make love, I suddenly had flashbacks to those old feelings of humiliation and self-loathing, and they just overwhelmed me. I wasn't ready to explain to you then what was going on in my head. Afterwards, though, I've repeatedly told myself that you aren't him, but I've been struggling to overcome these feelings. Can you ever forgive me?"

James didn't respond immediately. He seemed surprised by what she told him and started to respond before apparently considering further what he wanted to say, then remained silent. After what seemed to Jesse a long, painful pause, he said, "It's hard for me to understand anyone treating you that way, Jesse. But it's even more difficult for me to understand your having those feelings about yourself. You are the most capable and self-assured woman I know. I'm so sorry you went through that experience. I also wish you had told me about it before now."

"I do, too," Jesse responded, as James fell silent, obviously deep in thought about something, and Jesse wasn't sure what.

James took another sip of his wine, a thoughtful, faraway look passing over his face, before he returned his focus to Jesse. "Since we're trying to be totally honest tonight, I have to admit I haven't been perfectly honest with you, either."

"What do you mean?" Jesse asked, surprised by his admission.

He hesitated for a moment, apparently collecting his thoughts before beginning his explanation. Jesse could recognize the pain in his expression as he struggled to find the words to express what he wanted to say.

"I also had a relationship somewhat like yours when I was in medical school. I dated a student nurse for two years. Actually, it was more than just dating; we also had a sexual relationship, and we spent as much time together as we could—given the fact I was in medical school and she was in nursing school. This was no fling for me; I wanted to marry her. But I felt I should put medical school behind me before getting married. I was afraid the marriage wouldn't have a sound foundation with the extreme demands on our time while in school. So, I told her I wanted to marry her, but not until I graduated from medical school. It's interesting; she never took issue with that outwardly, but I sensed she wasn't happy with my decision. I soon got the feeling she was drifting away—nothing I could point to specifically—but that feeling persisted until about three months later when she broke off the relationship. It stunned me and caused me to be very sensitive to a woman I love seeming to pull back. I apologize for not telling you about my situation before now."

The light came on for Jesse. She wasn't the only one struggling with the fallout of a previous relationship. Yet neither of them had admitted to the other what they were dealing with. In fact, it appeared neither had completely admitted to himself or herself what they were dealing with, all the while soldiering on, trying to build a relationship without addressing the demons within each of them that were bent on destroying it.

James looked expectantly at Jesse, obviously anxious to get her response to what he had just told her—something that was clearly painful for him to admit. A small, kind smile finally spread across her face, and she leaned into him and whispered, "Thank you for telling me that." Then, with a broader smile she said, "It's nice to know I'm not the only crazy one in this relationship."

James chuckled at her comment, and the tension that had weighed on both of them evaporated, leaving them staring at each other with more love than either had ever shown. Jesse finally broke the smiling silence, saying, "Just so there's no doubt, I love you, and I want us to be together. I'm willing to do whatever it takes to make that happen."

James' eyes lit up with more joy than he could express. "I feel the same way, Jesse . . . And I don't want to end the night just saying, 'Let's see where this goes.'"

Delighted with his response, she reached across the table for his hand, and said, "So, what *do* you want?"

James squeezed her hand in return. "How about we set a deadline for making a decision about whether we're ready to take the next step—marriage. What do you think?"

Jesse's expression matched his—a smile that reflected pure joy. She reached across the table for both of his hands, squeezed them, and said, "I couldn't agree more. How about four months to reach a decision. I would say three months, but I have a new case that's going to take me out of town a lot."

"As you lawyers say, it's a deal," James said, smiling broadly. "And let's commit to getting together at least one night a week, as well as on weekends. I want to be sure you get to know all my foibles before saying *yes.*"

Jesse was about to explode she was so happy, and James' expression told her he felt the same way. Just then, the waiter appeared with their meals. After serving them, he asked, "May I get anything else for you?"

"Yes, indeed," James quickly replied. As Jesse looked on with an amused expression, he said, "Please bring us a bottle of your finest Champagne. And save us a piece of your tiramisu."

Chapter 8

Sarah began the attorney meeting at Jordan & McKenzie the following Monday by discussing the latest changes to the word processing software the firm was about to implement. Some of the changes were major—so much so that all staff would have to attend three one-hour sessions over the noon hour in the next week, with the firm providing lunch, to be properly trained. None of the lawyers objected, or even commented, but when Sarah said that the training sessions for the lawyers would be at 5:00 PM on three successive days the week after staff was trained, the grumbling was immediate.

"I've got too much on my plate to stop at 5:00," Steve complained. "I'm facing a deadline on two appeals."

"Yeah, I agree with Steve," Maggie moaned. "In addition to the discovery requests in the Conboy case, I have a summary judgment motion and memorandum that's due soon. I've been at the office every night until 8:00 for the past three weeks, with no relief in sight. No way I can carve out that much time for training sessions."

David and Jesse remained silent but nodded in agreement with Steve and Maggie while looking at Sarah. Her expression conveyed roughly the same amount of sympathy one would expect from a drill sergeant responding to a recruit's complaint over having to march in the heat.

"You did hear me say some of the changes are major changes, didn't you?" Sarah intoned. When no one took issue with her, she continued, "So how are you going to get all of that work done if you don't know how to use the firm's word processing software?"

Her logic was hard to argue with, but Steve gave it a try. "Can we at least agree that if any of us are proficient with the changes after the first two sessions, that person can skip the third session?"

Sarah glanced at David with an upraised eyebrow to see what his response was since this was a decision he would have to approve. After apparently thinking about Steve's proposal while ping-ponging his gaze between Steve and Sarah, David said, "I'll go along with that suggestion, but it will be up to the trainer and you, Sarah, as to whether any of us lawyers are sufficiently competent to skip the third session."

With a delighted smile, Sarah responded, "Perfect. I will gladly take on that responsibility." She recognized that David's approval reflected the confidence he had in her, as well as the authority she had to run the office as a tight ship. She could also tell from their expressions that Steve and Maggie weren't wild about her having the authority to decide whether they could skip the third session, but they apparently knew better than to take issue with David on this decision, and they held their tongues.

***

Once the administrative issues for the day were behind them, David asked Jesse to bring them up to date on the Conboy case.

"There've been some significant developments," Jesse

began. "I was just about to review Steve's draft motion to dismiss NMH's complaint when I got a call late last week from NMH's lawyer, Karl Stanton. Apparently, his office finally did the research they should've done before filing the complaint. He asked if we have any objection to their filing an amended complaint, which they can file within ten days. Since Judge Long would grant them leave to file an amended complaint even if we prevailed on a motion to dismiss, I told him I had no objection, and I doubted Bart Mayfield would either. Stanton will circulate a joint stipulation and proposed order among counsel for approval to send to Judge Long."

"I don't disagree with your decision, Jesse," David said, "but won't that also delay getting our discovery requests out? We can't know what to ask in interrogatories, or what documents to request, until we know specifically what they're claiming, particularly with regard to trade secrets and confidential information. And until we get the documents and answers to interrogatories, we won't be ready to start depositions."

"Yes, I agree, and I brought up those very issues with Stanton."

"What did he say?" David responded.

"Interestingly, he said he assumed I would be concerned about this issue. His suggestion was that we jointly ask the court to set the case for trial not six months after our pre-trial scheduling conference, but rather six months after we have filed an answer to their amended complaint. We, of course, reserve the right to file a motion to dismiss their amended complaint if it isn't legally sufficient. So, this should give us ample time to get all of our discovery completed."

David nodded in agreement, then asked, "What did you tell

him?”

“I told him I would discuss his suggestion with my co-counsel, Bart Mayfield. However, before I did so, I wanted to know whether this was a firm proposal on behalf of his client. We don’t want to agree to something and then have Ms. Robinson countermand his decision.”

“Surely he wasn’t surprised by this, given her behavior at the injunction hearing.” Steve commented.

“No, he said he understood where I was coming from; in fact, he chuckled when he said that. I gather Stanton is finding his client more challenging to deal with than he anticipated.”

“I think the injunction hearing proved that beyond doubt,” Steve said. “I’ve never seen a client take over a hearing like she did. I don’t think Judge Long had ever experienced that either.”

“Agreed,” said Jesse. “In any event, Stanton called later and said he had approval from Robinson regarding his proposal that the trial be set six months after all defendants file our answer. I have a call scheduled with Bart Mayfield later today and I think he will agree.”

“What about depositions?” asked Maggie. “Are they still insisting on taking fifty depositions? From what I’ve seen in this case so far, that’s a pretty outrageous number, obviously designed to grind our clients down and exhaust their resources.”

“Yeah, we discussed the number of depositions briefly,” Jesse said. “Robinson still contends they have that many legitimate depositions to take. So, we have no agreement there. I think Judge Long will limit each side to ten to fifteen depositions, plus one or two expert depositions. We’ll just have to resolve this issue at the pre-trial scheduling conference."

David took a final bite of his ham and cheese sandwich, glanced at the clock as the second hand moved past 1:00 PM, and brought the meeting to a close.

***

Later that afternoon, David dropped by Jesse's office just as she was getting off the telephone with Bart Mayfield. As David sat down in one of the client chairs in front of her desk, Jesse said, "As I anticipated, Bart agrees with allowing NMH to file an amended complaint, provided they file it within ten days. He also agrees that we ask Judge Long to schedule the trial to begin six months after we file our respective answers to the amended complaint."

"It's good we have co-counsel we work well with," David responded. "Some of my most unpleasant cases have been ones where I argued more with my co-counsel than I did with opposing counsel."

"I know what you mean," Jesse responded. "That's been my experience also." Jesse paused, looking expectantly at David. "Is there something else you wanted to talk about?"

"There is," David said, refocusing his attention on the reason for coming to see Jesse, but not before acknowledging to himself that one of the symptoms of the funk he had been in lately was that he was easily distracted, sometimes forgetting momentarily why he came into a room, or what he wanted to do next. "I mentioned to you that I was going to schedule a meeting with the principal of Jenna's school. Well, you and I have an appointment with her at 10:00 AM on Wednesday, day after tomorrow. I hope you're free then."

69

Jesse quickly confirmed her availability on her calendar, then turned her attention back to him. "How do you plan to approach this meeting, David? And what do we hope to accomplish?"

"That's what I want to discuss. The first thing I want to find out is whether the school is taking this situation seriously. Are they doing all they can to stop the bullying? Are they aware of the legal consequences if they don't do all they can to stop it?"

"I agree with that approach," Jesse said, nodding in agreement. "How the principal responds will determine how we proceed from there."

"To help her understand how serious the situation is, I'm going to talk about the effect the bullying is having on Jenna, and especially on her friend Wanda." As David said this, he could feel the anger arising within him once more. There were few things that angered him more quickly than someone trying to harm a young person. The fact that his own daughter and her friend were involved made it worse.

David continued, "Jenna spoke to Wanda over the weekend, and she tells me Wanda is becoming more and more obsessed with this situation. I'm proud of Jenna; she's trying her best to treat it as a bad joke by ignoring it, but Wanda can't seem to do that. There haven't been any further postings on the website or social media posts. But all of the other kids in school keep joking about it; they've nicknamed Jenna and Wanda the 'slut twins.'"

"That's awful, David. I don't know how I would've dealt with something like that at their age."

"Apparently it's affected Wanda so much she skipped

school on Friday. Jenna spoke to her over the weekend and said she's never seen Wanda so upset. She doesn't even want to go back to school."

"What are the teachers doing about this?" Jesse asked.

David shrugged his shoulders. "Jenna says they've warned the students about doing or saying anything to make the situation worse, but so far the kids—or at least some of them—are just treating the whole thing as a joke, not taking it seriously at all . . ."

David pondered the situation for a minute, then got up to go back to his office. At the door, he turned to Jesse, and said, "I forgot to ask. How did your dinner go with James last week?"

Even before she responded, David could tell from Jesse's expression that the dinner went well—perhaps very well. "It was better than I hoped for or reasonably could have expected," Jesse said as a broad smile covered her face. Jesse was not one to go into much detail about her personal life—even to David. But no detail was necessary; her smile said it all.

David was surprised into momentary silence, then smiled, said, "Good; I'm delighted to hear you're pleased," and walked back to his office, happy things were going well—at least for someone he knew.

Chapter 9

Maitland Middle School opened in the late 1950s in the middle of an explosion of suburban residential development as the City of Maitland became one of the primary bedroom communities for a burgeoning central Florida metropolitan area centered around Orlando. The school was totally rebuilt and updated with modern technology in 2010, enhancing its reputation for excellence, as reflected in its perennial "A" rating by the Florida Department of Education. It was fed by students from four different elementary schools for the transitional grades of six through eight and had demographics roughly comparable to the national averages. Jenna had been thrilled to attend Maitland Middle during the sixth grade—and during the seventh until the bullying issue arose.

David and Jesse arrived at the school shortly before their 10:00 AM meeting with Dr. Miriam Samuelson, principal of Maitland Middle for the past six years. They were greeted warmly by Dr. Samuelson's assistant, who ushered them into a small nondescript conference room adjacent to Dr. Samuelson's office. The only artwork to liven the room was a large, stylized painting of a hawk, the school's mascot.

The assistant invited them to sit at the round, plain conference table, which reminded David of the conference tables in the flight line building during his Air Force days where the pilots gathered when they were not actually flying—tables that were functional but not designed to enhance the room.

"May I get you coffee or water?" she asked. When David and Jesse declined, she informed them Dr. Samuelson would be with them momentarily and stepped out.

Almost immediately a tall, thin woman whom David estimated to be in her late forties entered, dressed professionally in a navy-blue suit, but with a pale pink silk blouse that lightened the look, making her appearance less business formal. She had medium short salt-and-pepper- colored hair, parted to the side, that matched nicely with her black horn-rimmed glasses. She wore little makeup—only a touch of lipstick—and flat soled shoes that kept her height from overpowering people meeting her for the first time. David didn't consider her a particularly attractive woman, but there was a warmth in her deep brown eyes surrounded by crow's feet when she smiled that was welcoming, inviting someone meeting her for the first time to get to know her better.

"Hello, I'm Miriam Samuelson," she said, extending a hand first to David, then to Jesse. "Welcome to Maitland Middle School. I wish you were here for a happier reason, but let me say up front, I'm glad you're here."

"We thank you for taking time to meet with us, Dr. Samuelson," David said, impressed she hadn't introduced herself as Dr. Samuelson, which made him more inclined to honor her title. As they all sat down around the table, David continued, "This is Jesse McKenzie; she's my cousin, my law partner, and my daughter Jenna's aunt. For all practical purposes she's the closest person Jenna has to a mother since my wife Carol died last year. You can discuss anything regarding Jenna as freely with her as you can with me."

The concern on Dr. Samuelson's face as David mentioned Carol's death appeared genuine. "I understand," she responded.

"And let me say how sorry I am for your loss and Jenna's loss. I met your wife on two occasions, and there is no one in this community I respected more than her. I've referred several young women to Women's Crisis Center, and the results each time have been remarkable." Turning to Jesse, she continued, "I understand you, Ms. McKenzie, are now chairman of the board for WCC. Thank you for your service in that capacity. I will certainly include you in any communications about Jenna."

Dr. Samuelson's openness convinced David she intended to be cooperative with them, which changed the somewhat confrontational approach he originally intended to take. Given his assessment they could be collaborative, he said, "Thank you for your kind words about Carol. Since I'm here primarily as a parent, not a lawyer, I would prefer you call us David and Jesse; do you mind?"

"Not at all; I prefer it also. Call me Miriam." She paused, took a deep breath, and continued, "I can't tell you how distressing this bullying situation is to me. In my entire twenty-year career in education, I've never experienced anything like it, although I'm well aware we aren't the first school to encounter this problem."

"We're scrambling to learn more about it, as well," Jesse interjected. "I must say, I've never seen Jenna so upset by a situation, other than her mother's death, as she's been over this one. And as bad as it's been for Jenna, it's apparently upset her friend Wanda even more."

"Yeah, I know it's been tough on both of them," Miriam responded. "Wanda has missed a few days of school because she's so upset." Turning to David, she continued, "One of our biggest challenges now is to convince all the other students this isn't just some big joke. It has to be taken seriously. So far, we haven't had much success."

"Maybe we can help with that," David said. "We've done our research. Cyberstalking or cyberbullying someone under sixteen years old is a felony of the third degree; so, it's extremely serious. Of course, if the cyberbullying caused harm to someone—especially a minor—it's even more serious. The students may not treat this situation so flippantly if they know that."

"Is that true even if the perpetrator is a minor?" Miriam asked.

"Well, a minor would likely be subject to juvenile court rules, although it's possible for a minor to be tried as an adult. But going through the juvenile courts is no picnic for a minor either." David gathered from Miriam's expression she understood how consequential the charges could be against the offender. He decided to get her sense of who was behind it. "Now that you've raised the issue, do you believe the perpetrator is a student here?"

Miriam slowly put both of her hands on the table, palms down and fingers extended, before responding to David's question, which seemed to trouble her. "As much as it pains me to say it, I do believe the person doing this is a student here—or at least a student who is cooperating with someone else who is doing it. There are references to things going on in the school that only a student would know—things concerning school events or happenings, particularly sports events. Someone outside the school wouldn't know such details."

This confirmed the conclusion David and Jesse had come to, but David wanted to explore one other category of suspects. "Don't take this as an accusation," David said, "but are you sure no faculty members are involved in this in any way?"

Miriam pondered his question before responding, which David interpreted as being a tacit admission she had asked herself the same question previously. "I can't be positive at this point, but my gut feeling is that no faculty member is involved. I've known most of our faculty for several years, and I'd be shocked if any of them are involved. Also, the comments being made by Ghostwhoknows seem quite juvenile to me."

David nodded in agreement with her last remark, adding, "But we must admit the juvenile doing this—if it is a juvenile—is smart, and quite knowledgeable about how to hide his or her identity."

"Unfortunately, I have to agree," Miriam said, returning her hands to her lap. "We were surprised our perpetrator was able to post what he did on our student electronic bulletin board on the school website. Somehow, he—or she—was able to navigate around the protections our information technology department had built into the bulletin board to prevent someone from posting anything on it until we reviewed what they wanted to post."

Her statement confirmed David's assumption that the school IT department had no clue as to whom the perpetrator was, but he wanted to know more about whatever investigation they might have undertaken. "I assume your IT department has also been trying to trace who posted on the bulletin board, and who has made the bullying comments on social media. Have they come up with any clues so far?" David was hoping for at least some sliver of information to inform his further efforts to bring this potentially dangerous situation to an end.

"No, nothing specific. . ." Miriam hesitated, appearing to be undecided about a further comment before adding, "but we've noticed all of the comments and postings have occurred soon after the girls soccer team has won a game. Both Jenna and Wanda are on the team, and they've been receiving a lot of praise for how well they've played lately. It may be nothing, but so far that's the only connection we've noticed."

David was surprised by this comment, and as he glanced at Jesse he surmised from her expression she was too. "Do you have any idea what the significance of that connection may be?" Jesse asked before David could get the same words out.

"It's only speculation, but the girls soccer team is having a very good season, whereas the boys team is having its worse season in all the years I've been here. They've only won one game. Could the bullying be the result of jealousy? I don't know; we're just speculating at this point," Miriam responded, shrugging her shoulders in frustration.

"It's a thought worth exploring further," David responded.

David and Jesse then went over some of the potential legal consequences for a student who engaged in cyberbullying, and offered suggestions how Miriam might present such information to the students. He had anticipated having to deal with an education department bureaucrat who would defend her power to address this problem exclusively without any interference from even well-intentioned outsiders. But Miriam was proving to be just the opposite. He was impressed by her attitude and grateful for her cooperation.

After they kicked around a few other ideas about how to deal with the situation, David felt they had achieved all they reasonably could during the meeting with Miriam. He urged her once more to emphasize to the students the serious nature of the bullying. She, in turn, said she would keep David and Jesse informed of further developments, and they brought the meeting to a close.

***

On their way back to the office, David asked Jesse, "What do you think of Dr. Samuelson?"

"My take is she's a sincere public educator who's been thrust into a situation she never anticipated, and she's as unsure how to respond to it as we are. She was less defensive than I thought she would be. . ." Jesse hesitated as she pondered how to accurately express some of the vague thoughts that were flickering about in her mind but remained just out of reach of coherence. Finally, she continued, "You know, I feel sorry for Miriam. She's trying her best to bring a first-class education experience to her students, after going through seven or eight years of college and grad school to be able to do so. Now, due to new technologies and new opportunities for bad characters to exhibit some of the worst traits of human nature, she's facing a situation for which she's unprepared but for which she will probably be held responsible to some extent, particularly if the outcome is a bad one. I think she senses this and is angry, frustrated, and fearful about it."

"Can you blame her?" David responded. "I feel the same way over this situation, and I don't have a doctorate in being a parent." After turning onto I-4 toward their office, David asked, "What do you think about her comment that all of the bullying episodes have come shortly after a soccer game?"

"It's perceptive of her to have picked up on that . . . I'm not sure what to do with this information, but we ought to look into it further."

"Yeah, I agree," David said. "And I have an idea where to begin."

***

Molly greeted David at the door when he arrived home promptly at 6:00 that night. She did her usual dance of jumping up and down and running in circles before plopping down at his feet to be petted. Since Molly had arrived at the Jordan household this had developed into standard protocol, and David had learned there was no point in trying to greet anyone else until Molly had received the attention she demanded. Only after petting her back, scratching behind her ears, and telling her, "Good girl" a few times could David give Jenna a hug and greet Angelita.

The aroma of the pot roast Angelita was preparing—along with mashed potatoes and green beans—reminded David how hungry he was after a demanding day. He and Jenna set the table for the three of them while Angelita finished her meal preparations. As they all sat down together—as they always did for the evening meal—David offered a prayer of thanksgiving for the food, and especially for the cook who prepared it. He often included her in the prayer when Angelita prepared an especially good meal, and tonight it drew her usual modest response: "This nothing, Meester David, just an old family recipe."

As soon as they began to eat, Jenna asked, "How'd your meeting go with Dr. Samuelson today, Dad?" David had told Jenna he was meeting with her principal about the cyberbullying situation, and that he would give her a full report. He also wanted Angelita in on the conversation since Jenna had kept her fully informed on all developments to date, and Angelita seemed as concerned as he was about the situation.

David put down his knife and fork and gave Jenna his full attention. "I thought it went well. Dr. Samuelson was more cooperative than I thought she would be. Usually when Jesse and I talk to someone who's not our client the person is wary, afraid we might sue them if we can find grounds to do so. But she seemed glad we were there and willing to cooperate any way she can."

"I'm glad to hear that, Dad. Did she say anything about who she thinks is doing this?" Jenna looked hopefully at her father as she asked the question and put down her fork as she awaited a reply.

"Not specifically," David responded, "although she did say she thinks the person doing this is probably a student at the school. She said only a student would know the details in some of the comments that have been made."

"Oh, there's no question in my mind—Wanda's either. The jerk is definitely a student!" Jenna stated emphatically as she picked up her fork again to continue eating.

"Why some student want to act like this, Meester David?" Angelita asked, clearly puzzled by what appeared to be random acts of hatred. David recognized that Angelita had been through some tough times in her life, but he suspected few, if any, of those tough times were due to malicious acts by someone designed purely to hurt her. This was apparently a new experience for Angelita, and not a good one.

"I wish I knew, Angelita. Unfortunately, some people just seem to get pleasure from hurting other people. It's sad. . . ." David said nothing for a few moments as he thought of someone so young—if the culprit was a student—acting like this.

David took another bite of the excellent pot roast, then put down his fork again as he looked at Jenna. "Dr. Samuelson did mention something else. She noticed that each of the bullying incidents has occurred shortly after the girls' soccer team has won a game. She also commented that the boys' team isn't having a good year, only having won one game. Do you think this may have something to do with why the perpetrator is doing this?"

Jenna was plainly taken aback by this idea. "I hadn't considered that, Dad. I mean, Wanda and I have played well, but other girls on the team have played well, too, and no one's bullying them. . ." She pondered David's comment for a few more moments, before continuing, "I also can't picture any of the boys on the soccer team being so jealous they would do this." She thought about Dr. Samuelson's comment a little longer before saying, "On the other hand, I can't think of any other reason why someone would do this either."

David could sense her frustration but decided to push further. "Where do the boys and girls team practice during the week? And are there other students around when you're practicing?"

"You've seen the soccer fields, Dad. They're next to the track, one field for the boys and one for the girls. The only people there during our practices are the boys' and girls' teams and our coaches, except for a few students who may be running around the track on their own. There's no interaction between the girls and boys teams during practice."

David nodded as he recalled seeing the soccer fields before on the occasions he took Jenna to practice. "So, no one else present during practice? What about during the games?"

"During the games we have a mix of students and parents, as you've seen when you've been to our games. Usually, the cheerleaders are at our games, except sometimes if the boys and girls are both playing at the same time, the cheerleaders alter which game they go to." Then, as a light came on in her face, she added,

"I forgot to mention, the cheerleaders are also at the area inside the track or occasionally by the soccer fields during our practices."

David hadn't thought of the cheerleaders being part of a suspect group, but at this point they had to consider everyone. "Any idea whether one or two of the cheerleaders might be involved?" David asked as he finished off the mashed potatoes on his plate.

"I can't imagine why, Dad. These are the most popular girls in school." Jenna played with the food on her plate as she seemed frustrated she couldn't think of any reason why someone would want to harm her or Wanda. Finally, she looked directly at David with moist eyes on the verge of tears, and with her voice only slightly above a whisper, said, "Whoever it is, Dad, we need to find the person and do something. Wanda can't take much more before she snaps."

"Jesse and I will do all we can, Jenna. Encourage Wanda to hang in there."

David felt as frustrated as he had since Carol's final illness. It was miserable feeling so helpless, as he painfully recalled from Carol's last days. But now the same feeling was mocking him once more due to his inability to protect his daughter from the cyberbully. The dinner ended on a somber note, with Jenna going upstairs to finish her homework.

As David helped Angelita clear the table, she said, "Jenna strong girl, Meester David. She get through this OK."

David just nodded and gave her a weak smile. *From your lips to God's ears, Angelita.*

Chapter 10

The purpose of the Florida Rules of Civil Procedure is, "to secure the just, speedy, and inexpensive determination of every action (lawsuit)." While Judge Sally Long may have believed the results—in her court, at least—were usually just, it was well known among Orlando lawyers that she believed cases often took far too long to resolve and were way too expensive for the litigants, and sometimes even for the court system. It was also well known among Orlando lawyers that Judge Long considered it her sacred duty to ensure lawsuits in her court were resolved speedily at reasonable cost, and woe be to any lawyer or litigant who interfered with that goal. She kept tight control over the proceedings, beginning with the initial case management conference, sometimes referred to as the scheduling conference, at which certain deadlines were set, limits were placed on discovery, and the date of the trial and its allotted length was determined.

When counsel for all parties met with Judge Long in her hearing room the following Monday for the scheduling conference, it was obvious she wasn't in a good mood. The joint stipulation in which the lawyers should have agreed on the number of depositions to be taken, the number of interrogatories that could be served, the number of experts each side would be permitted, and other such required items, left much to be desired. In fact, there were more items on which the parties disagreed than those on which they agreed. When she entered the hearing room through the rear door that connected to her chambers, Jesse could immediately sense her anger. The red splotches on her neck were already apparent, and the hearing hadn't even begun.

Judge Long found the electronic case file on her computer, opened her folder containing her notes, and asked the lawyers to state their appearances for the court reporter to record. She had required that a court reporter be present at all hearings in the case after the debacle that was the temporary injunction hearing. Karl Stanton announced his appearance and Rhonda Robinson's for the plaintiff, NMH; Bart Mayfield announced his appearance for Allan Brandon and Brandon Associates, Inc.; and Jesse announced her appearance and Steve's for Mark Conboy and the other six individuals—all the while Judge Long sat looking sternly at the lawyers seated around the long conference table from her own desk at the head of the table.

Once appearances were made, Judge Long referred again to her notes, then addressed Stanton and said, "I have the joint stipulation from all counsel agreeing to allow the plaintiff ten days to file an amended complaint. Are you sure you can meet that deadline, Mr. Stanton?"

"I can do better than that, Your Honor," Stanton replied. "Given the time constraints the parties have agreed to, we've worked overtime to bring our amended complaint to the hearing today. As soon as you sign the order granting us leave to file the amended complaint, we'll file it with you today."

Jesse was surprised by this, as both Bart Mayfield and Judge Long appeared to be. Jesse gathered that Stanton realized he had got off on the wrong foot with the judge and was trying to cure his bad impression from the first hearing. It appeared to be working because Judge Long promptly signed the order allowing the amended complaint to be filed, and then accepted the amended complaint from Stanton, who then handed a copy to Mayfield and to Jesse.

"The order I just signed gives the defendants ten days to file an answer or motion to dismiss. I realize the defendants haven't reviewed this new pleading yet, but you've had the original complaint for two weeks; do you anticipate filing an answer rather than a motion to dismiss? Before I set a trial date, I need some idea when an answer will be filed."

This comment by the judge surprised Jesse; she didn't recall Judge Long—or any other judge—ever pressing her for a commitment in advance on whether she would file a motion or an answer to a complaint, but she was plainly pushing the lawyers for an early trial date, and obviously preferred that an answer be filed as soon as possible. Jesse glanced at Mayfield who also seemed understandably surprised, and said, "Judge, may I briefly confer with my co-counsel?" When the judge agreed, Jesse and Mayfield walked out of the hearing room, briefly conferred and returned within three minutes.

As they sat down, Jesse said, "Judge, unless there is some entirely new claim pled in the amended complaint, the defendants will file an answer within ten days." As she said this, Stanton shook his head indicating there were no new claims, which the judge took note of, scribbling something in her notebook.

"Good," Judge Long announced. "This means we are going to trial in this case six months and ten days from today. There will be no continuances granted unless there is *very* good cause shown for a continuance. Do I make myself clear?"

As the judge glanced at each of the lawyers present, one by one, each nodded in agreement. She then continued, "One of the claims in the original complaint was that the defendants stole

NMH's trade secrets and used them to compete unfairly with the plaintiff. Is there a similar claim in the amended complaint?"

When Stanton confirmed there was, Judge Long said, "Then, there's an issue I want to get on the table right now, so it doesn't create a problem for us later. In several recent cases I've had we've had disputes over what the claimed trade secrets were. In those cases, the defendants protested they weren't able to complete their discovery before trial because the plaintiffs hadn't described the alleged trade secrets with enough specificity for them to be able to prepare a defense, so they asked for a continuance. I've reviewed the original complaint in this case, and the alleged trade secrets weren't sufficiently described; at least, I couldn't tell what they were from the vague descriptions. I don't want to run into a similar problem in this case." Turning to look directly at Stanton, she inquired, "Any questions about that, Mr. Stanton?"

"No, judge, we understand a claimant's responsibility to adequately describe what the trade secrets are that were stolen," Stanton responded.

"Good. So you understand NMH will have to describe the trade secrets clearly and with specificity in discovery so the defendants can timely complete their discovery before the discovery cutoff date; otherwise NMH won't be allowed to pursue the trade secret claim at trial."

Judge Long raised an eyebrow as she looked at Stanton for an expected affirmative response. "Yes, we understand, judge."

Jesse was observing Rhonda Robinson as Stanton said this. Her frustration with the judge's comments and Stanton's response was reflected in her stony, disbelieving expression. She looked like she was about to explode.

Sure enough, after only a moment's hesitation, Robinson interjected, speaking in a rapid- fire manner, "But judge, this case is about the defendants executing a plan to *gut* NMH's business by taking its key employees and *robbing* NMH of its business without paying for it. They *stole* customer lists, compensation schedules, know how, and key relationships. You can't prevent us from presenting evidence about these issues!"

Judge Long's eyes and gritted teeth reflected her stunned surprise, as the head snap by Stanton reflected his. He stuck out a hand to Robinson to get her to hush. No one said a word for nearly a minute, as even Robinson realized she had said too much. Jesse noticed the red splotches on the judge's neck, which had faded when Stanton produced the amended complaint, were now back in spades.

Finally, Judge Long took a deep breath, glared at Robinson with a countenance that would have intimidated a hardened criminal, and said, "Counselor, I haven't made any rulings on what evidence you may present. I have merely clarified that Florida law requires allegations of theft of trade secrets to be presented with sufficient clarity so defendants know what they are defending against, and so that all discovery can be completed by the discovery cutoff date. Do *you* understand this?"

"Yes, judge . . . I apologize." Robinson wisely appeared to be contrite.

After allowing herself a few seconds to cool down, Judge Long referred again to her notes, and said, "The next issue I want to address is the number of depositions. In the submission by counsel, I note that plaintiffs are suggesting they may need to take fifty depositions, whereas defendants believe only fifteen per side should be sufficient. Mr. Stanton, why in the world does the plaintiff need to take fifty depositions?"

This was a question Jesse had asked herself, and she was anxious to hear Stanton's response. He nodded his head before responding, apparently conceding this was a reasonable inquiry. "Your honor, we recognize this is a larger number of depositions than most cases require, but we have essentially alleged that the defendants conspired together to steal NMH's material handling business without paying for it. They hired away our entire management team, the very people who had been dealing with our customers, and who, we believe, told our customers and prospective customers, 'Hold off on your projects until we get to Brandon Associates, where we can do the job cheaper.' Mr. Conboy took customer lists, salary lists, and my client's pricing protocols to Brandon Associates, while still working for NMH, to secure his job and recruit the other individual defendants to Brandon Associates. There are a lot of customers and prospective customers around the country we're going to have to depose since we can't subpoena them to come to Florida to testify. When you add all of those depositions to at least nine depositions we will have to take just to see what the defendants have to say, it quickly adds up. Of course, if we don't need to take that many depositions we won't, but we shouldn't be artificially limited in advance; that could inhibit our ability to prove our case, which would be a denial of justice."

Jesse could tell Judge Long seemed somewhat persuaded by Stanton's argument. She and Bart Mayfield had discussed in advance what arguments they should make to prevent a discovery assault by NMH that might eventually exhaust Brandon associates' resources with which to fight the lawsuit. Mayfield had agreed they would need to address this effort by NMH head on and that Jesse should make the argument for all defendants. She felt prepared as the judge turned to her for a response before deciding what limit, if any, the court should impose on the number of depositions.

Referring to her notes, Jesse began, "Judge, it's important to remember that none of the individual defendants had non-compete agreements, so just as NMH was free to fire them at any time, they were free as at-will employees to leave at any time to go work for a competitor. Prior to the individual defendants leaving to work for Brandon Associates, NMH didn't have much of a business in *commercial* material handling contracts. The vast bulk of their work was on *government* contracts, and the evidence will show that the economics of government contracts and commercial contracts are distinctly different. In fact, that's one of the primary reasons my clients left NMH; it wasn't very competitive in the commercial market. The small number of commercial contracts that NMH obtained were originated mostly by Brandon Associates who didn't have an integration services division at the time, even though Allan Brandon was a consultant in that business. Brandon Associates would either refer the customer to NMH or hire NMH directly as a subcontractor.

"The prospective customers NMH refers to? The names of virtually all of those prospects were obtained by NMH from Brandon Associates. So, it would be an irrelevant goose chase for NMH to take depositions all over the country of potential customers with which NMH had a relationship when that relationship—if there was one at all—existed only through Brandon Associates' efforts."

Judge Long was following Jesse's argument attentively, but Jesse decided she couldn't just leave the number of depositions open for the judge to determine without a recommendation from the defendants. "So," she continued, "we suggest that each side should be limited to fifteen depositions, plus expert depositions, with each side being limited to two experts."

The judge pondered Jesse's argument while leaning back in her high-back chair before asking, "Any response, Mr. Stanton?"

"Yes, Your Honor. We disagree with Ms. McKenzie's statement that there were no relationships between NMH and its customers and prospects, except though Brandon Associates, and we should have the opportunity through discovery to produce the necessary evidence to prove our case. We can't do that if you limit the number of depositions we can take. What none of us wants to happen is that we go all the way through trial only to be told later by an appellate court that the case must be tried again because plaintiff was denied its right to take the depositions of *all* relevant witnesses."

Jesse gathered from Judge Long's wry smile that she recognized the not-so-subtle warning by Stanton that NMH was ready to take any adverse decision they didn't like to an appellate court. Jesse smiled inwardly at this—another blunder by Stanton due to a lack of local knowledge. *This judge is not one who responds well to a threat.*

After leaning back in her chair once more, scanning the ceiling and pursing her lips, she returned her gaze to the lawyers. "Here's what we'll do. Each side can take up to twenty depositions, plus two expert depositions per side. No deposition shall exceed seven hours of actual testimony. If any party believes there are good grounds for taking additional depositions, you can file a motion for leave to take a specified number of additional depos. Each side is limited to fifty interrogatories, including subparts. Any questions?"

When there were no questions about her ruling, the judge

proceeded to set the dates and times for counsel to submit their pre-trial statements in which they would list all issues for trial, and each party would submit their witness list and exhibit list for trial, together with objections to the other side's witnesses or exhibits. Finally, she brought the hearing to a close by reminding counsel that she expected all parties and their counsel to adhere to the schedule to bring this case to trial on time. She was living up to her reputation, and Jesse noticed all of the lawyers present appeared to recognize that fact.

***

Back at the office, Jesse shepherded Bart and Steve into the conference room and asked David and Maggie to join them. With the deadline for the defendants to file an answer to the amended complaint only ten days away, it was time to make some decisions about how to coordinate their defense to this lawsuit that had the potential to ruin the lives of all of the defendants.

Jesse brought David and Maggie up to speed on the scheduling conference they had just attended, then addressed Steve, "Have you had an opportunity to review the amended complaint?"

Looking up from the notes he was taking, Steve said, "Yes, briefly. I'll analyze it further this afternoon, but it appears they've alleged the same causes of action that were in the original complaint. Mostly, it appears they've just cleaned up the language and added some factual detail to the allegations."

"How soon can you have a draft answer ready?" Jesse asked.

"I had already begun drafting an answer to the original complaint, so I should have a draft answer to this one ready in a couple of days. I just need to do a little research regarding some of our affirmative defenses."

"When the draft is ready, would you send a copy to my associate, Regina Paxton?" Mayfield asked Steve.

"Of course. Regina and I have already had several phone conversations about our respective answers following the temporary injunction hearing," Steve replied. "We're coordinating our answers."

"Excellent. Let's address our discovery efforts then," Jesse said. "David and Maggie are working on those efforts. Where are we, David?"

Turning to Bart, David said, "We plan to serve a set of interrogatories and requests for production of documents within the next week, even before we file an answer. I was pleased to hear Judge Long addressed the issue of getting specific descriptions of what NMH claims are their trade secrets."

"Yeah, what was that issue all about regarding defining the trade secrets that the judge mentioned at the hearing? I haven't had that issue come up in any of my cases, which have all been in Georgia courts."

"It's an issue that has come up frequently in our cases here in Florida," David replied. "The definition of a trade secret is more limited than some people think. The legal definition is 'information that has either actual or potential independent economic value by virtue of not being generally known, has value to others who cannot legitimately obtain the information, and is subject to reasonable efforts to maintain its secrecy.'"

"Can you give me a good example?" Mayfield asked.

"Sure," David responded. "Perhaps the best example is the formula for Coca-Cola. It has all three elements necessary to be a trade secret. First, there is secret information—the formula for the drink; two, there is economic value to the formula because no one else has it—others have tried to copy it but can't quite do it; and three, reasonable efforts have been taken to protect the trade secret—Coca-Cola has fiercely protected the secrecy of the formula."

"That definition sounds to me more exacting than what NMH has alleged as trade secrets in their complaint," Mayfield suggested.

"Precisely," Maggie intervened, and that's why we're asking for specific details about what they claim to be trade secrets in our interrogatories. We believe we may be able to have the judge dismiss their claim for theft of trade secrets by showing NMH has nothing that actually qualifies legally as a trade secret."

"I understand," Mayfield replied. "Are you also coordinating with Regina?"

"Oh, yes. We've already discussed this issue several times. We should be able to serve our interrogatories and requests for production of documents on plaintiff's counsel by the end of the week, and Regina told me she would be able to serve hers then as well," Maggie said.

"Sounds like we are all on the same page," Jesse said. "Let's just keep in mind that although we're busy now, we're going to be extremely busy once depositions begin, and they will probably begin within about forty-five days."

The seriousness of the case and its possible consequences to all of their clients added excitement to the discussion among them as they planned their strategy and the next steps they would take over the coming months in this challenging lawsuit. Like any good trial lawyer, Jesse could feel her competitive juices ratcheting up, and she could tell David's were also. She was pleased to see David was acting more like his old self at work than he had recently, although she could tell that Jenna's bullying problem was tugging at his heart.

***

By late afternoon the rush of the day's events had finally slowed, Bart Mayfield had left to return to Valdosta, and Jesse finally had time to catch her breath. As she assessed her workload for the remainder of the week, she realized she was slammed. While she had been so busy with the NMH case, several of her other cases had heated up and were demanding her attention. Glancing at her calendar, she reminded herself that Tuesday evening was committed to Jenna. She and James had recently decided that Wednesday would be their evening during the week to spend together. *That's not going to work this week, though. I'll be working until 10:00 or later every night this week. I'd better not wait until the last minute Wednesday to let James know.*

Jesse dialed James' cell phone, hoping to catch him between procedures. Mondays were usually a heavy surgery day for him, often extending into the evening hours. He picked up on the second ring. "Hey, Jesse, I've just got a minute before going into surgery. What's up?"

She could tell he was rushed, and now probably wouldn't be the ideal time to cancel their Wednesday date. "After the day I've had I just wanted to hear your voice and tell you I love you."

"Aw, that's sweet, Jess. I love you, too. And I can't wait for our dinner date Wednesday night. Let's go to Ruth's Chris

94

Steakhouse in Winter Park."

"Uh, about that . . ." Jesse replied, hating to cancel but knowing it would be less painful to do it now rather than on short notice. A last-minute cancellation always irritated James. "There's just no way I'll be able to make it Wednesday. I'm so sorry, but I'm just overwhelmed at work. I promise I'll be free Friday, Saturday, and Sunday nights."

There was a long silent pause from James. Finally, Jesse asked, "Are you still there?"

"Yes, I'm here, Jesse. Didn't we just promise at Antonio's that we're going to set aside one night during the week for each other?" His disappointment was palpable.

"We did. . ." Jesse replied weakly. "I'm as frustrated as you are about this, but my caseload is over the top right now." She started to say she hoped things would calm down soon, but caught herself, realizing there was little chance her schedule would improve while the NMH case was pending.

After another long pause and a sigh of acceptance, James said, "Okay. I understand." Then, with mock seriousness he added, "But don't you dare cancel Friday night."

"It's a deal. I'll make reservations at Ruth's Chris for Friday night. I love you."

"Gotta go. Surgery's about to begin," James said as he clicked off, disappointing Jesse he didn't respond with a profession of love. As she turned back to her cases, the thought crossed her mind: *I can't keep cancelling on my promises to him or I'm not going to have a relationship with this man. How did life get to be so complicated?*.

<h1 align="center">Chapter 11</h1>

By Friday of the same week, Steve had drafted an answer to the amended complaint, and painstakingly revised it several times before giving it to Jesse for her perusal. She was as notorious as David for her exacting review of any pleading submitted to her by Steve or Maggie. They had heard both David and Jesse say, "A complaint or an answer we file is often the first exposure the judge has to our side of the case. So, there can be no mistakes—no typos, no misstatements, no grammatical errors—in our pleadings. Furthermore, our legal research must be thorough; we will only assert legal theories or defenses for which there is a sound legal basis. And finally, the pleading must be persuasive, leading the judge to see that justice is on our side."

Steve and Maggie had heard this spiel so many times they had it memorized; in fact, they recited it to each other from time to time. But they also recognized the truth of David and Jesse's other favorite quote, "It takes a long time to build a solid reputation, but it can be undone, or at least diminished, in an instant by a sloppy pleading, or one that overlooks a recent opinion by an appellate court that eviscerates our legal theory in a case." Steve wasn't about to overlook anything in a case of this magnitude.

Once Jesse's comments on the answer had been incorporated, Steve sent a copy to Bart Mayfield and his associate, Regina. It was critical that the defendants didn't contradict one another in their respective pleadings. In short order, all involved in preparing the answers for the respective defendants were in agreement, and the pleadings were timely filed.

In the meantime, Maggie was working furiously on the discovery documents. In most civil lawsuits the discovery phase is the longest, and often the determinative stage of the lawsuit. No more than two or three percent of civil cases filed ever make it to trial. During the discovery phase each side has the opportunity to submit written questions to the other side—called interrogatories. They also submit requests for production of documents to the other side, which, despite being called "requests," must be produced. And they can interrogate the witnesses under oath in the presence of a court reporter—called depositions—which enables the lawyers to know what the witnesses will testify to at trial. By the time this extensive (and expensive) stage of the case is over, each side knows the strengths and weaknesses of both sides of the case, and they can better estimate their chances at trial. The result is that the vast majority of cases settle without going to trial.

Maggie was nothing if not thorough in drafting interrogatories and requests for production of documents. In fact, it was rare for Jesse or David to significantly revise her discovery drafts. Once Maggie drafted the interrogatories and requests for production, she ran them by David and then Bart and Regina, who essentially copied Maggie's work, and all defendants served their discovery requests at the same time they served their answers.

While Maggie and Steve were completing their work, David and Jesse were interviewing their clients in depth. They both followed the practice David developed early in his career of creating a separate file—a paper file backed up by an electronic file— for each witness. The file would include extensive notes of an interview of the witness, including information regarding his or her background, and any important reminders for the witness's testimony. Gathering all of this information about their own clients early in the case was essential to establish all appropriate defenses and to properly prepare them for their depositions. It was time consuming, sometimes tedious work, but David and Jesse had both learned long ago to never allow a client's testimony to be taken without thorough preparation.

Soon after the answers were filed and the discovery requests served and received by all parties, Jesse scheduled a conference call with Bart and Regina, and asked David, Steve and Maggie to join. "Given the volume of documents we've requested from NMH, we suggest their documents be delivered electronically in a searchable format to a designated website in the cloud that your firm and ours can each independently search," Jesse said. "And we suggest we each produce our respective documents to plaintiff electronically, in a searchable format, to a website of their choosing. Is that acceptable to you?"

When Mayfield replied that it was, Jesse suggested that Maggie draft a confidentiality agreement to submit to the other side to ensure that all parties keep the documents confidential and used only for this case. "If you agree to handle production of documents in this manner, I'll contact Karl Stanton to get his agreement." Mayfield agreed, deferring to Jesse's extensive experience in handling document-heavy cases.

To her surprise, Jesse was able to get Stanton to agree to the terms of the confidentiality agreement Maggie drafted with only minor changes. Thus, the stage was set for the onslaught of discovery. Jesse anticipated a document dump of hundreds of thousands of documents from NMH, followed by notices of depositions in far-flung places.

***

Friday night was David's favorite night of the week. Each Friday as he drove home from the office, he felt the tension of the week slowly ease from his mind and body. Even on those Fridays when he knew he had to spend part of the weekend working, he still looked forward to getting home, having a relaxing dinner, and enjoying family time. Tonight was no exception. The week had been tedious as he and Maggie had worked on finalizing and serving the discovery requests. Several of his other cases had required extensive deposition preparation, including reviewing a mountain of important, but deadly dull, documents, and he had to stay at the office an extra two hours Thursday night to complete a continuing education course before his Florida Bar imposed deadline for completion, which was at midnight that very night. In short, he was glad to have this week behind him.

As he navigated the usual I-4 traffic congestion, David's thoughts turned to Jenna. The girls soccer team won their most recent game on Thursday—and the boys lost again—so he was anxious to learn from Jenna whether whoever was cyber bullying Jenna and Wanda was up to their old tricks again. There hadn't been another episode since David and Jesse visited Dr. Samuelson at Maitland Middle School Wednesday of the previous week. This had led Jenna—the optimistic one—to cautiously hope the cyber bullying was over. According to Jenna, however, the effect of no word from the Jerk had had the opposite effect on Wanda. She was more nervous than ever, fearful of when she and Jenna would be mocked or bullied again. According to Jenna, the tension was wearing on Wanda, and she was having trouble concentrating in class. Even her soccer game wasn't as sharp this week as it had been before the bullying started.

As David wondered once more why anyone would want to bully a couple of teenage girls, another thought crossed over from his subconscious into his conscious mind. He hadn't been in as much of a funk this past week as he had previously. Although he found it unintuitive, the fact he was spending so much time contemplating how to help Jenna seemed to push thoughts of his own situation into the background, arousing in him the parental defensive mechanism that would allow no competitors, such as his own feelings of inadequacy, guilt or loss. So long as he had his daughter to defend, he could put off focusing on how much he missed Carol.

Just as he was about to turn into his driveway at home, another thought crossed David's mind. Well, it was more a feeling than a thought. He was actually jealous of Jesse and her situation with James. It was obvious she was in love, and from all David could discern, James was in love with her. *Do they really understand how fortunate and blessed they are to be in this situation?* David was happy for Jesse but seeing her so happy tended to remind him of his loss of Carol. *Come to think of it, however, she was more than a little frustrated this week as the work piled up and she couldn't meet James for dinner.* David resolved to give her some brotherly advice—whether she wanted it or not—to avoid skipping a date with James for work, unless absolutely necessary.

As David reached for his keys to open the front door, he reminded himself once more how blessed he was to have his daughter, Angelita, and even Molly in his life. He was also fortunate to have his second family—the lawyers and staff at the law firm. Since Carol died, they had carried him emotionally, and he was grateful.

***

Before the door was halfway open, Molly was jumping up

and down, twirling in circles, and making a minor spectacle of herself to welcome David home. He finally had to rub her tummy for a few minutes to calm her down. Angelita had taken her to the groomer that day. Molly looked like a white ball of fur and smelled faintly of honeysuckle.

Jenna was right behind Molly to greet David at the door. "How was your day, Dad? Just to get this out of the way right up front, we haven't heard anything further from the Jerk. So, let's hope he has moved on."

This was a relief to David, whose only fear for the day was that he would arrive home to learn of more cyber bullying by the anonymous person they were calling the Jerk. The relief he felt from learning that hadn't happened surprised him and reminded him once more how much this issue was bothering him. "Glad to hear that," David commented. "How's Wanda holding up?"

"A little better, I think. She wasn't quite as nervous today, but I still worry about her. She has really let the bullying get under her skin."

"Good evening, Meester David," Angelita said as David entered the kitchen, engulfed in the aroma of the dinner she was preparing. It was what Angelita called her "Friday night special"— chicken fajitas—a dish she had perfected when she worked as a cook at a diner. She had the cast iron pan filled with strips of chicken, bell peppers and onions, enhanced with several spices that he couldn't identify. After she poured the contents of the pan onto a large platter, she cut avocado slices and arranged them around the entree. She then squeezed lime juice and sprinkled grated cheese lightly over the contents. Side dishes included cilantro rice and black beans. She had both corn tortillas and butter lettuce available to use for wraps, together with sour cream and pico de gallo for toppings. To finish off a perfect meal—at least in David's opinion—Angelita had made sopapillas for dessert, with honey, a favorite dessert of his since his Air Force days when he visited so many Mexican restaurants in Texas.

The meal set the perfect mood for the evening. David was feeling especially grateful tonight. Although the pain of losing Carol was still with him, it was outweighed by the joy of being with his daughter and his gratitude over having found Angelita. She was more than a housekeeper. She had taken charge of the household and brought a stability to it that was badly needed in the emotional turmoil following Carol's death. She ensured they had nutritious—and delicious—meals; she kept the laundry fresh and the house clean; and she was both tutor and chauffeur for Jenna, getting her wherever she needed to go on time. And the house was always cheerful with her around. Yes, indeed, David was counting his blessings tonight.

As Angelita poured David a cup of coffee to go with his sopapillas, David asked Jenna, "So, what's the team's record now?"

"We are twelve and one, with only one game left—next Thursday. If we win that one, it will be the best record any girls soccer team at Maitland Middle School has ever had. We're pretty proud of that."

"Wow! Impressive; you *should* be proud," David said, delighted his daughter was experiencing success at the sport at which she had worked so hard just to make the team.

After pondering the thought for a long moment, David asked Jenna, "Would you like to invite Wanda to spend the night here with you next Friday? If her mom is OK with it, you and Angelita could pick her up at her house after school, and you two could celebrate your great season. We might even convince Angelita to make chicken fajitas for us again next Friday."

"Oh, Dad, that's a great idea," Jenna said. "She's really had a tough year, moving to a new school, and then being cyberbullied. I think she would really like that."

Chapter 12

The following week passed quickly at the Jordan household. David had resumed his morning runs as he felt himself slowly returning to his old self at work, gradually feeling less in a funk, with his former enthusiasm for his cases returning. Jenna's invitation to Wanda for a sleepover with Jenna on Friday was welcomed and promptly approved by Wanda's mother. There was no further word from the Jerk to distract from the anticipation of the big final game. Jenna was stoked as the team made their final preparations, knowing that with a win they could set a school record for victories in a season. To add to the excitement, they were playing their biggest rival, Glenridge Middle School.

With so much on the line, there was no way David could miss the game. He left the office with just enough time to make it to Maitland Middle School as the game began. The two teams were evenly matched, with both teams playing outstanding defense, keeping scoring to a minimum. Glenridge went up by a goal shortly before the end of the first half, but Maitland fought back, scoring early in the second period on a goal by Wanda, with an assist from Jenna. From that point on, the teams were in a defensive struggle with neither team making a serious scoring threat.

David was wrapped up in the game as much as any parent in the stands. As time was winding down, the Maitland cheerleaders were urging the fans to get on their feet—and get loud! David got on his feet—along with all the other fans in the stands—yelling encouragement to Jenna and her teammates to bring home the victory. At this level of competition, the teams didn't go to penalty shoot-outs to determine the winner; a tie score at the end of regulation would result in a tie game. That would still result in a great season for Maitland, but not the record-setting season that a victory would bring. All of the Maitland fans were acutely aware of this, and the clock was slowly ticking away their opportunity for a win and a record setting season.

With only thirty-five seconds left, Maitland had Glenridge bottled up at their own end of the pitch. The Glenridge forwards were trying to break out to get the ball to the other end of the pitch and run out the clock. A tie for them would be a moral victory. As one of the Glenridge forwards tried to dribble the ball past Jenna, she managed to steal the ball, leaving an opening for her to take a shot at the goal. Just before she could position herself for the shot, however, one of the Glenridge defenders made an outstanding play to get to the ball first and kick it out of bounds over the Glenridge goal, leaving Maitland with a corner kick.

By now, the game clock was down to fifteen seconds. Wanda was Maitland's designated kicker for corner or penalty kicks, and she quickly got in position for the corner kick. David was well aware it was extremely unlikely Maitland would be able to score a goal in the little time remaining, but he was screaming encouragement along with all the other fans. As all the players on both teams jockeyed for position, David watched Wanda confidently kick a high slightly curving ball that appeared to be just a little too long. But as the players from both teams looked up spellbound, the spin Wanda put on the ball was just enough to cause it to dive into the far sidebar just below the crossbar, barely out of reach of the Glenridge goalie, and into the net for the winning goal.

As time expired, all the Maitland fans streamed down from the stands to celebrate with the team. The Maitland girls lifted Wanda and Jenna onto their shoulders as the fans and cheerleaders surrounded them, deliriously happy. David was so surprised by the dramatic victory, he remained in the stands, taking in the exuberant celebration and recording it on his iPhone to share later with Jenna. He knew this was a victory Jenna would remember for the rest of her life.

***

Dinner at home that night was one big celebration. When Angelita learned of the dramatic victory and Jenna's role in it, she prepared a small cake she called her "Victory cake," to celebrate, and she promised to make another one the next night when Wanda would be there for the sleepover when they could continue the celebration.

"Jenna, I so proud of you," Angelita exclaimed after every detail about the match that Jenna mentioned.

"I am, too," David said over and over, before remembering his recording. "I forgot to mention that I recorded the celebration following the game. Would you like to see it?"

"Yes!" Jenna and Angelita said simultaneously. David pulled up the video setting on his iPhone and began playing it. The recording picked up as the parents and other fans were streaming down onto the field as time expired. The team members surrounded Wanda and Jenna and lifted them onto their shoulders as the cheerleaders and then the fans gathered around the team. The video focused in narrowly on them, then moved back to a more wide-angle view.

"Meester David, who these two cheerleaders standing over there away from the team?" Angelita asked. "They don't look happy like everyone else."

David hadn't noticed the two cheerleaders standing slightly away from the crowd. He rewound the video to see whether he could find them in the earlier part of the celebration. In fact, they were there, but once Wanda and Jenna were lifted onto teammates' shoulders and were being honored as heroes, these two cheerleaders had drifted off to the side. *Angelita's right; these two seem to be frowning. What's going on with them?*

David couldn't identify them, but Jenna could. "Oh, they're Marsha Lloyd, our head cheerleader, and Becky Rawlings, both eighth graders," Jenna said. "Those two are probably the most popular girls in school. Maybe that's gone to their head a little; neither of them has been very welcoming to Wanda, but I'm surprised they're frowning; maybe someone from Glenridge made a nasty comment or something."

"Yeah, maybe . . ." David muttered.

"Dad, you may know Marsha's father. He's the vice-Mayor of Maitland," Jenna commented.

"Oh, really?" he responded. David considered asking more questions about Marsha and Becky, but then decided he wasn't about to spoil the mood of the evening. He redirected the conversation to how well Jenna and her teammates played in the biggest game of the year.

***

The entire Maitland Middle School gathered in the school auditorium late the following morning to celebrate the victory over

107

Glenridge, and the girls' record-setting season. All of the girls on the team were introduced, with Wanda and Jenna getting the most applause. Jenna was a little embarrassed at all the attention and felt especially bad the boys team was not even mentioned, although what could be said for a team that won only one game all season?

It was lunchtime as soon as the assembly was over, and all of the students headed to the lunchroom. The girls' team all sat together at a long table. There was more than the usual buzz in the lunchroom as the celebratory mood from the assembly carried over into the lunch period, but after fifteen minutes or so, Jenna noticed the buzz began to change. Students were looking at their phones and laughing. Some of them began pointing to the table where the girls' team was sitting.

Puzzled, Jenna asked a boy at the next table, "What's going on? Why's everyone looking at their phones and laughing?"

"It looks like the Ghostwhoknows is back . . . on the student bulletin board on the school website."

Jenna, Wanda, and the rest of the team members promptly pulled out their phones and went to the website. Jenna peeked at Wanda as she pulled up the website and could see the panic forming in her eyes. The bold headline was "Congratulations to the Girls Soccer Team," but the text below the headline was anything but congratulatory.

"The slut twins led the girls soccer team to a victory over Glenridge yesterday. Jenna Jordan and Wanda Sparling teamed up to steal the ball and make the winning kick as time expired. They've been teaming up to steal boyfriends with booze, sex, and parties all season, so they were ready for the big moment. Speaking of stealing, Wanda comes from a family of pros. Her father is currently an inmate at Raiford Prison at Starke, Florida for stealing from his employer. She has kept this secret from everyone, but you can't keep secrets from the Ghostwhoknows."

"Lies, all lies," Jenna said out loud as she finished reading what was posted. But as she looked back at Wanda, it was obvious something in the statement had struck a chord with her—a bad one. "No one's going to believe this dribble, Wanda," Jenna said, as her teammates nodded in agreement.

Tears were forming in Wanda's eyes, and her lips began to tremble. She was struggling mightily to maintain her composure, but Jenna could tell she was about to lose the battle. Rather than let the other students observe Wanda having an emotional breakdown in front of them, Jenna grabbed her by the hand and marched her out of the lunchroom, as Wanda struggled to keep up. Once they were out of the lunchroom, Jenna kept their backs toward the school building and walked slowly toward the athletic fields.

As soon as they were alone, while still holding Wanda's hand, but without turning to her, Jenna asked in a quiet voice, "What is it, Wanda? What is it about those lies that upset you?"

When Wanda didn't answer, Jenna turned to her. The tears were flowing now, and she put her hands over her face to hide the shame she was obviously feeling. Jenna put her arm around Wanda's shoulder and stood quietly beside her until she could gather herself. After what seemed like several minutes, Wanda said weakly, "It wasn't all a lie. . ."

Jenna was shocked into silence and waited for a further explanation from Wanda. After a few moments, she continued, barely above a whisper. "My dad *is* a prisoner at Raiford. He stole some money from his employer and got caught. When he went to prison, my mom couldn't handle it; that's when they got divorced, and we moved to Maitland. I didn't want anyone here to know about this; neither did my mom. Now, everyone knows. . ."

She kept her eyes to the ground as she began sobbing almost uncontrollably. Jenna had never been around anyone so inconsolable and felt helpless to comfort her friend. She put her arms around Wanda and held her as she continued to sob.

***

Jenna took Wanda to the school counselor and explained the cause of her being so distraught. The counselor, observing Wanda's fragile mental condition, allowed her to stay there, rather than return to classes, until she could catch the school bus home. Before leaving her with the counselor, Jenna confirmed that Wanda was still up for the sleepover with her that night—Wanda wasn't anxious to tell her mother what had transpired that day— and promised she and Angelita would pick her up at her house at 4:30.

The rest of the afternoon dragged by for Jenna. Although she went to her math class, she couldn't concentrate. Thoughts about Wanda and her confession about her father kept interrupting. *How did the Jerk find out about this? How could he—or she—be so cruel to Wanda? I'm really worried about her now.*

***

As Angelita drove Jenna and herself to Maitland's Dommerich neighborhood to pick up Wanda, Jenna brought Angelita up to date on the events at school that day.

"Why this Ghostwhoknows so hateful to Wanda—and to you?" she asked.

"I don't know, Angelita. Some people are just mean and spiteful." Jenna thought about Angelita's question further as they turned onto Thunderbird Trail, where Wanda lived. It was one thing to make up the stupid lies about booze, sex and stealing boyfriends. But Ghostwhoknows had actively researched Wanda's family background, apparently looking for something to embarrass her with, and found it. Wanda had always seemed a little fragile to Jenna, lacking self-confidence even though she was a talented athlete and a reasonably good student. Jenna had suspected there was something in her background that caused the fragility but had no idea what it was. Until now.

***

When they arrived at Wanda's house, Angelita remained in the car as Jenna went to the front door and rang the doorbell. After she waited for a minute or so, Angelita saw her ring the doorbell again, wait a few seconds more, then knock on the door, calling Wanda's name again and again. Jenna looked back at Angelita and shrugged; then, as a last resort, she tried the front door, which opened, called out for Wanda once again, and disappeared inside.

No more than fifteen seconds later, Jenna came running back outside, clearly panicked, and yelled, "Angelita, come quickly! It's Wanda."

As fast as she could, Angelita unbuckled, jumped out of the car, and ran into the house, fearful of what she might find. Jenna had re-entered the house, which had a foyer that led back into a family room, and she was standing next to Wanda who was lying on the carpeted floor, apparently unconscious, with an open Advil bottle on the floor next to her. Angelita examined it, noting it originally had 100 pills, but was now half empty.

Dios mio. "Call 911, Jenna. Tell them teenager overdosed on Advil. Come quickly."

111

As Jenna grabbed her phone to call 911, Angelita checked Wanda's air passages to ensure they were clear. She slapped Wanda not-so-lightly on the cheek to try to get her to respond, which brought her eyes faintly open, though she showed no sign of recognizing where she was or what was happening. When Wanda began gurgling as though she was about to throw up, Angelita rolled her onto her side so she wouldn't choke on her own vomit. Within seconds, Wanda began upchucking—everything from her breakfast cereal, the chili that was served in the school lunchroom that day, to what looked like twenty to thirty pills.

"The EMT team of the Maitland Fire Department should be here soon," Jenna informed Angelita, transfixed by the condition of her friend. "Is she going to be okay?"

"I think *yes*. She threw up most pills. But she need medical care real soon." Angelita didn't take her eyes off of Wanda, making sure all air passages remained open and she was able to expel anything she was trying to throw up. Even though she had thrown up what Angelita assumed was most of the pills, she was still only semi-conscious and not aware of her surroundings. Angelita had Jenna get a towel soaked with cold water from the kitchen and wiped her face and forehead with it, which brought Wanda slightly out of the fog.

"Jenna, is that you. . ." Wanda muttered so quietly they could barely hear her, but before Jenna could respond Wanda drifted off again with her eyelids closing. Angelita kept her on her side in the event she began vomiting again and cradled her head gently with her hand.

Within ten minutes of the 911 call, the Maitland Fire Department showed up, was briefed by Angelita on what she had done, and had Wanda on the way to Winter Park Hospital for emergency treatment. The Fire Department person-in-charge lingered behind once Wanda was on her way so he could get all of the facts he would need for his report. "I must say, I'm quite impressed with what you two did. You probably saved a life today with the emergency care you provided. How did you know to give such care?"

"I had to take course on emergency care at a former job," Angelita said. "I review my notes from course when I become housekeeper for Jenna and her father."

"Well, it paid off today. Good job. We will notify Wanda's mother about what happened. But I'm sure Wanda and her mother will want to thank you as soon as she can have visitors."

As Angelita drove them home, Jenna called her dad. As she related the story to David, the emotions of the day overwhelmed her, and she had to pause several times to stop the tears and gather her thoughts. She had the phone on speaker mode, so the first time she had to pause, Angelita intervened. "Meester David, I so proud of Jenna. She remain calm and call 911 when we find Wanda."

"No, no, Angelita is the hero today, Dad," Jenna responded. "Even the Fire Department man said so. Wanda wouldn't be alive if it weren't for Angelita."

"Well, I'm extremely proud of both of you," David said when all the details had been covered. "And I promise both of you, we are going to get to the bottom of who has caused this to happen."

***

Dinner wasn't the celebratory event the family had envisioned for that night with Wanda's planned sleepover. But there was an atmosphere of gratitude that a complete disaster had been avoided, accompanied by hope that the events of the day might finally lead to justice being served.

Chapter 13

Everyone at the Jordan & McKenzie attorney meeting the following Monday was full of questions for David. The Orlando Sentinel had run a story on Saturday detailing the history of the cyber bullying by the mysterious Ghostwhoknows, which led to Wanda's suicide attempt and the heroic actions by Angelita and Jenna to save her. The article also mentioned that Wanda and Jenna had been the stars of Maitland's victory over Glenridge on Thursday.

While helping themselves to the pizza being served that day, everyone expressed their admiration for Angelita and Jenna and how well they handled the situation. But it was Steve who captured the unexpressed thought of everyone present. "I had no idea cyber bullying was a problem in middle schools."

"Neither did I before this episode," replied David, "although Maggie educated me about the problem when I mentioned to her what Jenna and her friend were going through."

"Yeah, I've been exposed to this issue in a couple of my legal aid cases," Maggie said. "The problem even extends down to elementary school. And although it's still rare, there are an increasing number of attempted suicides by minors who have been cyberbullied. The method most often used in the suicide attempt is what Wanda used—non-prescription medicines like aspirin, Advil or Aleve."

After others also expressed their ignorance of cyber bullying being a problem in the schools, Steve asked the other question on everyone's mind. "David, do we have any idea who this Ghostwhoknows is?"

"Yes, thankfully we do," David replied, pausing to take a sip of coffee before continuing. "In fact, there will be another story about this episode in the evening edition of the Orlando Sentinel today, revealing who the Ghostwhoknows is."

This comment landed like a bolt of lightning, and everyone stopped eating to focus on David. "How do you know this?" Steve asked.

David smiled, folded his napkin and glanced around the room at the eager attention he garnered with his last comment. "It's an interesting story, although truly a sad one," he said as he began, happy to finally have answers to who was behind the cyberbullying against his daughter and her friend. "As most of you know, once this problem arose, Jesse and I went to speak to the principal of Maitland Middle School. She was fully cooperative and pledged to use all resources of the school to learn who the cyberbully was. I called her Friday night to mention something we noticed in the video I took of the victory celebration by the girls' soccer team and fans on Thursday. What we noticed was that two of the cheerleaders not only didn't participate in the celebration but seemed unhappy with it."

"Why did that catch your attention?" Maggie asked.

"Well, this was a record-setting victory for the team, and it seemed strange that the cheerleaders who were cheering the team on to victory weren't happy with the result. Seeing that on the video reminded me of something Dr. Samuelson, the principal, had said—namely that she and her IT department had noticed that all of the postings by Ghostwhoknows had come after a victory by the girls soccer team, and they suspected jealousy might be the primary motivation for the bullying. So, I called her and sent her a copy of the video. Apparently, the IT department had found something in the way the postings had been made on the school website that pointed toward these two cheerleaders being involved. When the video seemed to confirm her suspicions, Dr. Samuelson gave all of this information to the Maitland police who obtained a search warrant on Saturday to examine the girls' phones. The police completed the search on Sunday, and what they found left no doubt these two cheerleaders were the Ghostwhoknows."

"Wait, two eighth-grade girls had the technical skills to carry on this cyberbullying anonymously all this time?" Steve asked David, apparently dumbfounded this could happen.

"That appears to be the case at this point. Whether they obtained advice from someone older is unknown, but anyone who's proficient at searching the internet can find almost anything they need to know."

"So, who are these two cheerleaders?" Jesse asked.

David paused before responding, thinking to himself how painful it must have been to the families involved to discover their own daughter was the cause of another girl attempting to take her own life. "Marsha Lloyd, the head cheerleader, and Becky Rawlings. You may recognize the family names. Both girls come from well-known and well-respected families in Maitland. Marsha's father is the vice-Mayor of Maitland."

"Oh, my God, David!" Jesse exclaimed. This is awful. What explanation is there for what these girls did?"

Good question, Jesse.

***

Jesse's question had been on his mind since David learned the search warrant led to conclusive evidence of what the two cheerleaders had done, and they were arrested. How could these two girls, who had enjoyed all of the benefits of what were—at least outwardly—stable, upper middle-class families, and who were smart, capable, and popular girls, commit such purely evil acts of cyberbullying which nearly led to fatal results? What could possibly generate so much jealousy in these girls they were willing to anonymously bully other girls who were ostensibly their friends? And whereas David could somewhat understand someone committing a similar single evil act out of momentary anger or jealousy, this had been a campaign of malevolent intent carried out over weeks with multiple acts of bullying having no purpose other than punishing two girls who had performed well on the soccer team, thereby drawing praise from their peers, and—in the warped view of the cheerleaders—diverting attention from them. *My God! What have we come to? And what are we teaching our children?*

Jesse's question also reminded David of a conversation he had with his Episcopal parish priest, Father John Williams, during a meeting with him. Father John's wife died of a heart attack four years before Carol died, and for over a year David met him for breakfast every Wednesday to offer comfort and support. Their conversations covered an expansive range of topics, many of which were spiritual or philosophical. One such conversation David vividly recalled was in response to his question to Father John, "In the course of my work as a lawyer I have seen men and women commit some heinous acts that were utterly evil, even though no one had previously considered them evil people. What causes ordinary people to commit such evil acts? How do you explain such evil?"

118

Father John sighed, as an expression of great sadness passed over his face. He pondered the question, apparently searching for the right words to express his thoughts about a topic he had wrestled with often in the course of his ministry. After a long pause, he said, "We tend to view people as mostly good, while recognizing that we do bad things from time to time. When we do bad things, we tend to justify ourselves or make excuses for ourselves by blaming others or circumstances that have caused us to act in a manner we believe is inconsistent with our true character. We say, 'I wasn't myself when I did that,' as if that excuses our bad act.

"But that isn't the picture of human nature that the scriptures describe. Both the Hebrew Scriptures and the New Testament present mankind as being capable of wonderful acts of kindness and mercy but also being capable of unabashed evil. The truth is we are all capable of greater evil than we can imagine, and we usually don't even realize it.

"The book of James in the New Testament addresses this very issue. Verse 14 of chapter one says, 'One is tempted by one's own desire, being lured and enticed by it; then, when that desire has conceived, it gives birth to sin, and that sin, when it is fully grown, gives birth to death.' _1/ My understanding of this verse is that evil is the result of our own ungodly desires for power, prestige, revenge, sex, jealousy, or some other improper desire, that we give in to. When we yield to one of these desires as we are tempted, it will grow and fester within us until it transforms from a vague thought or feeling into concrete actions that can only be described as evil—what scripture calls sin. If we allow the evil to continue within us, it will eventually lead to spiritual or even physical death. In other words, we give birth to what is in us, and temptation to evil comes only because of one's own desires.

"I'm not sure that *explains* evil, but it does describe how evil acts originate. We tend to be self-centered people primarily interested in what we want or what makes us feel good, even if it might be harmful to other people. Not always, but far too often," Father John concluded.

"So, how can we contend with evil if it's within us?" David asked.

"That's where the gospel comes in, David," Father John replied. "We have to recognize our tendency to live our lives trying to satisfy our own desires, even as evil and misguided as they may be. Jesus said we need to change from being someone who is self-centered to being someone who is God-centered in our priorities, our relationships, and our commitments. This change must be so fundamental that he called it being 'born again.' Just as the alcoholic can't get off the booze solely in his own power, we can't seem to change our sinful desires solely in our own power. We need God's power in our lives to make such a fundamental change. So, how do we contend with the evil within us? We ask God to change us, which he has promised to do if we repent—which means commit to change—have faith in Jesus and be obedient to him. He will graciously forgive our sins and change us at the core of our being. Others have suggested different solutions—politics, education, the right philosophy, or strict laws—but none of these have proven very successful over time to root out evil; it remains with us and in us."

At the time, Father John's remedy for the problem of evil seemed more theoretical than practical to David, but now, having observed the mystifying behavior from these two privileged girls that almost led to permanent tragedy, he couldn't come up with a better one.

***

David repeated Jesse's question to him, "What explanation is there for what these girls did?" No one else at the attorney meeting spoke up to offer an answer as David considered how to respond. Finally, he took another sip of his coffee, shrugged, and said, "I don't think there is a satisfactory *explanation* for something like this. It boggles our minds to think two young girls who were so popular they were elected cheerleaders could be so callous and hateful to two of their schoolmates. It reminds me of what my priest once told me. We are all capable of irrational and evil acts, more so than we even imagine. And we have seen that play out in what these two girls did, as well as in what is reported in our newspapers every day."

David's somber comment lingered over the meeting for a long moment before Maggie asked, "What will happen to these girls?"

"As I said at the beginning, this is a sad story," David commented. "Although it's possible the girls could be tried as adults, I think that's unlikely. However, they will be prosecuted through the juvenile court system, and it could result in time spent in a juvenile correctional facility. Cyberbullying is increasing among all age groups, and authorities are anxious to make examples of those who bully, especially when minors are involved. And the fall-out isn't limited to the girls. I understand that Marsha Lloyd's father plans to announce his resignation as vice-Mayor and a member of the Maitland City Council to 'spend more time with his family.'"

Another hush fell over the meeting until Jesse asked, "Is there any good news to report? How's Wanda?"

"Ah, yes, there is some good news," David said. "Wanda

was released from the hospital Sunday morning. Jenna, Angelita and I visited with Wanda and her mom Sunday night. They wanted to personally thank Angelita and Jenna. Wanda seemed in good spirits, knowing that this episode is finally behind her, but she will need counseling to work through the trauma of it."

"How's Jenna holding up?" Jesse asked.

David tried to respond, but choked up before he could get a word out. He bit his lip to get control of his emotions, then said in a quiet voice, "She's as strong as her mother was. I couldn't be prouder of her. She's already talking about how she can help Wanda over the next few weeks."

David fell silent again, as another thought occurred to him. Looking over his second family sitting around the conference table, he said, "You know, events in our lives often seem to occur randomly, without any higher purpose at the time. But later, in retrospect, we see how fortuitous those seemingly random events were. I shudder to think how the Ghostwhoknows episode would have turned out if Angelita had not become our housekeeper."

With this comment, David brought the meeting to a close, and the attorneys returned to their problems of the day.

Chapter 14

The remainder of that week and the next were devoted to interviewing witnesses and reviewing documents being produced by NMH and by Brandon Associates. Jesse had to be familiar not only with her own clients' documents but also those being produced by Brandon Associates; otherwise, she would not fully understand how her clients came to be employed by Brandon Associates and whether there were any pitfalls in that process that could impact their defense. Additionally, she also had to review the NMH document production. As she conducted her review, it became quickly apparent NMH had performed a "document dump" in response to her requests, with NMH's intent obviously being to inundate and overwhelm the defendants with a deluge of documents that would drive up the cost of defending the lawsuit. In short, this was a tedious, at times mind-numbing experience for Jesse and the other Jordan & McKenzie lawyers, but one that was critical for their preparation for the depositions about to begin.

The first deposition Karl Stanton scheduled, not surprisingly, was that of Mark Conboy. He was the key manager Brandon Associates needed to get the integration portion of their material handling business up and running, and without whom the new business would have likely failed. Having Conboy well prepared for his deposition was so critical Jesse decided she and David should both be involved in getting him prepared; they would split the preparation for the other six clients.

When Conboy showed up for deposition prep he was wearing jeans, a faded flannel shirt with the sleeves rolled up, and well-worn construction boots; he appeared to be younger than his actual age—early forties. An inch or so over six feet, his 185 pounds seemed mostly muscle distributed over a lanky frame. His dark blond hair, with only light sprinkles of gray, spilled over his ears, and when he smiled boyishly, sun-weathered skin crinkled around his hazel eyes, giving him a warmth not previously apparent. Jesse's impression was that he looked like a southern good ole boy, quite different from his buttoned-up look for the initial court hearing.

David and Jesse welcomed Conboy into the firm conference room, served him black coffee—very strong as requested—and settled in around the conference table. Since Jesse would be defending his deposition, she and David had agreed she would take the lead in preparing him.

"Have you ever had your deposition taken, Mark?" Jesse asked.

"Naw. In fact, this is the first lawsuit I've ever been involved in," he replied in his southern drawl which was not unexpected given he had grown up in Marianna, Florida, only some 65 miles west of Tallahassee, as Jesse recalled from his resume. "I must say, it's an experience I hope I don't ever have to repeat in the future."

She could tell he was nervous about his forthcoming deposition, as most first-time witnesses are, particularly when one's livelihood is on the line. She decided to begin by getting him to talk as much as possible to help him relax, although she would emphasize the importance of *not* being over-talkative when being deposed. She would go over all the rules after he had loosened up and was more relaxed.

"So, how did you get to know Allan Brandon?" Jesse inquired.

The mention of Allan Brandon seemed to relax him immediately. He smiled in apparent reminiscence, took a quick sip of coffee, and replied, "I met Allan our freshman year at Georgia Tech. We pledged the same fraternity, and we were best friends throughout undergraduate and graduate school there. Both my undergraduate degree and master's were in industrial engineering, as were Allan's. After grad school, he returned to Valdosta, where he grew up. I got a job in the Orlando area, but we stayed in touch and saw each other from time to time, mainly at Georgia Tech football games. We both tried to catch one or two games a year. I've always considered him one of my best friends, and I think he feels the same."

Jesse noticed that the more he talked the more relaxed he seemed, so she pressed on with open-ended questions. "When did you two first begin discussing the possibility of your going to work for Brandon Associates?"

"We've talked about the possibility of working together ever since our college days. In grad school we often discussed how cool it would be to start a business together. It seemed pie-in-the-sky talk at the time, but nearly every time we saw each other one of us would bring up the subject and say, 'Some day. . .'"

"Well, when did the pie-in-the-sky talk turn into something more concrete?" Jesse could tell he was warming up to the subject, so she wanted to get into details that could be critical to the lawsuit.

He paused to consider when they began their discussions.

Jesse liked the fact he was thoughtful in his responses, taking his time to think before speaking. "That came about roughly five years ago. Allan had taken over his family's construction business about six years before that. His father had started the business, and they handled a wide range of construction—single-family homes, apartments, and business structures, including warehouses. When Allan took over the business, he decided Brandon Associates needed to be more specialized due to changes that were occurring in the construction industry at the time, and due to unique opportunities he foresaw for the Valdosta area."

Puzzled, Jesse asked, "What opportunities were there which were unique to Valdosta?"

"Yeah, I was also skeptical the first time he mentioned it to me," he drawled. "But Allan believed the economy was changing, and the economic changes would lead to the construction of more warehouses and distribution centers all over the country, and particularly in fast-growing states such as Georgia and Florida."

Still puzzled, Jesse followed up, "But how would that benefit a business in Valdosta?"

"Again, I was skeptical also, but as he pointed out, Valdosta is only fifteen miles north of the Florida state line, and I-75 runs right by it. As you know, I-75 is the major north-south interstate highway running through the middle of Florida and Georgia. Its location is ideal for a distribution center to serve Georgia, Florida, and even Alabama, although it's not a major metropolitan center. This wasn't just Allan's theory; the local chamber of commerce also touted this idea and made overtures to a number of major corporations that were considering distribution centers to serve Georgia and Florida."

Becoming slightly less skeptical, Jesse asked, "So, what did

Brandon Associates do?"

"Well, as Allan told me, this was Brandon Associates' opportunity to become more specialized, something he had wanted to do for some time. Several companies did, in fact, decide to construct distribution centers in the Valdosta area, close to I-75, and they sought bids from local construction companies as well as statewide companies. Allan cut his profit margins to the bone to get these initial contracts and wound up getting four of the six major contracts for warehouses. All four of Allan's projects came in on time and under budget, whereas the other two had problems and cost overruns. Word apparently spread quickly, and soon Brandon Associates was getting requests for bids on warehouse construction projects from Florida, Georgia, Alabama and the Carolinas. Their warehouse construction business exploded, and soon they limited themselves to warehouse construction because by specializing they were more efficient, making the company more profitable."

"Is that when he contacted you to work for Brandon Associates?" Jesse was beginning to understand what led to Conboy going to work there, but she was still unsure of the timeline.

"Naw, there was nothing for me to do for Brandon Associates at that time. Most of their initial contracts were solely for constructing warehouses. There were no material-handling contracts associated with them. If the companies needed material handling systems installed in the warehouses, they looked to other companies for that."

"So, when did that change?" Jesse asked, realizing this story might be more complicated than she originally thought.

"I discussed this issue with Allan once their warehouse

business took off, maybe five years ago. He was happy with the success they were having with the warehouse construction, but he noticed that more and more of the companies building warehouses also needed material handling systems in the warehouses. Brandon Associates was getting none of that business."

"Tell me about that conversation," Jesse said, curious to understand how her client's input may have contributed to Brandon's expanding business.

"Allan called to get my thoughts on the material handling business in general. He reminded me we had written a paper in grad school that was actually published in a trade journal about recent developments in the design of material handling systems and the new technologies that were being developed at the time. He had also consulted in the design phase of material handling systems for several of their customers that were building warehouses. His idea was that if Brandon Associates could become more involved in the design of material handling systems as well as the construction of warehouses, they could market the company as providing a turnkey service and be able to expand their business. He wanted my input since I had been working in the integration services segment of the material handling business for most of my career."

"What are the integration services you mentioned?" Jesse asked, looking up from the notes she was taking.

"Basically, the integration services include selecting the material handling equipment and software, installing it, and bringing it to the point of having an operational material handling system."

"So, did you and Allan discuss your going to work for Brandon Associates to handle the integration services if his idea worked out?" Jesse asked.

He clasped his hands on the table, shook his head at David who asked if he wanted more coffee, and responded, "No, not yet. At that time Brandon Associates didn't intend to handle the integration services in-house; they were just going to handle the design and planning phase. Allan wanted to have several reliable companies he could subcontract with to fulfill the integration element of a project."

"Well, did you make a pitch for NMH to be one of those subcontractors for the integration services?"

Convoy grinned, apparently enjoying taking Jesse on a lengthy journey to get to the heart of the story that led to the lawsuit. "Again, not yet. First, I was not with NMH at the time. I was with Acorn Integration Services, which was a relatively small, independent company performing integration services solely on government contracts, primarily for the U.S. Postal Service."

Jesse was furiously taking notes now to ensure she understood the history of Conboy's relationship with Brandon. "When did you go to work for NMH?"

"Actually, I didn't change my employment. Acorn Integration Services was purchased by National Manufacturing Company, and they renamed Acorn 'National Material Handling Company.' National Manufacturing was primarily interested in obtaining contracts with the U.S. Postal Service for mail handling systems, which is what Acorn had been doing for several years, so it was a good acquisition for National Manufacturing. In fact, Acorn had just recently submitted a bid for a contract with the USPS to install a major mail handling system in Tampa when we became NMH; that was the largest contract we worked on over the first year we were NMH, and I was in charge of that installation."

By now, Jesse wasn't sure when they were ever going to get to the point of discussing Conboy going to work for Brandon Associates—although this background was important—so she decided to cut to the chase. "When did you finally begin discussions about working for or with Brandon Associates?"

He unclasped his hands and leaned back in the high-back chair. "Those discussions began about two years after Acorn became NMH, but I need to give you a little more background. We were very busy with USPS contracts the first year, mainly on the Tampa project, but there were fewer new USPS contracts coming up for bid in the second year, and no other ready source of government material handling contracts to pursue. Having just paid a lot of money to acquire NMH, National Manufacturing was so concerned about the decrease in potential government contracts that—according to rumors both within the company and in the Wall Street Journal—National Manufacturing was considering selling NMH. Any company buying NMH would probably relocate the headquarters from Orlando and neither my managers nor I was interested in moving. So, we decided we needed to come up with new sources of income. The best way to do that, in our opinion, was to get into commercial material handling contracts."

Surprised at this statement, Jesse asked, "Weren't you already trying to get commercial contracts?"

Shaking his head, Conboy responded, "No, the commercial material handling field is different, primarily because the rules and regulations applicable to government contracts run the cost up so much that companies performing government contracts usually aren't competitive on price in commercial contracts."

"Well, if NMH was only performing government contracts, how did you plan to get price-competitive enough to compete in the commercial market?" Jesse was struggling to understand how NMH would ever make the transition from government to commercial contracts.

"That's where my relationship with Allan Brandon came in," Conboy replied as if that explained everything. "Although most commercial material handling contracts are awarded after a bid process, not all are. A significant number are sole-source contracts in which a company is told, 'This contract is yours if you can do it for this specified price.' I mentioned that we weren't usually competitive on price, but we did have some advantages. We could respond more quickly than most small commercial companies, and we offered better guarantees on our work than most companies. So, I asked Allan to give NMH an opportunity to show what we could do by awarding us a couple of sole-source contracts for integration services."

"How did that work out?" Jesse asked.

Conboy smiled wryly, apparently recalling those early contracts. "Allan did award us the jobs, but the prices he quoted were so low NMH would incur a loss on each of the contracts. Nevertheless, I was able to convince management to take the jobs to get an entrée into the commercial market, with the idea we would slim down our operation later to make it more efficient and profitable. And we brought the jobs in on time and within budget."

"Did those jobs lead to other commercial contracts?"

"Yeah, some. Over the next two years, we continued to get some contracts from Brandon Associates, and that work led to other companies considering us for sole-source contracts, although they were all relatively small projects. And over those two years we finally got to the point we were profitable on the most recent contracts."

Jesse scribbled a note about becoming profitable on the sole-source contracts before asking, "Did NMH ever try to win contracts through a bid process?"

Again, a wry smile from Conboy. "Oh, yes. We bid on more than thirty contracts over a two-year period. We didn't win a single bid. The closest we came to being the low bidder was ten percent above the low bid on one contract. It was discouraging, particularly when management at National Manufacturing refused to allow NMH to restructure the company to become more competitive."

"What eventually happened to the relationship between NMH and Brandon Associates?" Jesse asked.

"Well, just about the time we were finally becoming profitable on the commercial contracts, I got a call from Allan Brandon. He said he and his board of directors had decided to expand their company to include integration services in-house so they would be able to provide a full turn-key product, from the design of the warehouse and material handling system to its installation. This would require a major expansion of their company, and he wanted me to be the person to head up their new integration department."

Now we're finally getting somewhere. "What did you tell him?"

"At first, I tried to talk him out of the expansion into integration services. I told him I thought NMH would be able to continue lowering its prices as we became more efficient, and continuing to use NMH as a subcontractor would avoid the massive capital outlay creating a new department would require."

"I take it he didn't buy that argument?" Jesse inquired.

"No; he cut me off immediately and said they were going to expand whether I joined them or not, but I was his first choice to lead the new department. He also reminded me we had discussed working together since our undergraduate days."

"What was your response?"

He shrugged and hesitated momentarily. "What could I say? I knew that if all the work from Brandon Associates dried up, NMH's venture into the commercial business would almost certainly fail. National Manufacturing was still reluctant to allow its subsidiary NMH to restructure sufficiently, afraid it would hurt their reputation as a government contractor. I also knew that if the commercial venture failed, all of NMH's employees, including myself, would likely be out of a job. So, I did what anyone would do in my position. I told Allan I wanted to go to Valdosta to talk to him about it and understand fully what he had in mind."

Jesse glanced up from her notes. "Tell us about that meeting."

Conboy pushed back slightly from the conference table, squinting as he recalled the details. "We met on a Saturday morning several weeks later at the Brandon Associates offices on the outskirts of Valdosta, close to I-75. Allan told me he and his accounting staff had come to the conclusion they needed to perform the integration portion of their material handling system contracts in-house to achieve the profitability levels they sought. They were leaving too much money on the table by subcontracting out the integration contracts. Plus, the ability to provide a complete turnkey operation to a client from construction of the warehouse to design and installation of the material handling system would give them a big marketing advantage. It was the next logical step and a great opportunity for Brandon Associates—and for me if I headed up the integration department."

"What was your reaction to his pitch?"

Conboy seemed to be warming up to his story now. "Oh, I agreed with what he said. I was surprised it took him as long as it did to realize how much of the profitability of a material handling system project came from the integration portion. Plus, I liked the idea of working for a private company whose management I knew well and respected. One reason Allan and I often talked about someday working together was we trusted each other so much. But I had some demands of my own that had to be met before I was willing to accept his offer."

"What were your demands?"

"The first demand was that the integration department, if I were to lead it, would be based in Orlando rather than Valdosta. Neither my wife nor I was interested in relocating. Plus, I knew all of the managers working with me at NMH felt the same way. If Brandon took all of its integration contracts in-house, they would be looking for a job, and I viewed them as potential employees of the integration department Brandon wanted to set up. There were other reasons to be in Orlando as well, one of the main ones being Orlando has an international airport with direct flights to most of the population centers around the country, which is important for an integration department that might be handling projects all over the country."

Concerned about Conboy's comment that he hoped to hire most of the NMH managers, Jesse glanced at David for his reaction before asking Conboy, "What were your other demands?"

"The main other demand I had was to have the opportunity to acquire an ownership interest in Brandon Associates, or to have a bonus arrangement based upon profitability that would provide financial rewards similar to what an ownership interest would provide. I was reluctant to make a major move to a much smaller company without such an opportunity."

Nodding her understanding of his wanting an ownership interest, Jesse asked, "How did he react to your ownership demand?"

"Much better than I anticipated actually. He said, 'Since this would be a start-up operation for the integration department, let's come up with a bonus arrangement for the first two or three years, and then decide on an ownership arrangement.' I was satisfied with that given my personal relationship with Allan. Thankfully, he was also amenable to having the integration department located in Orlando, even though he hadn't anticipated that demand."

"So, did you come to an agreement once he met your key demands?"

"Not quite. There was one other topic I wanted to discuss before I was willing to make a commitment. After Allan called to tell me he wanted to hire me, I knew all six of my key managers at NMH would be interested in working there. With NMH losing the work from Brandon, and my leaving NMH, I thought it highly likely they would be out of a job. So, I came up with a business plan that included all six of them in it, with salaries included, to present to Allan. Part of my reasoning in coming up with a plan was to give him my idea of how the department would operate and how it could be profitable. If he disagreed with my plan, that would be a red flag for my joining Brandon Associates."

Jesse frowned at the mention of the business plan with all of the NMH managers included in it—with salaries no less—

before asking, "How did he respond to your plan?"

"He liked it; in fact, he said it filled in some problem areas he anticipated in his own business plan."

"One other question, did you use the salaries the six managers were paid at NMH for your business plan?"

He shook his head. "No, actually what I included as potential salaries were a little more than they were making at NMH because what they were making there was slightly under what corresponding positions were paid in the commercial market. I included salaries I thought were appropriate in the commercial market, not what they were making at NMH."

By now, they were an hour and a half into the deposition prep, and Conboy asked for a bathroom break. As soon as he left the conference room, Jesse asked David, "What do you think of his story so far?"

David glanced at the extensive notes he had taken before saying, "His story makes sense, although providing a business plan with salaries assigned to the people he was working with at NMH to start Brandon Associates' new integration department will likely be cited by Karl Stanton as a violation of Conboy's duty of loyalty and evidence to support NMH's other claims. We need to find out when the other defendants learned of the opportunity with Brandon, and what the details of their recruitment were."

"Agreed," commented Jesse, as she got up to pour them more coffee, stretch, and make a few notes to cover with Conboy.

When he returned, Jesse asked Conboy, "How did the meeting in Valdosta conclude? Did you agree to go to work with Brandon?"

"I agreed in principle to join Brandon Associates. We discussed compensation, benefits, and a few other items regarding how the integration department would operate, but I wanted to see a formal offer in writing and an employment agreement before making a final decision. Allan was fine with that, so he said he would get the offer and employment agreement to me as soon as the company lawyer could draft them."

"Anything else of note covered in that meeting?" Jesse asked.

"No, we concluded the meeting, and then we went to his house for a backyard barbecue where the heads of his design team and construction team joined us. Allan wanted me to meet the key players in his company that I would be working with."

"What happened next?" Jesse was ready to move into the details of his actual departure from NMH and the hiring of the other six defendants.

"Within ten days I received the formal offer and employment agreement from Allan, and I signed it. The day after I signed it, I met with the president of NMH and told him I was resigning. I gave him two weeks' notice but told him I was willing to stay another week or two if requested."

"What was his reaction?" Given the allegations in the lawsuit, Jesse anticipated the response would be negative.

"He was surprised, although he shouldn't have been given all of the recommendations I had made to streamline NMH so we could be competitive in the commercial market, nearly all of which got vetoed by National Manufacturing management." As Conboy said this, Jesse could sense the frustration in his voice that his efforts to streamline NMH were thwarted repeatedly. After pausing for a few seconds, he continued, "Oh, he also mentioned that he was sure the rumor mill about National Manufacturing selling NMH would crank up again. He reminded me that company protocol required the senior vice-president of National Manufacturing responsible for overseeing NMH to meet with me personally, so I flew to Atlanta two days later to meet with the senior vice-president."

"How did that meeting go?"

"In most respects, it went as expected. He tried to talk me out of leaving NMH. I told him what my concerns were, namely that the Post Office business was decreasing and NMH would be unable to compete effectively in the commercial material handling market unless significant changes were made to streamline the company to make it more price competitive. He was non-committal on any such changes so that just confirmed I was making the right decision. What was unexpected about the meeting was who joined us—Rhonda Robinson, the general counsel for NMH. The legal staff for National Manufacturing and its subsidiaries are all based in Atlanta. I'm unsure whether she asked to join us or was asked by the vice-president. In any event, she said very little but just sort of glowered at me throughout the meeting. I had the sense she felt I was committing treason by resigning, particularly when the rumor mill had circulated rumors that National Manufacturing would shut down the Orlando office of NMH if I ever left."

"Yes, as you know, I've met Ms. Robinson. The glowering look seems to be a permanent part of her personality," Jesse commented, somewhat comforted that Conboy's assessment of Ms. Robinson matched her own. "Did you tell either of them you were joining Brandon Associates?"

"No, neither asked where I was going, and I didn't see the need to volunteer that information."

"What happened next regarding your departure from NMH?" Jesse asked.

"After I returned to Orlando, word got out pretty quickly that I had resigned. Each of my six managers approached me over the following week. They all knew about my efforts to get NMH more competitive in the commercial material handling world, and they were concerned about their jobs after I left NMH. Each of them asked me about the possibility of an opening for them at Brandon Associates."

Jesse glanced at David for his reaction to this comment. It was one thing for Conboy to leave NMH to go to work for a competitor, but if he began recruiting for that competitor, he could run afoul of his duty of loyalty and his fiduciary duty as an officer to NMH. "What did you tell them when they asked?" Jesse inquired.

Conboy smiled knowingly, apparently fully aware of her concerns. "I was very careful not to give them any information except the phone number for Brandon Associates. I simply told them to call Allan Brandon if they were interested."

Relieved, Jesse followed up with questions about how soon each contacted Brandon, what feedback he got from them, and what further communications he had with Allan Brandon about hiring them. The response she got was not what she had hoped to hear. Conboy invited all six to his house for a barbecue to meet with Allan Brandon personally about possible jobs with Brandon Associates while he was still employed by NMH.

"Whose idea was it to have the meeting at your house?"

Jesse asked Conboy, her concern growing.

He shrugged. "It was my idea; Allan wanted me to rent a van at Brandon's expense and drive all of them to Valdosta for the meeting, but I thought that might not look so good. Instead, I told Allan he needed to come to Orlando—particularly since the material handling office would be in Orlando—and we could meet at my house. We have a big backyard, and barbecue is my specialty. He agreed."

"Okay, so tell me about the meeting," Jesse said.

"We met on a Saturday afternoon about 6:00. Over drinks and barbecue, Allan told them about the history of Brandon Associates, how they became more specialized in the warehouse construction business, which in turn led them into the material handling business, and now into the integration portion of that business. He painted an encouraging picture of how fast Brandon Associates had grown in recent years and how optimistic he was that the number of their material handling installations would increase once they were providing the integration services in-house. I thought he made a compelling presentation, and my managers apparently thought so too. Every one of them asked for a personal interview with Allan."

"When did the interviews take place?" Jesse asked, anticipating they took place right then, in Conboy's home. She was right; Brandon met with each one individually in Conboy's study immediately after the barbecue dinner.

Warily, Jesse asked, "Did you sit in on those interviews?"

Again, Conboy smiled, seeming to anticipate her concerns. "No, Allan met alone with them. He came up with his own calculation of what salaries to offer. I had suggested salaries for them, but Allan made some adjustments to my recommendations based upon the salary structure at Brandon Associates."

"What decisions, if any, were made that day about when the managers would give their notice to leave?" Jesse asked.

"Yes, we did discuss timelines that night," Conboy responded. "There was some ongoing work at NMH that would keep some of the managers busy for a few more weeks. They wanted to complete certain portions of the projects they were working on rather than leave NMH in the lurch, and Allan agreed with that. So, I think two of them gave their two-week notice a week later; two gave notice a week after that, and the final two planned to give their notice three weeks thereafter. As it turns out, NMH got another U.S. Post Office job about that time and the final two of the managers stayed at NMH for two additional weeks, making their departure six weeks later."

By now, their meeting had lasted over two hours. Jesse decided she had covered about as much ground as she could with Conboy for one day. She went over the rules regarding depositions that she and David always covered with their witnesses, gave Conboy a batch of key documents to review before their next gathering for deposition prep, and wrapped up the meeting.

***

As soon as Conboy had left, Jesse asked David, "What do you think about our key witness? Are your concerns the same as mine?"

"I think my concerns probably are the same as yours," David commented, as he reviewed some of his notes. "I wish he had held off having the meeting at his house until after he left NMH, but it is what it is. I'm also sure Karl Stanton will waive the

141

business plan with all the managers' names and salaries on it to the jury every chance he gets. On a positive note, I didn't recognize anything he referred to as coming even close to being a trade secret, unless there's something we've overlooked. But I'm sure there will be some surprises at his deposition that we'll just have to deal with the best we can. In the meantime, we need to get Maggie to do some additional research about when an employee who has no non-compete agreement crosses over the line when he agrees to go to work for a competitor and urges his fellow employees to join him. That line is a little fuzzy to me, and I have concerns over how all of this will play out before a jury."

"That pretty much summarizes my sentiments exactly," Jesse said. With that, they went back to their respective offices to wrap up any final tasks for the day before going home.

Chapter 15

The following Saturday David woke up with a slight headache, feeling depressed. His emotional funk had returned, and he wasn't sure why. Even Molly jumping in bed to get him up for her usual Saturday morning walk didn't cheer him as it usually did. He rolled over to try to go back to sleep but Molly was insistent; she wanted her walk. After she licked his face for the second time, he reluctantly got up, put on his jogging gear, and headed out with Molly for their three-mile walk around two of the local lakes.

David was pleasantly surprised upon his return to find Angelita in the kitchen making huevos rancheros for breakfast. Saturday was a day off for her, but he recalled she mentioned during dinner last night she would make his favorite breakfast the next day to try to cheer him up. He gave little thought to her comment then, but this morning her gesture was most appreciated.

"How you feeling this morning, Meester David?" she asked, concern evident in her furrowed brow.

"I'm OK. I'll be better once I have my coffee," he said, as he put a coffee pod in the Keurig and hit the "strong" setting. David appreciated the fact Angelita was concerned about him, but it irritated him at the same time, primarily because her concern reminded him he had been unable to shake his funk. He would seem to get better, gradually returning to his optimistic, focused self, but then he would descend again into his funk which he could only describe as a combination of depression and disorientation.

He was beginning to feel like Sisyphus from Greek mythology, who was forced by the gods to repeatedly roll an immense boulder up a hill only for it to roll back down every time it neared the top. *How long will this go on?*

"Meester David. . ." Angelita's voice brought him out of his musings. "After Jorge died, I had very difficult time. I had trouble just doing my chores. Couldn't concentrate. I finally went to see my priest, and he helped me. Maybe you should talk to Father John?"

David hesitated before responding. His frustration over the persistence of his condition made him resent Angelita telling him what he needed. But his resentment dissipated quickly when he reminded himself of her good intentions. Angelita had become like a loving aunt whose main purpose in life was to look after her niece and nephew. He was amazed how quickly she had adopted Jenna and himself as her own family, to say nothing of Molly on whom she doted more than he or Jenna did. How could he ever resent anything she did? Besides, she only told David what he had been telling himself for the past several weeks.

"Maybe you're right, Angelita," David admitted. "I do need to talk to somebody."

"Talk to somebody about what?" Jenna asked as she walked into the kitchen.

"Angelita thinks it would help me to talk to Father John about the depression I've been in for the last five or six months," David responded. "You might as well offer your opinion also."

"I'd say it's about time," Jenna said, not unkindly but firmly. "I've been worried about you, Dad. I've never seen you so down for so long. And it couldn't hurt to talk to him." While saying this, Jenna gave her dad her best smile, one he couldn't resist.

Before he could respond, David felt Molly nudging his leg with her nose. She sat down in front of him and stared at him with those big brown eyes that would melt anyone's heart. "So, do you have an opinion about this, too?" he asked her.

Without a moment's hesitation, Molly responded with an insistent, "Arf . . . arf."

"It seems the opinion is unanimous," David commented dryly. "I'll set up an appointment for next week."

***

The following Thursday David was at Father John Williams' office at 8:00 AM. Despite his posture appearing worse than David remembered, Father John greeted him warmly. His weathered skin and wrinkles around his eyes had deepened over the past year, but that just added to his welcoming persona. He seemed to be looking directly into the soul of anyone he greeted, but in a way that encouraged opening up to him rather than being defensive. David had continued to attend church regularly, but this was the first time in several months he had met with Father John personally, and his warm greeting reminded David he had waited too long to seek counsel from his good friend.

They traded small talk and reminiscences while Father John poured them coffee before they sat down around the small conference table in his office. "I've been expecting your call for some time, David. What took you so long to come see me?"

Surprised, David said, "I don't understand. Why have you been expecting me to come see you?"

The warm smile and understanding gaze captured David's attention. After only a moment's hesitation, Father John said, "The pain on your face at church over the recent months has been obvious, at least to me, particularly anytime the sermon or an announcement mentioned family."

"Has it really been that obvious, John?"

"Yes, it has been to me, but perhaps it's because I'm more sensitive than most to the pain of losing a spouse," he replied. Father John's wife, Sonya, had died unexpectedly of a heart attack nearly five years ago. "I knew that sooner or later the pain and frustration of losing Carol would bring you in for counseling. I just thought it would occur a little sooner."

David nodded in recognition of the pain and frustration he had been experiencing. "I haven't been in for a counseling session recently because I kept thinking I was getting better. But each time I thought I was getting better—getting past the intense pain her death brought me—I would have a relapse, and the pain, depression, and lack of focus would return. It's been so frustrating, and it's affecting my work, my relationships, and my confidence. It didn't surprise me that I went into the funk I've been in, but it *has* surprised me it's lasted so long; and so far, it doesn't seem to be going away."

"David, I was in exactly the same condition you find yourself in. When Sonya died, I was so shocked and bewildered I wasn't sure I could go on. I've never told anyone this, but I strongly considered resigning my position as the rector of All Souls Church. There's perhaps no worse tragedy that can disrupt someone's life and equilibrium than the loss of a spouse, leaving the person depressed, bewildered, unfocused, and in pain."

"That's certainly been my experience," David admitted.

"What makes it even more frustrating is that every time I think I might be getting past the worst of this condition, it keeps coming back. I'm beginning to feel like Sisyphus."

"This isn't uncommon, David. Many people have a similar experience after the loss of a spouse or a child. Sometimes, it goes on for years. But whether for a short time or long, everyone needs a time to heal. What have you been doing to cope?"

Shrugging, David responded, "I've tried everything I know to try. I've been reading my Bible regularly, concentrating on the Psalms for encouragement. I've been praying daily. I've read books on the subject of dealing with the loss of a spouse. I even went to a counseling session with a psychologist I know. All of these have been helpful for a short time, but then I have a relapse, and I feel like I'm right back where I was emotionally shortly after Carol's death."

"These are good coping strategies after such a significant loss. Keep doing them. Over time, you'll get better. However, there *is* one other thing I recommend you try. It was helpful to me in my recovery from Sonya's death. Think back to significant events in your life where you have really helped someone—perhaps a court victory or some good deed you have done that has had a huge impact on another person's life, particularly if you had to overcome adversity or major challenges to help the individual. When you identify that event, meditate on it. Try to remember how you felt afterwards; remember how important the outcome was to the other person. Give thanks to God that you were in a position to help that person."

"Do you really think that will help me overcome the relapses I've had?" David asked, skeptical this would help.

"Well, I know it helped me," Father John replied with his

warmest smile. "It gave me confidence that I was on the track I was meant to be on in this life. It reminded me that life is not just a collection of random events; it's a journey in which there is no higher calling than to serve other people. Once I realized I had helped people before, and I could again, my confidence came back, and some of the pain began to go away; I was able to focus more on the joy of the time I had with Sonya than on the pain of losing her. I can't explain it logically or theologically, but it worked. It just may work for you also."

David nodded approvingly of what this practice had done for Father John. He was still not sure this would help him overcome more relapses, but he was willing to try it. He resolved to identify as many events as he could in which he had acted unselfishly to make a real difference in someone's life. In fact, a few came quickly to mind, but he had his doubts these events would make the difference Father John promised. Nevertheless, he was going to try.

***

On the same Saturday morning David awoke in his funk, Jesse was as frustrated as she had felt in several weeks. She had traveled to Tallahassee for an early afternoon hearing the previous day, and her 3:30 PM return flight was delayed for four hours, causing her to miss her date with James that evening. This was the third time she had missed a date with him in the past three weeks, and James wasn't happy about that, despite the fact he had also missed one of their dates due to an evening emergency surgery he performed. *Is this what our lives together are always going to be? Are both of us doomed to have our personal lives totally controlled by our professional lives?* Jesse had been having this internal debate with herself ever since their recent dinner at Antonio's when they committed to giving themselves four months to decide

148

whether to take the next logical step—marriage.

Given their limited success over the past two months of carving out time for each other, Jesse wasn't sure how James felt about committing to the next step. To be truthful, she wasn't totally sure how she felt about it, either. The question wasn't whether she loved James; she knew she did. And she was pretty sure James felt the same about her. But in her view, love alone, while essential, wasn't enough. There were other things besides love she felt they had to agree upon—sex and children, money, and religion. Not that they had to have perfect agreement on each of these topics, but they had to know, understand, and be willing to live with the other's views on them. Otherwise, conflicts over these issues would quickly overwhelm their marriage.

As to sex and children, she knew there was a strong physical attraction, which they had kept under control while considering the next step, but they hadn't really discussed the children issue. Oh, they had hinted at maybe having two or three children, but no real discussion of what that would entail. She wasn't ready to give up or even curtail her career for full time parental duties, and she knew James wasn't either. Who's going to take care of our kids? Would we be willing to just farm out their care to a nanny?

Money shouldn't be a problem for them—two professionals in highly compensated fields. But from what Jesse had observed about money issues among couples, the question was usually not whether there was enough money to meet the couple's needs, but whether there was agreement, at least generally, on how whatever amount was available would be spent, saved or invested. From what little discussion they had so far, she didn't foresee a problem, unless one of them decided to become a full-time caregiver to the children, an unlikely but possible scenario, which meant the amount of money available would be reduced by roughly half. She needed to ensure that James was not assuming she would give up her law practice as soon as the children came along.

Then there was the religion issue. She and James had had no discussion yet whatsoever on this topic. And it was no wonder. She hadn't attended church with any regularity in over five years. Sure, she would usually attend services around Christmas and perhaps Easter—often with David and Carol—but rarely, if ever, at other times. So far as she knew, James didn't even attend church that often. Jesse had to admit that to a disinterested observer, religion appeared not to be a very important topic for either of them. Yet, that really wasn't true for her. Jesse had grown up in the Methodist church and had been faithful in her church attendance throughout high school, and most of her college life. Not until she went to law school did her church attendance decline, and even then she told herself she would resume regular participation in church life once she settled down. Obviously, now that she thought about it, this was a promise to herself she hadn't kept.

In any event, Jesse now realized, she and James had to discuss this topic. It not only affected them directly, but they also needed to reach agreement on how they would deal with the religion issue with their children. She didn't want to be in a family where the parents just dropped the kids off at church and picked them up later. She had always anticipated she would be part of a family in which they attended church together. *Why have I just assumed that James feels the same way about this? How can I be so thorough in my professional life, yet be so mindless in my personal life?*

Yes, there were issues to discuss with James—significant issues—and the four-month deadline was not far off. It was time for another important dinner at Antonio's, Jesse realized. And the stakes were as high as they were at the previous dinner there.

Chapter 16

Mark Conboy's deposition was scheduled for the Jordan & McKenzie offices on Wednesday of the following week. Jesse had met a second time with Conboy to ensure he was thoroughly prepared, and she was confident he would perform well. Nevertheless, there were a few questions nagging at her. She and Steve had reviewed all of the documents NMH had produced, although many of them seemed irrelevant to any issue in the case or only vaguely related. Was NMH just trying to overwhelm the defendants with their document dump, or was there some relevance she wasn't aware of? She had discussed some of these apparently irrelevant documents with Conboy, but he didn't seem concerned, nor did he have any explanation as to why they might be relevant to the lawsuit.

Conboy arrived for the deposition thirty minutes before its scheduled beginning of 9:00 AM for last minute instructions and joined Jesse in the conference room. Fifteen minutes later Karen Overton, the firm's receptionist, announced the arrival of Karl Stanton and Rhonda Robinson, followed five minutes later by the court reporter and videographer. Bart Mayfield decided to attend the deposition remotely from his office in Valdosta via a streaming link from the videographer since he didn't plan to ask any questions of Conboy.

As the court reporter and videographer set up their equipment for the deposition, Stanton engaged in small talk with

Jesse and Conboy, while Robinson was her usual sullen self. Jesse was pleased that in the notice of deposition Stanton had specified the deposition would be videotaped, which any party had the right to request, provided they were willing to pay for it. If Robinson acted up during the deposition, Jesse wanted to ensure it was captured on video so Judge Long could actually see the unprofessional behavior. As she watched the limited communication between Stanton and Robinson once they arrived, the thought occurred to Jesse that Stanton might have decided to videotape the deposition to help control his own co-counsel.

After the court reporter swore in the witness, Stanton slowly and methodically went through the rules for the deposition, specifically getting Conboy to agree to let him know if any questions were vague or ambiguous. As Stanton then questioned Conboy about his education and business background, Jesse was pleased to see he was following her advice to keep his answers short and responsive without going beyond the scope of the questions. She also noticed his drawl wasn't quite as pronounced as it was during their preparation sessions.

Once he addressed Conboy's college education, Stanton homed in on the relationship between Conboy and Allan Brandon. "Mr. Conboy, when did you and Mr. Brandon first meet?"

"I met him during our first week at Georgia Tech when we were both going through rush week with the fraternities there. We wound up pledging the same fraternity."

"Did you remain friends throughout your time at Georgia Tech?"

"Yes."

"And during your time in graduate school there as well?"

"Yes."

"Is it a fair statement to say he was your best friend during your years at Georgia Tech?"

"Yes."

"You both got your master's degree in industrial engineering from Georgia Tech?"

"Yes."

"While you were getting similar degrees with your best friend, isn't it true that you discussed going into business together at some point in the future?"

"We discussed that it would be fun going into business together, but we never talked about what kind of business or where that might happen." Jesse was pleased with Conboy's answer. She had warned him that Stanton would try to get him to admit he and Allan had planned since their college days to go into business together some day. He needed to be clear in his answer that the idea of working together was nothing more than a hope and a dream until Brandon Associates decided to enter the material handling integration business.

Undeterred, Stanton asked, "Although no specifics were agreed to while you were at Georgia Tech, isn't it true that during that time you formed a lifetime goal of going into business together?"

"No, the correct answer is that I, and I believe Allan, formed hopes and dreams of someday being in business together; I didn't consider it a lifetime goal." As Conboy said this he smiled slightly, which suggested to Jesse he was signaling that he understood where Stanton was going with this line of questions.

Stanton then pivoted to Conboy's time leading up to his work with Acorn Integration Services. "Prior to going to work for Acorn Integration Services, had you been working in the material handling business?"

Conboy nodded. "Yes, I had worked for two other material handling companies before Acorn, starting shortly after getting my master's degree. However, I was more involved in planning and consulting on material handling systems than on integration services until I worked for Acorn."

"What were your duties at Acorn?"

"I was usually the senior project supervisor for Acorn on its integration contracts, all of which were government contracts as I recall. As such, I was responsible for the acquisition and installation of the material handling equipment and software and getting the system operational."

"How long were you with Acorn?"

"I was there for five years before Acorn was purchased by National Manufacturing Co." Jesse noticed that Stanton had been taking very few notes, but he scribbled some in response to the last few questions.

"During your time at Acorn, did you ever have any discussions with Allan Brandon about the possibility of working together?"

"Not really. Allan had called me to discuss the material handling business in general before Brandon Associates expanded into it. But Acorn was only working on government contracts for material handling, and Brandon Associates was just beginning to get into the commercial material handling business. There was no discussion then about working together."

Stanton took a few more notes before asking in a somewhat skeptical tone, "Is it your testimony there was no discussion about—as you put it—your hopes and dreams of working together during that time?"

"We would see each other once or twice a year, usually at a Georgia Tech football game, and catch up on each other's lives, but there was never anything more than, 'Some day maybe we'll have the opportunity to work together. . .'"

Jesse noticed that Stanton paused and stared dubiously at Conboy before consulting his notes, then asked, "You mentioned the purchase of Acorn by National Manufacturing. Were you in favor of it?"

"Yes, Acorn was a relatively small, privately held company. I thought that with the added resources of a large publicly held company experienced in winning government contracts, we should be more competitive. That proved to be true. About the time Acorn became National Material Handling, we bid on and won a large material handling contract with the U.S. Postal System in Tampa."

"Other than the Tampa contract, did NMH continue to win more government contracts?"

"We did, but the size of those contracts was smaller. The Post Office was not issuing as many requests for bids after the Tampa project, and the volume of our work was down after our first year as NMH."

"In fact, by the second year of NMH, you were pushing management of NMH to get into the commercial material handling business, weren't you?" Jesse had wondered when Stanton would get to the subject of NMH moving into commercial material handling. She had explored that subject in depth with Conboy and thought he was well prepared to deal with such questions.

"Yes. Once I realized the volume of available government contracts was decreasing, I understood we had to look for other sources of income, and commercial material handling was the best alternative."

Stanton reached into the pile of documents he had placed on the conference table, found the one he was looking for, and asked the court reporter to mark it as the next exhibit. Turning to Conboy, he said, "I show you what has been marked as Plaintiff's Exhibit 5. It's a report from you to Arthur McDonald, the president of NMH recommending the purchase of a company named FastSort, Inc. Can you identify this document?"

Conboy appeared to be somewhat surprised to see the document, but after briefly reviewing it, he responded, "Yes, it's a report I wrote after I recommended to President McDonald that we explore buying FastSort. It was a small company involved in commercial material handling systems and a leader in sorting system technology. I thought their technology would be helpful with our government contracts, and their material handling experience would give us an entrée into the commercial material-handling world. He told me to investigate FastSort thoroughly and give him a written report."

"Did he agree with your recommendation that NMH purchase FastSort?"

"He did, but he didn't have the authority to make the purchase. He forwarded my report to the executive committee for National Manufacturing, which had to approve any purchase of this size. They vetoed the sale."

Jesse was pleased with Conboy's response, but she was becoming concerned about the scope of the questions. She hadn't discussed the FastSort report with Conboy, and he hadn't mentioned it in any of their discussions. She didn't know where Stanton was going with this line of inquiry, and no trial lawyer is comfortable with her client answering questions about a subject she's never discussed with him.

"After the FastSort purchase was vetoed, you began looking at other alternatives, didn't you?" As he asked this question, Stanton had a slight grin on his face as though he knew something Conboy and his counsel didn't. As Jesse glanced at Robinson, she seemed almost gleeful, and Jesse could also tell Conboy seemed uncomfortable with the question as he admitted he did look at alternatives.

Stanton picked up another document from his pile, had the court reporter mark it as exhibit 6, and presented it to Conboy. "Exhibit 6 is a business plan apparently authored by you a few months after the FastSort purchase was vetoed. It addresses the potential purchase of a company named Perfect Conveyor Systems, Inc., which I will refer to as 'PCS.' Do you recognize this document?"

What is this? Conboy never mentioned PCS to me. But it has NMH's identifying Bates stamp numbers on it, so it was part of their production. Jesse had learned through bitter experience never to reveal her surprise with the appearance of an unfamiliar document at a deposition, and she managed to suppress evidence of her concern as she read exhibit 6. It was not addressed to President McDonald, and it appeared to contemplate NMH being an independent company rather than a subsidiary of National

Manufacturing.

Conboy carefully reviewed the document before responding a little less confidently than he had previously. "Yes, this is a business plan I prepared not long after the FastSort purchase was vetoed."

"Isn't it true that this plan contemplates NMH being independent from National Manufacturing?"

"Yes."

"Isn't it also true that this plan includes most of the managers of NMH being a part of the company at their then-current compensation levels?"

"Yes."

"You knew and understood that compensation levels of its employees has always been considered confidential information by both NMH and National Manufacturing, correct?"

"Yes."

"At the time you prepared your business plan, you were an officer, a vice-president of NMH, weren't you?"

"Yes."

"As such, you understood that you had a fiduciary duty to NMH to always work in its best interest, didn't you?"

"I'm not a lawyer so I can't express an opinion on what my legal duties were."

"Well, you certainly understood that you had a duty of loyalty to your company, as all employees have, correct?"

Conboy shifted in his seat, appearing to Jesse to be uncomfortable with the question before offering a weak, "Yes, I understood I had a duty of loyalty."

"This business plan also includes a number of contracts that NMH would perform to generate revenue. Those contracts included ones that were already in process with NMH. True?"

"Yes. It included contracts in process with NMH and contracts in process with PCS. It also included contracts we hoped to get with potential customers."

"This business plan also includes profit margins and price points on the contracts in question, doesn't it?" As Stanton asked this question, Jesse noticed Rhonda Robinson had a smirk on her face that looked like the cat that cornered the canary.

"Yes."

"You agree that information such as price points and profit margins were considered confidential and trade secret information by NMH?"

Shifting again in his chair, Conboy responded, "I agree that profit margin information was considered confidential, but I don't know that such information is a trade secret."

Stanton gazed at Conboy doubtfully, as if to say, "You know better than that," before asking, "Mr. Conboy, what did you do with this business plan?"

"I showed it to three private equity firms to see whether they had any interest in funding the acquisition of PCS or all of NMH after acquiring PCS." With this answer, the alarm bells in Jesse's head were getting louder. In all of her talks with Conboy he never mentioned having discussions with private equity firms.

Rhonda Robinson's smile was getting bigger and more sinister at the same time. Jesse had an intense desire to punch the smile off her face, but she knew better. Besides, she was beginning to think Robinson might have reason to smirk. *Why didn't Conboy tell me about the private equity discussions? Why didn't I push Conboy harder to tell me about any potential issues that may come up during his deposition?*

By now, Stanton seemed to believe he had Conboy cornered in his testimony. With an air of arrogance, he asked, "Who authorized you to take this business plan with NMH's confidential information to private equity firms?"

Sitting up a little straighter, and looking directly at Stanton, Conboy responded, "President McDonald—who had also been our president at Acorn— did. Let me explain. When National Manufacturing turned down our purchase of FastSort, both President McDonald and I interpreted that as a lack of commitment by National Manufacturing to our material handling business. Furthermore, as our revenues decreased after we completed the Tampa job, rumors were rampant in NMH that National Manufacturing was considering selling NMH. An acquaintance of mine with National Manufacturing confirmed the rumors by informing me they had retained an outside consulting firm to perform a study on the pros and cons of selling NMH. That information eventually appeared in an article in The Wall Street Journal after it had reported for months there were rumors of a sale."

Conboy paused to take a drink of water before continuing. "President McDonald told me we'd have to assume we're on our own with respect to raising capital to acquire a company such as PCS. Alternatively, if National Manufacturing decided to sell NMH we would need to raise capital to keep NMH independent rather than being absorbed into another conglomerate company. He asked me to come up with some contingency plans. He knew I favored purchasing PCS, so he told me to come up with a business plan for NMH that included PCS and to look into the possibility of getting a private equity firm to fund the acquisition."

"Did you actually give President McDonald a copy of the business plan?"

"I don't recall. I know I discussed it with him, but I don't recall whether I actually gave him a copy."

Stanton smirked at Conboy's inability to recall whether he had delivered such an important business plan to the president, but he didn't ask follow-up questions—probably saving those for the trial, in Jesse's opinion. Instead, he said, "Tell me about your discussions with President McDonald regarding private equity firms."

"There wasn't much discussion. He told me to explore whether any private equity firms were willing to invest in NMH and to keep him informed of any interest."

"By the way," Stanton said, "did you prepare the business plan during work hours and on your NMH computer?"

Conboy stiffened, sitting up straighter before responding, "No. I prepared it on my home computer after work hours. Only later, when I needed some information from that plan for another business plan the president asked me to write did I put it on my company computer."

Stanton then took Conboy through all communications and meetings with the three private equity firms in excruciating detail. Although the end result was that none of the firms were interested in investing in NMH, Stanton repeatedly got Conboy to admit there was confidential NMH information included in the materials provided to them. Even with a confidentiality agreement in place with each of the firms, Conboy didn't know what they did with such information.

The other significant event that Stanton uncovered was that Conboy took representatives of one of the private equity firms to Tampa to go through the Post Office installation there to demonstrate what a material handling system actually looked like and how it functioned. The significant factor was not that the demonstration occurred but that three of the NMH managers—all defendants in this case—were part of the demonstration. So, Conboy had brought some of his top managers into his search for capital in hopes of keeping the team at NMH together, an admission that generated another smug smile from Robinson.

***

By now, it was noon. It had been a long morning, and Jesse was ready for a lunch break. She imagined Conboy was also. Stanton agreed to break once they finished discussing the Tampa demonstration, which he treated as if it were a smoking gun supporting his case.

Jesse followed her usual practice of ordering lunch in for herself and Conboy so they could discuss in private how the deposition was going while eating. They retreated to Jesse's office where she had a small round table in addition to her large traditional desk. After they enjoyed their sandwiches and poured coffee for themselves, Jesse pulled out her notes and reviewed them before addressing Conboy.

"I was a little surprised by the questions about FastSort, PCS and the private equity firms. Why didn't you mention them during our prep sessions?" she asked.

"Honestly, Jesse, it never occurred to me that any of those discussions were relevant to the case. Nothing ever came of the business plan I drafted or from the discussions with the private equity firms. No investments were made, and we didn't acquire PCS. So, how is any of that relevant to this case?"

Jesse pondered the question for a long moment and took a sip of coffee before responding. "I gather Stanton asked those questions to try to paint you and the other individual defendants as being disloyal to NMH. He will probably argue at trial that you and your colleagues had been disloyal for a long time, and when the opportunity to go to Brandon Associates came along, your recurring disloyalty resulted in significant damages to NMH."

"That argument seems to be a stretch to me. Could that actually hurt our case?"

"I don't think the case will turn on those facts, but I believe Judge Long will allow Stanton to make that argument to the jury."

Conboy shook his head in disbelief before asking, "What do you think Stanton will ask about this afternoon?"

"I anticipate he will concentrate on how you and the other managers at NMH came to be employed by Brandon Associates."

***

As expected, Stanton's first question once they resumed the deposition was, "When did you first have any discussions with Allan Brandon about NMH providing integration services to Brandon Associates?"

"That occurred sometime late in the second year after

becoming NMH, when NMH decided to get into the commercial material handling business."

This seemed to surprise Stanton. He asked, "Why didn't you discuss working with Brandon Associates before then?"

Jesse had assumed that Stanton had researched the material handling business thoroughly upon getting into this case, as she and David always did with their cases. The fact he didn't seem to understand the difference between the government contracts world and the commercial world was a surprise to her. *They haven't done all their homework.*

Conboy was ready with his response. "Because NMH and Acorn had only been involved in government contracts. Due to all of the rules and regulations applicable to government contracts, those contracts tend to be far more expensive than a comparable commercial contract. The cost difference was so great we never even attempted to bid on a commercial contract before then."

"What changed to enable you to provide integration services to Brandon Associates on commercial contracts?"

Appearing more confident than he did this morning, Conboy responded, "When NMH decided to get into commercial contracts, I knew we would be unable to win a bid. We just weren't structured for commercial competition. But not all jobs went to the low bidder. Some jobs were sole-source contracts, which would go to a specific company if they would agree to the quoted price. Such contracts were sole source rather than bids due to time constraints, a particular type of expertise required, or other unusual circumstances. I knew our entrée into commercial contracts would have to come from getting sole-source jobs, and I believed our best chance of getting such jobs was with a company run by my good friend, Allan Brandon. So, I called him, told him

NMH was getting into commercial material handling and asked
him to give us a chance to show how well we could handle the
integration portion of their material handling contracts."

"How did your good friend respond? Did he send some
lucrative contracts your way?" Jesse's perception was that Stanton
was hoping to find evidence the commercial integration business at
NMH was highly profitable from the beginning.

"Hardly. He offered us a couple of contracts if we would
agree to the prices he quoted. The prices were so low they were
below our direct costs for the job, but I convinced President
McDonald that these contracts would give us an entrée into the
commercial field where we had no presence previously. I told him
we would become more efficient as we obtained additional
contracts and, with some restructuring of our operations, we could
become profitable. He agreed; we got the jobs and came in on time
and within budget."

"Isn't it true that over the next two years NMH got
commercial contracts from other companies besides Brandon
Associates?"

Conboy nodded. "Yes, but they tended to be smaller
contracts. The majority of our contracts during this time always
came from Brandon Associates. Furthermore, even some of the
other contracts we obtained were the result of a recommendation
from Brandon."

"What about bidding on commercial jobs during this time?
Did you try to win jobs through a bid process?" *Again, he should
know the answer to this question without asking. He hasn't done
his homework.*

"Oh, yes," Conboy drawled. "We bid on over thirty

contracts over the next two years. We only came within ten percent of the winning bid on one contract. On the others, we were usually twenty to thirty percent over the winning bid. National Manufacturing allowed us to restructure somewhat to reduce our overhead, but they never allowed us to fully restructure in a manner that would allow us to be cost competitive. They said they couldn't do anything that would hurt their reputation as a government contractor because the bulk of National Manufacturing's business was from government contracts."

Apparently unhappy with this testimony, Stanton responded, "But isn't it true that by the end of the second year NMH was handling commercial contracts that were profitable?"

"It's true that we had a small profit on a few of the contracts, but nothing close to the profitability we had on the government contracts."

Obviously wishing to push harder on the developing profitability, Stanton asked, "But you touted to President McDonald in writing the fact the commercial material handling contracts had become profitable, didn't you?" *Maybe Stanton has done more homework than I gave him credit for.*

Conboy nodded. "Yes, I was pleased we finally had some profitable contracts, and I sent the president a memo informing him. I was encouraged with the progress we had made, and I was hopeful we would continue to become more profitable. I was also hopeful that by becoming profitable it would encourage National Manufacturing to allow us to take further restructuring steps to reach the profitability levels we wanted."

Stanton had the memo Conboy mentioned marked as an exhibit before continuing. "And yet at the very time NMH was becoming profitable with commercial contracts, you began discussions with Allan Brandon about taking your entire management team to Brandon Associates to create an integration department for them. Isn't that true?"

To Jesse's relief, Conboy appropriately countered the accusation. "No, that's not correct. Allan Brandon called to inform me the board of directors of Brandon Associates had decided to expand into integration services so they could truly provide a turnkey project to customers wanting to build a warehouse with a material handling system in it. I tried to talk him out of it, emphasizing that it would require a large capital outlay to create such a department. But he and his board had already made up their minds. They intended to create an integration department."

"Well, he didn't just call to inform you; he called to recruit you and your team at NMH, didn't he?"

"It's true that he offered me the job of heading up their integration services department, but he said nothing about hiring anyone else at NMH."

Jesse glanced at Rhonda Robinson. She had a strange expression of both disgust and delight on her face as Stanton reached into his stack of documents and gave a document to the court reporter to mark. "Mr. Conboy, I show you what has been marked as exhibit ten, a copy of a business plan apparently prepared by you for an integration department at Brandon Associates. It shows your name, office, and salary, as well as those of your fellow defendants in this case. Do you recognize this document?"

Conboy glanced over the document before responding, "Yes, it's a business plan I prepared after Allan Brandon called to offer me the job of head of the new integration department at Brandon Associates."

"Did Mr. Brandon ask you to prepare such a plan?"

Conboy was adamant. "No. After he told me Brandon Associates was going into the integration services business whether I joined them or not, I realized several things. First, if Brandon Associates took all their integration work in-house, NMH would lose the bulk of its commercial integration business. Second, the rumors about National Manufacturing selling NMH were still swirling, and the loss of the bulk of our business would likely guarantee a sale or at least the closing of the Orlando office, with the remaining government contracts being handled out of Atlanta. So, I decided to talk to Allan Brandon about his offer for me to join Brandon Associates."

"And he asked you—his good friend who had experience in integration services—to come up with a business plan, right?" Jesse noticed Stanton was pressing hard to show Brandon Associates had intended all along to raid NMH's key employees to create their own integration department.

Shaking his head, Conboy responded, "No, it was my idea to create the business plan. I knew that all of my managers would likely be out of a job if we lost the Brandon Associates work. And Brandon would need experienced managers to succeed in their new integration business. So, I came up with a plan to include them. As you will note, I also assumed the integration department would be in Orlando rather than Valdosta. I didn't want to move, and I knew my managers didn't either. Furthermore, having a large airport with direct service to most bigger cities around the country made Orlando a better location for the integration department. If Allan Brandon wasn't willing to accept what I included in the business plan, I wasn't interested in the job."

"Your plan also included salaries for your managers as well

as for yourself based upon the current salaries at NMH—all of which were confidential information, correct?"

"No, I listed salaries I felt were appropriate for their positions in the commercial material handling field regardless of what they were making at NMH."

"But all of the salary information was based upon knowledge you obtained while working as an employee and vice-president of NMH, wasn't it?" *He is attempting to label any information Conboy learned while at NMH confidential or trade secret. I'd better have Steve or Maggie research this issue further.*

Frowning, Conboy said, "Well, I did learn what current industry standard pay scales were while at NMH, but I've never considered that to be confidential information."

After consulting his notes for a minute, Stanton asked, "So, you went to Valdosta to meet with Allan Brandon? Tell me about that meeting."

"We met on a Saturday at the Brandon Associates office. We discussed the business plan, which Allan hadn't anticipated. To my surprise, he was willing to consider having the integration department located in Orlando, and he was willing to talk to the managers about joining his company. He also gave me more background on their business, and why they decided to include integration services in-house."

"Is it your testimony that Brandon Associates never considered having integration services in-house until about the time he called you to join his company?" Both Stanton and Robinson had highly dubious expressions as he asked this question.

"That's my understanding, but you'll have to ask Allan."

"So, within two weeks of that meeting with Allan Brandon you signed an employment agreement with Brandon Associates, didn't you?" When Conboy admitted he did, Stanton had his employment agreement marked as an exhibit.

"You immediately gave a two-week notice to President McDonald that you were resigning, and then you got all of your managers together to meet with Allan Brandon, didn't you?" As he said this, disgust once more covered his face. Robinson gave Conboy a look that could melt steel.

"That's not how it happened," he responded. "When I gave my two-week notice, I offered to stay longer if President McDonald wanted me to. As to setting up meetings by the managers with Allan Brandon, I didn't do that. When the managers heard I had resigned, each expressed an interest in going to Brandon Associates with me. I simply gave them the phone number for Mr. Brandon; it was up to them to decide if they wanted to apply for a job there. Allan wanted them to go to Valdosta for a meeting, but when I heard this, I told him they would prefer to meet with him in Orlando, especially since they anticipated the integration office would be in Orlando. He agreed and came to Orlando the following Saturday."

Stanton nodded his head and said, "And that meeting was held at your home, wasn't it?"

Conboy had to admit it was.

"And that meeting occurred at a time you still were a vice-president of NMH, weren't you?

Conboy nodded. "Yes, I was, but I had given notice, and

the meeting was not held during work hours."

"Did you participate in the interviews with the managers by Mr. Brandon?"

"I did not; he met alone with each one individually."

"But he had your recommended salaries from the business plan to offer them?"

"Yes, he had the plan, but the salaries he offered them were not the ones I had recommended; he came up with salaries on his own that were consistent with Brandon Associates' salary structure."

Smirking again, Stanton asked, "Isn't it true that over the next four to six weeks all six of the managers gave notice to NMH and went to work for Brandon Associates?"

"Yes, but each of them offered to stay longer if needed by NMH."

"Well, there wasn't much need for them to stay longer because you took all of the work with you to Brandon Associates, didn't you?"

"No. Two of the contracts about to start wound up going to Brandon Associates, but those two contracts were obtained through Brandon. All of the contracts obtained from companies other than Brandon were completed by NMH. And there were still some U.S. Post Office contracts NMH was working on; all of that work stayed with NMH."

At this point, Stanton asked for a short break in the deposition. It appeared to Jesse he was close to wrapping up. When he returned, he gazed at Conboy intently for a few moments before saying, "Let's see if I can summarize your testimony today, Mr. Conboy. You and Allan Brandon attended Georgia Tech where you both joined the same fraternity, got similar industrial engineering degrees and master's degrees, and expressed to each other the hope you could work together some day. You stayed in close contact over the years, and when Brandon Associates decided to get into the material handling business, he consulted with you. You decided NMH should get into the commercial material handling business, and your good friend Mr. Brandon gave you some sole-source contracts which enabled you and your team to learn to work together from the beginning of a material handling contract through the integration stage to full operation. Then, Brandon Associates decided to get into the integration business and hired you and your key managers at NMH to crank up that business, leaving NMH without most of its leadership to obtain or perform material handling contracts, and enabling you and Mr. Brandon to fulfill your long-held hopes and aspirations of working together. Do I have that right?"

Jesse immediately objected to the question as being compound and misstating the witness's previous testimony. Once her objection was made, Conboy said, "No, you don't have that right. I believe I have answered every part of your question previously, and I stand by my previous testimony."

"Is it your testimony that you really believe you have fulfilled your fiduciary duties and duty of loyalty to NMH?"

"It is." Conboy said this with confidence, to Jesse's relief.

"Is it your testimony that you and the other individual defendants didn't conspire with Brandon Associates to interfere with NMH's relationship with its customers and potential customers and take that business with you?"

After Jesse again objected, Conboy said, "I believe each of us had the right to go to a company with better opportunities for us, and the customers that went with us were all Brandon customers all along."

"And do you honestly believe you protected NMH's confidential information during your discussions with Brandon Associates and all the venture capital companies you met with?"

"I do. I don't believe I disclosed any confidential information that would harm NMH."

Stanton just stared at Conboy for a long moment before stating, "I have no further questions for this witness." As usual, Jesse decided to ask no questions of her own witness now; she would save her questions for the trial.

Stanton reverted to his customary courteous self once the deposition was over, but Ms. Robinson quickly left, slamming the conference room door behind her.

Chapter 17

Valdosta, Georgia owes its existence, as well as its current prosperity, to its location along transportation corridors through South Georgia. When the Atlantic and Gulf Railroad laid an east-west line through Lowndes County that ran four miles south of Troupville in 1859, the good citizens of the county decided to relocate their county seat to a new site directly adjacent to the railroad line. They named the new town "Valdosta," after Val d'Aosta, a plantation belonging to George Troup, the namesake of the former county seat. Some seventy years later U.S. Highway 41–the Dixie Highway—ran through Valdosta along its route from Miami all the way to Michigan. The Dixie Highway was later replaced as the most important road through Valdosta by Interstate 75, which was constructed in the 1960s. Valdosta's location close to the Florida-Georgia border and along I-75 contributed to its steady growth over recent decades, particularly for businesses like Brandon Associates, which benefitted from its strategic location.

David Jordan recalled the history of Valdosta on his way up I-75 the following week to meet with Allan Brandon and his lawyer, Bart Mayfield, to prepare for Brandon's deposition. But what he recalled most vividly about his time in Valdosta was his life as an Air Force pilot at Moody Air Force Base, located only ten miles north of town. Moody was established during the early days of World War II, was deactivated following the war, and then reopened when the Korean War broke out. It had been a continuously operating base since then, although under a variety of

Air Force commands. While David was there, it was an Air Training Command base, responsible for undergraduate pilot training.

David had not returned to Moody or to Valdosta since he left the Air Force to attend law school, and he found himself feeling nostalgic as he remembered his time there. It wasn't just thoughts of flying that brought back these feelings; it was while he was there that he met, courted, and married Carol. They lived in Valdosta for the first few years of their marriage, and he recalled those days fondly. Carol had taught English at Valdosta High School, and he remembered vividly their attending Valdosta High School football games. The football team under coach Bazemore was perennially among the best high school teams in the country and was a source of great pride to the community. As these long-suppressed thoughts about the early days of his marriage washed over him, David was overcome with his feelings of loss once more, and he had to pull over at the next rest stop to steady himself over a cup of coffee before continuing on.

Once back on the road, David forced himself to focus on his reason for traveling to Valdosta. He and Jesse had divided the important witnesses among themselves, with him drawing Allan Brandon's deposition. Jesse had reviewed in detail with David the areas of inquiry Stanton covered in Conboy's deposition, and they felt they had a good idea what he would cover in Brandon's. In fact, Jesse had the court reporter print immediately a transcript of the summarizing questions Stanton posed at the end of Conboy's deposition because she felt they were a road map of what he would ask Brandon. She and David anticipated Stanton would emphasize Conboy's and Brandon's close relationship, which extended all the way back to college where they had spoken often of their desire to work together someday. They expected Stanton would try to get

Brandon to admit he planned to hire Conboy as soon as Brandon Associates got into the material-handling business and bring with him his entire management team, regardless of the impact on NMH. Brandon had to be ready to deal with this line of attack; if he were not well prepared, Stanton would get critical admissions from him and bring Conboy and the other managers down with him.

David was still contemplating the questions Stanton would likely ask as he turned off I-75 at the West Hill Avenue exit, followed almost immediately by a left turn onto Norman Drive. A few blocks later he made another left turn into the Hampton Inn where he had a reservation. After checking into his room, he left for the Brandon Associates' offices and warehouse less than a mile away, just off Norman Drive. The receptionist led him into a spacious conference room that was more upscale than David anticipated given the warehouse in which it sat. Mark Conboy and Allan Brandon were already in the room and greeted him warmly.

David had only met Allan Brandon briefly following the earlier hearing in the case in Orlando. Whereas he had worn a suit for court on the previous occasion, Brandon was now dressed casually in khaki pants, a plaid shirt, and work boots. He was of average height, with sandy brown hair that was beginning to recede, a slight paunch, and a round face with glasses that made him look slightly younger than his forty-two years that David knew him to be from his resume. What was most distinctive about him was his baritone voice, which gave him instant authority when he spoke. He had alert, intelligent brown eyes that combined with his baritone voice to impress David as someone who should make a credible and trustworthy witness.

Although he had spoken to Bart Mayfield several times by telephone with Jesse, David had only met him once on the same occasion he met Brandon. Mayfield was a lanky six-footer, attired in a conservative grey suit with a plain maroon tie. David assumed he had come directly to the meeting from court since the few local attorneys he had met when he lived in Valdosta tended to dress more casually. He had dark hair with a lean, angular face with sharp features that gave him a perpetual glower until he smiled or spoke in his soft South Georgia accent, which softened his visage. David's impression was one of competence, although he understood from Jesse that Mayfield's practice was more corporate than trial work, and he didn't have the same level of trial experience David or Jesse had. Nevertheless, he was a good co-counsel to work with on this challenging case.

After generous mugs of coffee were served, they sat down around the conference table to prepare Brandon for his deposition. David briefly reviewed the instructions he always gave his witnesses for depositions and was pleased to learn Mayfield had already given similar ones. They then reviewed the history of Brandon Associates which David was relieved to notice was consistent with the history Conboy had related. Brandon's account of the evolution of Brandon Associates from a construction company building various types of buildings to one specializing in warehouses and consulting about material handling systems also tracked Conboy's version.

David then turned to the key issue he anticipated Stanton would focus on. "When do you recall first discussing with Mark Conboy the possibility of working together?"

"Oh, that goes way back—all the way to our undergraduate days," Brandon said, clearly recalling fondly those early discussions. "We never had any specific plans, but we liked talking about different businesses that would be enjoyable—and hopefully profitable—to get into. We had more such dialogue during graduate school, but keep in mind I didn't decide to come back to Valdosta to work in the family business until my last semester of grad school. So, our talks contemplated doing business in various parts of the country in just about any industry that required industrial engineers. It was all very speculative."

David made a note of Brandon's last point, then asked, "What about discussions with Mark when Brandon Associates decided to get involved in consulting about and designing material handling systems?"

Brandon nodded. "I did have discussions with Mark then, but not about coming to work for the company. It's important you understand what led to our involvement in material handling systems. Our initial interest was only in building warehouses. I felt I had accomplished a lot just by getting my father and his brother—the owners then—to specialize in designing and building warehouses. What we learned as time went by was that more and more of our customers wanted material handling systems in their warehouses, and the design of the material handling system was often driving the design of the warehouse. I felt we needed to get heavily involved in the design of material handling systems or we might lose much of our warehouse construction business to other companies that handled both. We didn't want to actually install the systems—the so-called integration portion of the business—but we wanted some control over who did; otherwise, we thought we would be at a competitive disadvantage."

This was an important point, in David's opinion; it was a *defensive* move by Brandon Associates to get into the material handling business. David made a few more notes before asking, "So, what was the substance of your discussions with Mark at that time?"

Brandon took another long sip of coffee and squinted as he recalled those discussions. "My concept was that we would develop the expertise to handle or oversee the construction of the warehouse and material handling system all the way from breaking ground to full operation, including the design of the material handling systems. We would handle the construction of the warehouse, but we anticipated subcontracting the integration services for the material handling system. When we were considering whether to get involved in the material handling portion of projects, I called Mark to get the benefit of his experience. Our discussions were informative, but there was no offer for him to come work for Brandon Associates. The offer only came later when we decided to begin to handle the integration services in-house, and that was not something we even contemplated until shortly before we made the decision to bring that business in-house."

David decided to press him on this issue since it was a critical one. "But Mark testified that you and he discussed working together almost every time you got together over the years, which was an annual event at Georgia Tech football games. I'm sure you'll get a lot of questions from Stanton about those discussions."

Brandon nodded. "Oh, sure, over a drink we would say, 'Wouldn't it be great to work together someday.' But I was working in a family business in Valdosta, and Mark and his wife were very happy in Orlando. I had serious doubts he would accept my eventual offer to join Brandon Associates for this reason, among others, and I don't think he would have accepted if I had insisted he move to Valdosta. But to answer your question specifically, all of those comments about working together someday were just pie in the sky, nothing more than that until the specific offer was made."

David pondered his answer for a long moment before asking, "That raises the next question, why *did* you agree to locate the integration services division in Orlando?"

"One reason I always thought Mark would be a good partner is that he's thorough and rational in all of the business decisions he makes. He didn't just say, 'I want to have the integration services department in Orlando.' He brought me a well-thought-out plan with very good reasons to locate that division in Orlando. After thinking it over, I agreed with him and concluded we would have a better chance of success if it were located in Orlando rather than Valdosta."

The more Brandon talked the more David was impressed with him. His comments were credible, and his words were well chosen. David felt he should make an excellent witness for the defendants absent an unforeseen surprise, which is always a possibility in a lawsuit.

They spent the next hour reviewing various allegations of NMH's amended complaint and documents that Stanton might ask about. Mayfield had done a good job of reviewing the documents with Brandon, and David was impressed with his recollection of detail. Finally, as they were wrapping up the meeting, Mayfield said, "I've made reservations for an early dinner at a local steak house for the three of us plus one other person who says he knows you, so we've asked him to join us."

Puzzled, David asked, "Who is it?"

"Ah . . . that's a surprise. We'll meet you at the restaurant at 6:30."

***

David arrived at the restaurant on time, more than a little curious about the person who would be joining them for dinner. *Who do I know from my days at Moody that would remember me? And how would this person know I was in town?*

Brandon, Mayfield, and the surprise guest had already been seated when David arrived at the restaurant. When the maitre'd led him to the table, David tried to identify the guest as they approached. He had dark hair generously speckled with grey and a full, but neatly trimmed, beard also turning grey. David didn't recognize him, although there was something familiar about his eyes and his smile as he was talking to Brandon. The sense of familiarity increased the closer he got to the table, but recognition remained just out of reach.

All three stood when David reached the table, and Brandon said, "David, I think you already know our vice-president for business development at Brandon Associates, Marvin Walker. I think you knew him previously as Lieutenant Colonel Walker."

Walker extended his hand for David to shake it and said, "Hello, David. I couldn't believe it when Allan told me who was coming to visit us. It's truly a small world."

David was so surprised he was momentarily speechless. Once he was introduced, he instantly remembered Walker, although he had no beard the last time David saw him. Lieutenant Colonel Walker had been the head of the academic department for pilot training at Moody, and he taught David the basic aerodynamics course that all student pilots were required to take. When David returned to Moody as an instructor pilot, he had flown in formation with Walker and students many times. There was also a very vivid memory involving Walker that he immediately recalled upon seeing him, one that he was sure would be mentioned before the night was over.

"Colonel Walker, it's great to see you again," David said, genuinely pleased to see someone he had highly respected as a young Air Force officer. "How in the world did you come to be the head of business development at Brandon Associates?"

As they all sat down around the table, Walker replied, "Please call me Marvin. You may recall that I retired from the Air Force after you had been an instructor at Moody for two or three years. My wife and I returned to our hometown in Massachusetts where I got a job in business development. To my surprise, I really enjoyed the job, but neither my wife nor I was happy back in our hometown. After thinking about it, we realized we were happiest during our Air Force days in Valdosta, so we decided to look into job opportunities here and move back. As it so happened, Allan was looking for someone to lead their business development efforts, and he hired me. It's worked out well for both of us."

"Indeed, it has," Brandon commented.

They ordered drinks and continued to talk about how Valdosta had developed and grown since David last lived there. The conversation was convivial, and David was pleasantly surprised by how much he was enjoying the evening. Finally, after their dinner orders were placed, Walker said, "David, when I learned you were involved in the lawsuit and coming here for Allan's deposition, I told him and Bart that you were someone who played a rather important role in my life. But I haven't given them the details of what happened. Why don't you tell them the story? I want them to know who they're working with in this case."

David was taken aback. Once he recognized Walker, he assumed this story would come up during the night. He just assumed Walker would want to tell it. But Walker wanted him to tell the story. Suddenly he thought that was fitting, as he remembered Father John's words of advice about how to overcome the funk he had been in since Carol's death. "Think back to significant events in your life where you have really helped someone, particularly if you had to overcome adversity or major challenges to help the individual. When you identify that event, meditate on it. Try to remember how you felt afterwards; remember how important the outcome was to the other person. Give thanks to God that you were in a position to help that person."

A sense of calm and satisfaction came over David as he began to tell the story.

***

I had just landed with my student during the first flying period in the morning. We had been on what's called a "contact" training mission, which meant we were doing acrobatics, barrel rolls, loops, and other such maneuvers below 18,000 feet. Those missions burn up fuel pretty quickly. But this mission wound up being even shorter because bad weather developed. When we launched, the weather was partly cloudy. But as often happens in south Georgia, fog formed over the nearby Okefenokee Swamp and rolled in over the base. Suddenly, Moody was under instrument flight rules, and they had to begin recalling the aircraft early so all could land before running low on fuel. It usually takes longer to land planes in bad weather under instrument flight rules than when the weather is clearer and under visual flight rules. This was particularly true that day because the fog had joined with the clouds all the way up to just over 5,000 feet, meaning we were in the soup from 5,000 feet down to 500 feet. And the ceiling was dropping.

Just as I pulled my T-38 into the parking blocks, the duty officer of the day approached me and advised there was an emergency in progress. A T-38 from our squadron with the call sign Redstick 10–pronounced one-zero—was squawking the emergency signal on its transponder and was flying in an elliptical pattern over Moody at 15,000 feet. There was no radio contact. The duty officer said his assessment was that either Redstick 10's radios were inoperable, or it had an electrical failure. A T-38 couldn't land without electrical power because the loss of electrical power would also result in the loss of hydraulic power, preventing a safe landing. If only the radios were out—which was likely since the transponder still had electric power—they could safely land. But due to the weather, they needed to fly in formation with a plane having an operating radio that could fly a ground-controlled approach—a GCA—with directions from Moody approach control.

The duty officer wanted me to take off as soon as possible to join up with Redstick 10. Once joined, I had to determine through hand signals whether the problem was loss of radios or total electrical failure. If the latter, I was to follow them to the location where they would eject and provide whatever information I could to air rescue. If the problem were loss of radios, Redstick 10 would fly on my wing in formation as Moody approach control brought us home with a GCA. However, before beginning the GCA we had to determine how much fuel remained for Redstick 10. Running out of fuel on final approach could be a death sentence.

They had a T-38 nearby loaded with half the normal amount of fuel. I thought that should be plenty for the rescue mission. I didn't want more fuel because the weight of the plane affected approach speed and landing speed. Since Redstick 10 was at the end of its mission and low on fuel, it made sense for my plane to have less than full fuel so the two planes could have about the same landing speed.

As I strapped into the cockpit, I asked the duty officer who was assigned the call sign Redstick 10 today?

"It's Lieutenant Colonel Walker and a student on only his third flight in the T-38."

As soon as I started the engines, I contacted the tower. Using my assigned call sign, I said, "Moody tower, Redstick 17, requesting taxi to runway 18 and immediate takeoff for emergency."

"Roger, Redstick 17. We're aware of the emergency. You're cleared to taxi to runway 18 right. Cleared for immediate takeoff. Contact Moody approach control upon getting airborne on frequency 122.7."

I think I set a new taxiing speed record at Moody. Without stopping on the runway, I moved the throttles to full power and then into afterburner as I rolled down the runway. Normally, once airborne we would come out of afterburner at 300 knots unless performing a full afterburner climb to altitude. I left the throttles in afterburner and raised the nose thirty degrees while maintaining 400 knots to get to altitude as soon as possible. Moody approach control was ready with a vector directly to Redstick 10 as soon as I contacted them.

I broke out of the clouds at about 6000 feet and came out of afterburner. Within two minutes I spotted Redstick 10 making a 180-degree left turn back to the south on an elliptical flight pattern. They were supposed to be flying at 300 knots, so I used my speed brake to slow down as I approached. Within thirty seconds of spotting them we were joined up with me on Redstick 10's left, slightly rear of its wing, with three feet wingtip clearance.

I gave the hand signal to inquire whether their radios were out and received an affirmative response. First issue decided. He should be able to fly on my wing on the GCA. But how much fuel did he have? I gave the hand signal to ask, and he came back with five fingers then three fingers—only 800 pounds of fuel left, and 600 pounds was considered minimum fuel. If all went well, he should have just enough fuel to make our approach with a GCA and then land in formation with me. But if there were any delays or diversions, Redstick 10 would be dangerously low on fuel. Furthermore, if we missed our approach—in other words never broke out of the clouds before reaching the minimum altitude— they might not have enough fuel left to go around and get to an altitude to safely eject.

I was sure Marvin was aware of the risk of possibly running out of fuel on final approach but there was no hand signal to ask if he wanted to risk it. So, I made one up. I gave him a thumbs down and then patted my shoulder to inquire whether he wanted to risk flying the GCA in terrible weather to land in formation with me. He nodded his head up and down vigorously. I just hoped to God he knew what I was asking. Although there was risk to his decision, there was also risk in ejecting from an aircraft into the middle of the Okefenokee Swamp. I would have made the same decision he did.

He then gave the signal for me to take lead, which I did with him on my right wing. As soon as I was lead, I contacted air traffic control. "Moody approach control, this is Redstick 17, now a flight of two with Redstick 10 who is approaching minimum fuel. We are declaring an emergency. Request direct vectors to final approach for a GCA into Moody."

"Roger, Redstick 17, understand emergency. Turn left to heading 360 and begin your descent to 6000 feet." They were turning us back north of Moody so we could then turn south to land on runway 18, which aligned north-south, with landings being made to the south, into the wind.

As we reached an altitude of 6000 feet, we were only about 500 feet above the clouds. When the next instructions came to descend further, we would be in the clouds until making visual contact with the runway just before landing. Flying in close formation in the clouds is always challenging. It's sort of like swimming in muddy water. You can see your hand at one foot in front of your face but not at two feet. I knew Marvin would have to snuggle in closer than three feet wing tip clearance to keep me in sight. The one thing a wingman can't do is lose sight of his lead.

As soon as we were about fifteen miles north of Moody, approach control told us to make a descending left turn to 1500 feet and a heading of 180 degrees, which aligned us with the runway. We had been maintaining a speed of 230 knots. Once we leveled off at 1500 feet, I gave the signal to Marvin to lower our landing gear, which we did simultaneously and immediately lowered our flaps to allow us to reduce our speed to 155 knots. We were now in landing configuration ready for final approach.

Approach control announced, "You will reach the glide path in one mile. Be advised that the last aircraft to land reported breaking out at three hundred feet, but reported jagged edges to the clouds which could result in a lower ceiling."

That statement focused my attention. Normally, minimums for landing in formation in weather were a 500-foot ceiling and one-half mile visibility. But this was an emergency, and we had to get Redstick 10 down. Minimums for a single ship landing on a

GCA were 100 feet and one-quarter mile visibility. I had broken a 100-foot ceiling several times, and I had landed in formation many times, even in weather with the ceiling slightly below five hundred feet. But I had never landed in formation with the ceiling as low as 100 feet. Flying final approach at 155 knots, which is 178 miles per hour, it doesn't take very long from spotting the runway 100 feet above ground to touchdown. If I wasn't lined up perfectly on final approach, Marvin might have difficulty after breaking out to get aligned with the runway in time for touchdown. And he may not have enough fuel to get back to a safe altitude to eject.

I forced myself to forget these thoughts and focus on the approach as the controller said, "You have now reached the glide path; begin your normal rate of descent." I could tell from my peripheral vision that Marvin was in perfect position. The rest of the approach consisted of small heading and rate-of-descent corrections from the air traffic controller to keep us on the glide path and on the centerline of the runway.

"You are now passing 500 feet; on glide path, on centerline." Okay, we should see the runway soon. . .

"You are now passing 300 feet; on glide path, on centerline." Where is the runway? We must have encountered one of those ragged edged clouds.

"You are now passing 200 feet; on glide path, on centerline." Still no runway in sight, approaching the ground at 155 knots. How low is this ceiling?

"Passing 150 feet; on glide path, on centerline; you are approaching minimums." Still no runway in sight. . .

"You are now at 100 feet; if the runway isn't in sight, go around." Still no runway!

Just at that instant I saw the strobe lights in the overrun of the runway, which told me exactly where I was, and thankfully I was aligned perfectly on the runway. I eased my plane over to the middle of the left-hand side of the runway, giving Marvin plenty of room to land on the right-hand side. We touched down simultaneously, and I gave a big sigh of relief as we rolled out to the end of the runway.

As we turned off the runway onto the taxi ramp, Redstick 10's engines flamed out. They were out of fuel, and I had to call the tower to send a truck out to pick them up and tow their airplane back to the ramp.

***

When David finished the story, no one spoke for almost thirty seconds. Finally, Walker broke the silence. "Allan, I wanted you and Bart to know the lawyer you're working with on this case doesn't flinch in a crisis. I put my student's life and mine in his hands, and he got us home safely under difficult circumstances. It's a day I'll never forget; we landed on fumes. If we had run out of fuel just a minute or two earlier, I wouldn't be here with you today. I think you chose your co-counsel well."

From the look on their faces, David could tell Brandon and Mayfield agreed, with their respect for him obviously going up a notch or two. But David wasn't going to take all the credit. "Well, it was a team effort with air traffic control and all concerned, and you were steady as a rock on the wing, Marvin. It was an important day in my life also. As to the lawyers you chose for this case, you've already seen how capable my partner Jesse is. She's tougher than I am."

Back in his hotel room David reflected on the evening. It had been an enjoyable evening getting to know Allan Brandon and

190

Bart Mayfield better, and even more enjoyable seeing Marvin Walker again. It connected David once more to an earlier stage of his life, in some respects a happier stage, when he was newly married to the only woman he had ever loved.

But the evening was more than that; he could feel it in his soul. Just as Father John had predicted, when he focused on the story of how he helped bring Lieutenant Colonel Walker and the student down safely from their emergency, it reminded him that life is not just a collection of random events; it's a journey in which there is no higher calling than to do one's duty and serve other people. Telling the story also reminded him that no one was more aware of this than Carol. She performed her duty right up to the very end. He knew she expected him to continue to follow her example.

David's funk would no longer control him. He was sure of it now. He would still have the hole in his heart where Carol would always reside, but her voice would be cheering him on, not bringing him down into depression. It was a liberating realization, and he expressed his gratitude for it as he said a prayer before going to sleep.

Chapter 18

The deposition of Allan Brandon commenced promptly at 9:00 AM the following morning in the conference room at the Brandon Associates offices. David arrived thirty minutes early to review a few key issues with Brandon and Mayfield. The court reporter and videographer showed up twenty minutes later, followed five minutes thereafter by Stanton, with Rhonda Robinson in tow. Or was it the other way around? Based upon Jesse's comments to David about the interaction between Stanton and Robinson, he couldn't discern who was in control of NMH's case. Disagreements between the two had spilled into the open several times previously, and he anticipated more such incidents might occur today.

Once the witness was sworn in, Stanton took Brandon through an unnecessarily complicated explanation of the rules for his deposition before asking about his educational background. He then focused on the friendship between Brandon and Conboy, getting Brandon to admit they met during rush week at Georgia Tech and soon joined the same fraternity.

After questions about the activities they were both involved in with their fraternity, Stanton asked, "Not only were you close friends throughout college, but you were also often in the same classes, weren't you?"

"Yes."

"And that was also true when you took classes for your master's degree in industrial engineering at Georgia Tech?"

"Yes."

After meticulously going over a long list of courses they both took, Stanton asked, "Is it true that you and Mr. Conboy discussed the possibility of going into business together as far back as your undergraduate days?"

Brandon nodded his head slightly before answering in his baritone voice, "Yes, we had generalized discussions about working together, but it was all pie-in-the sky talk. It was sort of a game of ours to speculate on what types of businesses it would be fun to get into. We had lots of ideas about different industries, but there was never anything more specific than identifying the pros and cons of all the different ones."

"So, it's your testimony that during your entire educational experience you and Mr. Conboy never made any *plans* about working together in a specific industry, including the material handling business?" As he asked the question, Stanton's expression plainly said he didn't believe that to be the case. Robinson's sneer indicated she didn't believe it either.

"We had lots of discussions about a wide range of industries and businesses, but nothing I considered to be *plans*. If I could make an analogy, it was like discussing it would be fun to own a Rolls Royce, but there was no talk about where to find one, how much to pay for one, or how to finance it. I always considered our discussions about working together someday as pie-in-the-sky talk, and I believe Mark did also."

"Did these pie-in-the-sky discussions, as you call them, ever focus on a particular industry?"

David was beginning to sense that Stanton was leading Brandon into a trap, and the ever-increasing sneer on Robinson's face reinforced his uncomfortable feeling. Brandon must have also suspected danger because he paused before responding. "Well, our discussions would often focus on a particular industry before we would move on to discuss other specific industries. But I don't recall at any time either of us identifying any particular industry as the one we should pursue."

"Isn't it true that during graduate school you and Mr. Conboy discussed going into the material handling systems business together, including the integration portion of the business?" As he asked this question, David noticed that Robinson looked up from her note taking with a smirk on her face he could only describe as evil.

Brandon seemed puzzled by the question and paused before he responded, evidently trying to recall a specific discussion about the material handling business. He shook his head slightly and said, "As I mentioned, Mark and I did have a lot of generalized discussions about potential businesses for us—often over a beer— and those discussions may have included the material handling business, but I don't remember any specific discussion."

Shuffling through the papers in front of him to find the document he wanted, Stanton said, "Well, let me refresh your recollection. We found an article from twenty years ago in the American Journal of Industrial Engineering authored by Allan Brandon and Mark Conboy, entitled, 'Recent Advances in Material Handling Systems and Technology.'" Shoving a copy of the article across the table to Brandon, he asked, "Are you and your co-defendant Mark Conboy the authors of this article?"

David quickly reviewed the document, then glanced at

Brandon who was obviously surprised by the article. As he read it, the cloud of puzzlement in his expression passed to one of recognition, and a small smile emerged as he replied, "Yes, Mark and I are the authors."

Why did Brandon not mention this article to me? It's obviously relevant to the case.

"This article includes discussion of recent developments in the integration portion of the material handling business as well as other aspects, doesn't it?"

Without glancing at the document, Brandon simply replied with a weak, "Yes."

"Did you and Mr. Brandon have articles published regarding any other industries while you were pursuing your master's degree?"

Shaking his head slightly, Brandon responded, "No, this was the only article we wrote that was published."

Nodding his head, Stanton said with more than a hint of sarcasm, "So, let me see if I understand your testimony correctly. Out of all of the many industries that you say you and Mr. Conboy discussed and identified as ones in which you might like to work together, the one industry your only published article addressed was the material handling industry. And your article included developments in the integration portion of that industry. Do I have that right?"

Brandon's shoulders slumped a little as he responded, "Well, you're correct this was the only article we got published in grad school, and it did discuss developments in integration services."

"Did either or both of you even attempt to get an article published regarding any other industry while in grad school?"

His shoulders slumped further as he offered a weak, "No. . ." David noticed in his peripheral vision that Robinson's sneer was now malevolent, and she made no effort to conceal it.

As Stanton paused to review his notes before asking follow-up questions, Brandon spoke up. "But the only reason we wrote this article was that one of our professors urged us to write it. He had had many articles published in the American Journal of Industrial Engineering; he thought this would be a timely topic for such an article, and the Journal would be likely to publish it. We jumped at the opportunity. An article published in a trade journal looks good on a resume."

Both Stanton and Robinson appeared surprised that Brandon continued his response after he apparently had completed his answer to the pending question. Stanton and Robinson glanced at each other, and when Stanton made no objection, Robinson jumped up from her chair, and exclaimed, "I object; there was no question pending; the answer was non-responsive, and I move to strike everything after he said, "No."

Stanton appeared so stunned his mouth actually dropped open, but he said nothing. David was surprised also, but he retained the presence of mind to respond immediately, "Ms. Robinson, you have no right to make objections. Under the rules of our court, only one lawyer per party is entitled to question a witness. Furthermore, the witness has the right to explain his answer, particularly at a deposition. If there is another outburst from you, I will seek sanctions from the court, including reversing your right to appear in this case *pro hac vice.*"

Robinson appeared ready to explode; her face and neck had

turned red, and her eyes were tiny slits through which she stared at David with an expression full of venom. Before she could say anything though, Stanton interceded. "It's about time for a break. Let's take ten minutes." Turning to Brandon, he said, "Is there a room where Ms. Robinson and I can meet privately?"

"Sure," he responded. "There's an empty office two doors down the hall on the left." As Robinson marched off to the office, Stanton remained to pour himself a cup of coffee from the carafe on the credenza. As he was leaving the conference room, he looked at David, shook his head, uttered a long sigh, and then trudged off to meet with his co-counsel.

Once Stanton was out of the conference room, David asked the court reporter and videographer to give them some privacy. When they left, David turned to Brandon to encourage him because although he had performed reasonably well, David felt he seemed deflated at times in his responses. "Allan, you're handling his questions nicely. I particularly liked your explanation for the journal article. Don't hesitate to explain your answers as necessary and project confidence in your responses. There's always the possibility that portions of this video deposition could be shown to the jury; if so, we want them to see a witness who's confident because he's simply telling the truth."

Brandon nodded, apparently encouraged that David was satisfied with his performance thus far, and Mayfield offered additional words of encouragement.

Just as David and Mayfield finished their comments to Brandon, they heard loud but muffled shouts coming from down the hall. David couldn't understand what they were saying, but there was no doubt Stanton and Robinson were in a shouting match. They must have realized they were putting on a show because the shouting quickly stopped. Two minutes later, Stanton came back to the conference room, followed a minute later by Robinson whose jaw was firmly clenched and whose body language telegraphed that her anger had not diminished—at least not by much. She poured herself a cup of coffee, added three sugars, and then took her seat at the conference table, noticeably further away from Stanton.

As soon as the court reporter and videographer returned, Stanton looked around the room, offered a forced smile, and asked, "Is everyone ready to proceed?"

When everyone present affirmed they were ready, Stanton said, "Mr. Brandon, you have denied that you and Mr. Conboy planned to work together in the material handling business, but isn't it true that he began working in the material handling business not long after you both graduated from your master's program?"

"Yes, I believe he did."

"And you were aware of his experience in that industry because you visited with each other every year at one or two Georgia Tech football games where you would catch up with each other?"

A reluctant, "Yes," from Brandon.

"In the meantime, you convinced your father and his brother—the owners at the time— that Brandon Associates should specialize in building warehouses rather than a wide variety of buildings, didn't you?"

"Yes. It took some time, but they finally agreed to specialize."

"And by the time you bought the business from them,

Brandon Associates specialized in building warehouses?"

"Yes. . ."

"Furthermore, when you convinced them to specialize in warehouses, you were well aware that most material handling systems are housed in some type of warehouse, correct?"

Brandon squirmed in his chair before answering, apparently beginning to glean where this line of questions was going. "Yes."

"In fact, you recognized soon after Brandon Associates began specializing in warehouses that many of the warehouses you built were for material handling system operations, right?"

Again, Brandon couldn't disagree with the question.

"And when you decided the time was right for Brandon Associates to get into the material handling business, the first person you consulted with was Mr. Conboy?"

Brandon sat up straighter in his chair and said, "Yes, he was the first person I consulted about the material handling business, but the reason the time was right to enter that business had nothing to do with working with him. We were losing business because many companies building warehouses were consulting with designers of the material handling system before their warehouse builder. It was a defensive move on our part. If we didn't get into the business of designing and building material handling systems, we stood to lose a large portion of our warehouse construction business."

"But regardless of why the timing was right, you continued to seek Mr. Conboy's advice at every stage of Brandon Associates' entry into the material handling business, didn't you?"

"I did continue to seek his counsel, yes."

"You sought his advice even though Mr. Conboy was working on government contracts rather than commercial contracts for material handling systems?"

"Yes, the technical issues in material handling contracts, whether for the government or private companies are similar. The main difference is how you staff such contracts. Regulations applicable to government contracts drive the costs up considerably."

"But there came a time when Mr. Conboy wanted to get involved in commercial contracts for his employer—my client, National Material Handling. And when that time arrived, he turned to you to get an entrée into commercial contracts, specifically for the integration portion of material handling contracts, right?"

"Yes, he explained that because there were fewer government contracts—specifically fewer Post Office contracts available—NMH wanted to expand into commercial contracts for integration services. We were subcontracting all of the integration portions of our contracts. I knew and trusted Mark, so I said, 'Sure, provided you can meet our cost requirements.'"

A cynical smile crossed Stanton's face as he said, "Isn't it true that once Brandon Associates gave NMH the integration contracts, you and Mr. Conboy had finally reached the goal of working together—the goal you said was pie-in-the-sky, but one you had discussed all the way back to undergraduate school? And the business was the very one your published article addressed?"

Brandon shook his head. "No, this was not the sort of relationship we discussed in college. We had discussed *starting* a business together, not just having a contractual relationship through a publicly held company."

Uh, oh, I think I see where this is going, David thought to himself, unhappy with Brandon's last answer.

Stanton nodded, apparently pleased with the response. "You're right, Mr. Brandon. You needed to find out whether you and Mr. Conboy could actually work well together before taking the final step of bringing him in as a partner in your business, isn't that true?"

Brandon frowned. "No, I had given no thought to bringing Mark into Brandon Associates when we entered into the initial contracts. I simply did him a favor by offering NMH contracts to see if they could hack it in commercial contracts. Once I saw the quality and timeliness of their work, we gave NMH more contracts. It was in Brandon Associates' best interest to have good, competent subcontractors."

"But isn't it true that within less than two years after the first contract with NMH, Brandon Associates decided to handle the integration portion of the contract—the largest and most profitable portion—in-house?"

A cloud passed over Brandon's face as he seemed to grasp where Stanton was going with his questions. After a brief pause, he said, "We did decide to expand into integration services, but that was because we wanted more control over the entire process. We had encountered problems with some of our subcontractors. With integration being such a significant portion of any material-handling contract, our management team decided we would be better off having total control over the entire contract rather than having to rely on subcontractors. Their mistakes could damage our reputation and our business."

"But I haven't seen a single document produced in this case evidencing any complaints about the quality of NMH's work," Stanton said. "Did you ever complain to NMH about problems with their work?"

"No, we had numerous complaints about most of our other subcontractors, but I don't believe we had any with NMH. However, we didn't want to have our only reliable subcontractor be a large publicly held company who was also a competitor. That would give NMH too much influence or even control over our business. We preferred to be able to control our own future."

As soon as Brandon completed his answer Robinson let out a loud snort, and muttered something under her breath that David couldn't understand. The expression on her face, however, left little doubt about what she thought of Brandon's testimony.

David immediately spoke up. "Ms. Robinson, this is your final warning. Keep your reactions to the testimony to yourself, or you will have to answer to Judge Long." Since she didn't actually *say* anything—or at least anything David could understand—he decided not to immediately seek sanctions. However, he instructed the videographer to change to a wide-angle view so the camera would capture *all* those sitting at the conference table. He wanted to have a video record of any further outrageous conduct by Robinson so the judge would have clear evidence why Robinson should be sanctioned. David found it interesting that Stanton didn't object to David's instruction to the videographer.

Robinson didn't respond, but it was obvious she was seething. Stanton whispered something to her, but she shook her head and focused on her yellow pad in front of her while clenching her teeth so hard her jaw muscles protruded.

Stanton reviewed his notes and appeared to gather his

thoughts after the interruption before asking, "When Brandon Associates made the decision to expand into integration services, did you inform your board you intended to hire NMH's vice-president, Mark Conboy?"

"Well, I told them I knew Mark's capabilities, and I thought he would be a good person to head up our new integration services department. They agreed with my recommendation and authorized me to make him an offer. I didn't know whether he would accept."

This testimony brought a smirk to Stanton, who said, "Mr. Brandon, do you expect us to believe there was any doubt in your mind that your good friend with whom you had discussed working together since college days would say, 'No' to your offer?"

Brandon sat up straighter, looked Stanton directly in the eye and said, "Believe whatever you want; the truth is that I had serious doubts whether Mark would accept our offer. He had often told me how happy he and his wife were in Orlando, and I was unsure whether he would move to Valdosta, which was part of our offer."

"Is it your testimony that you had no discussions with Mr. Conboy about setting up an integration department for Brandon Associates in Orlando before your offer?"

Brandon shook his head. "There was no such discussion until Mark came to Valdosta to discuss our offer the Saturday after we made it. That's when he presented me with a business plan that specified the integration department would be in Orlando, not Valdosta. He was quite clear this was a condition of his accepting our offer."

Stanton reached over and pulled a document out of his

stack, had the court reporter mark it as an exhibit, and then presented it to Brandon. "Is this the business plan to which you referred?"

"Yes."

"Well, this business plan not only specifies that Mr. Conboy and the integration department would be based in Orlando, but all of the NMH managers would be hired to work there also, isn't that right?"

Brandon shrugged. "I don't know about all, but the ones identified would join us, according to the plan."

"And Mr. Conboy had salary recommendations for each of the managers in his plan?"

"Yes."

"Did Mr. Conboy tell you he knew that all of the managers were willing to leave NMH and join you?" David assumed that Stanton was fishing for any evidence that Conboy had been planning to take his managers to Brandon Associates or some other company *before* the offer was made.

"No. He told me he hadn't had any discussions with them about working for Brandon Associates; he only gave them my phone number so they could contact me. But he told me we had been the source of the vast majority of NMH's commercial business. If we no longer were going to send commercial contracts to NMH that would probably lead to NMH shutting down the Orlando office. NMH could handle the diminishing number of government contracts out of their Atlanta office. So, we both assumed these managers would be looking for jobs."

Stanton nodded and a small, knowing smile crossed his

face before he asked, "At the time Mr. Conboy told you this he was still employed by NMH, wasn't he?"

"Yes."

"Is this the kind of information you allow your employees to disclose to third parties about Brandon Associates, Mr. Brandon?"

David made an objection on the basis of relevance and it being a hypothetical question, which gave Brandon time to think about his answer. "I don't think the situation has ever come up at our company. I've always told our employees to just use common sense in deciding what they can disclose to third parties. Under the circumstances, I didn't think Mark disclosed anything improper to me."

David glanced at Robinson who was shaking her head, but she kept her mouth shut and continued writing her notes. By now, David was hoping she would have another outburst that would provide solid grounds for a sanctions motion, but she contained herself.

Stanton paused to review his notes and apparently to decide how to proceed. After a few moments, he said, "Let's see if I understand your testimony. Mr. Conboy came to Valdosta after you made him an offer of employment. He shows up with a business plan in hand, salaries included, to hire not only himself but his entire team of managers and set up the integration department for Brandon Associates in Orlando, not Valdosta, something you had never even thought about before that day. But by the end of the day, you had agreed in principle to hire him, all his managers, and to set up the integration office in Orlando?"

"I think I've answered all parts of that question, but the

answer is essentially, yes."

"From my review of your offer to him it appears you didn't include an equity interest in Brandon Associates for him, is that correct?"

"Yes."

"But from my review of his employment agreement he does have one. Was the equity interest also negotiated that day in Valdosta as well?"

"We agreed in principle there would be an equity interest, and the details were worked out by the time the employment agreement was ready to sign."

Stanton stared at Brandon for nearly a full minute before saying, "That was quite a day. Is it still your testimony there were no plans to be in business together before that day?"

"It is."

An awkward silence filled the air while Stanton consulted his notes, glanced at Robinson—who didn't respond—then announced, "Let's take a forty-five-minute lunch break."

***

When the deposition resumed, Robinson still seemed out of sorts with Stanton. She kept her distance from him and was sullen, focusing on her note taking. Stanton's demeanor, in the meantime, remained professional as he directed his questions to the hiring of the NMH managers.

"Soon after you signed the employment contract with Mr. Conboy you went to Orlando to recruit the NMH managers, didn't you?"

Brandon nodded. "Well, I did go to Orlando to meet with some of the NMH managers, but all of them had contacted me to express an interest in working for Brandon Associates."

"And each of them had obtained your contact information from Mr. Conboy?"

Shrugging, Brandon said, "I assume so, but you would have to ask them."

In a knowing tone of voice, Stanton said, "Tell us where you met with the managers, Mr. Brandon."

A slight pause before he responded, "We met at Mark's home. . ."

"At the time of this meeting, Mr. Conboy was still employed by NMH, wasn't he?"

"I believe he was, although he had already given his resignation notice to NMH. And this meeting was on a Saturday, not during working hours."

"And all of the managers were still employed by NMH?"

"Yes."

In a condescending tone of voice, Stanton said, "So, all of the people you met with were then NMH employees, and you were meeting at the home of an NMH employee?"

David objected to the question as repetitive, but Brandon had to admit Stanton's observation was true.

After pausing for effect, Stanton said, "Describe for me the pitch you made to the NMH managers."

Brandon sat up a little straighter, and David thought he noticed a sense of pride in his voice as he responded. "I gave them the background of Brandon Associates, how my father and his brother had founded a construction company building a wide variety of buildings, how we had transitioned into specializing in warehouses, and how that led us into the material handling business. I also told them we had initially thought we would have the integration services portion of the material handling contracts handled by subcontractors, but experience had taught us we should bring the integration function in-house so we could offer a full turn-key operation to our customers. That's why I was there to meet with them."

Stanton jotted a few notes as Brandon spoke, then asked, "Did you tell them you had been consulting with Mr. Conboy about the material handling business ever since you first started thinking about getting into that business?"

"No, not then. But when we gave the first integration contracts to NMH I told our managers of my lengthy relationship with Mr. Conboy. My managers were skeptical NMH would be an appropriate subcontractor, but I told them he would ensure the job was done well and on time."

David noticed that Robinson leaned back in her chair and glared at Brandon after his last comment. Her face was flushed, and the muscles in her jaws were bulging from her clenched teeth. It appeared she was struggling to suppress another angry outbreak, but somehow she managed.

Stanton apparently also noticed that Robinson was about to explode again and pivoted to asking Brandon about the meetings with each of the managers.   He spent nearly twenty minutes on each interview, going over in minute detail everything that was said, with emphasis on how the salary for each manager was determined. In response to specific questions from Stanton, Brandon had to admit he relied heavily on the salary recommendations from Conboy and only made minor adjustments to conform to Brandon Associates' salary structure.

When David thought Stanton had exhausted all possible questions about the interviews, he circled back to ask about discussions regarding when each manager would give NMH notice of his resignation. Although Brandon testified they determined when each manager would give notice based upon the work schedule pending at NMH at the time, he had to admit the notice schedule was also convenient for Brandon Associates.

Once that topic was exhausted, Stanton asked, "Mr. Brandon, you knew and understood that by hiring Mr. Conboy and the six managers who worked with him that you were essentially taking away NMH's ability to handle commercial material handling contracts, isn't that correct?"

"I didn't assume that. NMH is part of a large publicly held company that was still performing government contracts. I assumed they could continue to compete in commercial contracts if they were willing and able to get their costs competitive."

"But the people you were hiring—all of whom are defendants in this case—were the people who worked on the commercial contracts with Brandon Associates?"

He had to admit they were.

"And to your knowledge, NMH had no other teams working on commercial contracts besides the team working with Brandon Associates?"

Brandon shook his head. "I'm unaware of any."

"So, you knew and understood that when you hired these people you weren't just hiring some people, you were taking away NMH's entire commercial material handling business?"

Brandon clasped his hands on the table in front of him, looked Stanton in the eye and said, "No, Mr. Stanton, I knew I was offering an opportunity to capable workers who would probably lose their jobs when we took our integration services business in-house. They were free to leave their jobs, and we were free to hire them." Stanton started to ask a follow-up question but apparently thought better of it.

Once again, Robinson squirmed in her chair, obviously incensed by the testimony and by Stanton for not asking follow-up questions. She furiously wrote a note and handed it to Stanton, who read it, and shook his head before saying, "I have no further questions for this witness."

Neither David nor Mayfield had any questions for Brandon, which brought the deposition to a close.

***

On the way home, David called Jesse on his mobile phone. She immediately asked how the deposition went.

"I thought Brandon performed reasonably well. I also now understand the story that NMH will tell at trial; it's clear from the questions Stanton asked. Unfortunately, it's a story the jury could buy and return a verdict for NMH, although I still like our story better. But Stanton will present the Plaintiff's case well if Robinson doesn't interfere too much. Ultimately, the case is going to boil down to whom the jury believes."

Chapter 19

The digital clock on Jesse's BMW rolled over to 7:00 PM as she pulled into Antonio's parking lot. She didn't see James' car as she quickly scanned the lot and breathed a sigh of relief. She needed a few minutes to gather her thoughts before engaging James in what she anticipated would be a crucial discussion, much as she felt before their dinner a month or so ago. The issue then was whether they were committed to each other and their relationship. Tonight, it was whether they were in agreement on what Jesse felt were key questions if they were to be married. She had run this discussion over in her mind repeatedly during the past week, and she castigated herself for not bringing up at least some of these topics previously.

Jesse asked the maitre'd for a booth and was barely seated before James joined her, kissing her on the cheek before sitting down opposite her. She was relieved he seemed delighted to see her despite his inquiry earlier as to why they were dining at Antonio's tonight. Most of their serious talks had taken place at Antonio's, and James was apparently wary of another "Antonio's moment" at this stage of their relationship. She couldn't blame him. Since they had their breakthrough during their last dinner there, they had moved blissfully forward enjoying their time together—despite all the calendar conflicts—but without addressing any of the important matters she wanted to discuss tonight. *James probably thinks we don't have any serious barriers to getting married, but when I raise my issues, he may discover he*

211

has some of his own.

They enjoyed drinks and caught up with small talk until they ordered—swordfish for her and veal piccata for him. Jesse had scheduled this dinner, but she was nervous about raising her topics. Knowing she should be completely honest about what was on her mind only added to her stress. She waited until there was a natural break in the conversation, then chose her words carefully to encourage James to be candid as well.

"James, I apologize again for the times I've had to cancel our mid-week dates lately. It's just been an unusually busy time; it won't always be like this." She gave him her warmest smile and he responded in kind. "I understand, Jesse; I've had to cancel also. It's the result of both of us having busy professional lives."

"I get it, but it's so important that we set aside time for each other. I've regretted each time I've had to cancel, more than you know." James smiled and nodded, so Jesse paused, then said, "Thinking about how difficult it's been just to schedule a week-night date has made me think about other issues we might face. . ."

He appeared puzzled as he asked, "What issues, Jesse?"

"Well . . . how do we deal with our calendar conflicts when children come along?" After looking at him expectantly and noticing his eyes widened in surprise, she added, "You do want to have children, don't you?"

James seemed flummoxed and was speechless for a long moment before responding amiably, "This *is* going to be an interesting dinner, isn't it?" His expression turned serious as he reached for her hand and with sincerity riding on his words said, "Of course I want children. I can't imagine being married to you without having children."

Jesse let out an audible sigh, smiling with relief before turning serious as she hesitantly asked, "You don't expect me to give up my career to be a full-time mother, do you?"

James appeared even more flummoxed by this question. But he recovered quickly, and declared, "That thought never crossed my mind. Remember, I've seen you in action. There's no way I would ever ask you to give up your legal career, or even interrupt it for any extended period of time. We'll have to make some sacrifices to have sufficient time for our children, but we can work through those issues together and share the sacrifices equally. David and Carol both had careers, and Jenna certainly hasn't suffered from parental neglect. If they were able to do it, we can, too."

This answer thrilled Jesse, and she felt some of the tension that had gripped her all day begin to ebb. "This is going even better than I hoped," Jesse commented with a chuckle. "So, let's move on to a non-controversial topic—money."

"Oh, that won't be a problem. Just let me handle all of the financial decisions, especially who we choose to do our day trading for us." He kept his expression as serious as he could before his face collapsed into a wide grin. After pausing to enjoy his own joke, he continued, "I'm sure we can work through any financial issues that arise. We're both earning a good living. My only stipulation is that I don't want to live a luxurious lifestyle. I was raised to be conservative with money and never compete for the fanciest house or the most extravagant vacation. Not that I want to be Mr. Scrooge with money; simply living comfortably will satisfy me. How about you?"

"I think I can live with that," Jesse agreed, while wondering what James *really* thought about her driving an expensive BMW, which she dearly loved. It was her sole extravagance, one he apparently didn't share since he was driving a six-year-old economy car. "I like your desire not to live above our means, and if we discuss all of our major financial decisions, I'm confident we can find common ground."

"So, have I given all the right answers?" James asked playfully. "Have we covered all the key issues on your checklist so this relationship can take off and we can begin planning the next step?" The smile on his face told Jesse that he felt they were cleared for immediate takeoff, and he was ready to pop *the question*.

"Uh, not quite. There's one other topic we haven't discussed at all, but it's one I think we need to talk about."

His face went blank, without any apparent clue what she was referring to. When Jesse was reluctant to say more, he finally asked, "What is it?"

Cautiously, Jesse responded, "Religion?"

Jesse thought she saw James' shoulders slump slightly, and the corners of his mouth turned down as if he had swallowed some soured milk. He said nothing, apparently surprised Jesse raised this issue, but he seemed to realize he should respond carefully. He glanced down at the table, then looked directly into Jesse's eyes, which reflected disappointment at his reaction.

"Jesse, I thought you understood that I have little interest in religion. My education has been mostly in the sciences, and I view religion as incompatible with science. In fact, I'm rather surprised you've raised this topic; I thought you had no interest in religion either. You've never mentioned going to church."

Jesse dropped her gaze to the table, stung by her realization of the truth of James' comment. She *hadn't* mentioned religion, even in passing, nor could she remember the last time she had attended church. She was pretty sure it was at Carol's funeral, nearly eight months ago.

"You're right; I haven't mentioned church—or religion in general—and I'm not sure why not. I was baptized and confirmed in the Methodist church, and I attended services regularly growing up, all the way through college. It was in law school that I began skipping church and I'm sure the boyfriend I told you about had something to do with that. But I always thought I would get involved with the church again once married, and I've always assumed my husband and I would attend with our children. I definitely want to be married in a church. Is this something you're open to considering?"

The blank look on James' face told Jesse this was plainly something he had *not* considered, and he appeared mystified that he would have to consider it now. After a long pause, James started talking; it seemed to Jesse he was thinking out loud, trying to figure out how he felt about religion becoming a part of the relationship with the woman he wanted to marry and part of his parental responsibilities with any children they might have. "Jesse, I don't want you to think I'm a complete heathen. I was baptized as an infant in the Presbyterian Church, although I never went through confirmation. My parents never attended church more than a few times a year, and by the time I was in high school, they didn't even go that often, so I didn't either."

"I understand," Jesse replied, giving him the best non-judgmental look she could muster.

"Once I got to college, my course work was dominated by

the sciences. I was on a pre-med track, and I never took any philosophy or religion courses. I always felt science was something I could rely upon as being solid and true, whereas philosophy seemed just a matter of opinion and religion mostly myth. So, I didn't pursue learning more about either of them."

Jesse nodded. She could tell he was struggling to get a handle on the idea that religion may have to be a part of his life at some level, and he wasn't sure how he felt about that. The more he talked, the more convinced Jesse became that they definitely needed to work through this issue and find common ground. "Are you willing to have our wedding in a church if we decide to get married?"

"Of course, Jesse. If that's important to you, it's important to me."

"Good. It *is* important to me to be married in a church. But I'm willing to be flexible as to what church we choose. It doesn't have to be Methodist. I'm willing to get married in a Presbyterian church if you prefer."

A light came on in James' eyes; it was clearly an "aha moment" for him, although Jesse wasn't sure why.

"I know the perfect place. It's the only church I've attended in over twenty years. Let's get married at All Souls Episcopal Church. I was impressed with the priest—Father John—at Carol's funeral, and it's a beautiful church."

"You read my mind," Jesse responded with her biggest smile of the night. "I've been thinking the same thing. One point, though. He'll require us to go through pre-marital counseling with him."

"I assumed as much. That's not a problem for me. He may even have a good suggestion or two for us," James said jokingly as he finally began to warm up to the conversation they were having.

Jesse nodded. "There's another reason he may be a good person to counsel us."

"What's that?" James responded as he took another sip of wine.

"Well, he had to go to seminary to become a priest. But his undergraduate degree, I understand, was in physics, and he worked at NASA for several years before going to seminary. As a scientist himself, he may have answers to some of your questions about the reliability of the Bible and whether it's mostly myths."

James seemed surprised with this information, and he was momentarily speechless. But then something seemed to register in his mind. "It looks like the entire universe is conspiring to get me back into a church," he observed wryly.

Jesse laughed out loud, pleased with the way this evening's delicate conversation had turned out. She was reassured about all of her concerns, and although James hadn't fully committed to being a regular churchgoer with her, she was optimistic, particularly since he liked Father John.

After reflecting further on the decisions they had made tonight, Jesse playfully asked, "So, does this mean you've asked me to marry you? I mean, we *have* agreed to go to pre-marital counseling."

James seemed startled by the question. Then he put on his sternest expression of the evening and said, "No, not yet."

Jesse's frown reflected her shocked disappointment, but her

expression quickly turned into delight as James slipped out of the booth, dropped to one knee, and, staring lovingly into her eyes, said, "Jessica McKenzie, I love you. Will you marry me?"

Jesse was stunned but managed to exclaim loudly, "Yes! I love you, too." As she gave her consent, everyone in the entire restaurant stood up and applauded while James and his bride-to-be enjoyed a lingering, affectionate kiss.

***

Everyone was buzzing with excitement about Jesse's engagement the following Monday at the firm's weekly attorney luncheon. Other than David, no one was aware her relationship with James was this serious, and even he expressed surprise James had proposed so quickly. "So, when is the big day?" David asked.

Jesse was becoming more excited about the wedding every time she thought about it. She had always assumed she would marry someday, but those thoughts were more theoretical than real. Ever since James proposed, though, the reality had been a constant companion—in a good way—and she was delighted to announce, "It will be sometime in the fall. Neither James nor I want a long engagement. We have an appointment with Father John on Thursday of next week, and we'll hopefully tie down a date then." Looking around the room, Jesse said to everyone, "So, keep your calendars open for late October or November until we have a firm date. It won't seem right if any of you aren't there to celebrate with James and me. I want *all* family at my wedding."

The last point was a critical one because she had already decided to ask Jenna to be the maid of honor and Maggie to be a bridesmaid. James had decided to ask David to be best man and Steve to be a groomsman. They would extend the invitations to them as soon as they had a wedding date and the opportunity to ask. It truly was going to be a family wedding.

Everyone nodded their agreement to keep their calendars open as requested, but David interrupted the revelry. "Jesse, keep in mind that our trial in the NMH case is scheduled for the first week of October, and the trial could last up to two weeks. Judge Long would rather have her wisdom teeth pulled than grant a continuance, so I'm confident our trial will take place then. But you probably should select a date well into November to be sure."

"Good point! I'll keep that in mind when we talk to Father John."

Finally, the discussion turned to business, and everyone's workload. The first case for discussion was NMH. "Next week five depositions are scheduled in California, and you're covering them, Maggie. How's your preparation going?" Jesse asked.

Maggie looked up from her yellow pad where she had scribbled some notes. "Pretty well, I think. I've talked to someone from each of the companies being deposed. Two of the companies hired NMH to provide integration services for their material handling contracts, but both companies were hired at Brandon Associates' recommendation. The companies had no previous relationship with NMH. As to the other three companies, none has ever done business with NMH; two of them had Brandon Associates provide integration services. The other company has never done any business with Brandon Associates or NMH, although both have responded to requests for proposals from that company. I've pulled all relevant documents regarding the five companies. So far, I haven't discovered any documents that seem to be problematic."

Jesse marveled once more at how fast Maggie had developed as a trial lawyer. She had the maturity most lawyers only achieve by their tenth year at the bar, and Jesse was confident Maggie would handle these depositions competently. Turning to Steve, she asked, "How's your preparation coming for the four depositions in Texas the following week?"

"From what I've gleaned so far, the situation is similar to that for Maggie's depositions," Steve said, glancing at Maggie. "Two of the companies have used NMH for integration services, but in both instances, the work came through Brandon Associates. As to the other two companies, neither has done any work with NMH or Brandon. Frankly, it seems to me Stanton has scheduled these depositions just to make our clients spend money."

"Speaking of which," Maggie intervened, "I received a call from Regina Paxton, Bart Mayfield's associate, today. She said Bart has decided he's going to attend all of these depositions remotely. They're being videotaped for trial purposes, and Bart feels he can adequately cover them remotely since he's relying upon us to make most objections."

"That makes sense," David added. "No sense in Brandon Associates spending money unnecessarily. God knows, this case is expensive enough even with cost-saving measures in place." Then, "Oh, before I forget, be sure to object to any outbursts by Rhonda Robinson. We need to have a comprehensive record of all improper actions or outbursts by her so we can either ask Judge Long to revoke her order admitting Robinson *pro hac vice,* or to at least warn her that any improper action by her at trial would result in her being censured, possibly severely."

After they kicked around the question of how Judge Long might censure Robinson, a topic each of them seemed to relish, they moved on to discuss other cases.

***

Friday of that same week was Jenna's birthday. Although the math couldn't be denied, it still amazed David that he suddenly had a teenager in the house, a thirteen-year-old. He assumed she would want to have a big party with all of her friends in attendance, including boys. To his amazement and relief, when he had raised the subject Jenna said, "Dad, I don't really want to have a party. Please let me invite Wanda for a sleepover, and let's just have a small birthday cake celebration with family. I didn't think Aunt Jesse could come because Friday is date night for her and Dr. Faulk, but she said they could stop by for birthday cake after dinner."

Although there was no party, Angelita treated Jenna's birthday with the attention and thoughtfulness that her becoming a teenager deserved. The appetizer was her special ceviche with shrimp infused with lime, together with onions, cilantro, tomatoes, avocado, sea salt and olive oil. For the main course she prepared her special chicken and steak fajitas with vegetables—one of Jenna's favorites—topped with pineapple and shredded cheese. And, of course, there was her special salsa with chips. The aroma of the ingredients filled the entire downstairs of the house and helped create a joyful atmosphere that even Molly was responding to. Despite her increased tail wagging and mournful stares at Angelita, though, her dinner fare remained her usual diet.

No more than five minutes after the dinner dishes had been cleared, the doorbell rang announcing the arrival of the newly engaged couple. James had purchased a ring for Jesse several weeks previously, although he hadn't brought it to their dinner at Antonio's, failing to anticipate he would be moved to formally propose that evening. Now, she was ready to show it off, and even Jenna and Wanda gushed over how beautiful it was.

As soon as there was a break from everyone ogling Jesse's

ring, Angelita brought out Jenna's birthday cake—a two-tiered yellow cake with chocolate frosting and fresh raspberries spread liberally on top of and around the cake. Thirteen white candles, already lit, created a circle on top of the cake. As Jenna blew out the candles, everyone sang *Happy Birthday* to Jenna.

David couldn't help wishing Carol had been there to share in this important milestone in Jenna's life, and he could feel tears beginning to well up in his eyes. To his relief, however, he didn't feel himself slipping back into depression. This reaffirmed his confidence that his funk was behind him. He even overheard Jenna and Angelita commenting earlier in the evening that he had returned to his old self since returning from Valdosta.

Once the cake was served—with a side scoop of vanilla ice cream—everyone brought out the birthday presents they had for Jenna. When she opened the envelope Jesse had brought her—no wrapped present—there was a gift certificate for $350 at an upscale women's store known for its quality but hardly a store where Jenna would normally shop. She turned to Jesse with an expression of both appreciation and surprise, but before she could say anything, Jesse said, "Let me explain why I chose this store. I wanted to be sure the dress my maid of honor chooses goes well with my wedding dress."

Jesse's comment didn't register with Jenna for several seconds. Then, her eyes opened wide with surprise. Overwhelmed, she was obviously too shocked to say anything. Sensing this, Jesse said, "Yes, I want you to be my maid of honor. Will you do this for me?"

Jenna slipped into Jesse's arms, hugging her tightly. When she was finally able to control her emotions, Jenna stepped back, looked Jesse in the eye and said, "This is the best birthday present ever."

David was moved by Jesse's generosity toward his daughter. She had chosen Jenna to fulfill a role that a woman only offers to someone with whom she is especially close, whether a relative or a friend. Despite their age difference, David could tell, there was a special bond between them that led Jesse to this decision, and for which he was extremely grateful. *Who would have thought that my tough, litigator law partner would have such a bond with my thirteen-year-old daughter? But then, she isn't an ordinary thirteen-year-old.*

Chapter 20

Neither James nor Jesse had seen Father John Williams since Carol's funeral, some eight months ago. When he greeted them at his office at All Souls Episcopal Church, Jesse noticed his stooped posture was worse and the lines around his eyes had deepened. But his warm smile, quick mind, and deep, melodious voice reminded her he was someone she could trust, and she was thrilled James shared her confidence in him—at least to the extent James was willing to trust any clergyman.

"It's good to see you both again," Father John said as he shook hands with each. "I remember meeting you following Carol's funeral. And, of course, David has spoken of you often, Jesse. You've been a tower of strength for him, and for Jenna, this past year. David has frequently mentioned that he doesn't know how he and Jenna would have made it through these past months without you."

Surprised that David had shared so much of his struggles with Father John and somewhat embarrassed he had given her so much credit, Jesse replied simply, "They're family, and I would do anything for them."

Father John ushered them into his office and offered coffee, which they both accepted. Once they were seated around his small conference table, he said, "First, congratulations on your engagement. I'm happy for you. I'm pleased you've decided to get married in a church, and particularly happy you've decided to get married at All Souls Church." His smile as he said this reassured Jesse he was sincere, and a quick glance at James convinced her he felt the same.

"As happy as I am for you, though, my duties as a priest require me to ensure you understand the nature of Christian marriage and the obligations you will be asked to commit to in the wedding ceremony. So, I have to ask you some personal questions about your faith background and the role the church has played in your life. It's important that you're candid in your comments but rest assured that anything you tell me will remain confidential."

Father John paused, apparently seeking feedback from them. When neither objected to his emphasis on being candid, he continued. "Whereas in a civil marriage there are only two parties entering the nuptial covenant, in a Christian marriage God himself is considered a party to the covenant because he's the one who instituted marriage. This, of course, is different from a purely civil ceremony, so I need to know something about your religious commitment and how you view marriage if I'm to marry you. Why don't we start with you, Jesse. How important has the church been in your life?"

This was more than Jesse anticipated she would have to share, but she had no reluctance to respond. She glanced at James, whose eyes had widened in surprise, then turned to Father John. "I was baptized and confirmed in the Methodist church, and I was faithful in attendance throughout high school and college. To be candid, my church attendance fell off considerably while I was in law school, and I haven't been active in a church in recent years. But my faith has always been important to me, and I've always assumed it would be a part of my family life, especially once we have children." Jesse gazed at James as she said this. She considered how much more to reveal before continuing with an appreciative tone, "Getting married in the church is more important to me than it is to James, but I'm so grateful he's willing to have a church wedding." Jesse hoped she hadn't said too much about James' opinion of having a church wedding, but she wanted him to be candid with Father John.

"I see," said Father John, nodding as he spoke. "It isn't uncommon for one of the parties in a wedding to be more interested in being married in a church. Usually, it's the one who attended services regularly as a child who wants the church wedding." Turning to look at James, he asked, "So, what role has the church played in your life, James?"

***

As Father John asked this question, James felt as though the priest was looking directly through him into his very soul. It wasn't a disagreeable or vexatious feeling because Father John's demeanor exuded kindness, and his gaze seemed non-judgmental. Nevertheless, James felt naked and awkward in the presence of this man of God, which surprised him because he had never felt church attendance was important. One could be spiritual if one desired—which he didn't—without necessarily attending church. The whole religion thing had always seemed irrelevant to him because it seemed to be based on myths, legends, and cultural history. He was only interested in truth that could be confirmed through the scientific method or otherwise verified by something more than blind faith. *But how am I going to honestly convey my views about religion to Father John without sounding like an atheist, which may lead him to decide not to marry us? That could cause Jesse to reconsider whether she wants to marry me.*

With these ideas rumbling through his head, James said

nothing during an awkward pause. But Father John remained silent while looking kindly at him, apparently assuming James was collecting his thoughts before responding. A quick glance at Jesse convinced him to be candid in his comments. "To be honest, Father John, the church has played almost no role in my life. I was baptized as an infant in the Presbyterian Church, but I was never confirmed. My parents rarely went to church when I was growing up, so I never viewed it as being particularly important. When my parents finally stopped going at all, I did too. The few Bible stories I learned seemed to be based on myths, which didn't seem to be a sturdy foundation for someone interested in science and who wanted to be a physician since high school. But I love Jesse dearly, and if it's important to her to be married in a church, that's what I want to do."

As James made the last comment, he looked directly at Jesse whose expression was a mixture of gratitude and concern. When Father John didn't immediately respond to James' comments, he turned back to him and continued, "Jesse tells me that your background is in physics, and that you even worked for NASA before going to seminary. I would be very interested in learning how a physicist became an Episcopalian priest. Perhaps you had some of the same reservations I had?" James hoped his question wouldn't insult Father John.

To his relief, Father John's kind expression never left. "As a matter of fact, I had most of the same doubts you had. Despite the fact my parents were more faithful in church attendance than yours, my interest in a faith commitment was half-hearted at best, even when I was confirmed in the church. By the tenth grade, I knew I wanted to be a scientist of some type. In college, I quickly got on a physics track and graduated with a Bachelor of Science degree, with a major in physics. Getting a job with NASA right out of college seemed almost too good to be true and fulfilled my dreams, which were pretty much all based on science."

James straightened up as his curiosity overcame his reluctance to reveal to Father John the paucity of his spiritual life. . .to the extent James had one. "So, how did you get off the physics track and on the priest track? Those seem to be two entirely different worlds to me."

"Not as different as you might think, James. All truth is God's truth, whether scientific, historical or spiritual. Actually, it was science that led me to personally investigate the reliability of the Bible and get serious about the question of whether there is, in fact, a supreme being—God."

James didn't even have to ask the question. His expression invited Father John to explain. "My senior year in college I took a course in astrophysics, which I found to be fascinating. Later, at NASA I became interested in cosmology, and particularly the Big Bang. I learned that at the very beginning, all of the matter, space and energy of the universe was contained in a volume less than one-trillionth the size of a period at the end of a sentence in your newspaper. With the Big Bang the universe began expanding at speeds much greater than the speed of light, and in the first second of time a delicate imbalance between matter and antimatter of a billion-and-one to a billion somehow miraculously survived. Without this imbalance, all mass in the universe would have self-annihilated.

"Learning about all this raised questions in my mind. Where did the energy and mass come from? What caused the universe to proceed from that chaotic beginning to the more orderly one we have today? Where did the laws of physics—which appeared shortly after the Big Bang—come from, and why are these laws uniform throughout the universe? Although scientists continue to come up with theories, there are no definitive answers to these questions based on our current scientific knowledge. I came to the belief that science alone cannot answer all of these fundamental questions and that I should look elsewhere to understand the guiding hand that brought our world into existence.”

“Are you saying that you came to the Christian faith because science didn’t have all the answers you were looking for?” James asked with skepticism.

“No, not at all. These questions I had were just what spurred me to begin looking into what Judaism and Christianity have always contended—that we live in a universe created by God. We are not here by chance. I finally came to the realization that if we *do* live in a universe created by God, I may have to answer to him some day about how I’ve lived my life.”

“I haven’t thought about that before, but I see your point . . . Is that realization what led you to seminary?”

Father John’s smile broadened as he seemed to be remembering the process that led him to his current position. “No, that came much later. The next question I had to examine was whether the Bible is reliable. If it wasn’t—as I suspected at the time—there was no point in wasting time evaluating what it has to say. I would look elsewhere.”

This discussion was proving to be far more interesting than James had anticipated. He was impressed with the careful, systematic thought process Father John had gone through in changing the course of his life. He still couldn’t see such a profound change in his own future, but he was intrigued by a man who shared his own doubts and was able to reconcile his beliefs as a scientist with those of a priest. "Since you're now a priest, I gather you came to believe the Bible *is* reliable. How did you come to that conclusion?"

Father John nodded, and continued, "What I quickly discovered was that my uninformed opinion that the Bible was mostly myths and legends was way off base. No less an authority on ancient documents than C.S. Lewis was initially a skeptic on the reliability of the Bible until he investigated further. As a professor of Medieval and Renaissance English at the University of Cambridge, he was quite familiar with ancient documents and with myths. To his surprise, when he began examining the scriptures carefully, he found that the Bible wasn't similar to any ancient writings dealing with myths. The scriptures were much more similar to historical texts, and there were many more copies of ancient Bible scriptures than of any other genre of ancient documents. He was also impressed with the fact that all of the New Testament books were written within a single generation of the life of Jesus Christ, and all of the gospels were written by eyewitnesses, except the gospels of Mark and Luke. Mark's gospel is accepted by historians as being based upon the preaching and teaching of the apostle Peter, and Luke had access to all of the key eye- witnesses as he wrote his orderly account of Jesus's life and ministry. In short, if you apply the same standards for reliability to the Bible that you do to all other ancient documents, it fares very well by comparison."

James contemplated what Father John had said. The reliability of the Bible was a surprise to him, but he still wasn't convinced this compelled him to become a Christian. He asked, "Even if the Bible is as reliable as you say, that doesn't necessarily mean that all of the statements in the Bible are true, does it?"

Father John nodded his agreement. "From a scientific

standpoint, you're correct, James. The fact that an ancient document meets the criteria for being reliable does not automatically mean that every statement in the document is trustworthy. Now, the church *does* believe that the entire Bible is true and trustworthy, but this is based upon faith, not a scientific conclusion. God puts great weight on faith in our response to him. In the book of Genesis, God promised Abraham—a man over seventy-five years old with a wife well past child-bearing age— that he would have a natural heir, and his descendants would be as numerous as the stars. Who could believe a promise like that without faith? Genesis 15:6 says that Abraham, 'believed the Lord; and the Lord reckoned it to him as righteousness.' _2/ In other words, because of his faith Abraham was deemed to be righteous before God."

James wasn't familiar with the story of Abraham, although he vaguely knew who he was. But he had to admit, believing a child would be born to a couple that old took a lot of faith, far more than he had or could even imagine having. He was perplexed, but he was beginning to think it was time for him to at least look into what the Bible had to say, particularly since faith and church attendance seemed to be important to Jesse. "So, how does one come to have that kind of faith?"

Father John smiled the smile of a teacher finally receiving the question he had been hoping for from his student. In his deep baritone voice tinged with kindness, he replied, "James, it's time for you to examine closely the truth assertions in the Bible with an open mind that's not limited by all of your previous assumptions. That's all I ask—an open mind and a willingness to look honestly at the evidence. My suggestion is that you go through confirmation class because it will address the main issues that you'll have to consider in determining whether you want to become a Christian.

There are no classes currently scheduled, but I would be happy to lead you through the material personally; we can meet once a week for an hour or two for four to six weeks, or however long it takes. First, however, there are two books I want you to read. The first is C.S. Lewis's book, *Mere Christianity*. The second is, *The Case for Christ*, by Lee Strobel. He was a journalist who set out to disprove the validity of the Bible and wound up becoming a Christian. After reading these books I believe you'll be ready to evaluate the truth assertions of the Bible."

James felt cornered, but at the same time he was glad he was going to finally address the God issue in a systematic manner. As important as faith apparently was to Jesse, he didn't want to make a half-hearted effort or just dismiss her beliefs. Still, he wasn't sure what conclusions he would come to, and he wondered what impact it would have on Jesse and their marriage if he didn't want to be confirmed in the church after going through the sessions. "What happens if I still can't honestly be confirmed in the church even after going to the classes? Will that prevent you from marrying us?"

With more understanding in his voice than James expected, Father John shook his head, and said, "No, James. I appreciate your honesty, and I can tell you're prepared to make an honest effort to find the truth. If you don't want to be confirmed in the church after the classes, I'm still willing to marry you and Jesse at All Souls Church."

"That's a deal I can agree with, Father. I'm ready to start confirmation classes when you are."

***

Jesse was more than mildly surprised by James' decision to go through confirmation classes. In fact, she was thrilled. But there was another question she wanted to bring up with Father John that continued to nag at her. Although she and James had admitted they had trust issues as a result of the breakups with their significant others during law school and medical school respectively, there was lingering doubt —for her at least—whether the topic might resurface down the road. Jesse was dumbfounded when the issue originally arose with James—as he was as well—especially since it came in the middle of a romantic moment. But since the night of their candid discussion at Antonio's about their painful breakups, they hadn't directly discussed the issue, despite James' playful inquiry from time to time about how long he was going to have to remain celibate. Jesse felt the trust problem was still lurking below the surface of their relationship, and she wanted to resolve it now before permanent commitments were made. She just wasn't sure whether James was ready to discuss the situation now, particularly with Father John.

Jesse, however, had never been reluctant to be bold when she felt it was required, and this was one of those occasions. Once James and Father John agreed on a date to begin confirmation classes, despite her trepidation, Jesse spoke up. "There's one other topic I want to discuss today, Father. I have difficulty fully trusting someone I'm in love with because of a betrayal by a former boyfriend. We had a very intense relationship, physical as well as emotional, and I thought he was about to propose to me. Instead, he unceremoniously dumped me and took up with another woman. I know in my mind James is nothing like he was, and that James is trustworthy, but I still have flashbacks occasionally, and I don't want my past mistakes and wounds to damage our relationship. Do you have any advice for me?"

Jesse took a deep breath after these words seemed to tumble out of her mouth. And when she glanced at James, he seemed astonished she'd brought up the subject. But she shrugged her shoulders at him, indicating she had to put this issue on the table, and his expression gradually turned to resignation.

Once the surprise seemed to have passed, James admitted, "Yeah, I've had a similar experience . . . although I didn't expect to talk about it today." He gave Jesse a pointed although not unkind stare. Turning to Father John, he added, "I would like to hear any suggestions you have about how we can avoid any similar trust issues in the future."

Father John's expression never changed significantly, although his kind visage was now tinged with concern. "Yes, I definitely have suggestions for you. First, you have to forgive the others involved in your past experiences. Even if they have never apologized or said they regretted what they did to you. Forgiveness is a decision, not a feeling, and you must immediately remind yourselves any time these feelings begin to resurface that you've already made the decision to forgive; then, squelch those feelings. Similarly, you have to forgive yourselves. Even though you aren't the guilty parties here, our minds will often search hard to find any possible grounds to tell us it's really our fault. Again, make the decision to forgive yourself, and then squelch the feelings any time they try to rise up with blame. Forgiveness isn't a matter of justice; it's an act of grace, which is within your power to extend—to yourself and to others. If you don't forgive all parties involved now, you will have to fight this battle over and over, and it won't be pleasant."

"I see your point," Jesse agreed, as James nodded along with her. Jesse had never fully addressed the idea of forgiving someone who had—in her opinion—acted cruelly toward her, and apparently James hadn't either. But she could see now forgiveness was the only way to truly put this episode in her life behind her.

After pausing in thought for a long moment, Father John continued, "Upon further reflection there *is* one other thing I'm going to suggest to you. We're only about four months away from your wedding. My recommendation is that you remain celibate until after your wedding. Given the wounds you encountered from what you both said were intense physical relationships, I think it will help engender the trust you have already begun to develop with one another. It will also help you understand how different your marriage will be than these previous relationships. You don't have to tell me whether you're willing to make this commitment to each other, or whether you're able to keep your commitment. Those decisions are between the two of you. I'm not unaware this isn't a commitment most young people make to each other once engaged, despite the teachings of the church, but as a priest I want to be clear that the Bible tells us to reserve the sexual relationship for marriage. And I do believe this will be best for both of you, given your past experiences. It will help put your marriage on a sound footing."

James and Jesse looked at Father John with blank faces and glanced at each other with surprise. Jesse nodded thoughtfully at James with raised eyebrows as he gently took her hand. Then, both said, "We promise to discuss it. . ."

After agreeing on a wedding date at All Souls Episcopal Church on the first Saturday in November, they left for an early dinner and much to talk about.

Chapter 21

The depositions in California that Maggie covered provided no surprises. Two of the companies deposed had hired NMH for integration services but at the recommendation of Brandon Associates who had designed their material handling systems. Two other companies had contracted with Brandon for design of the material handling system but preferred another company for the integration services. The final company deposed had done no business with either Brandon Associates or NMH, although both had responded to the company's request for proposal. As Maggie predicted, no harm to the defendants' case resulted from any of these depositions. On the other hand, she was unable to come up with any additional evidence to justify a motion to revoke the order allowing Rhonda Robinson to represent NMH in the case. She and Stanton squabbled quietly with each other throughout the depositions, but she carefully avoided putting any statements on the record or committing any act that would be the final straw for Judge Long to kick Robinson off the case.

Steve's experience with the four depositions in Texas was similar. Two of the companies had hired NMH to provide integration services for them but only upon the recommendation of Brandon Associates who had designed the warehouse and the material handling system installed in it. The other two companies deposed had never hired either NMH or Brandon Associates; they had simply sent a request for proposal to both and chose other contractors. The only difference in these depositions was that

Robinson and Stanton squabbled more openly and loudly. Any time these two spent more than a day or two together, their apparent personal antagonism increased and their evident frustration with each other spilled into the open. As Steve commented at the next attorney meeting after returning from the depositions, "Ms. Robinson is a serious candidate for an anger management program."

Jesse responded, "There's no doubt about that. On the other hand, I'm rethinking whether we should file a motion to revoke the order allowing her to appear in the case *pro hac vice,* even if there's sufficient evidence to justify it. The conflict between Stanton and Robinson certainly won't improve NMH's jury appeal. We may benefit if they act up at trial."

The remainder of July and August were taken up with a variety of inconsequential depositions around the United States—two in Texas, one in Nebraska, one in Tennessee, and three in New York. These caused NMH to exceed the original twenty-deposition limit imposed by Judge Long in the case management order, but they were permitted because Stanton sought and obtained, over Jesse's objection, the right to take an additional ten depositions. Jesse's only solace over the judge's allowing the additional depositions was that she reminded counsel the cost of depositions could be included in an award of costs to the prevailing party. "And I will be liberal in awarding such costs," the judge had said while pointedly looking at Stanton.

In addition to the depositions, there were numerous squabbles over the production of documents throughout July and August. NMH's counsel insisted on the production of almost every single document, whether digital or in hard copy, that Brandon Associates had originated or received from the time they got into the material handling business until the suit was filed. Likewise,

NMH sought all work-related documents from each of the individual defendants whether on a work-related computer, a personal computer, a mobile phone, or in hard copy. By Jesse's count, the defendants had produced nearly one million pages of documents by the end of August. The cost of the electronic discovery firm alone that Brandon Associates had to pay to collect, review and produce all these documents was almost a quarter million dollars.

Brandon Associates was bearing the cost of NMH's discovery assault. During a conference call in early September, Allan Brandon observed that the combination of attorneys' fees and the electronic discovery firm bills through August was approaching three-quarters of a million dollars. Jesse and Bart Mayfield advised Allan Brandon that preparing for and handling the trial would come to at least another quarter-million dollars.

"Fortunately, we've been very profitable since we brought integration services in-house," Brandon replied. "So, we have the funds to see the case through trial, but if we lose, we could be facing bankruptcy. This has turned into an existential fight for Brandon Associates—and maybe for the individual defendants as well."

From her end of the phone call, Jesse commented, "It appears NMH has carried out Ms. Robinson's threat to litigate this matter 'until Hell freezes over.' We anticipated a discovery blizzard based upon the number of depositions they initially asked for, and that's what we've got."

"What's up next in the case?" Brandon asked.

"We just received the court's trial order today," Jesse said. "The pretrial conference is scheduled for Monday, September 30, and the trial is to commence on Monday, October 7. The judge also scheduled a hearing on the motions for summary judgment that both sides have filed. Those motions will be heard at the time of the pretrial conference."

"What happens if the judge grants our motion for summary judgment?" Brandon asked with a hopeful tone.

Jesse quickly responded because she wanted to tamp down expectations. "Well, if she grants summary judgment on all counts in our favor, there will be no trial. But you shouldn't expect such a broad ruling. My best guess is that the judge will grant our motion on the tortious interference claims and on the claim of conspiracy to use trade secret and proprietary information. She will likely reject our motion on the other claims because she wants to hear the evidence first before deciding whether the jury should decide the remaining claims. Remember, a summary judgment cannot be granted unless there is no genuine factual issue on the claim. If there are factual issues to be decided, that's the function of the jury, not the judge. If a judge oversteps and decides factual issues that should've been submitted to the jury, the appellate court will promptly set aside the summary judgment and send it back to the trial court for a jury to decide. We don't want any unnecessary detours to an appellate court that will just drive up the cost."

"I certainly agree with that," Brandon said, with resignation.

***

As promised, Father John contacted James about his confirmation classes right away, and they agreed to meet every Monday at 6:00 PM for as long as it took for James to decide whether he was prepared to be confirmed in the church. They met for the first time on the third Monday in July to give James time to read the two books Father John recommended. James' classes were different than the usual ones because he saw no need to study the doctrines of the church unless and until he was convinced the scriptures on which the doctrines were based were, in fact, reliable.

To his amazement, James learned that the Bible consists of sixty-six books that were written over 1600 years by more than forty kings, prophets, leaders, and disciples of Jesus, with thirty-nine books in the Old Testament (or Hebrew Scriptures) and twenty-seven in the New Testament.

Because the Bible was written before the printing press was invented, it had to be copied by hand, mostly by Jewish and Christian scribes, priests, and disciples. Their copies were amazingly accurate, as confirmed by the Dead Sea Scrolls and comparing the various copies. The Bible, James learned, is better preserved than the writings of Plato or Aristotle, and their reliability is seldom questioned.

Another surprise to James was how interesting the stories of the Bible were. The events of the lives of Abraham, Moses, and David, for example, were more compelling than most of the secular books he had read. And no one could accuse the authors of trying to sugarcoat the accounts of their subjects; they were presented warts and all. David, for example, despite being blessed and protected by God, committed adultery, murder, and corruption in his duties as king, and was less than an ideal parent. But, he noted, God always forgave him—as well as Abraham and Moses—when they genuinely repented.

Similarly, in the New Testament, the authors of the gospels always presented the twelve apostles as disciples who were struggling to understand their teacher, and often didn't get what Jesus was saying. This added to the credibility of the gospels in James' opinion. Only after the resurrection of Jesus did they finally seem to grasp what Jesus had been telling them. It was hardly the description of the main characters an author would record if he were creating a myth.

But as illuminating as these discoveries were, the key issue for James was whether we live in a world created by God or a universe that somehow came about as the result of time and chance without the guidance of a greater power. He reasoned that if we live in a created world, there must be a creator. And if this creator had the ability to create our universe, he also had the power to raise Jesus from the dead—the bedrock of the Christian faith.

As someone scientifically trained, although not in astrophysics or cosmology, James was surprised to learn that the idea the universe had a beginning was only first suggested by the general theory of relativity put forth by Albert Einstein in 1916. And he was even more surprised to learn that the Big Bang theory was first proposed in 1927 by Roman Catholic priest and physicist Georges Lemaitre, based upon the discovery of the expanding universe by Edwin Hubble.

"So, how significant is it to you that both science and the Bible now proclaim there was a beginning to our universe?" James asked Father John on their third meeting. "And how do you explain why the description of the beginning is so different in the two versions?"

Father John's eyes lit up as his countenance seemed to say, "We've finally reached the questions you should have asked all along." He took a deep breath and leaned forward as he said, "It's critically significant. Remember, I told you that all truth is God's truth. If an event such as the creation—or as science would say, the beginning—took place, both a scientist and a poet should recognize the fact of the event, even though they will describe the event far differently. Given that science was primitive at the time the book of Genesis was written, it's hardly surprising the author (generally accepted to be Moses) described the creation in non-scientific terms. Science now says that at the moment of the Big Bang, all the matter, energy and space of the entire universe was contained in a volume less than one-trillionth the size of a period at the end of a sentence in a book. The church has always said that God created the heavens and the earth *ex nihilo,* which means out of nothing. So, there is essential agreement that the world has not always been here. The Genesis account says the world was initially 'formless and void,' whereas astrophysicists describe the early universe as a cauldron of immense heat, a primordial chaotic soup of light and particles. Both describe in different terms how the beginning gradually transitioned into the more orderly world we have today."

"Wait, are you saying that science and the church are in agreement on how our universe came about?" To James, this still seemed a stretch, although he was beginning to warm up to Father John's explanation.

He shook his head before responding. "No, there isn't agreement on all points, but in my view, the Bible describes *what* happened in general and sometimes poetic language, whereas science describes *how* our universe came about and developed in technical, scientific language. Since the Big Bang theory originated—by a Roman Catholic priest and scientist, no less—the two camps have been much closer together. Thus far, science has been unable to come up with a plausible explanation as to how the chaotic nature of the beginning has gradually transitioned into the more orderly universe of today without a guiding hand. The Bible, of course—whether in the Hebrew scriptures or the Christian ones—has always proclaimed the heavens and the earth to be the handiwork of God."

James pondered what Father John said. His comments seemed to largely reconcile what James had previously thought were irreconcilable differences between science and Judeo-Christian accounts of the beginning of the universe. It was an unsettling thought, but if the Biblical account of the creation was essentially about the same event as the Big Bang, then his belief that the Bible was just a collection of myths was no longer valid. He would have to re-examine the evidence and take the Bible far more seriously than he ever had.

"I'm beginning to see your point," James finally said. "What other evidence should I consider to reconcile in my own mind whether we live in a world created by God?"

"There are many other scientific facts and discoveries you could consider, but frankly you will never come to believe in the existence of God based on science alone. It will take faith on your part to come to that belief. However, it's not a *blind* faith; it's a reasonable faith based upon the evidence, with the best available evidence coming from the Bible. Every book in the Bible proclaims that God exists, that we live in his creation, and that he loves us and wants a relationship with us. My recommendation is that you consider this and pray about it."

"Pray about it? I don't know how to pray," James responded, taken aback by Father John's recommendation.

"Just talk to God. Out loud. Tell him about your doubts. But tell him you want to learn the truth. Then, read some of the scriptures, such as the Gospel of John. Then listen. You might be astonished by what you will learn."

James was a little surprised to hear himself say, "Okay, I'll try it."

***

The end of August initiated a new school year, and to commemorate the fact she was entering her final year at Maitland Middle School, Jenna asked her father for a celebratory dinner with Wanda present for the dinner and a sleepover. Of course he agreed. Angelita recognized the significance of the event and treated it accordingly. She prepared chicken and steak fajitas marinated with her special spices, and served them with Mexican rice, refried beans, lettuce, pico de gallo, guacamole and flour tortillas. She even added a small portion of the chicken to Molly's usual fare; her tail-wagging went into overdrive as she downed the special delicacy, adding to the celebratory mood. To top off the evening, David opened a bottle of non-alcoholic wine for a toast to the eighth grade "seniors" at Maitland Middle School.

As Jenna and Angelita were putting dishes in the dishwasher after dinner, Angelita confided in Jenna, "I've not seen Meester David so happy in many months. He like his old self, no?"

"I agree," Jenna replied. "I'm not sure what happened there, but ever since he returned from his trip to Valdosta, I've had my dad back. He's still sad over losing Mom, but he *is* his old self. . . Do you think he will ever want to marry again, Angelita?"

"*Dios mio,* Jenna. I don't know," she replied, clearly surprised at being asked such a question. "Do you think Meester David should remarry?"

"I don't know. No one will ever replace Mom, but he's only forty-two. In five years, I will be off to college, and then he'll be all alone . . . Well, except for you and Molly. I think he'll need someone . . ."

244

"You probably right, Jenna. But these things can't be rushed. Meester David will know when it's time to start dating again and find right woman to marry."

Jenna thought about this for a moment; then a sly smile crept over her face, and she said, "Yes, but there's no reason I can't encourage things along when the right woman shows up."

Chapter 22

The stress in any lawsuit ratchets up as the trial date approaches. Claims that seemed well founded when the plaintiff's lawyers were drafting the complaint may now seem weak due to a lack of evidence. Affirmative defenses filed by the defendants may also suffer from lack of supporting facts once the depositions have been taken and the documents and other evidence reviewed. Some of the claims asserted may get dismissed before trial if a motion for summary judgment is filed and the court determines there is no genuine factual issue to be determined by the jury. The judge decides all of the legal issues in the case, so if only a legal issue remains in any of the claims, the judge can render judgment on those claims without the involvement of the jury.

On the first day in September, Jesse and Bart Mayfield jointly filed a motion for summary judgment as to all of the claims asserted against their respective clients by NMH, with the hearing on the motion to occur at the time of the pretrial conference with the judge. The following day, NMH's lawyers filed a motion for summary judgment in their favor, asserting that the evidence showed NMH was entitled to judgment on each of the six counts as a matter of law. To Jesse, NMH's motion was almost laughable and, in her opinion, a mistake for NMH to even file. Judge Long deplored lawyers wasting her time, and, in Jesse's opinion, she would likely give short shrift to their motion.

But it wasn't just the summary judgment motions that

added to the pressure on the lawyers. By the time of the pretrial conference, the lawyers were required to stipulate to all facts that were not in dispute, and to list the key facts that remain in dispute. Additionally, they were required to list all exhibits they might introduce into evidence and all objections to each item on the opposing side's exhibit list. Failure to list an exhibit or an objection precludes introduction of the exhibit—or an objection to it—unless the judge finds good cause to allow it, something Judge Long rarely did. In short, it was a tedious, time-consuming project to review each of the 1132 documents on NMH's exhibit list and itemize all objections. Steve and Maggie took the lead on the objections, but Jesse had to review their work.

In the meantime, David and Jesse had to come up with their own exhibit list—and assist Bart Mayfield with his. They were able to limit their list to only 125 documents, most of which were also on the plaintiff's list, and therefore could likely be stipulated into evidence.

In addition, throughout September David and Jesse were preparing their outlines for the direct examination of their own witnesses and the cross-examination of NMH's. They never put one of their own witnesses on the stand without explaining in detail what he or she will be asked to testify about and clarifying any questions the witness may have. For key witnesses they would videotape practice testimony sessions so the witnesses could see for themselves any distracting mannerism or phraseology in their testimony. David and Jesse also prepared their witnesses for cross-examination from opposing counsel through simulated cross-examination sessions. The goal, in short, was to have their witnesses well prepared and comfortable in the critical role they would play in the trial.

***

The morning of the pretrial conference was a brilliant early fall day in Orlando, with the high temperature dropping into the low seventies, a rarity in central Florida for this time of year. David, Jesse, and Mayfield went through the attorneys-only security line at the courthouse, then took the smart elevator to the 16th floor courtroom of Judge Long. They arrived before Stanton and his entourage and took the counsel table on the left facing the bench where the judge would preside. Five minutes later Stanton, Rhonda Robinson and two associate attorneys arrived, followed immediately by the court reporter, who took her position in front of the bench.

As they were awaiting Judge Long entering the courtroom, Jesse noticed that Robinson seemed unusually uptight, even for her. There was a strained expression on her face, and she said not a word to Stanton, or the associates, as she spread out her materials for the hearing. She also refused to join in the perfunctory greetings that all of the other lawyers shared as they set up.

Jesse whispered to David, "Robinson looks like she's about to explode. We may get some fireworks from her before the hearing is over." David nodded silently, but before he could comment, the clerk announced, "All rise," as Judge Long entered the courtroom, took her seat at the bench, and asked the lawyers to identify themselves for the record.

After pouring herself a glass of water from a carafe, the judge said, "The first order of business today will be the motions for summary judgment filed by the parties. I've reviewed the motions and the memoranda of law counsel have submitted, and I want to hear from the defendants first on their motions for summary judgment."

Jesse and David had agreed that Jesse would argue the

summary judgment motion as to the two claims for tortious interference filed by NMH, and David would argue the motion on the trade secrets and proprietary information claim. Mayfield would supplement their arguments as he saw fit. David would also handle the argument on their motion as to count IV—unfair competition by all defendants—and count V—breach of his fiduciary duties by Conboy for misusing NMH's confidential information and soliciting NMH's employees and customers. Finally, Jesse would handle the argument as to count VI—breach of their duty of loyalty to NMH by Conboy and the other six employees.

Jesse strode quickly to the lectern the judge required lawyers to speak from to begin her argument. "Your Honor, I believe I can address both counts I and II at the same time because both counts allege tortious interference. Count I alleges interference by Mr. Brandon and Brandon Associates with NMH's relationship with its employees, and Count II alleges interference by all defendants with NMH's relationship with its clients and potential clients.

"The Florida Supreme Court identified the elements necessary to prove a tortious interference claim in *Ethan Allen, Inc. v. Georgetown Manor, Inc.,* cited in our brief. The elements are: (i) the existence of a business relationship, (ii) knowledge of the relationship by the defendant, (iii) an intentional and unjustified interference with the relationship by the defendant, and (iv) damage to the plaintiff as a result of the breach of the relationship.

"Regarding count I, all NMH employees had at-will employment. Not a single one had a non-compete agreement, so they were free to leave NMH's employment at any time, and Brandon Associates was free to hire them. Furthermore, under Florida law a contract terminal at will cannot be the subject of a tortious interference claim where the alleged interference is lawful competition, as the *Unistar Corp v. Child* court has held. Only if there is physical violence, fraud, predatory litigation or criminal prosecution associated with the interference can it be considered wrongful. Offering persuasion, limited economic pressure or more money doesn't rise to the level of wrongful interference, as the Restatement (Second) Torts, section 768(1) points out. Not only has there not been a shred of evidence presented of physical violence, fraud or other predatory action, NMH hasn't even alleged such actions. NMH could have bound their employees to them through non-compete agreements, which would have provided lawful grounds for preventing the competition they now face, but NMH chose not to do so. Accordingly, defendants are entitled to summary judgment on count I.

"Count II alleges the defendants interfered with NMH's relationships with its clients and potential clients. To establish the first element of this claim, NMH must prove a business relationship with identifiable customers, as the *Ferguson Transportation v. North American Van Lines, Inc.* case held. There is no valid claim for tortious interference with a business's relationship with the community at large, as the *Ethan Allan* court concluded. Despite taking thirty depositions around the country, NMH has failed to establish a sufficient business relationship with specific identifiable customers or prospective customers. Indeed, NMH's corporate representative testified that the prospective relationship at issue is 'the entire market segment that we were going after.' In both *Ferguson* and *Ethan Allen,* the Florida Supreme Court rejected the argument that interference with all prospective customers in a market can support a tortious interference claim.

"Furthermore, the undisputed evidence shows that of the

specific companies NMH contends the defendants interfered with, all of those companies were customers of Brandon Associates before NMH had any relationship with them. Indeed, NMH only obtained business with those companies through the recommendation of Brandon Associates. As to the other companies on NMH's potential customer list, the 'relationship' with them consisted of nothing more than sales calls. Such hoped-for relationships are insufficient to support a tortious interference claim, as the *Ethan Allen* court decided.

"Finally, even if NMH could establish a sufficient prospective customer relationship, their claim would still fail because NMH cannot establish the third element of the claim—unjustified interference. As the *Langford v. Rotech Oxygen & Medical Equipment* case pointed out, competition for business by a competitor is not actionable interference, even if intentional. In that case a number of customers were solicited by a former employee of the plaintiff who had formed a competing company, and some customers switched. The court held that this kind of competition for business is to be expected from former employees who are not bound by a non-compete contract, and no claim for tortious interference is available in such circumstances.

"Once again, Your Honor, despite NMH taking thirty depositions, there has been no evidence—none—of Brandon Associates or any of its employees communicating with any prospective customer of NMH for any purpose other than to develop its own business and compete in the marketplace. Defendants are entitled to summary judgment on count II."

As soon as Jesse sat down, Stanton took his position at the podium. His argument in opposition to Jesse's motion was rambling, hard to follow, and ignored the central facts that NMH had no non-compete agreements with any of the defendants and all of the alleged wrongful acts by the defendants were in furtherance of legitimate competition for business in the marketplace. After ten minutes of listening to Stanton, Judge Long interrupted his argument to ask, "Mr. Stanton, I didn't find any case cited by you that held that an at-will employee not bound by a non-compete agreement can be sued for tortious interference as the result of lawful competition. Is there such a case cited in your brief that I have overlooked?" The expression on her face clearly suggested she didn't believe there was such a case.

Stanton shuffled his notes and appeared to be stalling while he searched for a coherent response. Finally, he replied, "Well, no . . . not precisely. But we have cited cases holding that a tortious interference claim can be filed where there is at-will employment."

"Yes, but haven't all of those cases included some type of fraud, physical violence or other such action?" Judge Long was allowing him no wiggle room.

"Um . . . yes, perhaps, but we submit that recruiting NMH's employees through an officer who had agreed to go to work for Brandon Associates but was still an employee of NMH—namely Mark Conboy—amounts to the same thing."

"Anything else, Mr. Stanton?" Judge Long inquired. When he demurred, she announced, "I find there is no genuine issue of material fact on counts I and II and that defendants are entitled to summary judgment on those counts. The issue of the recruitment of the NMH employees by one of their own officers is relevant to other counts of the complaint but not these. Let's move on to count III."

As David approached the podium, Jesse sneaked a glance at Robinson, who had leaned back in her chair and stared with pure disgust at Stanton as he retook his seat. She whispered something to him, which Jesse couldn't decipher, as he sat down, but from his expression she clearly hadn't complimented him on a job well done.

"Your Honor, I will address defendants' motion for summary judgment as to count III," David said as he began his argument. "In that count, NMH alleged a conspiracy by all defendants to misappropriate and use NMH's trade secrets and proprietary information, including customer lists to compete with NMH and unjustly enrich themselves. The first fatal flaw in this claim is one that this court warned NMH about at the case management conference, namely that they would have to describe the trade secrets they claim were misappropriated clearly and with specificity in discovery. NMH has failed to even remotely identify anything that falls within the definition of a trade secret. Section 688.02 of Florida Statutes defines a trade secret as 'information that derives independent economic value from not being generally known or readily ascertainable by proper means by other persons who obtain economic value from its disclosure or use, and the information is the subject of reasonable efforts to maintain its secrecy.'

"Having failed to identify any information that qualifies as a trade secret, NMH claims that all defendants have used its proprietary information to compete with NMH. The alleged proprietary information, it turns out, based upon the testimony of NMH's corporate representative, consists of only two categories, employee salaries and NMH's customer list, neither of which qualifies as proprietary information.

"With respect to salaries, an employee is entitled to disclose his salary to any potential employer or other third party. As the court stated in *Lockheed Martin Corporation v. Aatlas Commerce, Inc.,* cited in our brief, 'if such salary information were considered confidential, then no employee could ever fill out an employment questionnaire, resume, or credit application without breaching confidentiality.' The only salaries relevant to this case are the salaries of the defendants that went to work for Brandon Associates, and they had every right to disclose their salaries as part of negotiating their compensation at Brandon Associates. Furthermore, it's undisputed that the salaries offered to the defendants by Brandon Associates were not the same as their salaries at NMH. The salaries were based upon Brandon Associates' salary structure and were higher than NMH was paying them for every defendant.

"With respect to NMH's customer list, as my partner Ms. McKenzie has already pointed out, the evidence in this case confirms that NMH's customer lists consisted of nothing more than hoped-for customers with whom NMH had no previous business relationship, and existing customers for whom NMH obtained work through Brandon Associates. NMH has failed to identify a single customer for whom Brandon Associates has performed work that was a previous customer of NMH. Brandon Associates and the individual defendants have done nothing more than engage in lawful competition. Accordingly, they are entitled to summary judgment on count III."

Once again, Stanton's argument in opposition to the motion was rambling, vague, and lacking in any case law that would challenge David's legal arguments. This time, when he concluded his argument after ten minutes, Judge Long asked no questions. She simply said, "Defendants' motion for summary judgment as to count III is granted."

Robinson was even more agitated as Stanton returned to his seat. She quickly scribbled something on her yellow pad and stuck it in front of Stanton who waived her off. Jesse noted that

Robinson's jaw muscles were protruding as she was apparently grinding her teeth over the way the hearing was proceeding.

As Jesse stood up to begin her argument on count IV of NMH's complaint, Judge Long spoke up. "Have a seat, Ms. McKenzie. I believe any argument on the remainder of the defendants' motion for summary judgment is unnecessary. Likewise, I believe any argument on NMH's motion for summary judgment is unnecessary. I have carefully reviewed the motions and the briefs in support of your motions, and it's readily apparent to me that there are factual issues that must be resolved by a jury. If I granted any of the remaining motions, I believe the district court of appeals would promptly reverse me and send the case back for a jury trial. So, we will proceed to trial on count IV of NMH's claim (unfair competition), count V (breach of Conboy's fiduciary duty), and count VI (breach of duty of loyalty by the individual defendants who went to work for Brandon Associates)."

As soon as Judge Long concluded her statement, Robinson stood up and said, "Your Honor, may I be heard?" As she did so, Stanton leaned forward and shook his head, obviously irritated that Robinson would intervene.

Judge Long stared at Robinson for a long moment, before responding, "Not if you intend to take issue with the ruling I've just made. As I told you on your first appearance in my court, once I have ruled, I expect no further argument from counsel."

"But, judge, there is merit to our motion for summary judgment, and you are not even allowing us to argue our motion; it's a denial of due process." Jesse noticed the red splotches appearing on Judge Long's neck as Robinson addressed her. *You would think Robinson had learned how not to deal with Judge Long by now.*

"No, Ms. Robinson, I am not denying you due process. As I said, I have carefully reviewed NMH's motion for summary judgment. Although there may be merit to some of your arguments, a jury is going to have to decide certain factual issues before a judgment can be entered for plaintiff or defendants on the remaining claims. You can renew your motion as a motion for directed verdict at the end of defendants' case, and again at the end of all of the evidence at trial. Now, we are going to go over the other items to be addressed in the pre-trial order for us to be ready to begin trial next Monday. Do I make myself clear?"

Although she was obviously not happy with Judge Long's ruling, Robinson had the presence of mind to sit down and argue with the judge no further. Over the next hour, the judge and lawyers discussed the *voir dire*—jury questioning— procedures, the time each side would take to present their case, the identity of the witnesses each side really intended to call, as opposed to the large number on each side's witness list, and a myriad of other procedural issues likely to arise during trial.

Once they covered all items on Judge Long's checklist, she said, "Jury selection will begin next Monday at 9:00 AM in this courtroom. I anticipate we will have a jury empaneled by noon. Plan your prospective juror questions accordingly."

***

Back at the office, after they had debriefed the hearing and pre-trial conference, and Mayfield had left to return to Valdosta, David and Jesse remained in the conference room to plan their schedule for the final week before the trial. Once they had finished their planning and were about to wrap up their meeting, Jesse said, "By the way, there's something I forgot to mention to you."

"What's that?" David replied, his voice implying he

couldn't imagine anything that had gone unmentioned on such an eventful day.

"You probably recall that Father John convinced James to take confirmation classes before our wedding. Although he denies it, I think James was afraid Father John wouldn't perform our wedding ceremony if he didn't. As it turned out, Father John was the perfect person to talk to James about his personal faith and the church because as a scientist himself, Father John was able to talk to James in terms he could relate to."

"That doesn't surprise me," David responded. "Father John is one of the most intelligent and widely educated people I know. He can converse with anyone on just about any topic, especially scientific or religious topics. When I heard that James would be meeting with him for confirmation classes, I thought he would be the perfect tutor for James."

"As it turns out, you were right. Father John was able to present enough evidence to convince him the Bible was reliable; he even talked James into beginning to try to pray. Since then, James has been eagerly studying the history and doctrines of the church; he can't seem to get enough of it. When we go out to dinner, he wants to discuss theological issues. And get this, he's praying on a daily basis and says he finds it comforting. At dinner last Friday, I asked him, 'Who are you, and what have you done with my fiancé?'"

David's eyes opened wider with amazement. This sounded nothing like the James he had come to know. "How do you feel about this change in James? This isn't the same man you fell in love with."

"That's true; there have been changes, but in a good way. The changes have strengthened the good characteristics and minimized or eliminated the less desirable ones. For example, he's more tolerant of those he disagrees with, and he's not as dismissive of ideas he once would have given short shrift. He seems more genuinely interested in other people and their concerns. I've known for a long time that he loves me; now that love seems somehow deeper and more authentic. To be honest, I'm thrilled with the new James, and now I'm even more excited about the wedding."

David was gobsmacked by Jesse's comments. They caught him completely off guard. When he was able to collect his thoughts, he said, "I couldn't be happier for you, Jesse. You've been there for Jenna and me through some tough times. I'm delighted happier times are ahead for you."

"Oh, one more thing. James doesn't just want to be confirmed. He says he wants to be baptized again, this time knowing what he's doing. It's happening this Sunday. Think we can take a break from trial preparation to be there when Father John baptizes him?"

David couldn't have been more amazed if Rhonda Robinson had called to say she was sorry NMH filed suit, and they planned to dismiss it. "I can't imagine not being there," David nodded as he contemplated this surprising turn of events.

Chapter 23

The first day of trial was always an exciting one for Jesse. All of her firm's efforts to uncover and establish evidence that would disprove the plaintiff's case would turn out to be successful—or not. The validity of the legal defenses she and David had raised would carry the day—or perhaps not. Were the stakes lower in the case, the tension might not be so high, but Allan Brandon had candidly admitted to her that an adverse judgment could push the company into bankruptcy, probably a chapter eleven filing for reorganization under the supervision of the bankruptcy court. Furthermore, David had insisted on requesting a retainer of at least $150,000 to cover their time and expenses for the trial, and Brandon Associates had only been able to come up with $100,000, which likely meant that if they lost the case, Jordan & McKenzie would have to eat part of their fee.

The financial risks inherent in the trial also had Allan Brandon and Mark Conboy uptight as well. Jesse could sense they were nervous, so she kept her comments to them upbeat and optimistic, as did David. One of the things that belatedly concerned the clients was the makeup of the jury that would decide the case. They had assumed at least some of the jurors would have business experience, hopefully as an owner of a business. But when they finally raised questions about what to expect from the jury, they were surprised to learn that potential jurors are summoned from the Florida drivers license data base, and the jury pool would likely consist of housewives, a high school dropout or two, perhaps a student at a local community college, school teachers, common laborers, and perhaps retired senior citizens, some of whom *may* have had business experience during their working days. Jesse tried to reassure them that more often than not jurors exhibited a remarkable level of common sense, even if they were deficient in business or life experiences one would hope for in jurors.

But if Jesse's team and clients were feeling the pressure of the moment, they appeared absolutely low key compared to NMH's team. Rhonda Robinson and Stanton were sniping at each other from the moment they entered the courtroom. The tension was painted on their faces, and Jesse was having difficulty imagining how they were going to present any sort of united front once the jury pool entered the courtroom. Arthur McDonald, the president of NMH, was present, apparently to be the corporate representative for NMH throughout the trial, and he appeared to prefer to be just about anywhere else but this courtroom.

Promptly at 9:00 AM Judge Long entered the courtroom, inquired whether counsel were ready to bring in the jury pool, and then instructed the bailiff to escort them in. Each side was entitled to six peremptory challenges—which meant they could excuse a juror for any reason at all, with only a narrow exception for racial profiling. In addition, jurors could be dismissed for cause if they were relatives of one of the parties or the lawyers, if they had an interest in the outcome of the case, if they had been employed by one of the parties within thirty days of the trial, or if they had formed an opinion or bias about the case, as well as a few other disqualifying events. Accordingly, Judge Long had requested thirty potential jurors to form the jury pool from which six jurors, and two alternates would be chosen for the trial. Jesse could sense the increased tension as the parties and counsel assessed the potential jurors as they entered the courtroom.

Once they were seated in the public area of the courtroom behind the bar, the judge gave them a short summary of what the case was about, inquired whether any of them knew the parties, their lawyers, or the potential witnesses, and then had the bailiff call twelve to the jury box for *voir dire*—questioning of the jurors by the lawyers. As attorney for the plaintiff, Stanton was first to question them.

Jesse smiled inwardly as Stanton walked up to the podium. His $1500 pin-striped suit, polished wingtip shoes, maroon tie, and $10,000 Rolex watch, along with his distinct New York accent, screamed Wall Street lawyer, a genre these jurors would likely have difficulty relating to. She had always kept her dress for trial simple, with no expensive jewelry—only a single strand of pearls or a thin gold necklace. In her experience, jurors listened more intently and seemed more receptive to lawyers they could relate to, so she dressed and conducted herself accordingly, as did David.

Despite his New York persona, Stanton was able to communicate effectively with the potential jurors, aided by two of the twelve currently in the jury box being New York natives. It only took him about an hour and a half to question them, and his thoroughness reduced the number of questions Jesse wanted to ask. After forty-five minutes she was satisfied that she knew enough about the potential jurors to excuse those who might not be receptive to the defendants.

Judge Long's procedure for selecting a jury was to call the lawyers to the bench so the potential jurors couldn't hear what was being said and require the lawyers to declare whether they wished to strike each member of the panel, beginning with the first person called. The plaintiff's lawyer would declare whether the first was acceptable; if so, the defendants' lawyers would either accept or strike juror number one. For juror number two, the defendants' lawyers would go first, and so on until six jurors have been accepted. Additionally, either side could backstrike, meaning, for example, that although both sides may have initially declared juror number one acceptable, either side could later move to strike that juror, provided they still had a peremptory challenge available.

Each side told the jurors they were just looking for a fair and impartial jury who would not be biased. But as Jesse had told Conboy during trial preparation, each party wanted jurors who would be fairer to them than to the other side. And the strategy as to how to get such a jury got more complicated as each side was down to their last challenge or two and considering whether the next potential juror who could be called for questioning would be better or worse than the ones already deemed acceptable.

After all the machinations played out, a jury of six, with two alternates in the event a juror got sick or otherwise had to drop out, was selected shortly before noon. Juror number one was a thirty-one-year-old female history teacher at Winter Park High School; juror number two was a twenty-year-old male Puerto Rican roofer; juror number three was a twenty-six-year-old male cast member at Disney World who played Disney characters; juror number four was a forty-five-year-old housewife who had previously been in real estate sales; juror number five was a fifty-six-year-old male carpenter who was also a retired Army sergeant; juror number six was a thirty-eight-year-old black nurse with an internal medicine practice in Orlando; and both alternate jurors were women retirees, one a former elementary school teacher and the other a former clerical worker.

Following a lunch break, the judge gave general instructions to the jury about their conduct during the trial, informed them that the opening statements by the lawyers they were about to hear were not evidence, but the statements would outline what the lawyers intended to prove. She then instructed Stanton to proceed with his opening statement.

Stanton took his position at the lectern, looked each juror directly in the eye before saying a word, and then began. "This case is about the breach of former employees of my client, National Material Handling Corporation—NMH—of their duty of loyalty to NMH. Led by defendant Mark Conboy, who was the boss of the other six defendants while they worked for NMH and who breached his fiduciary duty as an officer of NMH, all of the defendants entered into unfair competition at Brandon Associates to effectively take away NMH's material handling business.

"Although these events have taken place over the past year, the origins of this case go all the way back to the year Allan Brandon and Mark Conboy began college at Georgia Tech, some twenty-five years ago. They met during pledge week their freshman year and joined the same fraternity. They became fast friends, usually taking the same classes as part of their major in industrial engineering. During those years they began discussing what the evidence will show were plans to eventually go into business together. Although they discussed a variety of businesses to pursue, they narrowed their focus to the material handling business during graduate school at Georgia Tech while they both got their master's degree in industrial engineering. The material handling business involves processes, equipment and computers to enable a business such as e-commerce companies to locate the item being ordered, retrieve it and send it on its way to the purchaser. Likewise, the U.S. Postal Service requires material handling systems to process and get mail to the intended recipient in an efficient manner.

"There are two distinct parts to the material handling business. The first part is the *planning* and *design* of the system in which the designer determines what is needed, draws plans, and identifies the appropriate hardware and software, as well as the equipment to store the product until it is retrieved. The second part of the business is the purchase and installation of the system that has been designed and getting it to operate properly. This is called the *integration* portion of the business, and the installers are providing *integration services*.

"One of the exhibits you will see is an article Mr. Brandon and Mr. Conboy had published in the American Journal of Industrial Engineering while they were still in graduate school entitled, *"Recent Advances in Material Handling Systems and Technology."* Even before getting their advanced degrees, they had identified the business they wanted to be in together.

"Following graduation, Mr. Brandon returned to Valdosta, Georgia to work in the construction business that his father and uncle had started. They had always built a variety of buildings, including warehouses, but once Mr. Brandon joined the company, he encouraged them to specialize in warehouses. Given Valdosta's strategic location just twelve miles from the Florida border along Interstate I-75, it was a prime location for distribution centers to service Georgia and Florida, and any distribution center would need warehouses. Although he didn't emphasize this to his father and uncle, Mr. Brandon knew the warehouses would also likely need material handling systems to process what was being stored there.

"In the meantime, Mr. Conboy went into the material handling business shortly after getting his master's degree. In his first two jobs he worked primarily as a consultant on the planning and design of material handling systems. His third job, however, was with Acorn Integration Services where he was usually the senior project supervisor on its integration services contracts, all of which were government contracts. While he was still employed there, National Manufacturing Company purchased Acorn and renamed it National Material Handling Corporation, the company I now represent. Thus, by this time, Mr. Brandon and Mr. Conboy were well on their way to having the experience to work together in the material handling business. Brandon Associates was specializing in building warehouses that could house material handling systems, and Mr. Conboy had experience in all aspects of the material handling business. While all of this was happening, Messrs Brandon and Conboy were well aware of what each other were doing because they would meet at one or two Georgia Tech football games each year. Their plan was on track.

"Not long after Brandon Associates began specializing in warehouses, Mr. Brandon bought the company from his father and uncle. Once he was in control of Brandon Associates, Mr. Brandon was ready to get into the material handling business, and the first person he contacted was—you guessed it—Mr. Conboy. He continued to consult with Mr. Conboy frequently as Brandon Associates moved into the material handling business. The defendants will contend throughout this trial that government contracts and commercial contracts for material handling systems are different, but Mr. Brandon always consulted with Mr. Conboy alone, even though Mr. Conboy had worked solely on government contracts and Brandon Associates worked only on commercial contracts.

"Aided by Mr. Conboy's advice, Brandon Associates had a successful entry into the commercial material handling business, and it soon became profitable. Brandon Associates initially performed only the planning and design of material handling systems, subcontracting with a variety of companies for the integration services to complete the project. Since integration services was the part of the business NMH was involved in, Mr. Conboy contacted his good friend, Mr. Brandon, for an opportunity to work together on some commercial contracts because NMH's government contracts had declined, and they wanted to get into commercial contracts. This would also give Mr. Brandon and Mr. Conboy an opportunity to 'test drive' their working relationship before joining forces. But unlike the way Brandon Associates usually decided who their integration subcontractor would be, Mr. Conboy asked for a sole-source contract, which meant NMH would get the job without having to bid for it. His good friend, Mr. Brandon, agreed. Although the price point was low, NMH agreed to the price, and completed the job on time. There was never a complaint by Brandon Associates about the quality or timeliness of NMH's work on any of their contracts. By the end of the second year of handling commercial contracts obtained from Mr. Brandon, NMH became profitable on the commercial contracts.

"Once they knew they could work together well, Mr. Brandon reversed course and decided Brandon Associates would no longer subcontract the integration services but would handle that part of the contract in-house. The time had arrived for Mr. Brandon and Mr. Conboy to fulfill their plan to work together. Mr. Brandon asked Mr. Conboy to become the head of the new integration services division of Brandon Associates. The following weekend, Mr. Conboy went to Valdosta to discuss the proposal. He took with him a business plan he prepared for the new integration services division. It not only included himself but all of the managers at NMH who worked with him on the integration contract, which would leave NMH with no managers with commercial experience. It also specified that the integration division would not be located in Valdosta, but rather in Orlando, where he and all the managers then worked. Finally, the plan also included an equity interest in Brandon Associates for Mr. Conboy. Mr. Brandon agreed to everything Mr. Conboy proposed. Their long-term plan to work together had finally come to fruition—at NMH's expense.

"Shortly thereafter, Mr. Brandon came to Orlando to meet with all of the managers of NMH who were interested in working for Brandon Associates. They met at the home of Mr. Conboy one evening while he was still a vice-president of NMH, and all of his managers agreed to leave NMH to work for Brandon Associates, crippling NMH's ability to handle commercial contracts. Several customers that had agreed to have NMH provide the integration services reneged on their agreement and had Brandon Associates perform the integration.

"Based on these facts, NMH has filed three separate claims. First, we have sued all the defendants for unfair competition by the way they essentially stole NMH's commercial material handling business. Second, we have sued Mr. Conboy, who was a vice-president of NMH, for breach of his fiduciary duty to NMH for his role in wrongfully taking NMH's material handling business to Brandon Associates. And third, we have sued all of the former employees of NMH—the six managers and Mr. Conboy—for breaching their duty of loyalty to NMH, their employer, for their role in wrongfully taking NMH's entire commercial material handling business.

"The damages NMH has suffered have been significant because we have lost the entire commercial integration services team. We will present evidence of the full measure of damages it will take to make NMH whole, and at the end of the case, we will ask you to return a verdict in favor of NMH against all of the defendants. Thank you for your attention."

***

David had been observing the jury as Stanton made his opening statement. All of the jurors were paying close attention, and several of them seemed to be persuaded by the story Stanton was telling, particularly juror number four, who had previously been in real estate sales, and juror number five, the retired Army sergeant. He decided he was going to have to strongly rebut the spin Stanton had cleverly woven into the narrative of the events leading up to Conboy and Brandon working together. Otherwise, they would be playing from behind throughout the trial, a position no trial lawyer wanted to be in. Glancing at Conboy and his managers before getting up to address the jury, David could tell they were also concerned.

He took a moment to look directly at each of the jurors as he thanked them for their service as jurors in the case. Then he began, "The evidence you are about to hear will not support the story Mr. Stanton has told you or the claims his clients have asserted because Mr. Stanton has only told you part of the story. One of the reasons juries do such a good job of deciding factual disputes between the parties is they use their common sense to help decide what is true, so please use your common sense as you evaluate the evidence.

"What Mr. Stanton failed to tell you was that the so-called plans to work together some day were never anything more than pie-in-the-sky talk as two college friends had a beer together and speculated on what the future might hold. Plans involve specific goals, timelines, and what resources will be needed. There was never discussion of any of those things. The article they published about the material handling business in grad school? That was undertaken at the suggestion of one of their professors who thought material handling systems would be a timely topic, one that would likely get published, and would look good on a graduating student's resume. Neither Mr. Conboy nor Mr. Brandon had any intention of going into the material handling business at the time. In fact, when the article was written, Mr. Brandon had not yet decided to return to Valdosta to enter the family construction business.

"Once Mr. Brandon returned to the family business, he was involved in the construction of single-family homes, offices, schoolhouses, and warehouses. The reason he urged his father and uncle to specialize was because they needed to be more efficient to be more profitable. Trying to build so many different types of buildings hindered the efficiencies they needed because it required so many different skills. Warehouses offered the best opportunity for specializing because of the interest Valdosta had generated as a good distribution location for Georgia and Florida.

"The possibility of getting into the material handling business was never considered until after Brandon Associates had specialized in warehouses. They learned they *had* to consider it because many of their customers were consulting their material-handling designers *before* they consulted Brandon Associates for the design and construction of a warehouse. So, it was a defensive move to protect their primary business of building warehouses.

"In the meantime, Mr. Conboy did obtain experience in the material handling business shortly after grad school, but not because it was pursuant to some strategic plan the two friends had concocted years before. He needed a job, and the company that offered him one was involved in planning and designing material handling systems, along with other services, but not integration services. Mr. Conboy had no involvement with integration services until he was hired by Acorn Integration Services. Significantly, all of his work at Acorn was solely on government contracts; he didn't work on a single commercial contract at Acorn.

"So, of course Mr. Brandon contacted my client when Brandon Associates decided they had to get into the material handling field. The *design* and *technical* aspects of material handling systems are similar for government and commercial contracts. Where they differ is in how the jobs are staffed. The government regulations for their contracts are onerous compared to commercial contracts, and they require heavier staffing. Mr. Conboy was only asked to advise on the technical aspects of the business. And why wouldn't Mr. Brandon contact him—a friend with experience who wouldn't charge a huge fee just to answer some technical questions. What would any reasonable person do in those circumstances?

"Mr. Stanton mentioned to you that the company Mr. Conboy was working for, Acorn, was purchased by National Manufacturing Company. What he didn't mention is that National Manufacturing is a large publicly held company primarily active in government contract work in a variety of fields. They wanted to get contracts with the U.S. Postal Service for building post offices and material handling systems for the mail. Buying a small company like Acorn was their entrée into government contracts for material handling systems. And the plan worked initially. NMH, formerly Acorn, got a huge contract for a mail distribution center in Tampa that was the largest in the country at the time. But once that contract was over, the USPS work declined, and rumors were rampant throughout NMH that National Manufacturing was considering selling NMH unless they improved profitability. The rumor was even mentioned in the Wall Street Journal.

"As Mr. Conboy will explain, he soon realized NMH would not be able to get enough government contracts to meet the high profit levels National Manufacturing expected of its subsidiary company, NMH. He discussed this problem with Mr. McDonald, the president of NMH and formerly the president of Acorn. Mr. McDonald was also aware of the rumors of the possible sale of NMH. He agreed with Mr. Conboy that they should get into the commercial material handling business while still maintaining their government contracts. They even identified a small company to purchase named FastSort that built commercial material handling systems and was a leader in sorting system technology, which could also help on their government contracts. Mr. McDonald approved the purchase, but his superiors at National Manufacturing vetoed it.

"The veto by National Manufacturing left NMH with limited options. Somehow they needed to increase revenue and profitability on their own or, as the rumors predicted, NMH might be sold—or possibly even shut down. Their only potential source of additional work was in commercial contracts, but given their corporate structure based on their government contract work, Mr. Conboy knew they probably couldn't win a competitive bid. In fact, this proved to be true. NMH never won a single bid for a commercial contract while he was there.

"But Mr. Conboy did have one avenue left to try to get commercial material handling contracts for NMH. Brandon Associates was subcontracting all of the integration services for its material handling contracts. Although NMH wouldn't be able to win a competitive bid, he could ask his friend Mr. Brandon to hire NMH on a sole-source basis that avoided the bid process; they just had to meet the price quoted. Mr. McDonald approved the price quoted by Brandon Associates—even though it was below NMH's actual costs for the job—and this became NMH's first opportunity to handle a commercial contract for integrations services.

"Over the next two years, NMH did get additional contracts

for integration services from Brandon Associates—all sole-source contracts, and they performed them well. However, Brandon Associates was having problems with its other subcontractors, which was causing customer complaints. To protect their business, they decided they needed to handle the integration portion of their jobs in-house. Even though NMH had performed well, it didn't make sense to have a large company like NMH—which also could handle *all* aspects of material handling contracts and was therefore a competitor—also be their only subcontractor.

"The first Mr. Conboy learned of this was when Mr. Brandon called to inform him Brandon Associates was taking the integration work in-house. Mr. Conboy immediately knew what that meant. NMH would lose its primary source of commercial work, and it had no way of replacing that work because they couldn't win in a bid process. When Mr. Brandon offered him the job, he knew he had to consider it.

"But he wasn't going to accept it under just any circumstances. He knew the integration business would be more successful if based in Orlando due to its large airport with direct flights throughout the country, and he wasn't interested in moving. He also knew most of his team would likely lose their jobs if NMH were shut down, so he drafted a business plan and took it with him to Valdosta to discuss Brandon Associates' offer to him. The salaries he listed in the plan? Those weren't the current salaries the managers were making at NMH. They were based on industry standards, and the proposed salaries were more than they were making at NMH. Mr. Brandon recognized the wisdom of Mr. Conboy's recommendations, and an agreement was reached on all points.

"Mr. Stanton suggested that Mr. Conboy recruited the managers to Brandon Associates. That's not true. He didn't even tell them of his decision, but word got around after he resigned, and the managers approached him; he simply gave them Mr. Brandon's number to call if they were interested in working for Brandon Associates. They each negotiated their own deal with Mr. Brandon.

"There's something else Mr. Stanton didn't tell you. None of the defendants had an agreement not to compete with NMH if they left to work elsewhere. They were free to leave to work anywhere else and Brandon Associates was free to hire them. Likewise, NMH was free to fire them at any time. Mr. Conboy and his managers are guilty of nothing more than taking an opportunity to make more money at a company that offered more job security. This is all part of normal competition, nothing more.

"NMH complains that when Mr. Brandon met with the managers to discuss working for Brandon Associates, they did so at the home of Mr. Conboy. But this took place *after* he had given notice he was leaving NMH, and the meeting occurred in the evening, after work hours. This was no sinister act, nor was it a violation of any duty Mr. Conboy owed to NMH. It was nothing more than preparation for competition, which they had every right to do.

"So, after you have heard *all* of the evidence, we will ask you to find there has been no unfair competition, no breach of any fiduciary duty Mr. Conboy owed to NMH, and no disloyalty by Mr. Conboy or his managers. We will ask you to return a verdict for the defendants.

"Thank you for your attention."

***

Jesse watched the jurors closely throughout David's

opening statement. They seemed to realize there were two sides to the story Stanton had presented to them. Two of the jurors had even nodded slightly at some of David's statements. Although it was always risky to try to predict how jurors were leaning so early in a case, she believed they were no longer skeptical of the defendants' case and would listen closely to the evidence.

Since David had mentioned much of what Bart Mayfield needed to present on behalf of Brandon Associates and Allan Brandon, Mayfield's opening statement was shorter than the previous two. When he finished, Judge Long announced that she had an emergency hearing that would begin within the next hour. Therefore, she adjourned the trial for the day, with the plaintiff's case to begin at 9:00 AM the following morning.

Chapter 24

The first witness the next morning was Arthur McDonald, the president of NMH. Stanton efficiently led him through his education and business background, including the years he was president of Acorn Integration Services, Inc. He had McDonald explain the different aspects of material handling services—planning, design, and integration services—and McDonald helpfully described his personal experience in each of these areas. Within fifteen minutes, Stanton had established that McDonald was a seasoned professional in all aspects of material handling.

"Did you hire Mark Conboy while you were president of Acorn?" Stanton asked.

Nodding, McDonald replied, "Yes, we needed someone with experience in material handling to be our lead integration supervisor. Given Mr. Conboy's master's degree in industrial engineering and his previous experience with material handling, I thought he would be well qualified. During grad school he even co-authored an article in the American Journal of Industrial Engineering with Mr. Brandon dealing with all aspects of material handling, including integration services, the area in which we hired him to work."

Jesse thought she observed a slight smirk on Stanton's face

when McDonald slipped the testimony in about the article in the Journal. She declined to object to the testimony being non-responsive to the question asked because that would have just called more attention to the testimony.

Stanton then asked McDonald about the purchase of Acorn by National Manufacturing. He had been one of the larger owners of Acorn as well as its president, and this line of questions allowed Stanton to emphasize all of the benefits to Acorn of becoming part of a large conglomerate company that had the capital and other resources to compete with virtually any other company for contracts in the material handling field. "What type of contracts were you competing for—government contracts or commercial?" Stanton asked.

Shifting slightly in his seat, McDonald turned to the jury and said, "All of our contracts at Acorn and later at NMH were government contracts until Mr. Conboy convinced me that we should also try to secure commercial material handling contracts."

"Did Mr. Conboy tell you why he thought NMH should get into commercial contracts?"

"Yes. After our initial contract for the U.S. Post Office in Tampa was completed, new Post Office contracts were few and smaller. Mr. Conboy was concerned about rumors that were circulating at the time that National Manufacturing might sell NMH if profitability didn't improve. He recommended to me that we explore handling commercial contracts. I wasn't as concerned about the rumors of NMH being sold as he was, but he convinced me it could be a good idea to explore increasing our business by handling commercial work."

Stanton nodded with an understanding expression, then asked, "Did he have a specific recommendation about how to get into the commercial work?"

"Yes, he recommended that NMH buy a company called FastSort, Inc. It was a small company involved in commercial material handling systems, and it also was a leader in sorting system technology, which could be helpful with both government and commercial work. Purchasing it would give us an entrée into commercial contracts."

"Did you approve the purchase?"

"Yes, but due to its high cost, the purchase also had to be approved by National Manufacturing's executive committee. They felt it was just too expensive and vetoed it. I was disappointed but not surprised."

Again, Stanton nodded in an understanding way. After a brief pause, he asked, "Did Mr. Conboy recommend any other purchases?"

"Yes, he did. Shortly after the FastSort purchase was vetoed, he recommended that we purchase a company named Perfect Conveyor Systems, Inc., which we referred to as PCS. They had some unique technology for material handling systems, and they were engaged in both government and commercial material handling contracts."

"What was it about PCS that made you believe the executive committee would approve the purchase of this company when it had just vetoed the purchase of FastSort?" As Stanton asked this question, he had a genuinely puzzled expression. Jesse couldn't help admitting he was a good actor in the way he framed this question for the witness with the jury in mind.

McDonald shrugged and said, "Oh, I didn't believe the

executive committee would approve the purchase of this company either. But Mr. Conboy suggested there might be another way to pull it off. He said we should come up with a business plan for NMH that included the purchase of PCS to show how we could achieve a healthy return on our own. With such a plan, we could approach private equity firms for the capital to acquire PCS in return for an equity interest in NMH."

Stanton's expression passed from puzzled to dubious. "Did you really believe the executive committee would approve having joint ownership of NMH with a private equity firm?"

"Well, I had my doubts, but Mr. Conboy convinced me we had to do *something*. He also pointed out another benefit of drafting such a business plan. As I mentioned, there were rumors, unconfirmed at the time but widespread, that if we didn't improve profitability, National Manufacturing was going to sell NMH. If that were the decision, we would be prepared to work with a private equity firm to hopefully keep NMH independent rather than be purchased by another conglomerate company."

"And you went along with this?" Stanton asked, summoning what appeared to be genuine surprise.

"Yes, Mr. Conboy was very convincing. Plus, he said he just wanted to draft the business plan for our discussion purposes. We could decide later whether to present it to the executive committee. He said he was concerned we would learn NMH was being sold before we had an opportunity to come up with our own plan. And, of course, if we were able to obtain enough new Post Office contracts in the meantime, we wouldn't have to worry about being sold. So, he claimed the business plan was a defensive strategy."

Stanton had the plan marked as an exhibit and then covered

the highlights with McDonald. Under the plan, NMH would no longer be a subsidiary of National Manufacturing; it would purchase PCS with capital from an unnamed private equity company. Stanton focused his questions on the fact the plan included all current managers and officers of NMH at their current compensation levels. Additionally, all contracts in progress at NMH and anticipated to be obtained by NMH were part of the plan, including price points and profit margins.

"Did you actually discuss all of these aspects of the plan with Mr. Conboy?" Stanton asked.

"Yes, in general terms. I had a draft copy of his plan in front of me as we discussed it, but he took all copies back to revise in light of our discussions. I never saw a physical copy of the revised plan until documents were produced in this lawsuit."

"To be clear, is this exhibit the revised plan?"

"It is."

"What did you intend to do with this plan?"

"Well, once he revised it, we were supposed to meet to decide whether or how to use it. Given the amount of confidential and proprietary information in the plan, I wanted to have strict protocols in place regarding what could be done with it."

"What did you actually decide to do when he came back with the revised plan?" Stanton asked in his most nonchalant manner.

In an exaggerated tone, McDonald replied, "The next thing I heard, Mr. Conboy had showed the business plan to three different private equity firms."

"What about all of the confidential and proprietary information in the plan?"

"It was all disclosed to those firms. One of the protocols I wanted in place before the plan was shown to any third parties was that our comprehensive confidentiality agreement would be signed first, with strict protections for our confidential and proprietary information. Instead, Mr. Conboy just signed the confidentiality agreements prepared by those three firms, which were oriented toward protecting them rather than NMH. That was quite upsetting."

"Any other problems with Mr. Conboy failing to follow your protocols?"

"Yes, without my knowledge he took representatives of one of the private equity firms to Tampa to go through our Post Office installation there to demonstrate how a material handling system operated. What upset me most about that was he took three of our managers, who knew nothing about my discussions with Mr. Conboy, to the demonstration. In all my meetings with Mr. Conboy about seeking outside funding to acquire PCS we never talked about bringing any of the managers into those discussions."

Stanton nodded as if contemplating what McDonald had just said. Then he pointed toward the jury box and said, "Please tell the jury why what Mr. Conboy did was harmful to NMH."

McDonald shifted his gaze to the jurors before responding. "Mr. Conboy was a vice-president of NMH and my most trusted manager. He had a fiduciary duty to keep our proprietary information—such as our price points, profit levels, salary structure, and staffing protocols—confidential and out of the hands of our competitors. He not only passed this information on to the private equity firms without adequate protection against its disclosure, he brought several of our managers into the demonstration in Tampa which wound up inflaming the rumors about NMH possibly being sold."

"Is there anything else Mr. Conboy did to harm NMH?"

"Yes, while still an officer of NMH he later recruited all six of our managers who were working on commercial contracts to go to work for Brandon Associates. He used the proprietary information of NMH to compete against us unfairly once he and the managers joined Brandon Associates and undercut our prices. It was a violation of his duty of loyalty to NMH, and it has gutted our commercial material handling business."

McDonald's voice vibrated with controlled emotion as he made his last statement. Jesse glanced at the jury as McDonald concluded his testimony. They had paid close attention to his testimony throughout, and he seemed to be connecting with them. He had been a more compelling witness than she anticipated based upon his deposition testimony, and she knew she needed to take the wind out of his testimony, or it could influence the jurors' understanding of all of the remaining testimony to come.

As soon as Stanton took his seat, Jesse stood, and even before arriving at the podium, asked, "Isn't it true that none of the three private equity firms expressed any willingness to invest in NMH?"

McDonald shifted in his seat before muttering a weak, "They expressed interest but ultimately decided not to invest."

"The executive committee didn't approve purchasing PCS either, did it?"

"No."

"You have no knowledge of any proprietary information being conveyed to any competitor of NMH by any of the private equity firms, do you?"

Squirming in his seat, he replied, "Well, nothing specific, although we have our suspicions."

"So, you have suspicions but no evidence?"

"Yes. . ."

A bit more sternly, Jesse said, "With regard to Mr. Conboy speaking to the private equity firms, isn't it true he told you he intended to see if there was any possibility of raising capital for the purchase of PCS, and you told him to keep you advised?"

"Well, yes, but I didn't think he was going to show them a detailed plan with all of the information he put in the plan."

"Really?" she responded. "Mr. McDonald, in your business experience have you *ever* known a private equity firm or other investor to make a substantial investment in a company *without* being provided a complete disclosure of all important information—what the securities laws call 'all material facts?'"

He appeared to realize there was no wiggle room out of responding candidly to this question. "No, I guess not. But I thought he would get my permission before conveying the plan to any lenders or investors."

"And yet, we have seen no memo, no email, no text or recorded voice mail, telling him to do so. There is no such directive to Mr. Conboy, is there?"

If looks could kill, Jesse would be in mortal danger. After staring at her for a long moment, McDonald shook his head.

"Now, with regard to rumors spreading about NMH being sold as a result of the demonstration in Tampa, you were able to confirm that National Manufacturing had actually formed a committee to look into the question of whether they should sell NMH, true?"

McDonald twisted in his seat again. "Yes. . ."

"So, the rumors weren't just rumors; they were based in fact?"

Again, a reluctant, "Yes. . ."

Pivoting to another topic, Jesse said, "You also testified that Mr. Conboy recruited all six managers to go to Brandon Associates. You have no personal knowledge that Mr. Conboy recruited them, do you?"

"No, but I think it's pretty clear what happened."

Showing a little exasperation, she said, "Mr. McDonald, if all six managers testify they first contacted Mr. Brandon about a job, you have knowledge of no facts which dispute their testimony, do you?"

Once more, a reluctant, "No. . ."

"When Mr. Conboy resigned, you were the first one he spoke to regarding his resignation, weren't you?"

"I believe so."

"You knew he had no non-compete agreement and could go to work anywhere he wished?"

McDonald hesitated while apparently considering how to respond before admitting that was true.

"And he told you he was resigning because he was frustrated that the executive committee had not allowed NMH to acquire FastSort or PCS and restructure in a manner that would enable you to be competitive in the commercial material handling world?"

"He said something to that effect."

"Now, you also testified that Brandon Associates used NMH's proprietary information to compete against it after Mr. Conboy went to work there. Isn't it true that *all* of the commercial contracts NMH obtained while Mr. Conboy was with NMH were sole-source contracts obtained from Brandon Associates or upon their recommendation?"

"Well, they were all sole-source contracts. I don't know whether all were obtained through them."

"In order to submit a bid or proposal to a potential client, Brandon Associates needed to include the prices of its subcontractor, NMH, with all of the back-up that required, true?"

Again, a reluctant, "Yes."

"So, Brandon Associates already knew NMH's price points before Mr. Conboy joined them because that information was necessary for Brandon Associates to obtain contracts for NMH and themselves to work on?"

"Yes, I suppose that's true."

Turning to another topic, Jesse said, "Mr. McDonald, isn't it true that during the two years Mr. Conboy was trying to obtain commercial material handling contracts for NMH, the company submitted bids on over thirty different jobs?"

"I believe that's correct."

"Please tell the jury how many of those bids you won."

"Uh, I don't recall us winning any contract via the bid process." After pausing briefly, though, he continued, "But I didn't consider that unusual. Most companies rarely win more than one out of six bids, and we had not yet restructured to the point where we were likely to win jobs via the bid process rather than by sole-source contracts. I was confident we would eventually begin winning bids or requests for proposals."

"In fact, NMH only came within ten percent of the winning bid on a single contract, isn't that true?"

By now, McDonald was clearly uncomfortable, shifting repeatedly in his seat. "That may be true; I don't recall the details."

"On most of your bids, NMH was twenty to thirty percent above the winning bid, wasn't it?"

"As I said, I don't recall the details."

Jesse decided to press on with this point. "Yet, despite your inability to compete for contracts via the bid process, the executive committee still refused to allow NMH to restructure to compete more effectively for commercial contracts, didn't they?"

"They allowed some restructure, and more was in the pipeline when Mr. Conboy left."

"But not enough to enable NMH to win a single contract via a bid process while he was still there?"

McDonald's shoulders slumped as he quietly muttered, "Well, we never won one. . ."

***

As Jesse returned to her seat the judge declared a break. As soon as the judge and jury left the courtroom, Stanton and Rhonda Robinson got into a heated, but muffled, dispute. Jesse couldn't hear what they were saying, but it took no imagination to glean they disagreed over strategy and how the case was proceeding. Robinson had been smug during Stanton's opening statement, but sullen during David's opening. Similarly, she seemed delighted at the end of McDonald's direct testimony, but now appeared upset about how he testified on cross-examination. As best Jesse could make out, Stanton's decision not to present re-direct testimony of McDonald was particularly irksome to Robinson.

When the jury returned, Stanton put on deposition testimony from some of the out-of- state witnesses who were with companies for whom NMH had performed integration services. The sole reason for this testimony, as best Jesse could determine, was Stanton wanted to show the jury their customers were pleased with their work and understood they were a separate company from Brandon Associates, even if they were a subcontractor of Brandon on the job. While Jesse could understand why Stanton might want to put on one or two witnesses via reading their depositions into the record—an uninspiring method of presenting evidence—she thought it was an error by Stanton to put on six different witnesses via deposition to make this point, particularly when the effort took the rest of Tuesday and all of Wednesday morning. Glancing at Robinson after each of the depositions was read into the record, Jesse concluded from her expression that Robinson agreed with her on this point.

Wednesday afternoon brought an even more surprising witness from Jesse's perspective. He was a member of the executive committee of National Manufacturing. Stanton asked him to explain the role of the executive committee in supervising NMH, then had him describe in numbing detail why, from the executive committee's viewpoint, neither FastSort nor PCS was worth the substantial price NMH would have had to pay to acquire either company. He testified, "The anticipated return on investment for either company failed to meet our normal standards, and the return would have been less than NMH had earned in the two previous years."

Stanton also solicited testimony from him to minimize the importance of the executive committee conducting a study of whether they should retain or sell NMH. "We are constantly analyzing whether we should retain or sell all of our subsidiary corporations—of which there are twelve—and also constantly analyzing whether we should sell or retain all of our divisions of National Manufacturing—of which there are six."

Finally, Stanton asked him about National Manufacturing's commitment to NMH's efforts to succeed in the commercial material handling business. He said the executive committee was fully committed to NMH's efforts and that they had a number of proposals under consideration when Mr. Conboy and the six managers left which would have improved their price competitiveness. Stanton had him briefly address each such proposal and explain why it would have improved efficiency, helped achieve desired profit levels, and would have made NMH more competitive.

Stanton then asked him what NMH profits had been for commercial contracts for the period of time Conboy and the managers were there. He responded that they averaged about $2 million per year for that time period, which was just over two years. They anticipated an increase in revenues of ten percent per year for the next seven years, which would result in a twenty-five percent increase in profits per year. When asked what profit level they anticipated over the next seven years now that NMH's entire management team for commercial contracts was hired by Brandon Associates, he said they would be hard pressed to earn $2 million per year, but they thought it was achievable.

In short, his testimony was that NMH would have arrived at the desired profitability level given a little more time. But for Mr. Conboy's impatience, he believed NMH would have achieved the efficiencies it sought and been fully competitive in the commercial market. But as a result of the defendants' actions, they didn't anticipate any increase in profits in commercial contracts; they would do well to keep profits level.

Jesse and David had agreed he would handle this witness. "Isn't it true that either FastSort or PCS would have provided experience in commercial material handling contracts that NMH did not have at the time?" David asked.

"Yes. NMH hadn't handled commercial contracts previously."

"Isn't it true that you expected the return on investment to improve as NMH gained experience in the commercial market, just as it did when NMH gained experience in the government contract world?" David tried to appear as reasonable as he possibly could as he asked this question.

After pausing to think about the question, the witness responded, "I suppose that's true."

"You also testified the executive committee is always analyzing whether to retain or sell all divisions and subsidiaries. But there hasn't been an article in the Wall Street Journal within recent years about National Manufacturing possibly selling any other subsidiary or division except NMH, isn't that true?"

"Well, yes, but of course we can't control the press."

"You also testified that given a little more time, the executive committee would have allowed some restructuring to make NMH more profitable. But isn't it true that timing is often an important, even critical, factor in many business decisions?"

He paused, thoughtfully, for several seconds before saying, "It can be."

David felt it was time to address where most of NMH's commercial work came from. "Isn't it true that NMH had obtained roughly eighty percent of its commercial contracts through Brandon Associates as of the time Mr. Conboy resigned?"

"I believe it was somewhere in that range."

"Wouldn't you agree it would have been difficult, if not impossible, to improve NMH's profitability in commercial contracts after losing eighty percent of its revenue?"

"Perhaps. But we have confidence that with time, we can do it."

"In fact, since Mr. Conboy and the managers left, NMH has focused its efforts on obtaining more government material handling contracts, not commercial contracts, true?"

"Yes, we've been forced to in order to keep NMH's doors open. However, we've continued to pursue our commercial material handling business, and we believe we can achieve our previous profitability level within twelve to eighteen months."

David paused before reacting to the witness's statement

because he wanted to let the testimony settle in. As he did so, he contemplated carefully his next questions to demonstrate the fallacy of the inference that NMH was *forced* to concentrate on government contracts. "When National Manufacturing purchased Acorn and changed its name to NMH, it was handling *only* government contracts, right?"

"Yes."

"You weren't concerned about keeping the doors open then as you handled only government contracts because NMH had an acceptable profit level, isn't that true?"

"Yes."

"It was only once the government contract revenues decreased that NMH even considered handling commercial contracts?"

"That's correct."

"And the only way NMH was able to get into commercial contracts was by obtaining sole-source contracts because you couldn't win any bids for contracts?"

"Well, we haven't won any bids yet."

"And, eighty percent of your sole-source contract revenues came from a single company, Brandon Associates, isn't that true?"

"Yes. . ."

"Do you also agree that Brandon Associates was under no obligation—legal or otherwise—to continue sending sole-source contracts to NMH?"

"I'm not aware of any such obligation."

"And when NMH lost its primary source of commercial contracts, you didn't believe you could compete effectively in the commercial material handling business; isn't that the reason you have prioritized government contracts?"

"I think the best answer to that question is we determined that, under the circumstances, the best deployment of our remaining personnel and capital would be in the government contracts arena until we could fully replace our commercial team."

David stared at him for a long moment to allow that answer to register with the jury. He started to ask a follow-up question but decided he had made his point that NMH was not fully pursuing commercial contracts, and he didn't want to argue with the witness. He turned to the judge and said, "No further questions, Your Honor."

As David returned to the counsel table, Jesse noticed Robinson whispering something to Stanton. Her face was red, and she was obviously agitated. For once, Stanton's calm demeanor cracked briefly; he was apparently equally agitated in responding to her, although Jesse couldn't make out what either said. Their heated but low volume conversation continued until Judge Long asked, "Any re-direct examination, Mr. Stanton?"

Stanton stood, and through clenched teeth, said, "No, Your Honor."

***

The squabbling between Stanton and Robinson continued on Thursday morning before the judge or jury entered the courtroom. Although Jesse and David were both used to their arguing, it seemed particularly strident this morning, and McDonald, who was NMH's corporate representative for the entire trial, was also part of the squabble. From what little Jesse could pick up, their strategy over whom to call next as a witness was the bone of their contention.

Once the jury was seated, Stanton called Allan Brandon as an adverse witness. When an adverse party is called as a witness the lawyer can ask leading questions, something a lawyer normally cannot do on direct examination. Despite Stanton's ability to ask leading questions, though, his examination of Brandon was ineffective. Brandon was thoroughly prepared, including how to carefully respond to leading questions. He deftly downplayed the discussions he had during grad school with Conboy about working together someday. Before Stanton could raise the topic of the published article he and Conboy wrote, he slipped in his testimony that their professor had suggested they write the article for publication, and the professor even suggested the topic. Several times Stanton objected to his testimony as being non-responsive to his questions, but each time Judge Long overruled the objection.

When Stanton led Brandon through a lengthy series of questions about Brandon Associates transitioning to building only warehouses in an attempt to show this was part of Brandon and Conboy's plan to work together, Brandon was able to logically rebut any such suggestion. He ably provided statistics demonstrating Brandon Associates had become more profitable as they specialized in warehouses. And his explanation of why they had to transition into planning and designing material handling systems for their clients to protect their warehouse construction business was a masterpiece of common sense.

Jesse glanced at Robinson periodically as Brandon was testifying. The longer he testified, the more agitated she became. It was obvious that Stanton was frustrated with how little progress he was making with his examination of Brandon, but Robinson was beyond frustrated; she appeared about to explode—so much so that even the jurors were glancing at her occasionally. Judge Long also noticed and cautioned her to stop distracting from the questioning of the witness. Robinson retained sufficient presence of mind to realize she couldn't get crosswise with the judge in the presence of the jury, and she outwardly calmed down, although Jesse could tell she was still boiling within.

Stanton's efforts to paint Brandon's consultations with Conboy over the years likewise failed to demonstrate there was an ongoing conspiracy, in Jesse's opinion. Brandon's innocent appearance, with his youthful face and round glasses, together with his deep baritone voice, gave him credibility that would be difficult to discredit even with an effective examination, and this effort was going nowhere.

After a mid-morning break, Stanton continued his examination of Brandon, turning to why he decided to give sole-source contracts to NMH for integration services. Stanton, of course, was attempting to show that Brandon did so to have a trial run on working together with Conboy before Brandon Associates hired Conboy and all his managers. Brandon countered this argument by pointing out that the prices he paid to NMH were so low that the profits to Brandon Associates were higher than on the contracts they bid out for integration services. When Stanton then tried to get Brandon to admit they would have earned more profit subcontracting the integration services to NMH than handling them in-house, Brandon once again had facts and figures to demonstrate that was false. The most profitable way, by a significant margin, to provide integration services was for Brandon Associates to handle them in-house. Additionally, that gave them total control of the contract from initial planning and design all the way through integration and getting the system operational, an important factor in ensuring quality control and client satisfaction.

Brandon even superbly addressed the portion of his testimony Jesse was most concerned about—his hiring Conboy and the managers. He mentioned up front that he inquired whether any of them had a non-compete agreement. If so, he would never have employed them. But without one, he believed he was free to offer any of them a job, and they were free to accept. This was, in his view, normal competition. He denied asking Conboy to pressure any of the managers to join him at Brandon Associates; he even told them to co-operate fully with NMH before leaving, staying longer before leaving if needed. Furthermore, the salaries offered were determined by him based on company guidelines and industry standards, not anything Conboy suggested.

In short, Brandon's testimony turned out far better than Jesse had anticipated. Bart Mayfield asked only a few clarifying questions on cross, and Jesse decided to ask no questions at all. His testimony had been so good she didn't think any further questions would improve it, and she could call him as a witness during the defendants' case if it later proved necessary.

After Stanton told the judge he had no redirect examination of Brandon, she dismissed the jury fifteen minutes early for lunch. As soon as the jury exited the courtroom, Stanton stood and announced, "Your Honor, I have a matter to take up with the court. Do you prefer to hear it now or after lunch?"

Judge Long paused, looked at her watch, then said, "Since we released the jury for lunch early, let's take it up now. What's your issue?"

Stanton stepped up to the podium, and in his best New York accent said, "My client has just informed me they no longer want me to be their counsel in this case. Accordingly, I hereby request that my law firm and all our lawyers, including myself, be permitted to withdraw as counsel for NMH, effective immediately. Obviously, I can't represent a client who doesn't want my representation, but I can't withdraw without the court's permission, which I respectfully request."

Judge Long's eyes widened in surprise. A change of counsel in a case is not unheard of, but at this point in a trial it's extremely rare. The judge turned her gaze to Robinson and said, "Ms. Robinson, is this true? Has NMH fired Mr. Stanton and his firm?"

"It has, Your Honor," she replied.

"Before I ask Mr. McDonald the same question, let me make it as plain as I can that I will not entertain a continuance of this trial to allow NMH to hire new counsel. We're going to complete this trial during the time allotted for it. Mr. McDonald, do you still want to fire Mr. Stanton and his firm? If you do not, I will require him to continue as your counsel through the remainder of the trial."

McDonald stood, appearing somewhat unsure of himself, but after looking at Robinson, who nodded at him, addressed the judge. "Yes, Judge. We thank Mr. Stanton and his firm for their services, but we prefer to continue this trial without him."

Turning to Robinson, Judge Long said, "Ms. Robinson, am I to assume you will be the sole counsel for NMH for the remainder of this trial?"

Robinson quickly stood up, and said, "That's correct, Your Honor."

"Before I rule on the motion, Ms. McKenzie and Mr.

Mayfield, do you have any objection to Mr. Stanton's motion?"

Before responding, Jesse glanced at Mayfield, who was apparently as surprised by this turn of events as she was, but he seemed to view it as favorably as she did. They both responded, "No objection, Your Honor."

With resignation, the judge turned to Robinson and said, "I hereby grant the motion to withdraw by Mr. Stanton and his firm. However, let me remind you, Ms. Robinson, as I did when I granted your motion to appear *pro hac vice,* that you are required to be fully familiar with the Florida Rules of Civil Procedure, the Florida Evidence Code, the Florida Rules of Professional Conduct, and the rules of this court. If you fail to follow any of those rules, I can revoke the order permitting you to appear in this case. And I would remind you that a corporation is not allowed to represent itself in court; it must have counsel. Do you understand this?"

"I do, Your Honor," Robinson said confidently. The judge then declared the court in recess for lunch until 1:30.

Chapter 25

Over lunch, David and Jesse speculated with Conboy and Brandon about what would change with Robinson now NMH's sole attorney. "She'll be more aggressive in her questions than Stanton was," David mentioned to Conboy. "Yes, she will try to bully you into the answers she wants," Jesse added. "Don't let her put words in your mouth that you don't agree with."

"What makes her so pugnacious?" Brandon asked. "I don't think I've ever run across anyone quite so ready to argue and fight even if it's not in his or her best interest."

"I had very few dealings with her at NMH," Conboy replied. "But her reputation was similar to the way she's behaved in this lawsuit. The rumors were that she had been hired by a prominent Atlanta law firm out of the University of Georgia that hired mostly Ivy League grads. She always had a chip on her shoulder because she felt they got preferential treatment, and when she rubbed the senior partners the wrong way one too many times, they let her know she wasn't on the partnership track. They helped her get a job with National Manufacturing's legal department, but she had similar problems there. Finally, when National Manufacturing bought Acorn, her boss assigned her to be the general counsel for Acorn, renamed NMH.

"She understood the assignment as NMH's legal counsel was a low-rung position that offered little chance of advancement, but when NMH got off to a good start with the Tampa Post Office project, she apparently thought NMH could prove to be a success story and catapult her career onto a better trajectory. The few dealings I had with her before my resignation were pleasant; she seemed to view me as part of the team helping her get her career back on track. But when I met with her and the senior vice-president of National Manufacturing to discuss my resignation, she treated me like I was a turncoat. I think she believes Allan and I are the latest people to torpedo her career, and she's looking for some serious revenge.

"The other thing that has her upset, I suspect, is that National Manufacturing's legal department insisted NMH hire Stanton and the Paul & Ramey law firm for this case. I'm sure she viewed that as the latest snub to her. The only possible reason the legal department allowed NMH to fire Stanton at this late date is that she has been bad-mouthing him and has finally convinced McDonald to join her. I suspect her legal department boss has reluctantly given permission to fire Stanton but has told her in no uncertain terms that an unfavorable result will be her swan song with the National Manufacturing legal department."

"So, we now have an angry, insecure, loose cannon as our opposing counsel for the rest of the trial," David commented. "That explains a lot about her behavior to date, and we can anticipate more of the same. We have to be ready for anything."

***

When they returned to the courtroom, Robinson convinced the judge to make a simple announcement to the jury to explain Stanton's absence. "Due to unforeseen circumstances, Mr. Stanton will not be present for the remainder of this trial. Ms. Robinson will continue to represent NMH." The surprised look on most of the jurors' faces convinced Jesse they at least suspected Robinson of having something to do with those "unforeseen circumstances."

As expected, the first witness Robinson called was Conboy. As soon as she directed her questions to his discussions with Brandon about working together someday, she became argumentative and repetitive. Jesse objected to her badgering the witness three times, each of which Judge Long sustained. Despite her best efforts to get Conboy to admit a plan to work together with Brandon in material handling was hatched in grad school, he repeatedly denied it, saying there was nothing more than beer talk and fun speculation on what the future might hold. It apparently never occurred to her that the fact she kept repeating her questions and getting the same answers was doing her more harm than good with the jury—a lesson most trial lawyers learn early in their career.

Turning to her next area of inquiry didn't improve her effectiveness. She suggested that Conboy's primary purpose in accepting a job with Acorn had been to gain the experience he would need in integration services to team up with Brandon in the material handling business. His response was a model of common sense. "I took the job with Acorn because I needed a job at the time, not because of some college pipe dream about working together. Besides, I was unaware at the time that Brandon Associates was even thinking about getting into material handling services."

Rather than accept his answer and move on to a topic that might support her case, Robinson badgered him with questions about their discussions at Georgia Tech football games in an attempt to define precisely when they first discussed Brandon

Associates getting into material handling contracts. The more unhelpful answers she got, the more frustrated she became and the angrier her questions sounded. Each time Jesse glanced at the jury, she could tell Robinson was losing them.

She finally settled on a topic that could bear fruit for her. "Mr. Conboy, why did you push Mr. McDonald so hard to move NMH into commercial material handling jobs when all of your experience at the time had been in government contracts? Wasn't it because you knew Brandon Associates handled material handling contracts and would need a subcontractor to provide integration services?"

Conboy was cautious in his response. "No, I just realized that we needed additional sources of revenue since our government contract work was decreasing. The rumor mill was telling us we had to do something, or we would be sold. Handling commercial contracts was the logical extension of our business."

When Robinson tried to get him to admit his primary motive for moving into commercial work was to give him and his team experience in commercial work before joining Brandon Associates, he countered with the fact his first recommendation was to buy FastSort and then PCS. Neither purchase would have been necessary just to get some experience before joining Brandon Associates. He could have simply asked for a few sole-source contracts from Brandon Associates before joining them. He also pointed out he spent considerable time and effort in preparing the business plan for NMH and talking to private equity firms, none of which was necessary if his plan was to go to Brandon Associates.

Conboy's mention of the private equity firms led Robinson into an extensive inquiry about every aspect of his discussions with those firms. In Jesse's opinion, the fact none of these firms were willing to invest in NMH rendered this line of inquiry mostly irrelevant to the plaintiff's case. Instead, it gave Conboy an opportunity to point out that three separate independent firms in the business of investing in sound, profitable companies all declined to invest in NMH's commercial material handling business, confirming his belief that far more restructuring would be necessary to successfully compete in commercial work. Rather than minimize the impact of this point by moving on quickly to another topic, Robinson testily argued with him, which brought more sustained objections and allowed him to drive home his point.

Even with regard to not getting NMH's preferred confidentiality agreements signed—a point Stanton competently developed during his deposition, she asked the proverbial one too many questions. This allowed Conboy to point out that the confidentiality agreements actually signed by all three firms were basically the standard forms used in the industry. Besides, no one had yet identified even a single improper disclosure, he emphasized, which suggested this issue was a red herring.

Robinson had, by now, questioned Conboy for nearly an hour and a half in what Jesse considered one of the least effective examinations she had witnessed. The longer a lawyer examines a witness—particularly an opposing party—without success, the less impact it has on the jury when the lawyer finally gets some helpful testimony. In Jesse's opinion, Robinson should have led with the most helpful testimony she could get from Conboy. But her biggest mistake was her failure to realize that the strength of NMH's case was not the *fact* that Conboy and the managers all left NMH— which they had the right to do—but rather *how* they went about it.

By the time she got around to addressing topics that could help her case—Conboy's trip to Valdosta, business plan in hand, to convince Brandon to hire not only him but also his managers; inviting his managers to his house for an interview with Brandon while Conboy was still an officer of NMH; and actually coordinating the managers' departure dates—the jury was barely paying attention. Furthermore, her questions were so poorly worded that Jesse's objections were usually sustained, interrupting the flow of the testimony.

Reviewing her notes as Robinson completed her examination of Conboy, Jesse noticed he had worked into his testimony most of the points she had planned to address with him. So, she asked only a few clarifying questions on cross-examination and sat down, taking less than ten minutes.

Never one to pass up an opportunity to speak when she should remain silent, Robinson questioned Conboy extensively on re-direct, despite the fact that questions on redirect are supposed to be limited to the scope of the cross-examination. After Jesse's fourth objection to Robinson's questions being outside the scope of cross-examination, all of which Judge Long sustained, the judge called all counsel to the bench for a sidebar conference where the jury couldn't hear them.

Judge Long was as stern as Jesse had ever seen her; her patience seemed nearly exhausted. "Ms. Robinson, I have warned you repeatedly about the scope of your questions. You are on redirect. You cannot go over all of the topics you addressed on direct examination again, only those addressed on Ms. McKenzie's cross. I shouldn't have to remind you of this. If you continue to refuse to follow the rules and my instructions, I will hold you in contempt of court. Do we understand each other?"

The tone of the judge's voice combined with the red splotches on her neck apparently convinced Robinson she was

serious, leading to a meek reply. "Yes, Your Honor. . ."
Nevertheless, Robinson continued her redirect for an additional
fifteen minutes, although she did limit her questions to the scope of
the cross-examination. When she finally concluded her redirect,
Judge Long declared a recess for the day, and an obviously
exhausted jury was released until the following morning at 9:00.

***

The trial was delayed Friday morning for an hour due to
another emergency hearing before Judge Long. When the trial
resumed, Robinson announced NMH's final witness, a CPA, who
was called as an expert to opine on the damages NMH had suffered
as a result of the defendants' alleged wrongful conduct.

David was surprised by how Robinson competently took
her witness through his background and qualifications to express
an opinion on NMH's damages. He suspected Stanton had
prepared an outline before he was fired. Robinson kept her
questions short and open-ended so the witness could use his own
words to explain how he arrived at his opinion. Using an overhead
projector, he presented graphs showing the revenues and profits
earned while Conboy and the six managers were still with NMH.
He then assumed that but for the wrongful acts of the defendants,
revenues would have increased for the commercial contracts work
over the next seven years at a rate of ten percent annually, but he
assumed increases in profits of twenty-five percent annually. He
explained that profitability would increase more rapidly than
revenues because NMH already had most of the staff they would
need due to their government contract work.

The damages, therefore, were the difference between the
total anticipated profits over the seven-year period compared to the
total if profits were flat (no increases) over that time frame. The

difference was then reduced to present value at an eight percent per annum discount rate, all of which was summarized in a chart containing the actual numbers.

NMH's Damages

Anticipated profits @ 25% annual increases	$37,683,716
Less profits w/o annual increases	-$14,000,000
	————————
Difference over 7 years	$23,683,716
Net present value @ 8% discount rate	$13,211,880

On cross-examination David went immediately to the assumptions underlying the CPA's opinion. "What was the basis for your assumption that revenues would increase at ten percent per annum?"

"I was instructed by my client to make that assumption."

"Well, assume that Brandon Associates stopped sending work to NMH—which they had the right to do—and that work accounted for eighty percent of NMH's commercial contract revenues. Do you agree that the potential of losing some or all of Brandon Associates' work—which actually happened—rendered NMH's assumption their revenues would increase by ten percent a year highly speculative and not probable?"

"Losing Brandon Associates' work would make it more difficult to increase revenues, but that possibility is one of the reasons they only assumed a ten percent increase per year. I believe their assumption of a modest increase in revenues of ten percent a year is not unreasonable, particularly given the vast resources of National Manufacturing."

Shaking his head, David said, "But it's not reasonable to assume NMH would continue to get eighty percent of its revenues in commercial work from a single client through sole-source contracts, is it?"

"No, but it's not unreasonable to assume NMH would get enough business from other sources to replace any reduced percentage of their revenues from Brandon Associates."

David then pivoted to another assumption. "In forming your opinion, what portion of NMH's commercial contracts did you assume came from winning bids?"

Frowning slightly, he said, "I assumed NMH would gradually increase the portion of their revenues coming from bid jobs to a similar portion won by the average company seeking commercial material handling contracts. That would be winning about one bid in six."

"What percentage of commercial contracts are awarded via bid or request for proposals versus direct negotiations?"

Warily, he responded, "That varies considerably, but in a typical year between thirty to fifty percent, or more."

Pleased that he got the answer he hoped for, David asked, "Are you aware that NMH has never won a single commercial material handling contract via a bid process?"

Initially taken aback by this question, the CPA glanced at Robinson whose gaze was fixated on her notes, then at McDonald who also seemed preoccupied with note taking, before turning back to David. "I assumed NMH had won few, if any, but given NMH's resources as part of National Manufacturing, I believe it's reasonable to assume they will win their share of bids in the future."

"But, I take it, you have not investigated nor formed an opinion as to what specifically it might take for NMH to win commercial material handling contracts via bid process in the future?"

His shoulders slumped, and he seemed more than a little perturbed as he glanced at Robinson and said, "No, not specifically, but anything that improves efficiency would help."

After getting the witness to admit some appraisers—although not him—would use a higher discount rate than eight percent on estimated profits on a new, risky business, which would reduce the amount of damages, if there were any, David saw no need to examine him further.

Robinson limited her re-direct to asking about each of the restructuring proposals the executive committee was considering and their effect on efficiencies that would improve NMH's chances of winning bids. After asking him about all of the proposals, she inquired how adoption of all of the proposals would affect NMH's chances of winning bids. "If all of these proposals were adopted, NMH would have about the same chance of winning a bid as the average company handling commercial contracts, which means they would win about one in six. I believe my opinion of NMH's damages is consistent with that."

As the CPA left the witness stand, Robinson announced that NMH rested its case.

***

As soon as NMH rested its case, Jesse stood to make a

306

motion for directed verdict. Such a motion asks the court to decide there are no genuine issues of fact for the jury to resolve based upon the evidence presented and that the moving party is entitled to judgment as a matter of law. Judge Long asked Jesse to state her grounds for the motion, without argument. Once she had done so, the judge said she would take the motion under advisement but likely wouldn't rule until all the evidence had been presented.

Judge Long allowed a shorter than normal lunch break in an attempt to wrap up testimony by the end of the day. When the jury returned from lunch, the defendants began putting on their case, which had been considerably shortened by all the favorable testimony they were able to present on cross-examination during the plaintiff's case. Bart Mayfield agreed with David and Jesse that they should call their clients to testify first, beginning with the six managers, whom David would examine, and concluding with Conboy, whom Jesse would present. Mayfield would then call Brandon to testify, if necessary, and then Jesse would present the defendants' economist expert who would testify about the damages claimed by NMH.

The testimony of each of the managers was short and to the point. All of them had heard the rumor that if NMH's profitability didn't improve, NMH would be sold. When they learned that Conboy had resigned, they felt the writing was on the wall concerning NMH being sold, or their being fired. Once they learned he was joining Brandon Associates, they asked him about a job, but he responded only by giving them Allan Brandon's phone number. Each of them interviewed separately with Brandon, without Conboy being present, and accepted his offer, which included a raise and slightly better benefits.

The testimony of all six could have been presented within an hour, including cross-examination, but Robinson was at her most verbose, argumentative self, which brought many objections, nearly all sustained. It was almost two hours before their testimony was complete.

During Conboy's testimony, Jesse concentrated her questions on NMH's reluctance and delay in allowing NMH to restructure sufficiently to compete in the commercial integration services world. Although NMH had achieved profitability of about $2 million per year in commercial contracts by the time Brandon Associates decided to bring the integration services in-house, Conboy emphasized that no further meaningful increases in profitability were possible without significantly restructuring their business operations. And without the restructure, NMH was unlikely to ever win a competitive bid. He also testified that the proposals to make NMH more efficient in their commercial contracts were a well-kept secret. No one ever informed Conboy any such proposals were under consideration by the executive committee.

As Robinson arose to cross examine Conboy, Jesse assumed that even Robinson could notice the jury was losing focus. Juror number two—the Puerto Rican roofer—appeared to be asleep, and juror number four—the housewife formerly in real estate sales—had a totally bored look plastered on her face. The remaining jurors appeared fatigued. Robinson did nothing to arouse the jurors with her ineffective cross-examination, but at least she kept it short.

Mayfield then had Brandon take the stand very briefly to round out his testimony, with Robinson once again accomplishing nothing on cross, followed by Jesse calling their expert as their final witness. Marcus Belmont had a PhD in economics and had taught economics at the University of Florida for twenty-two years. He had testified over thirty times in court on the issue of damages in commercial cases, one of which involved the material handling business.

After soliciting testimony to qualify him as an expert, Jesse asked, "Dr. Belmont, have you reviewed the opinion of NMH's expert as to the amount of damages he says NMH has suffered in this case?"

"I have, and I was in the courtroom listening to his testimony."

"Do you agree with his opinion?"

"No, I do not. In my opinion, NMH has suffered no damages. In fact, they would be better served by getting out of the commercial material handling business entirely and focus on government contracts."

"What's the basis for that opinion?"

"Up to fifty percent of contracts awarded in the commercial material handling field are determined by a bidding contest, as my research has confirmed. NMH was never able to win a single commercial contract via bid, so they likely would never be as profitable in the commercial world as they are in government contracts. They should stick to government work."

Jesse nodded, then said, "But Mr. Conboy admitted that NMH had a profit of about $2 million on their commercial work before he left NMH. How do you explain that?"

"An annual profit of $2 million in commercial contracts is insignificant for NMH, which is part of one of the largest conglomerate companies in the world. And they were able to achieve that modest profit level only due to the sole-source contracts that they received from Brandon Associates, thanks to the personal relationship between Mr. Brandon and Mr. Conboy. That simply wasn't a sustainable business plan. Without the ability to win contracts via bid, they had no chance of obtaining enough business to become acceptably profitable in their commercial work. In short, they simply weren't competitive, and a business that isn't competitive won't last in the long run."

On cross-examination, Robinson surprised Jesse by her competence. "Dr. Belmont," Robinson asked, "are you aware that Brandon Associates considered NMH's work to be of the highest quality of any of its subcontractors for integration services?"

In a dismissive tone, he responded, "Well, that may be true, but they were unlikely to win bids unless they became competitive on price."

In response, Robinson then took Dr. Belmont through each of the restructure proposals the executive committee had under consideration. He reluctantly admitted adoption of each proposal should improve efficiency and profitability somewhat, which could, in turn, improve their chances of winning bids. By the time she finished her cross-examination, he had to admit it was possible, even if he still believed highly unlikely, that NMH could have achieved profitability in commercial contracts at the level NMH predicted. This was a critical admission by Dr. Belmont because that level of profitability was what NMH's expert used to calculate the amount of damages NMH asked the jury to award.

When Dr. Belmont stepped down from the witness stand, Judge Long dismissed the jury until Monday morning at 9:00 AM, at which time final arguments would be presented. Once the jury was dismissed, Jesse renewed her motion for directed verdict, which the judge denied, saying there were factual issues for the jury to decide.

Chapter 26

Tension is always high for a trial lawyer about to present final argument in a case—not unlike the tension an athlete faces before a big game. For some, the tension spurs the lawyer on to better performance; for others, it clouds their judgment and hinders their performance.

David and Jesse spent the weekend preparing Jesse for her final argument. The evidence had been complex, so it was important that she remind the jury how the evidence supported the points David had made during his opening statement. They also spent several hours discussing the issues Robinson would likely emphasize and how to respond—a task made more difficult because she was a loose cannon who might make arguments that have emotional appeal but are irrelevant to the claims still pending. It was imperative, they decided, that Jesse object to any such arguments; otherwise, a legally irrelevant argument could influence the jurors when they decide whom to favor in their verdict. By late Sunday, Jesse was confident she was ready for the big moment.

One glance at Robinson on Monday morning as she entered the courtroom convinced Jesse that Robinson was wound even tighter than usual. Her jaw was clenched, and she began fidgeting with her notes as soon as she sat down. When David offered a cheery, "Good morning," Robinson ignored him, apparently lost in her own thoughts about what was about to happen. From Jesse's observation, Robinson seemed awed by the moment and overwhelmed by her emotions, not a helpful state for a trial lawyer.

As soon as the jury returned to the courtroom, Judge Long reminded them that what the lawyers were about to say in final arguments was not evidence but could be helpful as they evaluated the evidence; therefore, they should listen closely to the lawyers' comments.

When Robinson stood to begin her argument, she placed her notes on the podium, took a deep breath, and then stared at the jurors one by one for nearly ten seconds each before saying a word, creating an awkward silence. Then, the words came tumbling out of her mouth with a sense of outrage. "By now, it should be abundantly clear from the evidence that defendants Brandon and Conboy hatched a plan in grad school to run a business together in the future. And pursuant to that plan, they coldly and calculatingly *gutted* NMH's commercial material handling business by *illegally* taking all its key employees, *robbing* it of its business, and *stealing* its confidential information to unfairly compete."

Jesse was immediately on her feet. "Objection, Your Honor. . ." Before she could state the grounds for her objection, Judge Long pounded her gavel, and commanded, "All counsel, sidebar. Now!" The look on her face would have weakened the knees of any lawyer with even a modicum of understanding about what she had done wrong. When all counsel arrived at the bench, the judge stared at Robinson for what, even for Jesse, was a long, uncomfortable moment before saying just above a whisper so the jury couldn't hear, "Ms. Robinson, another outburst like that and I will hold you in contempt of court. Unless you want to spend tonight in jail, you will limit your arguments to the claims actually being tried. We're not trying a case about theft; your claims are for unfair competition, breach of fiduciary duty, and breach of duty of loyalty. Don't try my patience further."

"But judge. . ." Robinson began.

"No buts! I have ruled," Judge Long hissed, the red splotches on her neck apparent to everyone in the courtroom.

As the lawyers returned to their seats, the judge instructed the jury to ignore Robinson's statements about the defendants stealing the plaintiff's employees, business, or information, and reminded them what the pending claims were. When Robinson resumed her argument, she was clearly shaken by the judge's intensity and warning but managed to regain her composure after a hesitant start. She reminded the jury of the longstanding plans Conboy and Brandon had to work together and suggested they had even identified the industry as confirmed by their journal article in grad school. Brandon's decision to specialize in warehouses was a preliminary step to get into material handling, the industry in which Conboy had been working from shortly after graduation.

Jesse was monitoring the jurors' response to Robinson's argument and was somewhat surprised they weren't exhibiting as much doubt or skepticism as she expected, given Robinson's performance and the judge's rebuke.

Robinson briefly summarized her view of the evidence up to the point Conboy solicited sole-source contracts from Brandon Associates. Then, she went into more detail, pointing out the high quality of NMH's work—which Brandon Associates admitted— and the fact they always finished their jobs on time and within budget. Once they knew they could work well together, Brandon finalized the decision to bring all the integration work in-house and

Conboy and his team along with it —a decision that Robinson suggested had been informally made years previously. "How do we know that?" she asked. "Look at the business plan Conboy took with him to Valdosta. It not only included hiring his entire team to work at Brandon Associates; it also included an equity interest in Brandon Associates for Conboy. Finally, they would work together in a company they jointly owned, a fulfillment of their longstanding plan."

Robinson then took them through the interviews at Conboy's house while he was still an officer of NMH, the discussions about when each member of the team would resign, and how that left the team at NMH performing commercial contracts so depleted they weren't in a position to take on new commercial work. Finally, she displayed the chart showing the damages NMH claimed they had suffered.

Only once after Judge Long's warning to Robinson had Jesse objected, and that was on a statement Robinson attributed to the wrong witness, which the judge acknowledged as she sustained the objection. To Jesse's surprise, Robinson had done a better job presenting the evidence in a favorable light than she had imagined Robinson could. Even more surprising, she had done this in only thirty minutes and had held the jurors' attention the entire time.

As Jesse arose to make her final argument, she felt the full burden of being lead counsel on her shoulders. Her clients' futures depended on her ability to convince the jurors they had done nothing wrong. This was a case she felt her clients should win, but the outcome remained uncertain, and despite all of Robinson's missteps, she had presented plausible arguments to the jury. If the jurors bought those arguments, her clients would be devastated, with Brandon Associates likely in bankruptcy, and her clients along with them. As these thoughts flashed through her mind, her competitive juices kicked in, and she strode confidently to the podium.

After thanking the jury for their service, Jesse reminded them of David's admonition in his opening statement to use their common sense to evaluate the evidence. "There were good, sound, business reasons for every decision Brandon Associates made, and for every decision Mr. Conboy and the six managers made. The only thing they are guilty of is planning for and engaging in permissible competition. As the judge will instruct you, an employee without a non-competition agreement—even an officer of a company—has the right to *plan* for competition with his employer even while still working for that employer." Jesse also reminded them that NMH has the burden of proving by the greater weight of the evidence each of the claims they had asserted—a burden they had not met.

Jesse pointed out the so-called plans in college were nothing more than pie-in-the-sky speculation, and the article in the journal was written at the suggestion of their professor. Brandon hadn't even decided to return home to the family business at the time. She took them through the work experience of Brandon and Conboy after graduation, which gave no hint of any plan to work together.

Brandon's urging his father and brother to specialize in warehouses resulted in improved profits, as he predicted. What he hadn't anticipated, however, was how the material handling concerns of their potential clients began to interfere with Brandon Associates getting new warehouse construction jobs, requiring them to get into material handling as a *defensive* measure.

She reminded them Conboy got most of his experience in integration services at Acorn, but it was all on government contracts. After Acorn was purchased by National Manufacturing, NMH had a good start, but profitability fell off as new contracts were fewer and smaller. After the executive committee refused to allow the purchase of FastSort or PCS, Conboy sought commercial work the only way that was open to them—getting sole-source contracts from someone who knew and trusted him at Brandon Associates. "Remember," Jesse emphasized, "NMH couldn't win a bid. They never won a commercial bid while Mr. Conboy was there, and they presented no evidence that NMH has won a bid to this day. National Manufacturing's executive committee claimed they were considering restructuring NMH to be more competitive, but no one at NMH, including its president and Mr. Conboy, ever heard about it. What Mr. Conboy did know was that they never won a bid, and when they lost their only reliable source of sole-source contracts, their commercial endeavor was surely going to fail."

Jesse then reminded the jury of why Conboy prepared the business plan to take to Valdosta and why he thought all of them would soon be out of a job at NMH's Orlando office. The plan was nothing more than preparation for competition, which is perfectly permissible as the court would instruct them. She carefully pointed out that Conboy took pains to avoid any communication with the six managers about going to work for Brandon Associates, simply telling them what Brandon's phone number was when asked about a job there. "Common sense tells you that's not recruiting. Furthermore, Mr. Conboy didn't participate in the interviews with the managers. Each met separately with Mr. Brandon alone, which they had every right to do."

Turning to damages, Jesse pointed out they shouldn't even have to consider the issue of damages since the evidence didn't support NMH's claims of liability by the defendants. "But if you do reach the issue of damages, the evidence reveals their calculations are all pure speculation. NMH's own expert didn't even attempt to project their revenues over the seven-year period. His testimony was that NMH instructed him to *assume* revenues would increase by ten percent per year for seven years, with profits increasing each year by twenty-five percent. But NMH presented no evidence to show *how* they could reasonably achieve a ten-percent *increase* in revenues when they had just *lost* the source of eighty percent of their commercial work. Common sense says this is all speculation, highly unlikely to come to pass."

As Jesse returned to her seat, she noticed that Robinson was again apparently agitated. Her jaw muscles were bulging from clenching her teeth so tightly, and her eyes were tiny slits through which she was shooting daggers at Jesse. Robinson's reaction to her argument convinced Jesse she must have done something right. She just hoped the jury agreed with the points she had made.

After Bart Mayfield made a short but effective final argument, which reinforced and supplemented Jesse's, all eyes were on Robinson as she arose to make her rebuttal argument. Since the plaintiff has the burden of proof, the plaintiff's lawyer has the opportunity to make a reply or rebuttal argument to respond to the points the defendants' lawyers have made. Jesse had glanced at Robinson several times while Mayfield was making his final argument, and it seemed to her Robinson was about to explode.

As soon as Mayfield sat down, Robinson rushed to the podium, grabbed it tightly with both hands and leaned forward as she began, "You've now heard all the pitiful excuses the defendants have made for their unlawful but successful efforts to take NMH's entire commercial material handling business. They claim it's just all part of normal competition, but the truth is they should all be in jail for what they've done!"

"Objection!" Jesse and Mayfield were both on their feet simultaneously. Before either could state their grounds for objecting, Judge Long ordered counsel to the bench. Jesse had never seen the judge so stern, and she seemed to be struggling to control her emotions as she spoke. "Ms. Robinson, I've warned you repeatedly against such improper statements. The objections are sustained. You are to remain in the courtroom once the jury retires to deliberate; you will then have the opportunity to show cause why I should not hold you in contempt of court for repeated violations of the rules and my instructions to you. Do you understand?"

Somehow through the fog of her own anger, Robinson finally seemed to realize she had angered this judge one too many times. She took a deep breath before replying, "Yes, Your Honor. I apologize."

As counsel returned to their seats, the judge instructed the jurors to disregard counsel's statement that the defendants should be in jail and then allowed Robinson to continue her rebuttal argument. To her credit, Robinson controlled her emotions and, in Jesse's opinion, made a few reasonable arguments—mostly dealing with damages—before making a final plea for the jury to return a verdict for NMH that "fully compensates my client for the damages they have suffered."

***

After final arguments, Judge Long followed her usual practice of providing the jurors with a copy of her jury instructions, which she then read aloud. She covered the jury verdict form that was included in the instructions so they would understand how to complete it once they reached a decision, gave instructions to elect

318

a jury foreman who would sign the verdict, and then sent them to the jury room to begin their deliberations.

Once the jury was out of the courtroom, Judge Long turned to Robinson, and said, "Ms. Robinson, you have repeatedly violated the rules of this court and my specific instructions to you. As I told you when you sought permission to appear *pro hac vice* in this case, you were responsible for knowing the applicable rules of this court, and yet you have repeatedly continued to violate them and my specific instructions. I have another matter I must address in chambers while the jury is deliberating so there is no time now for you to present evidence why you should not be held in contempt of court. I will hold such a hearing at 9:00 AM in this courtroom tomorrow. In the meantime, once the jury has returned with its verdict, you will surrender yourself to the bailiff who will escort you to the Orange County jail to be incarcerated there until time for the hearing tomorrow morning. It is so ordered."

Robinson appeared stunned to Jesse, as did all other counsel in the courtroom. The anger that had apparently been driving her behavior throughout most of the case now seemed dissipated, replaced by what appeared to be fear and regret.

***

Awaiting a jury verdict is one of the less enjoyable aspects of being a trial lawyer. No matter how confident the lawyer is that the jury will return a favorable verdict, there are always nagging second-guesses about a myriad of decisions made throughout the trial that could tip the jury against you. Furthermore, experience has taught most trial lawyers that juries are unpredictable; they don't always base their decisions on what the lawyers believe is the key evidence in the case. These thoughts were flitting through Jesse's mind as the defendants and their lawyers all waited on the

319

jury's decision in a conference room on the same floor as the courtroom.

Some of the managers made a small bet on how long it would take for the jury to return, with the most optimistic selecting forty-five minutes, and the least optimistic saying three hours. The jury left the courtroom to deliberate shortly before noon; the bailiff brought in lunch for them, so some thought the jury would return with their verdict by 1:30. That time passed with no word from the jury, as did 2:30 and then 3:30, causing concern to rise in the conference room. Finally, at 4:45 the bailiff rapped on the door and announced, "The jury's reached a verdict."

Few feelings are as helpless or scary as watching a jury file back into the courtroom to render their verdict, which may alter the entire future of the losing parties. As the jurors returned, they all stared straight ahead, offering no clue as to whom they had favored in their verdict. Once seated, Judge Long asked, "Has the jury reached a verdict?"

"We have, Your Honor," announced the jury foreman, juror number five, the fifty-six-year-old male carpenter who was also a retired Army sergeant. The judge then instructed him to publish the verdict.

"As to count I for unfair competition by all defendants, we find for the defendants." Jesse quietly let out a sigh of relief and heard Conboy's sigh which was louder than her own.

"As to count II for breach of fiduciary duty by defendant Conboy, we find for the defendant." This time Conboy's sigh was louder, and Jesse's relief was palpable.

"As to count III for breach of duty of loyalty by all the individual defendants, we find for the defendants." Several of the managers expressed their relief just above a whisper. "Yes! Thank God."

Judge Long then polled the jurors to ensure they all agreed with the verdict. Upon learning they had, she thanked them for their service and told them they were dismissed from jury duty. Before anyone could move, however, Jesse stood and asked Judge Long for permission to interview the jurors to get feedback on the trial and what had led to their verdict. This was entirely within the discretion of the judge, but she granted permission while instructing the jurors they had the right to decide whether to be interviewed or not.

Due to the late hour, only three of the jurors hung around for Jesse and David to question them. After discussing briefly what the jurors had found most convincing, the jury foreman brought the session to a close with the statement, "You should know that during our deliberations we agreed that until Ms. Robinson took over as the lawyer for the plaintiff, we were all leaning in favor of NMH." Surprised and humbled, David and Jesse thanked them again for their service and left for a low-key celebration with their clients.

***

At the firm meeting the following Monday, the trial was the biggest topic for discussion. David and Jesse had taken off Tuesday and Wednesday of the previous week to rest up after the grueling trial, and they had been so busy catching up with other cases on Thursday and Friday that there had been no time to discuss the trial.

"So, the jurors were actually leaning in favor of NMH before Robinson took over?" Steve asked.

"That's what the jury foreman said," Jesse replied. "David and I were both surprised, but it shows how unpredictable juries can be. Our clients were surprised as well, but they were grateful for the outcome and appreciative of the job we did."

"What happened to Ms. Robinson?" Maggie asked.

"Good question," David responded. "I learned from our court reporter who covered the trial and the show-cause hearing that Robinson apologized profusely and promised the judge she had learned her lesson. Judge Long repeated her finding of contempt of court, but she said one night in jail was punishment enough. She also revoked her order permitting Robinson to appear as counsel for NMH in this case, so we won't be seeing her again in any post-trial motions or on appeal."

"So, NMH is now without counsel to decide whether to appeal and to defend against our motion for costs and attorneys' fees?" Maggie asked.

"Not so," Jesse said. "I received a phone call from Karl Stanton this morning. He's been rehired to represent NMH. He said his client would prefer not to appeal the case, and if we're reasonable about costs and attorneys' fees we should be able to wrap up the case in short order."

"That's good news for our clients; I'm sure they're relieved," David commented.

"They are," Jesse replied. "He also told me that Ms. Robinson has been fired by NMH. Apparently, President McDonald was quite upset he allowed her to convince him to fire Stanton, and he asked the National Manufacturing legal department to assign a new in-house lawyer to NMH."

They all fell silent for a few moments as they considered the surprising turn of events in the trial, which led to the tragic results for their opposing counsel. Finally, Jesse broke the silence. "You know, despite her being such a pain in the rear throughout the case and one of the more unlikeable lawyers I've ever litigated against, I feel sorry for her."

"Why?" asked Steve, obviously mystified why Jesse wouldn't be happy that Robinson got what she deserved.

"First, she was in over her head once she became lead counsel in such a complex case due to her limited trial experience. Second, most of her mistakes were due to her anger management problem. She simply couldn't control her emotions, and that led to the acts which resulted in her being held in contempt of court. She showed enough ability at other times during the trial to convince me she could become a competent trial lawyer. But until she gets her anger under control, she'll never reach her potential."

"You're right, Jesse," David said. "There's a lesson there for all of us. We all get angry from time to time in our cases, but if we don't release that anger immediately it could lead to mistakes harmful to both our clients and ourselves."

They all contemplated David's comment briefly before he turned the conversation to a happier and more important topic—Jesse's forthcoming wedding.

Chapter 27

After a cool spell during the second week in October, central Florida enjoyed a delightful Indian summer for the rest of the month. The first cool weather of fall in Florida is as welcome as the first hints of spring in the rest of the country, and the beautiful weather added to the excitement Jesse and all her co-workers at Jordan & McKenzie were experiencing as the wedding day approached.

The run-up to the wedding included several parties thrown by friends of both James and Jesse. But the party that brought them the most joy was the one hosted by David and Jenna in their home. All employees of Jordan & McKenzie were invited, as were the nurse and two staff members of James' medical office. Molly—freshly groomed and sporting a pink bow on her collar—helped Jenna greet everyone as they arrived, and David escorted them through the house to the patio out back where the bar and hors d'oeuvres were to be found.

Steve regaled anyone who would listen with his observations from the early days of their representing James when he noticed a chemistry between James and Jesse that couldn't be explained by the attorney-client relationship. He also reminded James—to much laughter—that when James invited them both to dinner to celebrate the victory over his former employer, he had cut out after drinks so James and Jesse could have some time alone. "Don't I get at least a little credit for helping bring about this relationship?" he asked facetiously.

Others from both James' office and from the law firm offered humorous anecdotes about them, including how they could tell their relationship was sailing along smoothly or had hit stormy waters. All admitted, however, that since they became engaged, the waters were calm, the skies were clear, and gentle breezes were softly blowing. Finally, David brought the celebration back to a serious moment, as he asked for everyone's attention to offer a toast.

"All of you know," he began while scanning the group gathered around the patio, "that Jesse is more than just a law partner to me. She's also more than a first cousin, once removed. She's like a sister and my best friend wrapped into one person. So, I've been more than a little interested in—and concerned about—what kind of man she would marry. I worried she would be unable to find a man worthy of her. After all, when someone is as smart, beautiful, and capable as Jesse is, it's hard to imagine who would measure up to her. But thankfully, she met someone who does measure up; I'm proud to say that James is my friend, and I am so honored to be his best man for their wedding.

"So, please raise a glass. To James and Jesse, may you have a long life together, filled with love and sustained by the commitment you're making to each other, and may you always be surrounded by family and friends who love you as much as everyone gathered here tonight does."

Jesse's eyes began to mist over as all joined in with a hearty, "Hear, hear!" She was especially moved by David's toast because he seldom expressed his emotions in public. Although she knew he cared for her as a family member and as a law partner, hearing him say she was his best friend touched her at a level that frankly surprised her. And to hear how completely he had accepted James convinced her yet again that she had chosen the right man to be her husband.

"On behalf of James and myself," Jesse responded as soon as she could suppress the tears from flowing, "I hope you know that each one of you was invited tonight because either James or I consider you family. Soon you will all be family to both of us. It's always good to be among friends, but it's wonderful to be among family as James and I celebrate our forthcoming marriage. Thank you so much for being here."

Having noticed a sign from Angelita that the food was ready, David invited everyone into the house where Angelita had prepared one of her specialties for a buffet dinner. She had diligently worked most of the day making pollo borracho—tequila chicken with grilled onions and cilantro, and served with lettuce, sour cream, pico de gallo, refried beans, guacamole and Mexican rice. For dessert, there were Mexican churros which, unlike Spanish churros, have the dough coated with a sugar and cinnamon mixture rather than pure sugar. They were served with chocolate dipping sauce. Angelita beamed with the compliments about her dinner, especially when James' nurse asked David how he had found his "professional cook."

As Jesse glanced about at the guests devouring the dinner, she was flooded with a conflicting mixture of a sense of loss but at the same time, a surging joy. The sense of loss, of course, arose from being in Carol's house. Carol had been her best friend and David's wife, a wonderful woman with a servant's heart who came to the aid of battered and drug-addicted women when they had nowhere else to turn. She had bravely fought the cancer that eventually took her life, but not before demonstrating to Jesse, David, and Jenna what true courage in the face of death looks like. Going through Carol's illness with her had changed Jesse at a fundamental level. She knew she would never fear death again as she had before, and she realized now, more than ever, how much good one person can achieve if she commits fully to serving others.

But her sense of loss was quickly overwhelmed by the joy filling her this night. She reminded herself of all the blessings that were hers in the moment. She would soon marry a man who met all of her expectations for a husband, and more—especially since he had become a man of faith after meeting with Father John. Her sense of joy didn't all arise from her own circumstances, however. She marveled at how well Jenna was doing. Only one year removed from her mother's death, she was a strikingly beautiful thirteen-year-old who seemed wise beyond her years but at the same time retained the bubbly optimism of a young woman. Even David had stabilized after a period of mourning over Carol. She knew the hole in his heart left by Carol's departure would always be there, but she could sense he was getting his life back to the point where he could look forward rather than back. She just hoped he would find the right woman to help him discover joy in his own life in the years ahead.

Finally, Jesse acknowledged once more how wonderful it was to have the opportunity to work in a meaningful job with the people in her firm every day. Steve was an outstanding young lawyer who made her, and David, look more accomplished every day, as was Maggie who was especially outstanding with electronic discovery. Sarah Garcia kept the office running, and Karen Overton made every client or visitor feel welcome. Rodrigo Alvarez was the best paralegal she had ever worked with, and their secretaries seemed almost as committed to the firm as to their own families.

The thought crossed Jesse's mind that it would probably seem strange to some people that on the eve of her wedding to a man she dearly loved she was expressing gratitude for the people she worked with as well as for her family members. This thought, however, reminded her of the goal she and David set when they formed the firm. They wanted a firm that was *family*. She realized as she looked around the room that was exactly what she now had. And these were the people she wanted to be present when she married James.

***

Early morning fog rolled in on Jesse's wedding day, threatening to spoil the uninterrupted lovely weather that had engulfed central Florida for the past several weeks. By noon, however, the fog had lifted, bringing yet another brilliant day of sunshine and mild temperatures. The weather seemed to Jesse to be a metaphor for the emotions she had experienced over the past two weeks. She had never been so sure about anything before as she was about her decision to marry James. Yet as she contemplated the enormity of the commitment she would be making, thoughts of what could go wrong or how could she *really* be sure rattled about in her brain, infusing her with a nervous energy and a hint of doubt that was unsettling. Not until the fog lifted, replaced by another glorious day, did the confidence in her decision overwhelm the nervousness and calm her, leaving her free to savor the joy that was building within her as the wedding hour approached.

Jesse and James had decided on a 5:00 PM wedding at All Souls Episcopal Church. That would allow time for the wedding ceremony and a reception dinner at a local hotel before they left at a reasonable hour for a nearby resort for two days before

328

embarking on a week-long Caribbean cruise for their honeymoon. Thoughts of the relaxing honeymoon ahead lingered in her mind as she gathered her vintage white A-line wedding dress with a soft train and clothes for the two-night stay at the resort. She and James would return home to pack for the honeymoon trip later. Just as she finished pulling the immediate clothing together, Maggie and Jenna showed up to take her to the church where they would change into their wedding attire and apply makeup.

All Souls included a chapel built in the 1880s in the Carpenter Gothic architectural style and a larger sanctuary built in 1967, which was designed to complement the chapel. As Jesse inspected the newer sanctuary before donning her wedding dress, she was overwhelmed by its beauty. The All Souls flower guild, with a generous donation from David, had filled the church with mixed-color chrysanthemums, interspersed with yellow and white roses. Flowers were placed on both sides of the narthex at the entrance to the church. There was a bouquet at both ends of each aisle, and the altar was surrounded by flowers, giving the church almost the appearance of a colorful garden. Jesse's maid of honor—Jenna—and her bridesmaid—Maggie—would carry a bouquet of yellow and white roses. Jesse would carry a bouquet of white roses.

When 5:00 PM finally arrived, Jesse, Jenna and Maggie left the dressing room for the main entrance to the church. From the narthex, Jesse could see Father John standing at the front of the church, dressed in his priestly robe with a stole that coordinated nicely with the colors of the flowers. Next to him stood James, in formal attire that emphasized his jet-black hair, awaiting the arrival of his bride. Although he was too far away for Jesse to see clearly the color of his eyes, she knew what a startling blue they were, reminding her he was the handsomest man she had ever seen, and her heart warmed at the sight. David and Steve also were striking in their tuxedos with broad smiles as they stared at the narthex where the bride and her maids gathered. Jesse also noted that the church was full, without an empty seat in sight, filled with friends whose love she knew would surround them as they took their vows.

Finally, the pianist began playing Pachelbel's Canon in D which was the signal for Maggie to proceed down the aisle, followed by Jenna, suddenly looking so grown up and beautiful she drew approving stares and quiet compliments as she passed. Once she reached the front of the church, the music switched to "Here Comes the Bride," and Jesse took a deep breath before gliding down the aisle to meet her bridegroom who was staring at her with awe—as was everyone else in the church, mesmerized by such a beautiful bride—and more love in his expression than Jesse could ever remember.

When she reached the front of the church, Father John began with the celebration and blessing of a marriage from the Book of Common Prayer. "Dearly beloved, we have come together in the presence of God to witness and bless the joining together of this man and this woman in Holy Matrimony." _3/

Father John continued with the liturgy until the point of the declaration of consent. "Jesse, will you have this man to be your husband; to live together in the covenant of marriage? Will you love him, comfort him, honor and keep him, in sickness and in health, and, forsaking all others, be faithful to him as long as you both shall live?"

As Father John posed this question, she recalled the faith journey that James had been on over the past months as he transitioned from a skeptic about God, having no interest in exploring whether He existed, to a man of strong faith who could be expected to reflect that faith in his love for her throughout their marriage. She was encouraged by his journey and it, in turn, strengthened her own faith, undergirding her belief that her marriage would be on a firm foundation. Without reservation, she responded, "I will." She stood beaming at James as he made the same commitment to her.

After Father John read the prescribed scriptures and offered brief remarks about marriage, they took the marriage vows. "In the Name of God, I, James, take you, Jesse, to be my wife, to have and to hold from this day forward, for better for worse, for richer for poorer, in sickness and in health, to love and to cherish, until we are parted by death. This is my solemn vow." She then made the same vow to James, followed by the exchange of rings as a symbol of their vows and the pronouncement by Father John that they were husband and wife.

Following the remainder of the liturgy, Father John brought the ceremony to an end with a concluding blessing upon the newly wedded couple. "God the Father, God the Son, God the Holy Spirit, bless, preserve, and keep you; the Lord mercifully with his favor look upon you, and fill you with all spiritual benediction and grace; that you may faithfully live together in this life, and in the age to come have life everlasting. *Amen.*"

***

As David came out of the church behind the newly married couple, he paused as they engaged in a passionate kiss, then giggled like high schoolers they were so happy. All the wedding party circled around to the back entrance to the church so they could re-enter the sanctuary from there for pictures of the bride and groom, and others in the wedding.

331

Standing nearby while the photographer took multiple pictures of James and Jesse, David couldn't help but reflect on the fact he was in this very place a year ago, almost to the day. That had perhaps been the saddest day of his life as he buried Carol, an event from which he thought he would never recover. To his surprise, he had recovered more than he thought he would over the past year. As he reflected on the year, he marveled at how much Jenna had grown up. Even though she was still only thirteen, she seemed like a young woman to him. He was also grateful that Angelita had come into his life. She was not just a housekeeper; she was more like a treasured aunt to him and to Jenna. She had brought stability to the family when David and Jenna needed it as much as Angelita did.

To David's amusement, he recalled one more family member that had helped him heal over the past year—Molly. David had never been especially fond of dogs, but Molly had won him over. She greeted him with excitement every day when he came home from work, and unless she was by Jenna's side as she did her homework, Molly would often come nuzzle him and insist he show her some affection, something he needed more than she did.

After the pictures in the church were taken, they adjourned briefly to David's house where they could take photos of the bride and groom and the rest of the wedding party with the charming lake as the background. After the photographer had taken all the pictures he thought were needed, David asked for several more for him personally. The first was with Jenna, Angelita, Molly, and him. The next picture added the bride and groom to the mix, and the final one added the rest of the wedding party.

As they departed for the wedding reception, David knew these pictures would always remain special to him. They marked the end of the most difficult year of his life, a year that, despite its setbacks and obstacles, had been a time to heal.

Epilogue

The wedding reception at the hotel was a lively affair. Everyone present was delighted to be invited to the wedding of this outstanding couple who seemed like local celebrities due to their being so beautiful and accomplished. The bar was open, the band was playing, and some couples were already dancing by the time the wedding party arrived. The master of ceremonies announced the arrival of David, Jenna, Maggie and Steve before the dramatic announcement of the arrival of the bride and groom, who entered to great fanfare and applause.

Delighted that everyone was having so much fun, Jesse encouraged them to carry on with their dancing and partying, and she and James began circulating throughout the room to thank every person present for attending their wedding. Just as they finished greeting all the guests, it was time for dinner, and everyone took their assigned seats. Toasts were made throughout the dinner, with David leading them off, followed by at least a dozen more.

After dinner had been served and they were waiting on dessert, James and Jesse had a moment to themselves away from the attention of others at the head table. "I'm the happiest I've ever been in my life," James whispered to Jesse. "I'm married to the most beautiful woman in the world, and I feel like the luckiest man alive.”

"I feel the same way,” she responded, locking her eyes on his in a way that made him believe she meant every word of it.

After a silent interval, James chuckled and said, “I never thought I would admit this, but I’m really glad we followed Father John’s advice and decided to wait until after the wedding to make love.”

"Yeah, I’m glad we waited, too, although, believe me, it’s been as difficult for me as it has been for you,” Jesse responded with a deeply loving look.

After another long gaze at each other, James gave her a knowing smile and slyly said, “But now we don’t have to wait anymore.”

The others at the head table seemed startled and turned to look at her when Jesse uttered a loud, one-word response: “Yes!”

***

After dinner and the toasts, David circulated among the guests. He hadn’t had an opportunity to speak to some of them earlier in the evening, and he didn’t even recognize several in attendance, including one exceptionally attractive woman whom he only saw in passing as the wedding party entered the hotel. Just as he finished speaking to one of his lawyer friends, Jenna approached him. “Dad, can I talk to you for a minute? I have something important to discuss with you.”

"Of course, Jenna. Hasn’t this been a lovely day?” He was still wrapped up in the joy of the occasion, but when he noticed she seemed a little nervous, he asked, “What is it, sweetheart?”

"I hope you don't mind, but I asked Aunt Jesse to invite someone to the wedding and reception who's sort of a friend of mine."

"That's perfectly fine, Jenna." Puzzled, he asked, "Why did you think I would be disappointed with you for doing that?"

"Well, she's one of my teachers."

Somewhat surprised she'd invited a teacher, David still reassured Jenna that was okay. "I'm sure your teacher was proud of how well you performed your duties as maid of honor."

"Uh, Dad, I didn't invite her because of me; I invited her to meet you. I think you might like her."

David was so shocked he didn't know what to say. He stared at her for several seconds, dumbfounded that his daughter was apparently trying to play Cupid for him. Finally, he began, "Oh, Jenna, that's not such a good idea. . ."

She quickly interrupted him. "Dad, please! Just let me introduce you to her. That's all I ask. You never have to speak to her again if you don't want to."

The pleading tone in her voice left David little choice. "Okay, Jenna, but please don't make a habit of this." As soon as he said this, Jenna quickly hurried off to find her teacher while David turned to speak to a nearby friend.

Within two minutes, David felt a tap on his shoulder. "Dad, I want you to meet Marlene Granger. She's my Spanish teacher and will be one of my soccer coaches next spring."

As David turned to greet Jenna's teacher, he was suddenly staring into the most incredible blue-green eyes he had ever seen staring right back at him just above a friendly smile. She was the woman he had only glimpsed earlier. Up close, she was stunning. Although he hadn't yet regained his voice to greet her, he noticed she was two or three inches shorter than him, with a fit and shapely body that her modestly styled dress couldn't hide. Her chestnut brown hair fell below her shoulders, but David's attention lingered on her mesmerizing eyes; they captivated him. Finally, he managed to mutter, "I'm pleased to meet you."

She seemed amused by David's awkward response but gave him an even bigger smile as Jenna stood by beaming that she had made what appeared to be a successful introduction. When David offered nothing further while continuing to stare, Marlene said, "Jenna tells me you've been through a rough patch recently and could use a friend to help cheer you up."

David glanced at Jenna, then gave Marlene his full attention, returning her smile before saying, "Yes, perhaps a new friend *would* be nice."

ENDNOTES

1. Pg 119. James 1:14. Used with permission Revised Standard Version Bible, copyright © 1989 by the Division of Christian Education of the National Council of the Churches of Christ in the United States of America.

2. Pg 231. Genesis 15:6. Used with permission Revised Standard Version Bible, copyright © 1989 by the Division of Christian Education of the National Council of the Churches of Christ in the United States of America.

3. Pg 330. The Celebration and Blessing of a Marriage, pp 423-432 The Book of Common Prayer Rite II. Used with permission. The Book of Common Prayer and Administration of the Sacraments and Other Rites and Ceremonies of the Church: together with the Psalter or Psalms of David According to the Use of the Episcopal Church. New York: Seabury Press, 1979

ACKNOWLEDGMENTS

It's a rare book that is written without the assistance of many people, and this book is no exception. Without the support and helpful suggestions from my wife, Mary—a better writer than I am—I would never have made it to the finish line. I am also grateful to Mark Godwin, the historian for Moody Air Force Base, as well as the troops at the visitors' center at Moody, for information about this important base. Donald Davis, President of the Lowndes County Historical Society, provided helpful information about the history of Valdosta, Georgia and Valdosta High School. Chris Carden supplemented my depleted memory of the rules and procedures applicable to a flight emergency like the one described in chapter 17. Linda Rooks, a successful author I know and trust, offered good advice and encouragement.

But most of all I want to thank my editor, Kathryn Livingston, for her steadfast assistance throughout the writing process. Her suggestions about structure, word choices, and plot always improved the written product, and her encouragement kept me going when my enthusiasm was flagging.

ABOUT THE AUTHOR

Darryl Bloodworth is a graduate of the United States Air Force Academy where he excelled academically and as an athlete. He lettered three years in football and in baseball and was captain of the baseball team his senior year. He served in the Air Force as a pilot and instructor pilot. He graduated with High Honors from the University of Florida Law School and is a retired trial lawyer after 50 years at the bar. He is a Fellow in the American College of Trial Lawyers and a former president of the Central Florida Chapter of the American Board of Trial Advocates. He is also a former president of The Florida Bar Foundation.

www.DarrylBloodworth.com

Other books by Darryl Bloodworth:

We Who Remain,
EABooks Publishing 2021

Core Values for the Young (and Not So Young) Christian
Insight Publishing Group 2010.